The Four Miniatures

I hope you enjoy this story
Kind regards
Kate Nelson
11.6.09

Kate Nelson

authorHOUSE®

AuthorHouse™ UK Ltd.
500 Avebury Boulevard
Central Milton Keynes, MK9 2BE
www.authorhouse.co.uk
Phone: 08001974150

First published by AuthorHouse 4/21/2009

ISBN: 978-1-4389-6192-7 (e)
ISBN: 978-1-4389-6189-7 (sc)

Library of Congress Control Number: 2009903177

Printed in the United States of America
Bloomington, Indiana

This book is printed on acid-free paper.

www.katenelson.org

Acknowledgements.

I should like to thank all those who have helped and encouraged me during the writing of this book. It has been worth the time spent travelling to workshops and writing groups working my way through a series of exercises and short stories before working on a novel.

I have also enjoyed listening to and learning from established writers.My friends, particularly Lois who shared her understanding and love of art which has extended my knowledge. Margaret, Jill and Pauline whose gentle encouragement to write a book have been much appreciated. To Kirsty who patiently interpreted my hand writing and Janet who read every page assiduously and supplied or extracted the bits of punctuation I missed! To Ann, who has patiently improved upon my limited computer skills! To all of you a really big thank you. To Timothy, Kara and Katie- hey guys I've moved the goal post again. Entering the world of publishing has been both exciting and at times a little scary so a big thank you to all who have helped me..

Chapter 1

Bar Lou was standing, admiring her autumn garden which was a riot of colour; the sun was shining – then she shivered. A sudden very cold blast of air passed over her. She felt her throat constrict.

The phone rang. She took a deep breath and tried to calm her jangled nerves.

She lifted the phone to her ear.
"Hello"
"Bar Lou?"
"Yes."
"It's TM. What are you doing?"
"I've just been in the garden collecting some flowers for my lounge. Why?"
"I have some bad news. Michael and Alicia have been involved in a car crash. No details so far. The Chief Constable will contact me as soon as there is more news. Can you make your way to Firedown School please? Someone must be with Nathan – I will send a car for you."

"Of course I will go TM."

It was minutes before she could control herself. "Oh dear Oh dear." Bar Lou, her full name was Barbara Louise Campion, knew Michael

Eversley from the war years, when they had worked together on special assignments. They were both extremely lucky to escape with their lives: neither spoke of that time. Bar Lou, as he called her, worked now as his Personal Assistant. Despite her rather dizzy exterior, she was an exceptionally clever woman, one of many who went to University but left before graduating to work for the war effort. She was especially gifted at code breaking.

Before she knew it, the car arrived. She had changed and donned her least outrageous hat:- she then started on her way to see Nathan. It was not going to be an easy meeting.

She was still figuring out what to say as they pulled up outside Firedown Preparatory School. The Headmaster, George Green, was waiting –

"I'm sorry, Miss Campion, word has just come through on the telephone. No one survived the accident!

Nathan is with my wife. He is really looking forward to seeing you. Shall we go in?"

"Of course."

As the study door opened, Nathan spotted Bar Lou. He ran to her.

"Are we going out? Can I bring a friend?"

He looked expectantly at her face.

"Bar Lou, what is the matter?"

Bar Lou held him close.

"Shall we sit down Nathan? I have so much to tell you. Mummy and Daddy have been in a road accident – a very serious one. They were badly hurt. The Ambulance men and women did their best but they died on the way to the hospital." The silence was agonising.

Nathan was just nine years old. He sobbed and sobbed.

"Bar Lou, what will happen to me? Can I live with you? Daddy always said that, if I was worried or frightened and Mummy or he were not there, to find you, because you loved me really as much as they do. Please Bar Lou!"

She looked at the Headmaster.

"We will see what can be done. Now we are going home to Garden Cottage."

She had noticed his trunk being put in the car as she looked out of the window.

"Come now Nathan. Thank you Headmaster, Elizabeth, we shall be in touch."

Nathan was very quiet on the way home. The silence was punctuated with the occasional sob. Bar Lou sat deep in thought – her arm around his small shoulders. There was so much to do. She really must settle Nathan's fears. He needed his questions answered.

James and Edward, who were Nathan's guardians, would have some of the answers. She remembered the day when Michael had told her of his decision to appoint guardians for Nathan.

"He said – It's better to be safe than sorry. Between the three of you, Nathan will be safe if anything should happen to Alicia or me. You are aware that Alicia's parents do not approve of our marriage and they have never met Nathan – no matter how we have tried to bring them together. So Alicia and I decided to make these arrangements-"

"A good idea" said Bar Lou. That conversation came back into her mind. The arrangements had only been in place for 12 months. She wondered if the grandparents would try to make contact. Nathan stood to inherit his parents' estate and from what she knew, he would be a rich young man. She wondered if that bit of information would sway the grandparents. She must talk to Edward about this as soon as possible.

The next week passed very quickly. Arrangements had to be made. Once the inquest had been opened and the bodies released for burial the date was fixed for the funeral. It was to be a quiet, family service in the Parish Church. Friends and neighbours came to the service as did people who worked with them. It was a lovely sunny day and the service went as planned. –

"Thank goodness" said Bar Lou.

This was the start of a much closer relationship between Nathan,

5

Bar Lou, James and Edward. None of the adults were married or had children of their own. It was going to be quite a learning experience.

Nathan went back to Firedown to finish the term.

"Christmas is going to have to be very special, Bar Lou informed Edward and James. We shall have to compare diaries".

This is where we start to look after Nathan. Planning came second nature to Bar Lou. James Eversley Browne and Edward Rayner were not so sure they liked being faced with disrupting their usually quiet Christmas at the Club. However, they were both honourable men and having given an undertaking would not back down. Despite their initial fears and concerns, they really enjoyed themselves.

They were right to be concerned. In the view of the Chief Constable it was no ordinary accident – too many loose ends and unanswered questions.

It was not until after the Will had been read that Bar Lou could hand to TM, the Circle Head, a package that Michael had left for him.

Once he had opened it and read the contents he knew that the death of Michael and Alicia was no accident. They had been murdered.

"Someone will pay" he vowed to himself, "And I do not care how long it takes".

Chapter 2

"Gentlemen," Bar Lou said. "We have a problem. It is now certain that Michael and Alicia were murdered. His car is with the forensic scientists now – hopefully we will find the 'mark' we are looking for and need. It is important that Michael's work continues. First of all we must keep this information tightly within this group. No notes, prompts or other information must leave this room. As is procedure any notes you have made will be shredded."

Bar Lou, James and Edward were deep in thought. Colonel Blundell, a member of the Circle, sat silently.

"TM," said Bar Lou, "What about Nathan and his protection? Is he at risk? Should he be moved from Firedown?"

"No. I think not at this stage. Do you know if his father sent him any letters or postcards lately or gave him an unusual present? Or has anyone tried to befriend him whom we do not know?"

Bar Lou shook her head. "Not that I know of but I shall have a good look around his room at Temple Meadows. There are some recent papers in the office as well. I shall go to Firedown on Saturday and see who Nathan asks to tea."

"Take Tiggy with you," said TM, "It will be quite good for Nathan to have her around. They are very close."

"Thank you, Bar Lou, gentlemen" said TM. "Please take care. Vary your routines. I am sure you know the score. If I have any news, I will let you know. It is a sad business. We will find out who did this and why. However we must be right and not quick. Thank you once again."

"Time for some light refreshments, I think" said Edward. "Shall we adjourn to the Club?" said James.
"Good idea. Let's go. Bar Lou, we need to finalise the Christmas arrangements. I have some ideas which you could discuss with Nathan on Saturday," commented Edward.

"Colonel, will you join us?" said James. "I will phone ahead and book a private room."

"Humph! A private room, James. I do not know why you need to book one. Room 7 is already known as your office." Edward smiled, offered his arm to Bar Lou and they left for the club.

Meanwhile, Nathan was busy telling Emir, his friend, what Christmas would be like at Temple Meadows. "We have carols around the tree, with the choir, on Christmas Eve. Tiggy and her family come and Bar Lou, the Brigstocks and the GGs."

"You invite horses to Christmas?", said Emir.

"No, stupid" said Nathan, "They are my Guardians Edward and James. Edward plays the piano for our games. James usually reads from A Christmas Carol. Whoever is the youngest in the room puts the Angel on top of the tree and we put Baby Jesus in the crib. It could be different this year. Do you think people will still laugh, Emir?"

"I should think so, Nathan. I wish I could go home but the Sultan has said I must stay here this year."

"Bar Lou is coming this weekend. I could ask her if you could stay with us – come to tea. She is crazy, quite dippy actually but I love her, so will you - we could have fun and there will be three of us to do the Brigstock Challenge."

"The what?" said Emir.

"The Brigstock Challenge. Well, Brigstock worked for Daddy. He drove the car, booked tickets and things like that. He used to be in the Army and was very good at escaping. He tells such wonderful stories and shows me how to do lots of things. Each holiday he organises a challenge day. Tiggy and I and other friends join in. It is such good fun. He keeps shouting at me, "Teamwork Nathan – "Teamwork." Bar Lou holds the clues – if we get stuck we go to see her. I think you might like it. Would you come and stay, Emir? Bar Lou will ask the Guardians but it should be OK. Golly, here comes Bar Lou. How many colours can you see in that dress? Wow! and we are going to tea with her! Oh great, Tiggy has come as well."

The visit was a huge success. Tiggy liked Emir. So did Bar Lou. When she saw the Headmaster she asked about Nathan's progress – she also probed a bit into Emir's background.

On her return to Temple Meadows, Bar Lou contacted TM. She told him that as far as she could see the only reference in Michael's notes was about four miniatures, possibly something he was considering buying. Also Nathan has a new friend, Emir, details along with Michael's notes are on the way to you.
Nathan wants Emir to come for Christmas. It would be a good idea. I hope it will be possible.

TM thought for a while – "four miniatures." He had heard that before and it was not from Michael.
"Well, well, who ever you are, we might just be getting closer".

Chapter 3

The first Christmas after the death of Michael and Alicia was by far the hardest. There was tension in the air, not always expressed, just an underlying atmosphere, words unsaid.

Fortunately Emir, Nathan and Tiggy seemed to accept that changes were fun but it was no surprise to Bar Lou when Nathan wanted to share his room with Emir and even offered to share his teddy bear. Bar Lou was not so sure about Emir. There was something about him that made her dig deep in her memory. "It will come to me," she thought.

Bar Lou soon settled into the routine of the school years and quite enjoyed being Nathan's special person. The Guardians began to enjoy being with him, sharing their interests and planning exciting activities. Nathan told Emir solemnly, "GG days are a bit up and down, sometimes a little boring, but they do try and I like them."

Brigstock challenges came and went. Bar Lou had carefully selected from her friends, people who could safely be entrusted with helping Nathan. She was inordinately proud of him and his achievements. He loved learning languages and had inherited his mother's talent for drawing – with a few strokes of his pen he could quickly catch the scene in front of him. It was three years on before Bar Lou asked the Headmaster what might be the best way forward for Nathan. She was not so surprised at his summary.

"Nathan is a good all rounder, with a lovely mind. Already at the age of 12 he is fluent in French and Arabic. His German and Italian are quite good too. He is a good mixer. I think with his mind and the right guidance he will make Camford University. Thereafter who knows – the Foreign Office, eventually the Diplomatic Corps or," thought Bar Lou, more likely he will take his place in the Circle and follow in his father's footsteps. She quickly concentrated again to hear the Headmaster say "He will be Head Boy here next year.

If you were thinking of further afield, you might like to look at the work Per Osmason is doing in Norway. It is an International College with a difference. Academically it is sound, a good mix of nationalities, a strong emphasis is on leadership, responsibility for themselves and others as well as making a contribution to the local community. Not only would he thrive in such an atmosphere but it would be a good foundation for the future."

During the next few years, the plans for Nathan's holidays will include time in the Middle East. He will experience many different cultures. The school will offer a year's exchange with a college of similar standing in America.

"Bar Lou, you are doing a wonderful job with Nathan but you must learn to let him fly the nest. He will always come back, you know" said the Headmaster.

On her return from Firedown, she went to see TM and told him of the Headmaster's comments. He seemed to be most impressed.

"Oh, by the way," said Bar Lou, "Nathan sent you this present. Four pen drawings on one page of Michael, Alicia, myself and Temple Meadows with just a hint of Brigstock in the grounds.

"My goodness" said TM, this is absolutely great. It will have pride of place in my office."

Then he mused – four miniatures. I wonder what prompted these?

"Bar Lou, I have been puzzling over something all morning. Can you remember, offhand, the name of the Austrian Diplomat in Italy, when Michael first joined the Circle?"

She thought for a moment. "Yes, I am almost sure it was Mikael Alinsky. If I remember rightly he changed his surname just before seeking asylum here in this Country. It is now Allinson, I think, or something similar. Why?" "It was just one of those things, a little niggle from the past."

On her return to Temple Meadows Bar Lou consulted the Guardians. They agreed to sound out Nathan as to what he wanted from his next school.

"Being Head Boy will challenge him," said James, "But he will come through it a lot wiser. It will be the first test of the way we have tried to manage his development."

"Good heavens, James, it is not a folio of stocks and shares. He is a young man on the verge of adulthood, about to face the first serious set of challenges since his parents' death. "Oh, and by the way, TM loved his miniatures."

"I'll bet he did" said James "and I wish I knew why Michael wrote 'four miniatures' on his pad."

What was their importance?

Chapter 4

TM was still puzzling over the 'four miniatures'. Why, oh why, had Michael written this down. He could not recall having discussed this with him at all. Then why am I constantly drawn back into working out their importance. There are other matters more pressing. Ah, well, time will tell, he said to himself.

The phone buzzed – TM pressed the button.

"Yes? It is the Prime Minister!
Ah – I was expecting him.
Good day, Prime Minister, how can I be of assistance?"

Then followed a conversation which jolted TM. If the intelligence was correct someone wanted to break 'The Circle'. MI5 had already discovered some information of a kind that could put their work at risk.

"It is serious, Prime Minister. May I come back to you?"

He put the phone down, called Bar Lou, James and Edward and arranged to meet urgently. If we are being targeted, then it is time to do more than observe the situation. We must act.

And so a process began, quickly and without alerting too much attention. Nathan would be home soon for the long summer break. Therefore it would be normal for Bar Lou to go travelling with him. Maybe the Far East. He knows the Sultan's son, Emir, so it is a good dropping off point. Bar Lou had the sharpest eyes and keenest ears of anyone he knew. If there is anything to know she will find out. They knew that Nathan's pet name for her was 'Dippy Dora' – nothing could be further from the truth. Now, as for the other trails, contacts were made, instructions given and the Circle members were re-screened just to be on the safe side, of course. Doubt if there is anything to find, but who knows?

Bar Lou heard Nathan before she saw him. "Bar Lou, Bar Lou, where are you? I've got some great news." Bar Lou emerged from the cottage. "Slow down, slow down, take a deep breath, my little doodlebug – now, what is this news?"

"I'm to be Head Boy next year. I never expected it, as there are so many good chaps in my year. Wow, Head Boy at Firedown. Do you think I will be good at it? I want to be the best. The Headmaster said I must choose my deputies – two of them very carefully, not just choose my friends. Then we give our list of names for Prefects to him."

"Well, well, young Nathan, that's quite a task."

"Yes," said Nathan, "It is going to be like a year long Brigstock challenge, only this is for real. Do you think James and Edward will be pleased? Oh, and is Tiggy home. I did not ask Emir to come here this summer just in case. I want him to be a Deputy. We have a lot of boys from overseas in school and he would be good."

Bar Lou let him ramble on, then said, "Do you want to stay at the cottage this weekend? The GGs are coming to dinner so you can give them your news."

"Oh, and I have a surprise for you"
"What is it?"

16

"Well two surprises really. I've got two new dogs, a wonderful funny Jack Russell which I've called Rumple and his brother is Stilskin." "What awful names," said Nathan. "I thought you would like them, as it was your favourite bedtime story for a while."

"What was?"

"Rumplestilskin of course!

Oh, by the way, Brigstock has left the challenge for this summer. He said it is in the usual place."

"Oh great, I will call Tiggy and go and find it."

"Take the dogs – whilst I get tea. Don't be too long."

So off he went, whistling, happy at last. What a clever man that Headmaster is – she breathed a sigh of relief.

It only seemed to be five minutes, in reality it was two hours or more when two hungry faces appeared at the window. Dogs yapping, children laughing, what a perfect day!

The challenge this summer was to train both dogs and enter them in the obedience class at the Summer Show. "Boring, "said Tiggy, who much preferred horses. It could be fun," said Nathan. "I think we have grown out of making bridges and dens. Wouldn't it be good if we both won rosettes at the show?"

"Tea is ready". "Are there crumpets for tea?" said Nathan, now an avid Betjeman fan. They giggled. "Isn't it just the best to be home, and have crumpets for tea, with honey and butter. It could not be better," said Nathan. "Oh yah", said Tiggy. Bar Lou smiled. Two little dogs looked up expectantly, shiny brown eyes watching every mouthful, hoping for just a taste.

"We are almost back to normal, whatever that is," she thought to herself. She looked at her watch – oh heavens and she had not even started dinner.

James and Edward arrived early, accompanied by TM.   Strange, Bar Lou thought – oh well, Nathan will be pleased.

She was right. "GGs," he yelled, "I've got so much to tell you." Then he saw TM. "Good evening, sir," he said, moving back into prep school mode.

"No need for formalities young Nathan. I just wanted to say thank you for the pictures you drew for me. They are very good."

"Yes, I like drawing – I feel Mummy is close when I draw. Did you know I am the Head Boy at Firedown?"

"No, but jolly good show – your father was the first Head Boy when the school opened – well done. Has Bar Lou told you where you will spend some of your holidays?"

"No," he said, looking up expectantly.

"You are going to stay with Emir and his family and travel around the Middle East."

"Wow will I ride a camel?" They all laughed.

"Well, Nathan, have you thought about which school after Firedown? It's your last year there, you know" said James.

"Yes, I know – I do not want to go to a Public School – even if I could get in – I have enjoyed being with boys from other countries – you know Firedown is great for that" – he went quiet.

"I will think about it and write down what is important to me. Did you know Emir is going to America and Jackson to some school in Australia? Soon I will have friends all over the world."

The adults were wise enough not to push the subject too hard. Bar

Lou had left a few prospectuses in his room. That would be enough for now.

Then Nathan looked up – "Edward, am I old enough to go to the Opera with you this summer. Are you going to Tidbourne? You see, if I am to be Head Boy, I need to know more about the Arts and I hear the picnics are sumptuous."

"I think so – I will look at the programme and see what I can do."

"Good – can we play monopoly please?"

TM rose – "I must move, Bar Lou. Well done all of you, he has the making of a fine young man, but I doubt if Firedown will know what has hit it. It will be interesting. Bar Lou, you know Nathan speaks Arabic?" "Yes." "Well, when I asked him he said both high society and bazaar. Another pair of ears maybe – goodnight."

Chapter 5

The summer holidays passed quickly. Bar Lou and Nathan really enjoyed their time in the Sultanate with Emir and his family. The Sultan and his wife, Patra, were such gracious hosts.

For Nathan and Emir, it was a magical time. Both dressed as local boys, they wandered through the bazaars, haggling for souvenirs. Nathan loved sketching the scenes. They went to the camel races in the desert, slept in rather super tents and ate all varieties of strange foods apart from sheep's eyes, a delicacy they maybe but Nathan baulked at the idea.

Bar Lou, well, she heard and saw more than she even admitted. Her hosts were fascinated with this rather eccentric English lady who was happy in any company. They talked freely in her presence. Sometimes they forgot Nathan understood the language. He thought it was a great game telling her what was said by the other people in the Palace.

The time passed too quickly for Nathan and Emir, but Nathan was looking forward to the final part of the journey from Abu Simnel to Cairo.

"You are so lucky," said Emir. "I only have the other Palace children for company. I will miss you Nathan."

Nathan was sad for his friend and spoke to Bar Lou. "Why can't Emir just make a longer journey back to school with us? He has not seen Abu Simnel. It would be so much fun – please, please, Bar Lou."

"I don't know, Nathan. Emir has to start preparing for his destiny as Sultan. There are many things he must learn, but I will speak to Patra and see what she says."

"You could say he was learning to be a foreign ambassador."

"Go away, Nathan. Remember, we are off to the races today. Go find Emir and change please."

Bar Lou dressed in her most colourful outfit, with big floppy hat and matching sun shade umbrella. She was getting impatient, waiting for Nathan. Didn't he know it was rude to keep people waiting? She smiled at the young Arab boy holding the umbrella over her – not really seeing him.

Then she looked again – it was Nathan, looking the part.

"Well, you said change, Bar Lou. Emir and I thought it would be fun – we could find out which horses stood the best chance of winning. You just might make some money."

"Monster," was all Bar Lou said.

It was a wonderful day – Bar Lou loved the hustle, the people and the winning and was thrilled when the Sultan's horse 'Ariel' won a race.

"Do you know," said the Sultan, "that man has asked if I would be prepared to sell Ariel."

"Why call this horse Ariel?," said Bar Lou. "Ah, well, my son learns your English ways and assured me that a horse with the name of Ariel will go like the wind. Emir would not sell this animal. He is the start

22

of Emir's own stable. He has many things to learn. How can I think a spell as a very junior foreign ambassador would be as you say, just the ticket, on the way back to Firedown. Teach him well Bar Lou – I trust you. If Nathan ever needs my help – you know he will have it. Now, let me see if I can point out this man. He has been asking many questions about you."

Bar Lou took a deep breath. Then it is true, she thought, someone was targeting the Circle. I wonder why. They did not have to wait long before she spotted the person the Sultan had described to her.

She froze – "Oh no, I'm sure it is Arpinsky." He did not use that name when speaking to the Sultan. She wanted to get closer. There was only one way she could be sure. She needed to get close enough, without causing a stir, to look at his hand.

If it was Arpinsky, she wanted to know. She would never forget those hands. They were the hands of the 'torturer', when she was captured during a special operation in France. He was, and in her view still would be, sadistic. Oh she hoped she was wrong. She recalled so vividly the pain, the fear and the suffering that she began to shake and needed to sit down.

Nathan was at her side in a flash. "Bar Lou, Bar Lou, what is it? Why are you trembling? Please, Bar Lou, tell me."

"Its only the heat, dear," she said.
"But you feel so cold," said Nathan.
"It sometimes happens like that."
"Oh well – I will get you some water."
"Thank you."

She saw the Sultan approaching with Arpinsky. Oh my goodness, it was him. "Miss Campion, may I introduce Mr Pinkerton. I've just told him he cannot buy Ariel – for it is not mine to sell."

Pinkerton offered his hand to Bar Lou. She smiled through her teeth.

"How nice to meet you," she said. She just about managed to touch his hand.

"Please do excuse me," she said, "I am feeling the heat and need to find some shade."

"Gentlemen, your majesty." She nodded and left.

So he had surfaced – she must let TM know.

"I don't think he recognises me – well, who would after all the extensive plastic surgery? Not quite like me any more. Why, oh, why, did that man have to come today? Nathan and I must move on. It is time anyway."

Patra approached. "Bar Lou, can I help?"

"Oh yes please. Could you arrange for me to go back to the Palace? Nathan and I must get ready to complete our journey. I believe Emir will come as well."

"Yes," said Patra, "as a junior foreign ambassador, I am told. That wouldn't be Nathan's idea would it?"

"Well who knows?" said Bar Lou.

"I only know this," said Patra, "sometimes we live in fear. My husband is a humane man and has done much for his people. I do not know if it is enough. We have both been so grateful to you and Nathan for helping Emir so much. One day I would like to visit with you. Please remember, if we can ever help you or Nathan you only have to say. Nathan will go far. To have lost both his parents at such a young age must have been so difficult. When I asked him about it, do you know what he said?" "Well, Patra, the second time around, I chose my new parents. Mummy and Daddy told me once, you can't choose your family but you can choose your friends. I have three special friends who have opened their hearts to me – I am so very lucky."

"Having spent some time with you – I know he is maturing into a fine young man. Well done."

"The job is not yet finished, Patra. This year as Head Boy will be quite a challenge for him. Hopefully all we have tried to do will put him in good stead. Then maybe his future is assured. Where on earth are those two boys?" "Oh, they are riding camels back to the Palace." "God help the camels," said Bar Lou. They both laughed.

When she returned to the Palace, Bar Lou went to her room. She always travelled light so there was not that much to pack. She went in search of Nathan.

He was in his room, sitting on the balcony finishing off some sketches.

"On hello, I won't be a minute. Thought it would be nice to give the Sultan and Patra some sketches I have done myself. There is one of Emir on a camel, the Sultan and Patra at the races, the desert camp and Patra's beautiful garden where once upon a time the ladies of the harem used to walk. I have four frames here. They are not quite miniatures. I hope he likes them. I am getting better at drawing. Shall I sign them?"

"Yes, of course, and I am sure he will love them.""I have two for Emir of his Mother and the Sultan. So they get two each, how about that?" "Very good, how thoughtful of you."

As she walked away she thought, not miniatures again. One day Nathan might remember the significance because I'm blowed if I can.

The dinner that evening was a quiet celebration. Nathan gave his hosts their presents – they were absolutely delighted.

"What a wonderful gift you have Nathan" said the Sultan. "Now I have a small gift for you. It is similar to the ring Emir and I wear. I am appointing you as my official Ambassador for young people. You see it will spring open if you do this." He showed Nathan how. "Inside is a token. If you are ever in need of help send that to me or Emir for now we are as one. Wear it with pride, my special friend."

"As for you, Bar Lou, with the help of Nathan here, I have a very special locket. Open it and look inside." She did and there were two miniature paintings of Nathan and his father. "I say to you as I say to Nathan, around the edge is an inscription. If you need my help, or in time Emir's, copy it out and send it to me. Now, let us enjoy the rest of the evening and safe journey my friends. I think, Bar Lou, you will need a holiday when you return to England!" She smiled. "Is Mr Pinkerton still around?" she asked. "No, I offered him a flight to Bucharest. He took it." "Good," said Bar Lou, "he is corrupt." "Oh, I know" said the Sultan. "But sometimes the enemy of my enemy has to be treated as a friend but that does not mean he is one."

So the journey home commenced. It was fun to see the two boys enjoy themselves and learn so much. They had arrived at Aswan. "We fly from here to Luxor," said Bar Lou. "The Nile is too low for the cruise boat to come this far. We are to be at the airport for 4 pm, so please pack."

"Before we go, Bar Lou, is it true Agatha Christie wrote one of her books here?" asked Emir.

"Yes, why do you ask?"

"Well, the lounge looks like a reading room in the library." She looked around and smiled. So they had noticed. They were beginning to see things for themselves. I will get them each a copy of the book.

They arrived at the airport in good time, checked in and the great wait started.

"Bar Lou, where is the plane? There is only one on the tarmac. Will we travel on that one?" said Nathan.

"I don't know. There are lots of people here, so it could be. Why don't you two boys go and ask, politely, please."

They came back giggling. "We have started another adventure," Emir said. "There is no plane to take us to Luxor. That one is for the Minister. A whole plane for 3 persons," said Emir. Nathan joined in. "Emir asked to talk to the Manager. He can be quite the thing, imperious!! the word." "He flashed his ring at the man in charge, so I did the same." "Wow, did things happen? It must be magic for it certainly had an effect. The Minister and the three of us will travel up front and everyone else here, going to Luxor, will use the rest of the plane. How's that?"

"Well done," said Bar Lou.

"Oh, and we all get the same food" said Emir.
Bar Lou sighed. What had she let herself in for now, she thought, commandeering planes at 13 yrs old. Nathan, please keep your feet on the ground.

The rest of the journey was really quite uneventful. They joined the cruise ship at Luxor, did all the touristy things, enjoyed shipboard life and arrived at Cairo, happy to go home.

"What a month," said Nathan.

"You could say that," said Bar Lou.

She wanted to get home too, to see her new dogs, whom she had missed, but most of all to see TM. There was so much to tell him. He had been right to ask her to go. Then he so often was. She was sure he would enjoy seeing Nathan's sketch book as he sees with an artist's eye, that young man does. She smiled "He'll do. Yes he certainly will."

Chapter 6

Bar Lou's meeting with TM raised many questions for them both.

"Are you sure it was Arpinsky?"

"Definitely, as if I could ever forget those hands. I can still hear him say I will make the little bird sing and feel his hands on my body. It is something I shall never be able to forget."

"Oh, I've borrowed Nathan's sketch books." TM raised an eyebrow. "Books?", he said. "Yes, books, all three. He really has inherited his mother's talent."

TM scanned through the pages, then stopped, took the book to the windows, turned and faced Bar Lou.

"It is Arpinsky, but more disturbing, is this man in the background. I thought he was dead as did intelligence agencies around the world.
Bar Lou, I need to copy a few pages from this pad. Will you tell Nathan?"

"I don't know, probably when the time is right. He is busy being Head Boy at Firedown."

"Oh, don't I know it? He came to see me, so many questions about the best way of getting things done. If he goes on learning at this rate he will be running 'the Circle' at 21. I did suggest he wrote his ideas down and talk to the Headmaster."

Bar Lou looked at her watch. "I must go," she said. "People to see, things to do, you know how it is."

"Yes" said TM "as always, Bar Lou, you must miss little. Thank you and thank Nathan."

TM picked up the scramble phone and spoke to his opposite number in Washington. "Arpinsky has surfaced, but more disturbing, he has been seen with Appleby. I am sending you, by special messenger, a pen drawing that Nathan, Michael's son, did in the Middle East. I think it will surprise you. Nathan, of course, is unaware of its significance. Have you checked out that other information I asked you to provide?"

"Yes, all clear thank you."

Meanwhile, Nathan had given the Headmaster his paper on how he would like to use his year as Head Boy. The Head was keen to see who Nathan would like as his deputy, as if he really needed to look. It was Emir.

When asked why, Nathan replied. "It reflects the run of the school. One day he will be very important in Middle East politics. So he needs to start taking some responsibility for others now."

"Why do you want a team around you Nathan?"

"Well sir, you will need a new Head Boy next year, so if we have 2 or 3 assistants, who are good at sport, arts or things like that, we may just find a good egg for next year."

Thirteen, going on thirty, thought the HM! He is mixing with too many adults. Must talk to Bar Lou about that.

"I find one of your choices strange. Hannaway! He does not make much of a contribution to the school as I see it."

"Oh, he will," said Nathan. "He sees, hears and knows more about what is going on than anyone. He looks so insignificant, people don't notice him. He will be great - at least I hope so."

"Well, Nathan, thank you. I will talk with the staff and let you know. You can however do one thing you suggest."

"Oh yes," said Nathan.

"The welcome evening for the new boys. Good idea that, so get on with it, but please, no Brigstock Challenge just yet!"

"Sir", said Nathan, as he left the room.

Bar Lou was sitting in her cottage reflecting on a time she would never forget as she looked at Nathan's sketch pad again.

"You never made me sing, she thought, "but you took away my looks and any hope I had of having children. I lived with the physical disfigurement which fortunately has been repaired, but the mental scars, never. I cannot forgive you. Perhaps one day you will meet your match. If there is a God in Heaven you may just sing like the little 'birds' you tortured and enjoyed doing it. You will not escape your fate, Arpinsky," she said to the room.

She called her dogs. "Rumple, Stilskin, walkies! Let's go find James and Edward. I fancy crumpets for tea."

Nathan had been told by the Headmaster that the staff, although surprised by his suggestions, had agreed to his requests. They would need some new badges. "Sir, why not ties? Badges are an awful bore, so non u."

"Alright, ties it will be. Let me have your ideas." "Thank you, sir."

Nathan asked Emir, Hannaway, Walsh and Jocelyn and Jackson to join him in his room.

"What are we doing here, Nathan?" asked Hannaway.

"Well, my friends, we are Team Firedown. Emir is to be my deputy and you will all be assistants. It is a new role, so we must get down to our plans for this year.

Emir, I will meet the new boys in half an hour. I would like you, Hannaway, to find 2 boys in each house who can befriend them, have tea sometimes, make sure that they are OK. Talk to the House Masters. Walshy, you need to start looking at our teams this year. We are a bit low down on the sports ladder. I need your ideas. Jackson, you will liaise with each of the Heads of House. We must know what is going on. Jos, old friend, have we got enough musicians for this year's Christmas Concert? You know we have a new teacher this term. See what you can do. Sorry, Emir, we have to go. Tea and crumpets on Sunday. Yes, it will be our Cabal evening." It created a bond that would last a lifetime.

James, Edward and Bar Lou were enjoying a quiet brandy after dinner. There was a companionable silence. All were assimilating the news that Arpinsky was still alive and the information they needed to gather in.

"Just think," said Edward, "life is going to change again. Pity I have enjoyed these last few years."

Chapter 7

Nathan's year as Head Boy at Firedown was the key to his future development. His handling of his fellow pupils showed a maturity beyond his years although some of his ideas went no further than a suggestion. The team approach for pupils involvement in school life was very successful and remains a standard today.

Nathan had to think long and hard about his move to a senior school. Two of his friends, Henry and Jocelyn, were to go to public school, Emir, to America, Walsh to a new private school with a sharp sports bias and Jackson to Australia. "We will still be the 'Cabal,'" thought Nathan. At half term, he asked Bar Lou if she would take him to meet Per Osmason at the International College.

The Guardians, TM and Bar Lou were delighted. James and Edward said they would like to return to Norway where they had many friends from the days of the Résistance. In reality they wanted to search out some contacts for Nathan, smoothing his path just a little. Not that he really needed that kind of help, but one never knew what might happen, especially with Arpinsky on the loose.

It was a great visit and as a treat Emir joined them. Per Osmason liked what he saw in the boy and was totally non plussed when he spoke to him and Nathan replied in Norwegian. So were Bar Lou and the GGs.

"When did you learn the language, Nathan?" asked James. "Oh, I borrowed some tapes from TM. There is a lot left to learn you know but I love learning new languages."

"Well," said Per Osmason, "Would you and your friend like to spend a day with boys here, just to give you some idea of our programme." "Oh please," was the reply from Nathan.

It was never in doubt that after the visit Nathan would attend the International College. Bar Lou was apprehensive. His talk was all about climbing, skiing and sailing but would he settle to the academic work? She hoped he would get his Baccalaureate and finish his education in England.

In the few years Nathan spent at the International College, the young man emerged, confident, caring and very bright. His year in America had afforded him the chance to meet up with Emir and to develop an interest in the Stock Market. James was delighted and suggested that he draw some money from the Trust Fund and start learning the hard way.

On one break from College, when he was 17 years old, he told Bar Lou, "When I make my first million, I will give you half and then start again."

"Well, we will see," said Bar Lou, not doubting for one minute that once Nathan turned his attention to a project he would give it much thought. Nathan loved the risk associated with share dealing, in fact he could be quite a bore with bulls, bears, cobblers and linkers. Not getting the reaction from fellow students that he wanted, he contacted the Cabal who agreed to meet and formed the Cabal Finance Club, each member buying one share at £100 which they would use to raise money to help

Firedown School and other causes which met with unanimous approval.

Whilst girls were definitely attracted to Nathan he was keener on his activities. Anyway, there was always Tiggy, who by now had started taking an interest in Emir. Their love of horses was the beginning, how it progressed would be for the future.

Nathan went on to Camford to read Political Sciences and Languages. Hannaway and Jocelyn arrived at the same time. As a threesome they were solid, still playing the stock market but involving themselves fully in the University life. They played hard and worked hard becoming expert at returning to College late and avoiding being caught. Nathan's years at the International College had certainly taught him a thing or two.

All these young men had taken a caring interest in the College Inner City project. Being set free in the capital city had been the original attraction but now the whole Cabal were involved. Hannaway wanted to use the Finance Club money to create scholarships to Firedown for some of the brighter boys. It was a big decision. They sought advice from co-workers, parents, guardians, the College Dean and TM. "It has to be done sensitively," said Walshy, himself a scholarship boy. "It is not easy, coping with your new life and your old one. My dad said that all I seemed to learn was how to swear in a posh accent. If I had not played rugby I could well have found myself ostracised!"

Well, Walshy old man, you sort it out, help us do it the right way. The one thing these kids do not get is a holiday. Perhaps we could do something on those lines, a lot of fun, a bit challenging but in a safe environment. It does not all have to be spent. We need to expand their ideas. Perhaps Brigstock could help." "I'll ask," said Nathan, "but he is getting old."

Thus the Cabal holidays were borne. It was a huge undertaking at first but Nathan, being Nathan, would not take no for an answer. The first year over 100 children had a week's break developing skills, coping away from the city and just having fun.

Hannaway spotted two boys and one girl who he thought might be in line for a scholarship. "A girl?" they discussed, "Firedown does not take girls". "It will one day," said Hannaway. "I was reading in one of the papers that it was the way to go."

"Well, we could ask Tiggy?" said Emir.

"Oh, smitten are we Emir?" said Jocelyn.

"It might work though." Tiggy always joined them for lunch on Sundays.

"It's a good idea guys, but please be careful how you do it. Some of the scholarship girls at school had a hard time, never had any money or the latest clothes and had to listen to other people's music. Clever they might be, and some were very clever, but there is more to school life than brains."

Tiggy was quickly co-opted on to the Cabal Holidays Team and introduced as you might guess - horse riding.

"Sorry guys, got to go," said Nathan. "I am off to the Rugby Ball with Walshy – should be fun and who knows ...?"

Before he left, Hannaway took Nathan aside. "Nathan, take care, Arpinsky has been in town posing as a journalist. He has spoken to me about the Cabal Holidays. Very keen to know who the organisers are. Contact TM before the ball. And try not to break too many hearts!"

"Oh, damn that Nathan, what a dampener to put on an evening. Soon forgotten though." The two friends had a super evening.

The Rugby Ball was the 'night out' at this time of the year. It set the standard for the May Balls and general end of term mayhem.

For Nathan, it was the evening he saw Maddy Alinsky, known to one and all as the 'ice maiden'. A little different to the usual jolly hockey stick crowd or the blue stocking brigade. "Careful Nathan," said Walshy, "you could get blown out." "Oh, well, I can look, can't I?" "Yes, but watch out. Go any further and you may weep."

It will wait," thought Nathan, who did manage one dance with her in the Paul Jones. Wow, what a smile she had, wants to go into journalism. Well Well! They met again at the May Ball. She was with her own set, not really attached to anyone as far as he could see.

He went over to the group. "May I have the next dance, Maddy, please?" He turned on the charm. "Please," he said again. Maddy stood up "Have we met?" "Yes, at the Rugby Ball, I'm Nathan Eversley. Come lets dance." He took her into his arms and knew that that was where he wanted her to be forever. Careful, Nathan, take your time. The dance over, they parted, Maddy to do a little research on Nathan Eversley and Nathan just to dream.

The pilot for the Cabal Holidays was very successful. The Cabal had funded it from the stock and shares fund and still had money over.

The scholarship idea was a definite plan, now that Firedown had opened its doors to girls. There were few obstacles in their way. The first three recipients would start next term.

Meanwhile TM and the Circle were patiently tracking Arpinsky and Appleby around the world. They were so confident. They had a few allies, mainly renegade ex officers from war torn areas. "They are planning something big," thought TM. "But what?" They know that the Circle stands in their way, so we will have to be vigilant." He did not like Appleby taking an interest in Nathan.

Nathan's last year at University was hard. There was not much time for, as he put it, jolly japes. Even holidays were spent studying, apart from a few weeks he spent with Emir.

"Nathan, do you know anything about some missing miniatures?" said Emir. Nathan froze. "Not really, but it is a topic that continues to emerge from time to time. Before my father died, he wrote '4 miniatures' on a pad in his office. It's a bit of an enigma."

"Oh," said Emir. "Arpinsky has been collecting auction catalogues and has let it be known he is making a collection. He has even asked the Sultan to help."

"Arpinsky, oh heavens. Why does he hang around like a bad smell? I'll tell the Guardians when I get home. Will you visit this summer?" "Oh, I hope so," said Emir.

"Still got Tiggyitis? Push off, Nathan, we have things to do. How is the venture in to the Stock Market?"

"Well, I've had a few bad buys but I should reach the million mark before I graduate. Keeps me independent you see."

Wow, you have done well! What is your secret?"

Nathan laughed. "Have friends all around the world and listen to what they say."

All the Cabal members received Firsts in their degrees and chose the same graduation date. Nathan had kept a weather eye on what Maddy did - she also got a first. "Clever, beautiful, intriguing," he thought. "One day Maddy, one day."

Graduation day dawned. Bar Lou, TM and the Guardians arrived. Punting and picnics were the order of the day and a final dinner at Temple Meadows.

There was a surprise in store for Nathan. He saw Bar Lou in a gown with the Honorary Doctorates. She looked so right. Well, the cunning old bird! But I have got a surprise for her. Tonight, I will be able to keep my promise.

No one clapped louder when Bar Lou was awarded an honorary degree. The cap was not quite her style, he thought. Equally Bar Lou, TM and the Guardians were so proud of Nathan.

After the ceremony and a very giggly punt trip down the river with champagne and a picnic, TM said to Nathan "What next?"

"Oh, I've been accepted at Harboard Business School. Emir and I will go together and what is nice, I am paying my own way."

"Are you now?"

"Yes, all those bulls came romping home."

They both laughed. TM thought, "You'll do, Nathan, you really will."

Their dinner party was good fun. Nathan presented Bar Lou with a super bouquet of flowers, a note attached containing a Banker's Draft for £500,000. The message simply said,
"You are really worth a million, my darling Bar Lou, my chosen mother".

His friends all received drawings encapsulating their years at University. It was becoming a tradition. He also outlined his ideas for Temple Meadow. "One day, I will bring my bride here but not yet as I want Edward and James to feel secure. Brigstock has told me he wants to retire to live with his sister near the sea. My idea is to link Temple Meadow and the Dower House and create a home for you both with plenty of room. It will be yours for life. I hope, James, that you will do the necessary legal work and sort out architects for me. I would like to add a gymnasium and pool. I have done some rough drawings, so my three super adopted parents, please do this for me whilst I am in America. James, to do this I need to release some monies from my Trust Fund to match the £250,000 I have made myself. I need to begin to take up my father's mantle, so I am going to spend time trying to sort out the enigma of the 4 miniatures. It ought to keep me busy. TM don't look so startled. I need another Brigstock and there is one more task I would like you to do, but I will discuss it with you privately.

So friends to the future, may it be as good to us as the past."

Strange toast thought Emir – wonderful friend though.

The men remained to drink their port and the ladies drifted into the small lounge to talk amongst themselves.

Nathan spoke to TM. "Please, will you run a check on Maddy Alinsky? One day, I hope to marry her but not yet. We have not yet even formalised our friendship but we will. I want to follow in my father's footsteps, so I am hoping it will be with Maddy."

"Is she the one referred to as 'the Ice Maiden'?" "Yes," said Nathan, "if you can help her realise her dream, will you?"

"Who knows?" said TM. "Good luck in America Nathan. Very good evening. I must leave now. Find time for some fun in America and don't break too many hearts."

"Hopefully not, sir, hopefully not."

Chapter 8

TM was trying to suppress his anger. ARPINSKY and APPLEBY had been sighted in London. No-one had informed him of their arrival, but he had seen them with his own eyes at High Holborn tube station. Although not standing together, it was clear to him they were looking for someone.

The crowd was moving so fast he was almost on top of them before he could stand to one side. "What are they doing here on my patch, and I did not know? Why stand in broad daylight? These two usually walk in the shadows."

He decided to wait. There was a small café where he could watch them and enjoy his second coffee of the morning. In the café, he used his phone to contact the office.

"Meet me at La Bistro, table near the window, quickly," he said, to the person on the other end of the phone. "Pinky and Perky (his code names for Arpinsky and Appleby) are in the capital."

The message was quickly sent to the Chief Constable of Surrey and the Commissioner of Police. Things moved swiftly, plain clothes officers settled into door ways and the Bistro. The long wait began ...

TM left the Bistro. He had to get to the office. The Prime Minister needs to know. There could be a security risk. He also needed to let the Circle know. On returning to his office there were messages on his desk from James Browne and Colonel Ince Blundell.

The Colonel had heard a rumour about some precious cargo arriving and James had seen Appleby at the Burbington Gallery, taking a great interest in an exhibition of miniatures owned by galleries and private families throughout the land.

"Not the miniatures again," thought TM. "We really have to solve this enigma once and for all. Michael has left a note on his pad. The Sultan has heard of 2 gents looking for miniatures, ready money available. We have to smoke them out, but how?"

He spoke to the Commissioner to ask if the Antiques Squad could assist with any information. Why miniatures, it was very strange?

The red light blinked on his scrambler phone. It was his friend from the FBI. One of his men had been trawling through some records of art thefts and desirable antiques. He had found mention of the disappearance, from the Roccoca Gallery in Austria, of a number of miniatures, mainly recovered stolen property looted during the war. The curator told the story that somewhere there were some miniatures which contained a riddle. If that could be solved, it would lead to the discovery of information regarding one of the biggest international fraud groups. He always insisted that some really big names were involved - people in key positions. In order to solve the riddle one needed all four miniatures. Unfortunately, no one knew where they were.

"What about the Curator?", he said. "Oh, he died in a road accident whilst on holiday, with no other cars involved." The phone went dead.

How could he work out what Michael knew? He would have to review his contacts and talk to James, Edward and Bar Lou. He could retrace Michael's last few months from his reports but he had done this many times. What was he not seeing?

Meanwhile, Emir and Nathan were settling in at Harboard Business School. Nathan was interested in forensic accounting and the many ways monies moved around the world. He needed at least a good working knowledge of 2 more languages. He chose Chinese and Japanese as he was aware, from his degree studies, that the Far East was a fast developing market.

The two young men roomed together, an arrangement TM and the Sultan approved of, as it made quiet surveillance somewhat easier.

The latest report suggested that the boys were as usual working and playing hard. Nathan's interest in the Stock Exchange around the world was quickly growing, as he began to get to grips with how business was transacted through the global financial networks. With a sound knowledge of accounting, money could move quickly and almost without trace, as audit trails would go cold.

His tutors were amazed at his grasp of the international money scene. They would be even more staggered, had they realised he was on his way to making his second million.

Emir had been specialising in Bloodstock Management ever since he had read of the disappearance, without trace, of a Derby winner. He had been intrigued. He promulgated the idea to Nathan that the buying and selling of horses was an easy way to launder money, especially as it was so easy to travel these days.

"Horses, as currency?" said Nathan. "No, Emir, I just do not see that happening". "Why not?" said Emir, "it is always happening in the Art World?"

"Fair comment," said Nathan. By the way, did you ever follow up on the purchase of that yard in Surrey?"

"Yes, it is mine. Ariel is here now" said Emir. "When did that happen. Emir?" "Last weekend". "How many horses are there now?" "About 12, mostly unknowns. I am looking for one experienced manager and an up and coming trainer."

What about Col Ince Blundell. He is not employed at present and perhaps Tiggy could work with him. If anyone could find you a good trainer, he could, with his connections."

"I'll think about it," said Emir. "How would you feel if they moved away?"

"Oh, I will still see Tiggy. She is like my sister - where ever we are, we keep in touch," said Nathan.

"Oh, is that so? You know that I would really like to get to know Tiggy. I just think she is wonderful."

"Oh, hearts and flowers," said Nathan. "But remember you will never buy Tiggy. She has one too many Brigstock challenges not to know what is going on."

"I know," said Emir. "In my country I would talk to my father and he would encourage such a marriage but life is very different for me now. I am worried about my parents. The Middle East is a dangerous place. Men who are not born to power are grabbing it and becoming very corrupt. People are disappearing."

"Ah, be gone. Dull care," said Nathan.

Emir lobbed a book in his direction.

"By the way," said Emir, "any progress with the 'Ice Maiden'?"

"No, the big thaw has not yet started. I hear she is making a name for herself in television journalism, very, very sharp. She does her homework well. There is always a chance that global warming will start the process for me."

"Arrogant sod," said Emir.

Nathan laughed. "Did you read about Jocelyn? He has been selected for the B Tour of India and Pakistan. Bet he packs his clarinet alongside his bats. Maybe we could go and see him play. I've a fancy to learn some Urdu and Gutjerati. Jackson is in the Foreign Office, but I've lost track of Hannaway."

"Oh, he is working in Hong Kong, some international banking group."

"How could I have missed that?" said Nathan. "Head in the clouds old boy. The 'Ice Maiden' has you in her spell."

"Rubbish, I've got so involved in this idea of forensic accounting. You know that is the subject of my Masters," said Nathan.

"Oh, I think I'll stick to Horse Trading, more fun and there is more choice. I will meet up with the delightful Tiggy."

"Let's go eat, Emir, and I do not mean hamburgers or pizzas, just a straightforward recognisable dish."

"Like Ice Maiden steak."

"Ha ha."

TM was receiving regular bulletins on the movements of Pinky and Perky. They really were on a cultural break. There was hardly a gallery not visited. The Art World was beginning to buzz.

"Dangerous," thought TM. "We need to get them out of this country. We need a false trail. I'll talk to Bar Lou," he thought.

Bar Lou enjoyed lunch with TM.

"Now, what is it you want?" she said.

TM explained about the idea of a false trail.

"Oh, I know just the person."

"Who?" said TM.
"Brigstock!"

"Brigstock, I thought he had retired."

"Well, he has, but he is bored to tears. I saw him last week. He would do nicely."

"Good," said TM. "I agree if he can bamboozle Nathan and that Cabal of his, Pinky and Perky may just be on their way home. Set it up, Bar Lou, but keep me informed. Have you spent all your money yet?" "No, indeed I have not." "Well, you can pay for lunch." "Scrooge" said Bar Lou. "Good afternoon."

Chapter 9

Maddy groaned. "It cannot be 4 am already! Oh why, oh why, did I agree to stand in for Annie? It just is not what I want to do. Just two more minutes," she thought.

The phone rang - who on earth was that at 4 am?

"Maddy, it's your friendly producer. There is a big story breaking. The car will be with you in 5 minutes."

"Five minutes. You must be joking."

"Well make it ten."

"OK."

Out of bed, showered and casually dressed, she quickly drank a very black coffee. "Oh, my hair," she thought as she glanced in the mirror. "No time now. I'll sort it out in the Studio." Fortunately she had chosen her outfit the previous night.

The entrance buzzer sounded, one, two, three rings. The car was here, thank goodness. She did not have to drive. "I wonder what the story can be." There was not much on the wires last evening.

In the offices there was pandemonium. The producer looked up. "Hi, Maddy, read this."

'Money laundering scandal exposed as stolen paintings come to light. Member of the Aristocracy involved. Ramifications not clear.'

"Why is this earth shattering?," said Maddy. "Because those paintings were stolen in broad daylight from Heatherbourne Castle, the home of the Foreign Secretary. It was a strange robbery, almost amateur, yet the three taken were small enough to be stowed under a jacket. There is almost a 30 second interval when the night alarms switch to the day setting. It was very clever. Too clever for many of our known villains. Heatherbourne Castle Gallery has only opened to the public this year. It has attracted the cogniscenti and a rather larger than usual overseas interest."

"Well, it is cheaper to fly to the UK at present," said Maddy. "Overseas visitors flock to our stately homes."

"Could be – but from my sources it is deeper than that. There was one video camera working. Heatherbourne have been trying out this new system so there might be footage of some assistance. Read the sequence of the morning news carefully and be prepared to change direction quickly. Just smile, Maddy, whilst Graham gets his feed. One of those 'news is coming in of a serious art theft etc'. We will not be able to prompt you."

"Oh, fine, I stand in for Annie, as a favour, then you expect me to perform miracles."
"Just perform Maddy, as only you can, please."

"Go away. How long have I got?"

"About 40 minutes – so hurry."

Graham was already reading the morning schedule when Maddy walked into the room. Oh no, not the Ice Maiden. The camera will be on her most of the time, little Miss perfect.

"Hi, Maddy, how do you like early mornings?" he said.

"Much better when they follow late nights and I am enjoying myself."

"You should be so lucky!"

Maddy shrugged her shoulders. Grabbing a coffee, she picked up her handbag and left for make up. Ready to face the world? "Just about," she thought. At the same time Neville Walsh turned on the TV. He had had a restless night.

"Wow, it's the Ice Maiden. The camera loves her. I'll video it and send it to Nathan. I wonder if he is still smitten? Well he will be when he sees this." He left the video running and ambled off to shower.

It was a big day for Walshy. He was reporting for a week of trials with the National Team. Oh, to pull on the Red Jersey of Wales.

Before he left home he put the video in an envelope, little knowing that the recording would start Nathan off on another world wide mission. He also put in some press cuttings about Jos and himself. "Look and learn, my boyo," he thought, "look and learn."

Back at Harboard Business School Nathan and Emir had returned from their meal and were sitting in companionable silence.
"I think I'll turn in," said Nathan. "Night."

Emir had a restless night. He had tried to contact Patra, his mother, with no success. Something was wrong, he thought. But what?

"I'll go for a run, blow the cobwebs away and collect the post on the way in. There may be a letter for me."

"A package here for you, Nathan. Another missive from Bar Lou and the scented envelopes. Why don't you put these girls and their mothers out of their misery? Want a coffee?"

"Yes please, and a bagel. It's about all I can cope with after last night."

Nathan opened the scented envelopes, read the invitations and put them on the desk. Next the package.

"Hey, Emir, it is a video from Walshy and some press cuttings. Walshy is in the Welsh trials." "He will Captain his country one day," he thought.

Nathan had a very sophisticated sound system with friends all around the world, using different video systems he had set his machines to cope.

"What is on the video?" said Emir as he walked into the room.

"Oh, not the Ice Maiden again." "Yes but listen to the news, if you can take your eyes off Maddy. Boy, the camera does like her."

'News is coming in of the recovery of the local paintings. Their discovery was made as a result of an undercover operation into money laundering. It is alleged that a member of the aristocracy is involved along with other public figures. This is a breaking story. We will give you further details as they emerge. Graham.'
"Thank you, that item will run and run, I think, which leads us nicely into the sports news." Maddy smiled.

"Emir, this is what we were talking about. Every time there is a lead the trail goes cold. This is not a local operation, we are in for an interesting day."

"More than interesting, my friend. The Dean wants to see you at 10 am. Nathan, do you know what it is about?"

"No, but I'll soon find out. I think I will re run the video and read Bar Lou's letter."

"When are you going to make contact with Maddy instead of just watching her on TV?"

"All in good time Emir, all in good time. I had better get prepared for the Dean's chin wag."

At one minute to 10 am Nathan presented himself at the Dean's office.

"He will be with you in a minute, Nathan". Now who's heart have you been breaking?" "Only my own," said Nathan.

The desk buzzer sounded. "Go in Nathan and good luck."

He knocked.

"Nathan, come in. There are some people I want you to meet. This is Perry Bracken, Chairman of Walls Bracken and Heath International Accountants and Brokers."

"Yes, I know the firm, sir. Good morning, Mr Bracken." "The gentleman standing next to him is someone I think you know."

"Edward, what are you doing here? Is everything alright at home? Is it Bar Lou?"

"No, Nathan, calm down. Perry, here, has been a friend of mine for many years. He read your dissertation as a member of the Assessment Team and as he will tell you himself, he was impressed. How much do you know about the breaking news of the money laundering scandal in UK?"

"Only what I have seen on a video Walshy sent to me."

"Perry, do you want to continue."

"Nathan, I am here to offer you an assignment for about 6 months. We need a keen young mind to examine all the information on this money laundering scandal. I was impressed with your insights in your dissertation and after a conversation with Edward and the Dean I think that young man could be you. How many languages do you speak fluently?" "About 8 sir, but I can get by in four others. How will this affect my Masters Degree, Sir? he addressed the Dean. "I still have to complete a field work assignment."

"It will not, Nathan. Your Degree is assured and has been for some time. It will be summa cum laude but do not rest on your laurels. Take this assignment. I do not know what you will eventually do, but the contacts you will make worldwide will stand you in good stead. Young man," said Perry, "Suppose we go for lunch. Edward is paying although from what I hear you could equally afford it." Nathan blushed.

"If you are head hunting, sir, it should be your bill. Then you could set it against your tax bill!"

They all laughed.

Lunch was taken in the private dining room at Walls, Bracken & Heath. As they reached the coffee stage, Perry turned to Nathan and said, "Well, Nathan, do you think you are up to the challenge?"

"I think so. I certainly would like to try. Edward will you give it your blessing?"

"Of course Nathan, of course". He kept his thoughts private but made one comment.

"Nathan, we are all so proud of you and I know Michael and Alicia would have been as well. Alicia would have warned you about taking on such a task, but I do not. It will be the making of you."

"Thank you, can I tell Emir?"

"Well, just say you have been offered the annual Walls Bracken scholarship to study International Finance for 6 months."

"Oh, by the way, will I get paid? The labourer is worthy of his hire, you know."

"Get out Nathan," said Edward. "I will see both of you and Emir before I go. Oh, I have just one bit of breaking news. Inter News have asked Maddy to follow through with this story, so you may meet sooner than you think and whatever you asked TM, he said OK."

Nathan smiled. "Yes," he said, "Just yes."

Chapter 10

Nathan returned to his room. Emir was busily writing at their desk.

"Oh, actually finishing an essay?"

"No," said Emir, "I am writing to my father and Tiggy. I have decided to leave Harboard. It is time for me to go to my father and start taking some of the strain. It has been quite an experience being your friend. No that is the wrong word, my chosen brother, our bond is now for life. Remember what my father said about the ring? As for Tiggy, I hope one day I may ask her a very important question, that is if my family approve. She may be your chosen sister, Nathan, but she is more than that to me. If her father takes the job at the yard, it will ensure their future and may be mine too."

Nathan replied "Emir, my brother, I hope all goes well with you. I too have learnt much from our friendship but I agree it is time for us to go our separate ways. May Allah always be your guide," he said in Arabic. "Wherever we are in the world, Emir, there will always be a special bond and who knows, if the Ice Maiden eventually thaws, I may ask you to be my best man!"

"Some hope, but if you do, I will be there."

Both young men knew at that moment they were now being called upon to really make their way in the world. Whatever the future held they would be there for one another.

"Emir, before I break up this moment, can I have one special request?"

"Of course, just say what it is."

"I would like a very special present for Bar Lou's birthday. She will be 70 in June. I think it is time she became a race horse owner. Have you got a suitable animal?"

"Oh, yes. I think I have. Ariel's son, out of Fly like a Bird, we have called 'Mercury'. Just right for Bar Lou, I think. "Will you be in England for her birthday?"

"Would not miss it for the world, Emir. Can you just imagine the outfit she would wear as the owner of a Derby runner?" said Nathan.

They both laughed.

"Talk to me, nearer the time, Nathan, and we will sort out the details. He will not come cheap."

"Then why not let Tiggy's father do the negotiations? Jos could act for me, then everyone will be happy. Hopefully Mercury can stay at your yard."

"When he wins the Derby."

"Don't you mean 'if'?"

"No, 'when'. We will have such a party."

"There is a long way to go Nathan."

"I know, but I shall enjoy travelling every mile, especially when the Ice Maiden thaws."

"When, not again, Nathan."

"Oh, didn't I say she is working on the same story as I shall be covering for Walls Bracken Heath? Then we shall see."

In the viewing room of Inter News, Maddy sat watching a video on the stolen paintings. She had the research in front of her. The provenance for the paintings raised many questions in her sharp mind.

"I wonder if we will ever get to the bottom of this," she puzzled. "I will need some help, that is certain. Now, who would be the best person? I will have to find out what the budget will be. Too much to do today. If I start with the information I have, collect the budget papers and decide where to start, that will be enough."

In New York, Nathan sat at his desk in an ultra modern office. "Not really my style," he thought. "I need a few home comforts.

Now, to the list of potential personal assistants. Should they be men or a women or one of each?" In his heart he knew what he would like and how to choose, but the weather was not warm enough. I don't know these applicants. I wonder if Edward is still in town. I could do with his help."

An idea was forming in his mind. If we chose the top five and all spent the day at the Ball Game then went on to a bowling lane, that would tell me more than a thousand questions asked.

It was not quite how things were done at Walls Bracken and Heath. "So what," Nathan mused. "I want to succeed and I have to know and trust the people I have in my team." He had no idea how his plans were being received and how one person in particular wanted him to fail.

Meanwhile, on the other side of the world Maddy was having dinner with her two closest friends, Esther and Mary Ann. She was going to broach the subject of working as a team on her new project. Mary Ann, quiet and studious, had read Art History and read archives like most people read a novel. Esther was perceptive and recently admitted to the Bar and was making her way in her chosen profession. "It is not going to be easy for her," thought Maddy.

"Maddy, did you ever hear from that guy you met at the Rugby Ball? What was his name? Nathan, yes, er that's right. Nathan Eversley," asked Esther. "I was reading a brief that Edward Rayner and Co. had prepared. It just dawned on me that they might be connected in some way. Nathan was in their offices when I went to collect our paper."

"I've seen him about. We have been at a few functions but he seems to have disappeared out of sight."

"No," said Mary Ann, "he hasn't. He has just won the Walls Bracken and Heath Scholarship. I saw a photograph in Time today. He is quite a hunk."

"A hunk!" shouted Maddy and Esther. "When did you become so hip? You are a dark horse, Mary Ann, tell us more."

"Have another glass of wine, ladies" said Maddy, "there is something I want to ask you both. I have this assignment and I need help. The kind of help you can offer, for the pay isn't much. It wouldn't affect your current work, well not immediately. There could be some foreign travel as a bonus."

"I would have to clear it with the Partners" said Esther. "Well, as I work from home for clients, I could offer some time."

"Is it a deal then?" said Maddy.

"Well yes, it could well be," said Esther.

On the other side of the world Nathan was at the Ball Game with his potential candidates. He already knew one would not make his final two. There was something about him. Nathan knew he did not want to be there. "I will find out," he said to himself.

Of the other four candidates he had already earmarked Gabriella, the first girl from her family to reach University of American African descent. The going had not been easy. Like Maddy she had a captivating smile. She was certainly the sharpest knife in the box. He smiled to himself. Her looks would open more doors than his keys and she was enjoying herself. But what role for her? She was not the secretary type. Anyway she would be wasted.

"So, what I need from my second team member alters my first thought. I need someone computer literate, a Hannaway type, see all, hear all, say nothing." He pulled out his sketch book and did some lightning drawings especially of Joseph Conrad-Parker the 3rd. He is an enigma.

At half time, Conrad-Parker indicated that he intended to withdraw his candidacy and he let Nathan know, in no uncertain terms, that this was no way to select staff. He would be making a report to that effect and submitting it to the Partners.

After an evening meal, Nathan spoke to the remaining candidates individually. He was almost certain he wanted Gabriella and Mark. As each candidate left the room, he made some notes. After the last interviews, he poured a malt whisky and switched on the cable news. Nothing much tonight and with that he went to bed. "Tomorrow will be interesting. The rumour mill will have the sails going so fast!!" Conrad-Parker, would be fuelling it.

At 10 am, he presented himself at Perry Bracken's office.

"Good morning, Nathan, my phone has been red hot. How do you conduct interviews in England – at a 'Rugby match'? I am not sure that this firm will take too many of your radical ideas - but we shall see.

Suppose you tell me who you would like on your team, and why."

"Well sir, I would like Gabriella Obotou and Mark Heaney."

"An Afro American and a third generation freshman. Well, your team will not lack charm. Now, why these two?"

"I like Gabriella's ambition. She is persuasive and a good conversationalist. With your approval she will be my PA. Mark, the darkly brooding freshman, well he will organise the business for me. He will therefore be my Business Manager. I feel we are on the same wave length."

"Good choices, Nathan, you have my approval, but try to avoid doing too much business at Ball Games."

"Well, I would much prefer a cricket match, but over here, well? Good morning, sir."

"Nathan, just one last thing. Be very careful how you tell the other three. Oh, I forgot to say Conrad-Parker III withdrew. He does not like ball games either." "I hear what you say, sir, and I will heed it." He thought to himself, it's like being back at Firedown. Well, if team work succeeded there, it will work here. Tomorrow will be the first day for the new team. If we get off to a good start maybe we will succeed but it will be pretty mundane as we work on the action plan."

Nathan spoke with David and Graham. He liked them both. He would assess how they took the news and maybe, just maybe, there could be a future role for one of them.

He went home to his loft flat. He had sold his grandmother's condo and bought the loft. "I really must start to finish the place. We will work from here sometimes, and I need a room for guests."

At the end of the day he, switched on the cable news. He had finally got the tuning right and could keep up with news from home. He was about to switch off when Maddy appeared. As quick as a flash, the record button was pushed. She had won an award for her journalism. Must send her some flowers. So he lifted the phone, dialled his favourite flower shop and ordered a bouquet, "mainly white and blue and just a touch of pink flowers please."

Message; '*warm congratulations, Nathan.*'

Just right for an 'Ice Maiden' he thought, as he switched off the light.

Chapter 11

TM was having lunch with James, Edward and Bar Lou. The Colonel joined them infrequently these days. He had moved to manage Emir's yard. Tiggy was in seventh heaven. "All this and horses too," she said to no-one in particular. She did miss Temple Meadows and particularly Bar Lou. She always had the latest news of Nathan. Now that they were both working, the time they had together was limited but precious.

"How is it at Temple Meadows at the moment?" asked TM. "Dreadful, builders, loud music, banging. I am staying at the club during the work," said James. "Whilst I have become Project Manager! Well, Brigstock does the work and I pay the bills," said Edward.

"It is a wonderful design. Nathan is so talented. There was little known about the architect, a friend of his from University. He has linked the hall with the Dower House via a conservatory with fantastic views and a fitness suite - not my territory I'm afraid."

"No, I can see that," said TM smiling.

"Well, to business. Pinky and Perky. Things seem to have gone quiet? – that is disturbing. That contact of yours, Perry Bracken in New

York, has got Nathan applying forensic accounting to all the cold trails. It was a clever move. Here in London Inter News have commissioned a piece on the missing Leidl story. Maddy Alinsky is heading the team."
"Oh, the 'Ice maiden'" said Edward.

"Oh yes, Nathan's muse. I take it he is still smitten?" "No doubt about it. But will it come to anything, I wonder, James?" "Well, he is serious and there is no reason why not. A golden couple one might say. Yes, one might. Bar Lou, how are your Middle East contacts fitting into this?"

"The Sultan has his fingers on the pulse. We are trying to locate the other 2 miniatures. It is difficult at the moment as we do not want to cause a stir. Ripples of information could leak out and that would be the last thing we need."

"We can only keep tabs on what is happening" said TM. "Perry will let me know what Nathan turns up, via Uncle Sam, my contact in Washington and I have asked an old friend at Inter News to find a way of keeping me up-to-date without compromising Maddy's work. Ice Maiden she may be, but so charming that people tell her more than they intend.

Bar Lou, how will you be celebrating your birthday?"

"I am told Nathan has planned the day and Brigstock is busy all of the time, so who knows? I may jump out of an aeroplane, drop in through the open roof of the swimming pool and land with a splash."

"That does sound a bit Nathanish. He owes you all so much and what is more he knows it. Is he aware of how many parachute jumps you have actually done?"

"No, I just do not talk about it. No point. I could only really talk to Michael. He understood. Please don't go there."

"Fine."

"Just to round off today, I have the forensic report and follow up actions over Michael's car accident and the Museum Curator's. We have found the 'mark'. The Austrian police have been wonderful. Guess where it leads? It is a classic FBI sting, so it should not be hard."

"Not Perky? Oh come into my parlour, said the spider to the fly" said Bar Lou, "I can't wait."

Maddy was very surprised to find the flowers delivered to her office and to receive an invitation to go to the Derby with Nathan and his friends. He must be coming back, but for a social occasion? Well, why not? Wait till I tell the girls. The 'Ice Maiden' and the hunk sounds like a cheap eye catching headline!"

Nathan, meanwhile, was in Hong Kong. Three cold trails finished in the money markets there. He was hoping to look up Hannaway. When he last spoke to him. 'Egg Head' seemed withdrawn and off balance. He might know something. Anyway, he would enjoy meeting Gabriella. "I might ask him to show her around whilst I spend some time with the Tsangs."

Hannaway was relieved to see Nathan. He had arranged for his friend Mai Lee to take Gabriella shopping. "We should be alright for the day," he thought.

At Nathan's suggestion they hopped on the ferry to Lantau and bussed it up the hill to the monastery.

"I could never be a monk," said Nathan, "but I so love this place. My father wrote about in his diary."

The bus journey to the monastery was quite an experience. "Go to the back, Hannaway. It is the only safe seat to really survive the journey. Now for the ear bashing." All of the pilgrims started to intone their favourite hymns, only they were all different, hens clucked and locals jabbered away.

"As you say, Nathan, quite an experience."

They paid their entrance fee, ordered lunch and walked into a most peaceful oasis. Both men walked around admiring the sunlight glinting off the statues of Buddha in the various Temples. They joined in the quiet contemplation and had the fortune sticks thrown for them.

Nathan asked in Mandarin "Well, what is the news, oh farsighted one?"
"You will make many journeys in your quest. You have enemies and friends. Keep your counsel. I have one future message. The 'Ice Maiden' will thaw". Nathan smiled. "Thank you, oh wise one."

"Come on, egghead, have a go. What do the sticks say for my friend, oh wise one?"

"Tell him a journey of a thousand miles starts but a simple step. He must take that step. His happiness does not lie here. Good fortune for him will come with the lotus flower." "I will tell him."

They moved on. As they stood in the garden, they heard such wonderful flute music. A young Japanese boy was playing for his Buddha. It was a haunting tune.

"Well, isn't it time you told me what is worrying you?" said Nathan. "I don't really know where to begin. At first when I was auditing some accounts I thought there had been a banking error, a wrong figure, a data input mistake. It is such a well respected Bank."

"So, what do you now think?"

"Not think, Nathan, know. One of our very prestigious clients has bought some well known paintings for well under their real market value. I think it is money laundering."

"What! how often has this happened?"

"Four or five times in the last year. It is so very clever."

"Have you told anyone?"

"No."

"Well, do not. This may just be the key to opening up one of our cold trails."

"Nathan, I cannot stay here but there is a complication."

"Your 'lotus flower'?"

"How did you know my name for her? Yes, it is Mai Lee."

Nathan thought quickly. "I will have to talk to TM but why not work for our Cabal Finance Company? Work out of London. I think TM will have a flat you could use. As to Mai Lee, marry the girl if she will have you. Then to all intents and purposes you will honeymoon in London so she can meet your friends. You could come back briefly, resign and settle your affairs. I can help pave the way." "We have talked of marriage. I am sure she would say 'yes' but her parents do not understand our ways," said Hannaway.

"I think I can help. I will talk to the Tsangs," said Nathan.
"Oh, please don't. It is the younger Tsang who is involved in the artwork scam."

"No, oh dear! Well, why not organise a farewell dinner for Gabriella and invite her parents. Get Mai Lee to cook and we will see if the Lees will be prepared to let Mai Lee marry you. I need to make some phone calls, so we should have lunch and head back."

On his return to the hotel, he heard much giggling in the suite. There were shopping bags everywhere. Gabriella and Mai Lee were really on the same shopping wavelength.

He smiled, went into his room and contacted TM.

The conversation finished. "I will be in London next weekend and stay for Bar Lou's birthday, so we can meet then."

"Good." The phone went dead.

"Mai Lee, Gabriella, have you had fun?" "Oh yes," they chorused, "we have so much in common. I hope one day Mai Lee will come to America and I can return the compliment."

There was a knock at the door.

"Come" said Nathan. "Oh, Hannaway, come in." Mai Lee ran to him. 'So far so good,' thought Nathan.

After a hurried conversation, Mai Lee turned to Gabriella and Nathan, saying "I know you have done so much for my man here. Would you and Gabriella come to dinner tomorrow? I could ask my parents. They would then perhaps understand what a good person Graham is."

"I'll bring the champagne," said Nathan, as he winked at Hannaway. "Graham eh?"

"Can I help you cook, Mai Lee. I could do one of my traditional dishes. It could be an East meets West meal."

"That would be great. So it is agreed. Come Graham, there are parcels to carry and food to buy. See you both tomorrow."

"That was fun," said Gabriella to Nathan. "Are we any further along the trail?"

"Yes, I think so. Gabriella, will you go back to New York without me. I have to go to London. It is Bar Lou's 70th birthday soon. I just have to be there. There are one or two other matters needing my attention.

I may even take in a few matches at Wimbledon, go to Lords and the Derby. Who knows, I might learn something useful?"

OK. Well, I have some notes to put together, I will liaise with Mark and see what we can find for your return."

Nathan returned to London full of excitement and anticipation. "Bar Lou will have a fantastic birthday - if I have anything to do with it. I really want to see the alterations at Temple Meadows. It has to be just right for my 'Ice Maiden.'"

His meeting with TM was brief but purposeful.

His reunion with the Cabal was long, raucous and fun.

"Well, Nathe", said Jos, "what about the 'Ice Maiden'?"

"She will thaw," was all he replied.

"How did it feel pulling on the red jersey of Wales Walshy?" "Like nothing I have ever experienced. I knew I was a last minute substitute, but may be the team will give me another chance."
"And Jos, what about the cricket? How was India?" "Great to both. There will be retirements at the end of next season, maybe next year?"

"Mark, how is the Army?" "My short term commission ends in July. Then who knows?"

"I saw Hannaway in Hong Kong. He will be here, in time for Lords, with his new wife."

"What?" "Yes, a very beautiful and clever Chinese girl, Mai Lee."

"Well, I never," said Walshy. "The old dog." "Same age as you Walshy," said Jos. They laughed.

"Whilst we are here, I have an idea to resurrect Cabal Finance. We have a considerable amount of money to disburse. How would you guys feel if I asked Hannaway to come here permanently and look after the funds with us?"

"Great, what a wonderful idea Nathan."

"We agree don't we? Yes."

"Good. Now I need to ask another favour."

"What?" said Jos. "Turn up the heat in the Pavilion at Lords in the hope that the 'Ice Maiden' will melt?"

"No, you daft lot. Mark, it concerns you. I need some help with an assignment I have been doing to complete my Masters. There are staff in New York but I want someone who can go off around the world without causing a stir. Could you work with me for 6 months or so?"

"Nathan, that would be great. It would give me time to renew some contacts and think about the future. Thank you."

"Well, guys, time for some serious drinking. Tomorrow we decamp en masse for Temple Meadows."

"What have you planned for Bar Lou?" "Wait and see. Oh and by the way, Emir will join us there." "Emir, wow, that will be good."

"I hope you like the alterations. We now have a conservatory and swimming pool and fitness suite linking the Dower House and the main house. There are a few innovations which I want to show all of you."

"What's it all in aid of Nathan?"

"What do you think, just preparing the nest!! Watch this space!"

"What have you bought Bar Lou" asked Walshy.

"A race horse."

"A race horse? Well, it's better than 'a handbag'. Which horse, and who did you buy it from?"

"Emir found it for me. It is one of Ariel's progeny and is called Mercury. Bar Lou and I and one other, I hope, will go by balloon to their yard, or helicopter if the winds are not right, where Tiggy and the Colonel will tell her that she is the new owner of Mercury who will be running at the Derby meeting. She is already the registered owner on the Race Card. If she doesn't die of shock, just imagine the outfit she will wear on Derby Day. We have a box and I will give you the various passes at Temple Meadows."

"To the Cabal," said Walshy, raising his glass. "And to you, my 'Ice Maiden,'" said Nathan under his breath.

.

Chapter 12

Arpinsky and Gregory were sitting at the centre of a sleazy bar in Soho. It was unusually quiet. It had not been as easy as they had thought to find the two miniatures needed to complete the set.

"We could be sitting on a fortune," said Gregory. "We know some of the 'names' involved. Talk about 'birdies singing' - it will be more like guilty consciences paying. We would be in clover living the life, girls unlimited, no fees, no bosses just a great fat off shore bank account. Even those old Gnomes of Zurich would have watery eyes thinking about our monies."

"Don't be daft; it is that kind of behaviour which would put our names in lights. We have to be discrete but that is not quite your style."

"Never mind," he thought, "you might enjoy the hunt but you will not be around for the kill."

"However, there is a gem of an idea in what you said. Before the war those in the know moved their assets to Switzerland, a neutral country so they say, to collect when it was over. Maybe that is where the miniatures are now. No-one would be stupid enough to keep them altogether.

We need to do a lot more research. Maybe, if you hadn't fixed Alinsky so quickly, we would still have a reference point.

You still in touch with your clever artists?"

"Yes."

"I need impeccable Jewish papers. A whole new life to learn about. We will get these miniatures one day."

Maddy awoke to find Nathan sitting by her bedside, sketching away.

"Where am I? Oh, Bar Lou's cottage!"

"Shush, you will wake her up. Those dogs can hear a pin drop." "Nathan, just tell me what I am doing here." "I invited you. Last night we met at the Jazz Club. My friend Jos was playing with his new band the Labac. Oh yes, they are good. Well I have an important date with a race horse and Bar Lou this morning. It is her birthday and we are all going to Epsom tomorrow." "Still," said Maddy, "tell me what happened." "After some persuasion, we drove here last night. I slept up at the house, just in case you are wondering."

"Go away," said Maddy, "I want to get up."

"Not until after breakfast, made with my own fair hands. You are not disappointed to be here are you? I managed to get passes for Esther and Mary Ann for Epsom. Hannaway will bring them. You will meet his beautiful wife Mai Lee. Sorry he will only have eyes for her. They are still on honeymoon. Now eat up. If you can face the champagne, I'll pour for you. There is fresh orange juice and just to complete the picture, a white rose in a vase." He smiled. She is really beautiful.

"Now to wake Bar Lou. It is a fine day and the balloon will be here soon. She will be having breakfast in the clouds or rather below them. We two are going."

"We two?"

"Yes, you as well, Maddy. She really will be in need of female company, so it's you, me and Bar Lou. The two most special ladies in my life. I mean that Maddy."

Maddy was for once silenced. "Did I just hear that? Well, well, Nathan, it is going to be an interesting day."

Knock
"Bar Lou, Bar Lou, may I come in?"

"Yes, if you can get past the dogs."

"Rumple, Stilskin, go catch a rat." He opened the door and out they went. He had taught them something then.

"Bar Lou, I did not want to share this special moment with anyone else but you. A very happy birthday. He gave Bar Lou a parcel, flowers and cards.

"Oh, Nathan it is special and always has been when we are together."

"Don't forget, Bar Lou, you are my chosen mum. Wherever Mum and Dad are now, they will understand, I am sure. Oh, and I brought a pot of green tea."

"Good, I need it."

The bed was soon awash with discarded envelopes and wrapping paper, as she laughed, oohed and aahed her way through the pile.

"Now for your present, Nathan." As she opened the paper, the tears rolled down her face. "Nathan, this is wonderful. Wherever did you get the time?" "Oh, a bit here and there and a trawl through my sketchbooks."

He had given her a drawing that looked a little like the front page of a comic but actually was a scene of miniatures depicting her life, people, places and memories.

"Now, wipe those tears. Wear something slightly warm, just to keep away the morning chill. Choose your hat carefully because we are breakfasting in the clouds and going to collect your birthday present.

Then its back here for lunch with all your gossipy friends. All the usual suspects will arrive for dinner at Temple Meadows. It will be the end of what I hope will be a perfect day.

We will go to Epsom tomorrow," said Nathan.

"When you say we, who do you actually mean?" "Well you, me and Maddy. I thought you would like a lady companion, particularly a beautiful one."

"Yes, that is fine but one word of advice, well two really. 'Festina lente' Nathan, if you can remember your latin. Maddy is special to you, I know that. She is an independent person, not quite ready to be swept up in your more outrageous goings on."

I know that, Bar Lou. It has been nearly four years since I first met her. She was called the 'Ice Maiden', you know. Maybe its something to do with global warming but I sense a slight thaw. When she has finished her latest assignment and I return from America, and if we still feel the same way, I will ask her to marry me, but not until then. Neither will I do anything, what was it you used to say 'untoward'? You have my promise of that."

At 9 am precisely the balloon arrived at Temple Meadows.

"We are going in that?" said Bar Lou.

"We must be crazy," said Maddy "but humour him today. He has been planning this for a long time.

76

"Yes he must have." "Once I was told by a good friend to let him fly the nest, for he would always come back. He is a free spirit, Maddy but a good man who could well become a great one."

"I'm beginning to see that," said Maddy.

"Please don't start something that you will not continue. It would be fairer to say now, if it is just fun and nothing else. I have nurtured him through one heartbreak, I am a little too old to cope with another."

"Oh, I think I hope I will be around for some time. He is special to me as well. I am only just beginning to realise how much."

With that Bar Lou made as dignified an entrance into the balloon, as she could, followed by Maddy and Nathan. James, Edward and Brigstock waved.

"Off we go, pilot. Nathan introduce me."

"Oh, I don't think you need an introduction."

The Pilot turned around. "Happy birthday, Bar Lou." Per Osmason, oh how wonderful, I thought you were away flying over oceans somewhere." "Well, not today. This young man said there could only be one pilot for today and I agreed."

"And who is this, Nathan" looking at Maddy.

Nathan blushed. "This is Maddy," he said, eyes smiling. She turned and smiled at him then he knew as did Bar Lou and Per Osmason that Maddy had been drawn into a very special circle.

"Breakfast anyone?" said Nathan. "Champagne, smoked salmon, scrambled egg and Beluga caviar. We have to start the day as we mean to go on."

It was a special 3 hour flight. It should only have been 2 hours but the cross winds affected the flight path.

"Nathan, this is just magical, but where are we going?"

"There and back to see how far it is" he said with a smile.

"Touché," said Bar Lou.

"Nathan," said Maddy, "please tell her, and me, where we are going."

"Well, we are starting the descent now." There was a slight bump as they landed. Colonel Ince Blundell was waiting with Tiggy and Emir.

"Happy birthday, Bar Lou."

"Thank you. Nathan why are we here? It is a lovely surprise what are you up to?"

"Wait just a few more minutes. Emir wants to show you his new yard."

She followed, chatting away to the Colonel. "Where is Angela?"

"Ah, she is coming. Here she is now."
At that moment Tiggy led out the most beautiful animal on four legs, coat gleaming, eyes bright, pawing the ground in expectation.

"This, Bar Lou, is a future Derby winner, Mercury, and you are his proud owner. Put his blanket on Tiggy," said Emir.

"Oh yes, I nearly forgot. What does it say, Bar Lou?"

She looked, 'Mercury'. Owner: Barbara Louise Campion.

"It's yours, from Nathan and all of us with love and"

"Not another surprise?"

"Well, yes, he runs in the 2.30 at Epsom tomorrow at the Derby meeting. Here are your passes. You, Bar Lou, will be able to go into the saddling enclosure. We have a box for the Derby. Your friends, and a few of Nathan's, will all be there. So choose your most outrageous outfit," said Emir smiling.

"No need," said Patra "the Sultan and I have a surprise as well. Come into the house". "I don't know how many more I can take," said Bar Lou.

"Patra, Sultan, how wonderful to see you. You are well?"

"Thank you, Bar Lou, yes."

"Now Patra take Bar Lou to our room and let her choose her present for tomorrow."

Bar Lou followed Patra. About 10 minutes later she emerged wearing the most fantastic outfit in myriad blues, tasteful, but just Bar Lou.

"Nathan, I have seven such outfits, one for every decade of my life. Isn't that wonderful?" "Brilliant," he said, as he winked at Emir, then turned to smile at Maddy.

After coffee and some of Patra's wonderful pastries, it was time to go.

Maddy and Tiggy were talking in the corner. Nathan frowned as he walked towards them. He heard Tiggy say to Maddy, "I thought you would be my rival for Nathan's time and love, now I see you together. I hope we are going to be special friends." "I hope so too Tiggy," said Maddy.

Emir appeared. "Come on people, we need to get back for the OAP lunch. Sorry Bar Lou, just joking."

They all laughed. It had been a wonderful morning. Bar Lou felt a new era was dawning. She hoped she would live to see it arrive.

The rest of the day passed quickly. Bar Lou loved being the centre of attention and having so many friends around her.

As she sat at dinner that night, wearing the third creation of the day, she looked down the table. Had it really been fifteen years since Michael and Alicia died? Yet look at Nathan now. At ease, any company fun to be with, a caring and very clever young man and how talented he is.

Nathan smiled across the table at Maddy and was glad when the dinner party broke up.

"Can I walk you back to the cottage Maddy?"

"What about Bar Lou?" "I think she will go with TM. She will need him tonight," said Nathan thoughtfully.

"Before we go, I would love to show you the conservatory and fitness rooms. They make a wonderful addition to Temple Meadows."

"Oh yes, and what else have you in mind?" said Maddy smiling.

"Me?" said Nathan. "There is so much I want to share with you Maddy, but maybe not tonight. Just come with me." They walked towards the conservatory hand in hand.

As they approached the door Nathan dimmed the lights. "Just look at that scenery. It is a starry night with a hunters moon. I hope it will be lucky for Bar Lou tomorrow. Now for the swimming pool. I designed in some special effects. We have a wave machine which children will love. Just look at the roof. See how the stars reflect on the water. Now, watch as I press this button. The roof rolls back and you really can swim beneath the stars. It is quite warm tonight. Shall we swim Maddy?"
She thought for a minute. "Why not?"

"Once you told me you had never been skinny dipping. Now is your chance. Don't worry about the windows. We can see out but, from the outside, no one can see in."

"I - I don't know."

"Yes you do. Just enjoy the feel of water rippling over your body, swim on your back and look at the stars. If you like, I will not even come into the pool."

Maddy started to strip. "Look the other way, Nathan." Then she slipped into the water. "It's wonderful" she said to herself. It was as though she was in a world of her own.

Nathan stood quietly, as much as he really wanted to be in the pool with her. Tonight was not the night. It would spoil the magic.
He stood ready with the towel, as Maddy emerged from the pool, wrapped the towel around her and held her close. My darling, darling, Maddy.

"I'll close up, whilst you dress and we will just be in time for hot chocolate and a shot or two with Bar Lou. Maddy I know that we are both busy. I will be in America until late September, October, then, who knows and you have your project to complete but we will see one another in between I hope.

Would you come to New York for the Bank holiday? I won't press you now, but I will send you two open tickets for World wide travel. Then you can join me anywhere.

Are your step parents coming tomorrow?"

"Yes, I hope so. They are very apprehensive. You are all so successful."

I know, it's a pity really, isn't it?" he laughed, "but so are you. It would be nice to meet them."

81

"Fine, but don't be too disappointed."

"How could I be? They brought you up as Bar Lou, Edward and James did for me. We have a lot in common.

Well here we are at the cottage, brace yourself for the hot chocolate with a kick." He turned, faced her and kissed her gently on the lips.

"Nathan is that you? Have you brought Maddy? Good, the hot chocolate is waiting. I just want to say 'a big, big thank you'.

Now about tomorrow."

Chapter 13

In the New York office, Gabriella and Mark sat perplexed.

"Something is not right, Gabs," he said. "There is a piece of information missing. I've been over and over the files. I've tried all I know about computers to find the gap but to no avail."

"This project is our enigma, so full of ghosts," said Gabriella. "You follow one trail halfway across the world, only to find it drops into a black hole. It is almost as if someone is playing with us."

"Yes, I know what you mean. When is Nathan back?" Today, he is flying 'redeye'. So, any minute now."

"He will breeze in and say, 'Who is going to bring me up-to-date'?"

They both looked round quickly.
Within the hour Nathan assimilated all the information they had gleaned and a little bit more.

"Nathan, I have a feeling that a file is missing and not only that, there have been 3 attempts to get into my computer, one from inside this building. At the moment it is 'hack proof'. I have designed my own programme. I have left the details, as you requested, in a deposit box. This key is yours."

"Good, well done. What we need to do is add to the team someone who has been working in International Banking ... I know just the person. I have to set up an office for an International Finance Company. If the Company appoints the person I think they will, we shall have all the information we need, but please do not broadcast this. I still have to talk to Perry Bracken."

"Fine by me," said Gabriella. "And me," said Mark.

Nathan's phone buzzed.
"Eversley," he said.

"Yes sir, right away. I am off to see the Boss. At the moment I am not sure which way to go, but we will talk on my return. Did you enjoy Hong Kong, Gabriella?"

"What do you think?" she said. "I had a letter from Mai Lee. She and Hannaway are so happy. Did you know she is working?"

"No," said Nathan.

"She has set up some English classes for the Chinese community, mainly women in a Community Centre. I think it is called 'The Den.'"

Nathan smiled. "A clever women is Mai Lee, keeping in touch with her roots."

"I must go. When 'he who must be obeyed' calls, I run. Well, walk quickly."
Nathan walked purposefully towards Perry Bracken's office.

"Come in, Nathan, please. Now fill in the gaps in your report. I am very disturbed about the Tsang connection. I have known his father for years. He has been a good friend of this country and yours."

"I gathered that, sir. Apparently Fing Wah got in over his head with gambling debts and had difficulty paying the piper. I was surprised that he did not tell his father but that is water under the bridge. From what I can discover, I will know more shortly, he was offered an opportunity, shall we say, to wipe the slate clean. Being the person he is, he took it. First of all, it involved buying antiques and selling them either in America or Hong Kong. From what I now know, they were all genuine. James organised that for me. He will be in New York next month. Fing Wah knows many collectors through his father's contacts. His gallery is doing well. His family are just so glad he has settled. Little do they really know. He is dealing in a lot of cash purchases that can only mean black money or money laundering. He certainly is not short. He is starting to travel. I saw him at Epsom. I have one of my colleagues in England doing a bit of homework on his 'friends' as one might say."

"How long will it take?"

"Who knows, but the chap doing the work is discreet and moves in the shadows, if you get my meaning."

"Take care, Nathan."

"Perry, may I mention two other points to you? There have been three attempts to hack into the computer in my office, one internal and two external. Someone or some persons are very anxious as to what progress we are making."

"That is disturbing news. Can anything else be done?"
"Well, yes, but please do not ask too many questions."

"Thank you Nathan. Did you have a good break in the UK?"

"Very definitely, sir. No doubt Edward will give you all the details."

85

"And the Ice Maiden?"

"Well, lets say a warm front is approaching."

Perry laughed. "And when will we meet this lady?"

"Maybe she will come here for Independence Day," he laughed. "It would be most appropriate, don't you think?"

"Well, bring her to lunch."

"That would be a treat for all of us, I expect."
With that the conversation ended.

Bar Lou, Edward and James were taking tea in the conservatory. It had been a busy week.

"Well, Bar Lou, how does it feel to be a winning owner?"

"Confusing really. It was a fantastic day. I doubt I shall ever forget my 70th birthday."

"What about the young lady, Maddy? What do you think of her? She is very beautiful, and that smile! Do you think," said Edward, "she might like to be an 'old man's darling'?"

"Well, she is definitely not courting a young foolish man, is she?"

"Far from it. Bar Lou do these dogs have to chase around so?"

Smiling, she said, "Yes. Unfortunately Nathan failed that Brigstock challenge."

"Don't we know! Talking about Brigstock, how is he doing? It was good to see him at Epsom."

"Yes, it was. We have lunch every now and again. Things to talk about. Let us say the 'spider project' is about to be launched."

"Don't get too clever, Bar Lou."

"What me? This will be a long match with definitely no tie breaks."

"I am off to New York next week. Would you like to come with me? You could see Nathan, we could make it a surprise. Just show him that the oldies can fight back."

"That would be fine, if we travel first class, of course, now that I am a winning owner."
"Of course."

"I've never flown 'redeye'. That might be an experience."

"It will be arranged."

"Rumple, Stilskin, go chase a rat." With that the two dogs ran for the door, barking wildly and Bar Lou smiled. "He does get some things right does young Nathan."

Meanwhile Nathan was back at 'the loft'. He had mounted his sketches of Maddy and was now looking for a suitable place to hang them. He settled on the bedroom. "One day we will share this room, Maddy, but now I shall just have to settle for the next best thing." He looked at his watch, too early to phone.

I need to contact her. "I hope she will come to Independence Day and not just for Perry's amusement."

He checked his voicemail, 6 messages, but only retained one from Maddy. Then he thought. "Stop it. You need a clear head, so concentrate old boy."

With that he faxed Jackson. "Any progress? Edward is due in New York next week. How is life at the office? Not getting too distracted?"

Nathan needed that information. He also needed access to a safe computer. Then he thought. "Yes, Cabal International Finance. I hope Hannaway will not mind coming to New York for a few months. Mai Lee will enjoy it. She could be very useful. Yes, we are beginning to move. I can almost hear Bar Lou saying 'festina lente', Nathan, 'festina lente.'"

Nathan found some discreet offices for Cabal. Mark built a computer and installed some very special programmes. Hannaway and Mai Lee were coming in September. Meanwhile Jackson would start to establish its credential, doing the rounds, meeting people, absorbing information, spending some time visiting antique galleries, buying a piece here and there.

Nathan had given up trying to finish the loft himself. He had met Patra and the Sultan at the Waldorf and asked her for help. She was delighted to have a project. She knew why they needed to travel but she would love to be back home. She liked Nathan. Emir and he were like brothers and very good for one another. If any thing happened to the Sultan or herself, Nathan would be there for Emir. That was good enough for her.

So helping Nathan furnish the loft was like helping a son set up home for the first time. Plus she could talk to him in Arabic, a much easier language for her to use. She was meeting Nathan for lunch at 'the loft'. It would be interesting.

Nathan had arranged a simple lunch and then, to her surprise, gave her drawings. "This is what I thought, but I am not sure. Maddy will be here in July. I want her to like it. What do you think?"

"Well," said Patra. "I am sure I can do something with it and the budget?"

"I have set up an account. Here is the card which will enable you to draw from it. Take it to the bank and they will exchange it for an active card. They are expecting you. Please, I ask only one thing. Leave my drawings of Maddy where they are. They are my inspiration at the moment. Can I give you a lift anywhere? I have to go to a gallery, to look at some antiques, or would you like to come with me? It would cause a stir, me on the town with a beautiful lady. It all adds to the mystique."

"That might be an idea. Thank you."

Edward was talking to Perry over dinner. "How is Nathan doing?"

"Very well. Not breaking too many eggs, so I am happy. He is a little unorthodox in some of the ways he approaches problem solving, but I can live with that. He also has an extensive network of contacts for one so young. Well, his early education has a lot to do with that. He has made some good friends. I hope we did the right things, Edward. Somehow there is a part of Nathan nobody reaches yet. Tell me about this Maddy."

"Oh, I wish she would be 'an old mans darling', if you get my drift. They are right together and for once, he is not rushing blindly into a relationship."

"Has he told you about the Tsang connection."

"Yes, he wanted some advice. I knew the father very well, he is quite the diplomat, but Fing Wah, he is another kettle of fish altogether."
"Do you think Petre Tsang knows?"

"In his head, probably, but in his heart, no, if that makes sense."

"Maybe! Maybe Nathan is closing in on that problem. We shall have to face the consequences, as will Petre one day soon."

"It is more complex than that. I think you may be simplifying the problem too much. This started because we are trying to find '4 miniatures' or at least find out what their significance is."

"The problem is like stacking a pack of cards. Pull the wrong one out and they all fall down. Don't you agree?"

"Is this too big an issue for Nathan?"

"No, call it an initiation or maybe a Brigstock challenge."
"What's a Brigstock Challenge?"

"Let me tell you," said Edward. "When Nathan was small ..."

Eventually Perry said, "So that is why he sees life as a boys own adventure ... dear dear what have I taken on?"

Chapter 14

Maddy had read and re-read every clipping, and seen every video which cross referenced with the money laundering scandal. It seemed to her journalist mind that, somewhere, there was a cover up or some person was calling in favours very effectively.

The print news had been all about the return of the Leidl paintings. It was in someone's interest to tell the story this way. But who?

She was due to meet Esther and Mary Ann this evening over a meal at her flat. "I'd better get a move on and prepare dinner."

All three young women knew that the food would be incidental, now that Esther had clearance from the partners at long last. "It does not affect my work," she grimaced.

Mary Ann was less forthcoming.

"Mary Ann, is there a problem?" asked Maddy. "No, but I am in a difficult position. You know that I have been verifying provenance information for one of the smaller auction houses? Well, something strange has turned up. Some paintings, mainly Victorian, which are on the missing list, have changed hands privately. I only know this from my work with Hammersteins. If it gets into the public domain, they will suspect me and finding work in the future would be very difficult. I could point you in the general direction, Maddy. Do you think you can handle this without implicating me?"

"If there is another angle, very definitely," said Maddy.

"Esther, what do you think?"

"Most galleries have catalogues. I know that the Met have copies of almost everyone in their Antiques & Art Squad. Maybe we could make contacts there."

"The other thought I had was to trawl through Company House records and see how many of the names that have been bandied around appear and if there are links, apart from the obvious ones."

"There is also a register in Europe. It is part public, part private, compiled by a young Jewish man, intent on finding War Criminals and, where possible, organising the recovery of works of art. He may help you in particular, Maddy, as you have family links to Austria and Germany."

"Not very strong ones, but I will give it a try. Thank you."

"Anyone for more wine?"

"Hey, Maddy, did I see you in Saluté magazine at the Derby meeting? Was Nathan there? Come on, we need the gossip."

"Not a lot to tell. He has gone back to New York. He still has over half of his scholarship assignment to go. It was fun though. He lives in a very different world so it's a case of 'watch this space'. But just to tickle your taste buds, I did go skinny dipping in the new pool at Temple Meadows. It was great."

"Was he there?"

"Yes, but not in the pool. There was just me swimming up and down. Sometimes I wish he was not such a gentleman so there!"

"Well," said Esther, "that takes the biscuit. It really does."

"Now, girls, we need to focus on this project. We could not fail, could we?"

"No, not us surely, but it is trickier than I thought."
"We can only do our best. Cheers!" she said, as she lifted her glass.

After her friends had left, Maddy poured another glass of wine. A plan was gradually forming in Maddy's mind. "What I need is a large sheet of paper and some marker pens. Perhaps if I put down all I know, some links might appear that I have so far missed."

She spent the next 4 hours collating all her information. Suddenly she felt very tired. "Blow the dishes," she thought, "I'm off to bed." She checked the time again. I might just catch Nathan on the phone.

She did not need to look up the number. She just dialled.

A voice said "Eversley."
"Nathan" said Maddy, "how are you?"
"Do you know what time it is?"
"No, but I have some news. I will be there for the 4th July. Is that okay?"
"Brilliant."
"What will we be doing?"
"Need you ask?"
"Nathan, I need to know what to pack."
"Just bring a toothbrush. We can get the rest here."
"No fear! I'll take a chance and give myself some options."
"Whatever. Maddy, I've missed you. 2½ months and I will be based

in England. At least I hope so. Til the 3rd of July. Don't forget, it, will be Independence Day and you know how I like mine. Well, I am off to bed, sweet dreams." The phone went dead.

Nathan already knew that Mary Ann was working for the Hammersteins but he had not told Maddy. It could be a conflict of interest. "I'll work it out. If not, I will see Edward. He will know the best way to handle it."

TM however was more worried. There were too many people in the field. That was not good practice. Problem was, Maddy was a journalist first and Nathan was only just about to realise how big the problem was. He has sensibly decided on a two prong attack which should offer some protection.

But Maddy, she is very exposed. If the names are correct, instead of being the Golden Girl of Inter News, she could be vilified in the press. Then Nathan would have a problem. We need to have a meeting of The Circle. It is time now to assess where we are and how we can influence matters.

'Not easy,' he thought, but that is the challenge.

Maddy woke with a start. Her door bell was ringing. Whoever could this be at 6.30 am? She almost fell out of bed, pulled on a dressing gown and answered the door.

"Alinsky?" the young man said.
"Yes, Maddy." "For you!"

He handed over a simple pink rose in a clear holder. She read the message, '*Just returning the compliment, see you on the 3rd, NE.*'

"Thank you," she said as she signed the form. Touché Nathan.

She made a coffee then went to look at the paper she had been working on until the early hours. Nothing so far, she thought. Then she looked again picked up a highlighter pen and started making the chart.

"Oh my goodness," she said to herself.

If this hits the fan, we will need to be in a nuclear bunker.

She thought about phoning Esther but did not. Something stopped her. She put her rose in water and smiled. "Only 5 days," she thought. "Then I will talk to Nathan. He will know what to do.

Now, what to take with me, or maybe I should go shopping, or I could wait until I get to New York."

For some reason Nathan was finding it hard to settle. Then he remembered that Mark Heaney was meeting Jackson today. He decided to join them.

Freddie Jackson was by the computer when Nathan walked in.

"HL. What are you doing here?"

"Looking for a missing link. Any news?"

"Not really. There are quite a few names beginning to emerge, if they prove to be involved. It is a bit too big for us, Nathan. You will have to push it up the line."

"Not yet. Maddy will be here soon. She may have some news."

"Nathan, you are walking a tightrope, so take care. One of Maddy's friends is on the edge of a buyers' circle. I'm not sure which one, but she needs help. Is Maddy sharp enough to cope, do you think?"

"I don't know but Bar Lou might just be able to ...

Bar Lou? Oh, she and Maddy have lunch every so often. I'll bet she has seen all of my baby photos by now."

Freddie laughed. "As long as that is all she has seen."

"Fair enough, Freddie. When is Mark due?"

"I'm here with the new programme. It gives us more security and will automatically trace back on any hacker routes.

"Is Gabriella ok, Mark?"

"Fine. She is chasing up some company information. Contacts at the Treasury, I think."

"Good heavens, I hope she is careful. IRS information is not that secure."

"Has Hannaway definitely accepted the job?"

"Yes. He starts in September but he will be over for briefing in August, the last week."

"Well, Maddy is here then. Jos is playing in some Jazz Festival here. Walshy might be free. I wonder if Emir will visit his parents. It would be good to be together again and a much better cover if we need one. I suspect that the next few months will be hectic and not quite the plain sailing I envisaged."

"What is this I learn about the 'loft' and a royal makeover?"

"Get away with you, but it could come in useful if the Sultanate falls. Patra is fantastic. The loft is great, just as I envisaged and the guest bedroom is beautiful, very soft colours. Maddy will love it."

"The guest bedroom?"

"Yes, why not? Softly, softly, catchee monkey, my friend."

"Oh, by the way, did you get the letter I left for you?"

"Yes, it's here in my case."

"Well, open it."

"It's my results from Harboard. I had forgotten they were out this week."

"Well, how did you do?"

"MA, summa cum laudé."

"A first again? Do you ever come second?"

"Not if I can help it."

"Mark, are you up for a few drinks tonight? We are having a celebration. Phone Gabriella. Tell her 'the loft at about 8 pm.'"

"Did you know Mai Lee is here, staying with Gabriella? Looking for somewhere to live, I think, and shopping!"

"Freddie, the Cabal ought to buy the flat. Can you organise it? And make sure Mai Lee comes over tonight."

"Sure, it will be an investment anyway."

"Now, Mark, where are we?"

"Well, you know the saying 'all roads lead to Rome'. I think we are making progress. So far, I can confirm 4 names. If we can link them up in some other way well, it's a wrap. We hand over what we know, sit back and watch the eggs hit the fan."

"As clear as that?"

"It could be. There is a massive amount of cross checking to do but we will get there. Say latish September for the report."

"Can you encrypt everything we have?"

"It is already done and only on this computer. Oh, by the way, we have the internal mole."

"Who?"

"Give you two guesses, no one."

"Don't lark about it – who is it?"

"Conrad Parker III."

"Well, well. Check out all his contacts, Freddie. We may have found a missing link. See if you can fix the get-together for the end of August. Now I must go do some shopping, personal shopping, if you get my drift."

"Anything we should know?"

"No. That will have to wait until October. There is too much at stake to jump the gun now."

The next morning, as he arrived in the Bracken Walls office, the receptionist said, "Nathan, Mr Bracken wants to see you as soon as you arrive."

"Fine, I'll go straightaway." He stood outside the door, straightened his tie and knocked.

"Come in, Nathan."

Nathan walked in and all the partners were there and Edward.

Perry Bracken offered him a glass. "Congratulations, Nathan, a Master Summa cum laudé. Whatever will you do next?"

"Well, that would be telling sir. James," said Nathan. "Bar Lou has sent you a gift. She has been keeping it for you. Now is the right time I think."

Nathan accepted the package from James.

It was his father's and mother's gold fountain pens. He choked back the tears. "Your grandfather Edward, commissioned them, especially when your father and mother married. First used to sign the Register. They were the only items to survive the crash. No doubt you will find a use for them."

"Certainly, but not just yet."

The partners moved away with, "well done, what a credit you are etc."

Nathan turned to the two men. "We have made rapid strides with the project. This refined accounting method works well. However the report will be explosive, I warn you now. It will be ready late September. It will take the team until then to verify everything we know."

"Nathan, how is this information stored?"

"I will show you sir, but as we have a mole, maybe somewhere away from here."

"A mole! Are you sure?"

"Yes, sir. He handed him a disk. "I think this is self explanatory."

"Nathan, have you time for lunch with two old friends?"

"Of course."

"Come with me, there is someone very special waiting to spoil you."

"Who?" "Bar Lou."

"Well, Nathan, you clever young man."

Bar Lou gave Nathan another present.

It was a watch. The very latest, very expensive and one he had always intended to buy.

"Its wonderful, I'll wear it on special occasions, and today is one such. How did you know?"

"Maddy told me."

"Oh she did, did she? She will be here on Friday."

"I know. She says she has her own very special present for you and she winked."

"I don't know what you are talking about!"

They all laughed and went to lunch.

Back in England Maddy was packing her holdall. Well, he said travel light so I will. Just one very special dress and the rest, mainly casual.

"Well, Nathan, let's see if you like your special present."

She folded her flow chart between two sheets of tissue paper and wrapped her dress in them. 'Best to be safe,' she thought. At least this holdall is cabin size so I will not have to wait at the airport.

She looked at the ticket. "Dam you, Nathan, it is first class. I will have to change. It's the redeye flight as well, so something that does not crush. Oh I know," she decided, as she opened the wardrobe.

As she left the flat, TM's team moved in to give her some added security. Not that she knew, of course.

All that she could focus on was seeing Nathan and discussing her paper with him.

She hoped he would be pleased but there was a lingering doubt. Was there a conflict of interest? 'Who knows, I hate to admit it but I am out of my depth.'

"Will the passengers for flight 112, please board."

"Miss Alinsky?" "Yes," said Maddy. "Will you come this way, through the VIP lounge?"

Her adventure was about to unfold.

Chapter 15

Brigstock was briefing one of his many contacts. "This is deep undercover and must be achieved whatever the cost."

"Quite," said the two men with him.

"We have been in many tight situations together and I know I can trust you absolutely. It is almost a matter of National Security. Our opponents are wiley, clever and completely without feeling. You will know one as the 'Torturer.'" Dave whistled then said, "Oh, I owe him more than one." Ken just smiled.

"Please be careful, you need clear heads. Have you been visiting galleries as I asked?"

"Yes. Eyes light up when we say we are cash buyers. We'll need stronger glasses if we look at any more miniatures. But we think the bait has been taken."

"Ta ra," said Ken. "Look what came in the post. An invitation to a private exhibition of miniatures at the Hammerstein Gallery."

"Where?" said Brigstock.

"The Hammerstein, very discreet!"

"And that is what you will have to be. Here are current photographs of the two people we need, to say, spoil their plans."

"Enough to smoke them out, or do we have them to choke?" said Dave.

"Not so quickly. You know what he did to Bar Lou. This one we will reel in very slowly, but reel him in we will. Watch your backs. I mean it. You can contact me through the usual channels."

"On how's your sister Briggie?"

"Stultifying me. It was a mistake to retire."

"Well, you seem to have escaped the leash."

"Yes. I think she will be relieved as well. Until Saturday then. I believe we are all going to the reunion?"

They nodded.

Meanwhile Maddy's flight had landed. The steward lifted down her bag.

"Miss Alinsky, will you come this way please? You will need your passport and visa at the ready. I do not envisage any problems."

Safely cleared through Customs and Immigration, Maddy started to look around.

"Are you expecting anyone in particular?" said a voice behind her. "Nathan, where did you spring from?"

"I just wanted to look at you before you spotted me. You look, well, fantastic. Come on. We will go to 'the loft' first."

"Nathan, I really need your help. This project I am working on. We are out of our depth and I do not know what to do."

"Well, forget it for a moment. My car is waiting, so just sit back and relax. I am sure if we put our heads together we can find a way to cope."

Nathan was really excited. Maddy here with him for three days. He hoped she would like 'the loft'.

She loved 'the loft'. It was beautifully furnished, understated but elegant.

"Which woman helped you do this, Nathan?"

"How did you guess?"

"Sensitive you may be, and artistic, but this is really something extra special."

"It was Patra, you remember, Emir's mother."

"Here is your room. My room, but where will you be?"

"Next door, do you like your room?"

"Yes, but why Nathan?"

"Maddy, there is nothing I would like more than to be with you, to watch you sleep, awake, smile there by my side. Just let me say, 'Let's start with the 'hors d'oeuvres' and wait for the main course until we are both free to make a very special commitment to each other." With that he kissed her, slowly and purposefully. Then she smiled. "Show me the menu," she said. "Well, if you put it like that, I have got the rest of the day clear."

"Go, unpack before I do something 'untoward', as Bar Lou would say."

"Right." A few minutes later she emerged, changed and holding a sheet of paper.

"Nathan, I want to enjoy myself for these few days but will you please look at this with me? There is no one else I can trust."

She spread the page out on the table. Nathan studied it. He blanched. Maddy had found the missing link, but how to tell her?

"Has anyone else seen this Maddy?"

"No, you are the first."

"How did you bring it here?"
"Between two sheets of tissue paper folded in my dress."

"Maddy, Maddy this is explosive."

"I know. It frightens me."

"Look, do you mind if I ask Perry, Edward and Bar Lou to look at this with us. Perry may decide to show you what I have been working on, but only he can do that. I hope you understand."

"Well, all right."

It was an hour before the three visitors arrived. Maddy explored 'the loft'. Then she went in to Nathan's room just as he finished changing. She saw the drawing by his bed. "It's the next best thing, Maddy."

"When did you do them?"

"From time to time. There is always a moment when you see the real person with an artist's eye."

"They are wonderful and the person who is modelling, is she my rival?"

"No, she lives in my dreams. You are the real thing. Come here, I want to kiss you."

At that moment the intercom buzzed.

"Foiled again," he said. "It will be our visitors. If I cope with drinks, there are some snacks in the fridge. Would you sort them out for me? I think we will sit on the garden terrace."

"Fine."

"Edward, Bar Lou, Perry, please come in." "So this is the ..."

"loft" said Nathan.
"It's beautiful," said Bar Lou, not too feminine. Not too male either, just a fine balance. Patra has done well, very well."

"Maddy," said Bar Lou. "Nathan, where are your manners? Edward you have met, and this is Perry Bracken, Nathan's boss."

"Shall we go out on to the terrace?" said Nathan. As he passed Edward he said quietly, "No, she does not want to be an old man's darling!!!"

The next hour flew by. Maddy and Nathan had been on opposite sides of the world but their work pointed in the same direction and to the same people.

"No Arpinsky," thought Bar Lou.

"Edward, we now know the missing link."

"Who? Perky?"

107

"Oh no, how is Brigstock doing?"

"Very well."

Perry looked at Edward. You will have to tell TM. I think he is in Canada. He could be here in 10 hours. I need to go to the top."

"Nathan, I would like what you have to date."

"I thought you might, sir. Mark is on his way with what we have."

"Thank you."

"You know, both of you have stumbled on the key to something very big. What you know, could, if it gets into the wrong hands, put your lives in danger. Are there any other copies of your work, Maddy?"

"No."

"Fine, we will see you tomorrow for lunch. Very informal, a barbeque, few drinks, swimming. Do you swim Maddy?. Before she could say a word Nathan said, "Oh yes, she does, just like a fish in the moonlight."

"I must go. See you both tomorrow. It has been a great pleasure to meet you Maddy." With that he left the room.

Bar Lou signalled to Edward, who was quite content to stay put.

"I think we should go. These two need a little time to think about what has happened. You really are your father's son, Nathan. I am so proud of you."

"Come, Edward, I want to see Patra. Perhaps she would like to have a look at my cottage."

Maddy turned and looked at Nathan. "We will get through this."

"Yes," said Nathan, putting his arm around her shoulder. Do you want to go out for dinner or shall we chill out here."

"I'm sure I could make us something to eat. Put some music on if you like."

They cleaned up and did the dishes.

"I know," said Nathan, "we need some fresh air. How about a horse and carriage ride around the City. It is wonderful in the evening light."

"We can just be a couple of tourists, enjoying ourselves. Let the others take the strain. We need some fun."

"Come on, get a jacket. No time like the present."

Maddy smiled. She knew for certain that Nathan was her soul mate and when it was right, they would make that commitment to one another.

"I'm coming," she laughed "but do we have to do everything at 100 miles an hour?"

"Not everything," he smiled.

"Now, no phones, no faxes, just the evening sun, a ride around the City and home. At least I hope that one day you will think of it as home."

"No doubt I will," thought Maddy, "but I could go grey before my time." She smiled her special smile at him. There was no need for words.

Chapter 16

Arpinsky and Appleby were sharing a drink in their usual sleazy bar.

"Not many in tonight," said Appleby.

"No, I think we will have to find another meeting place. What can you tell me about the miniature exhibition at the Hammerstein Gallery?"

"It is by invitation only. There will be about 100 miniatures that we have not seen before. Whether they will be of interest, I'm not sure."

"That young receptionist was telling me that there is a lot of interest. The catalogues will only be available at the exhibition. She said something interesting though. Apparently, there are two new prospective buyers on the market. New money types, loud voices, loud suits, know the cost of everything and the value of nothing."

"Do we know any more about them? If we do not we need to. It would be criminal if they were to spoil our little plan."

"Not so little really, not so little, but we can hardly warn them off, can we?"

"No, if necessary they will have to disappear."

Davy and Ken did not really understand all the implications of this job. On the surface, it seemed simple enough. Ken had an uneasy feeling.

"I think this one will get nasty," he said. "We really must be well prepared; a few little toys would be helpful."

"Toys! This is not a game!"

"Very special toys from a very special workshop."

"Oh, those toys. Yes, I wonder what new gadgets they have devised."

"There is only one way to find out. Let's go."

Back in New York, Nathan was sitting in a very high-powered meeting. His presence had been discussed at length. Perry and TM had insisted on his being there.

He really wanted to be with Maddy who had gone shopping with Mai Lee and Gabriella. He hoped she was enjoying herself.

"Nathan?" "Sorry sir, I was just thinking." "I do not know if we have all the information we need. There are some gaps which need filling." "Mark, on my team, is trailing the spending of two names who seem to flit in and out of the scene, Pinkerton and Appleby. There seems to be a connection but we are struggling to find it. They have a different agenda altogether."
"Told you he was good," said TM to his FBI contact.

TM said, "You are almost right, Nathan, very perceptive. Glean all of the information you can but, do not get too close."

"Nathan," said the FBI Chief. "Can you explain your connection with Cabal International Finance?" Nathan looked startled. "Yes, we are a group of friends who met at Firedown School and later at university. Whilst we were there we spent some time helping inner city children. We found that all our ideas were coming to nothing for lack of cash, so we used some of our own monies to play the stock market. Fortunately we were successful, very successful, so new projects were funded around the world mainly for the relief of poverty."

"What is the value of its assets? I need to calm some very nervous staff in my department."

"When I last looked, about 2½ million dollars."
"And you, Nathan, you are not yet entitled to your inheritance, yet you do not have any money worries?"

"That is true; Edward taught me all I know about stocks and shares. I used some of my allowance to play the market. Most of my friends think I am a wild life nut. Bulls and bears, you know, and I do have friends around the world. Bar Lou, Edward and James, who cared for me when my parents died, made sure I had the best education for me. It has paid off."

"Handsomely I believe."

"Very, sir" he said, without going into detail.

"May I say something; the key to some of our dead trails was provided by Maddy Alinsky, an English TV journalist and presenter. We met at Oxford. When, or if, there is a conclusion, will she be allowed access to sufficient information to complete her report and television programme? It seems only fair to me."

"If we break this ring and clear up a few other matters and she liaised with TM, I cannot see any major problems, but we will both have to clear it high up."

"Fine. That is good enough for me."

"Bar Lou, how is your project progressing?"

"We are making good progress. We have our first break through, a private exhibition of miniatures at the Hammerstein Gallery. It will be what you might call a 'cash buyers convention.'"

"Well, I think this is as far as we can go. Please follow up on any outstanding leads, but be careful. This is one operation that must be kept under wraps."

"Nathan, Edward, are you lunching with us?"

Nathan said, "I have to find three happy shoppers before they break the bank, so I must refuse, but thank you all the same."

"Three, Nathan, isn't one enough?"

"More than Edward, more than. She is flying back to UK tonight so, if it's okay with you all, I shall be otherwise engaged for the rest of the day."

He smiled and said, "Good morning, and thank you for including me. Just one piece of information. Before I go, Osmantia, in the Middle East. It might be worth investigating. The Sultan, or rather his wife, is perturbed." With that, he left.

Nathan met up with 'the girls' at his favourite fish restaurant. A regular client, he could always get his usual table overlooking the harbour, but discreet.

He ordered a drink then saw Maddy, Gabriella and Mai Lee approaching. He signalled to the Manager who met them at the door.

"Good day, ladies. Mr Eversley's table. This way."

"Nathan stood up. "Well, is there anything left in the shops? Perhaps it would help if these parcels were put in my car."

At that point, Mark Heaney and Freddy Jackson joined them, in time to load the car, and then sit down for a meal.

"Why are we on brain food, Nathan?" said Freddie. "Just renewing a few spent cells. Anyway, they do the best lobster this side of the ocean. Is that alright for everyone?"

"Now, a glass of wine." His hand glanced Maddy's. She smiled. Before we settle to our meal, Maddy flies back today, so 'Bon Voyage'. We will need to get back to 'the loft' in time for her to pack. You can carry on chatting after we leave."

"Now, how did the shopping go?"

That was all he had to say. It was non-stop repartee. Six happy young professionals enjoying a business lunch or were they?

Maddy looked at her watch and said to Nathan, "I think we should move." He agreed. Once back in 'the loft' he said, "Come here, Maddy. I just want to hold you close. Shall we sit on the terrace for a while and just talk?"

"Fine," said Maddy, "Are there any hors d'oeuvres left?"

"A few," smiled Nathan.

"Now, seriously Maddy, there are a few things I want to say." She gazed at him steadily, eyes smiling.
"Yes, about what?"

"Us."

"Go on."

"Well, I am finding it increasingly difficult to concentrate because you are so in my mind and thoughts. Maddy, I love you and hope that you would want to spend the rest of your life with me? Do you feel the same?"

"Yes," she said quietly, "Oh yes."

Then we have to be sensible for a while. I need to talk to your Guardians and do the traditional thing, ask for your hand in marriage?"

"Why?"

"Because I am a traditionalist at heart. I do so want to make sure, as far as I can, that we have a smooth path to a wonderful future. We will also have to tell James, Edward and Bar Lou, not that they will need telling!"

"I know we will be together at the end of August, so what about if I return to UK with you then, then we set the ball rolling."

"I have to be in New York until the 20th so I could be in London on 21st. We could have a couple of days together, see your guardians, then have a special dinner party on the Saturday and tell the World."

"And marry when?"

"In the New Year, say Jan 6th, which is the last day of Christmas."

"Do we have to wait that long?"

"Well, we could go to Las Vegas now and be married in 2hrs but that is cheap and far from the wedding you deserve."

"I suppose so."

"Maddy, write to me with your ideas. You can have the wedding you want, where and when you want it, and the guests, the breakfast, the trimmings, that is plenty to think about. But before we move inside, I have a little gift." He handed her a box.

"This is beautiful." It was a heart shaped locket. She opened it; there were two of Nathan's own drawings of him and her.

"Can I put it on for you?" He picked up the locket and put it around her neck. "It is with all my love." He kissed the nape of her neck, then said, "Shall we go inside?"

All too soon, Maddy had to leave for the airport. 'He is very clever', she thought. "Come to the Independence Celebrations," she smiled. This time she was quite happy not to be independent. She smiled, kissed Nathan and said, "Let's go. I am beginning to like travelling first class."

"I hope that is the way it will always be. I love you. Oh, I forgot. Whenever you want to talk to me, use this phone. It is on my bill and is the latest in mobile communications."

With that, she moved through the checkout, then turned and smiled. He watched her go.

Now back to work and this report. 'It will take all my concentration. It might just lead to other projects, who knows?' But there was only one he wanted to concentrate on.

Once back in England, Bar Lou contacted Brigstock.

"How are we doing?"

"Not on the phone. I will be at your cottage in half an hour."

Bar Lou looked around her cottage. It could do with a makeover. She must contact Patra.

She thought about Nathan. He has really matured and ready to manage his inheritance. It would be his on 25th September. James and Edward would need to explain the significance and the responsibilities it would bring. Never mind, Maddy would keep his feet on the ground. She hoped that relationship worked out.

There was a ring at the door.

It was Brigstock. "Bar Lou, how good to see you. I think you will be pleased with our project. It is turning up new information all the time. Apparently our Pinky and Perky have possession of 2 miniatures. So they tell the Hammersteins and they are looking for 2 more. They have been shown hundreds, but nothing suits. It is as though all four have to match in the same way."

"Do you know anything about this?"

"No, not really. I will need to talk to TM. Tea."

"Not green, thank you."

"English?"

"Yes, please. How was America?"

"Wonderful. Nathan got his Masters Degree. It was so special."

"I hear he has a steady lady friend."

"Oh yes, she is beautiful and clever."

"Good enough for Nathan?"

"Very definitely. You chaps must be careful not to antagonise Pinky and Perky. We really need them firmly in the trap with no room to escape."

"What will happen to them?"

"Who knows? I know what should happen, but I would find myself foul of the Geneva Convention!"

"I can really understand how you feel. I do not think Pinky and Perky are a life long partnership. If we follow this through to its natural conclusion, I doubt if Perky will be around."

"Why do you say that?"

"Because Pinky takes no prisoners, he is just there at the death."

"You could be right."

They carried on chatting about the house. "you must come and see what Nathan has done. We now have a conservatory, a swimming pool and a fitness suite!!"

"Well, I'll be blowed."

"You wouldn't, if you used the fitness suite!"

They both laughed, then Brigstock said, "Bar Lou. Hopefully this will bring an end to your demons. You deserve to be happy and as for Nathan, his natural parents could not have done better."

"Thank you, I hope so."

Then she reflected. 'Four miniatures. Michael, oh Michael, if only you had lived.'

Chapter 17

Once back in her flat, Maddy began to think about the last few hectic days. 'I am committed to Nathan and it feels great. Like all the best things that could happen rolled into a few precious moments. Really, we have had a similar life, both sets of parents died when we were young, both brought up by friends and other people's families. While he is so secure in the love around him, I feel that there is part of me I do not know. There is very little I know about my early childhood. I do remember that train journey from Prague through Europe and the boat to England. I remember the brown attaché case and the label. Where they are now, I do not know, probably ended up in a jumble sale somewhere. Michael and Angela have been so good, so caring but they will not talk about the past. I wonder what the big secret is. Why did they really change their surname? It is all questions, questions, questions and no answers? There is something nagging away inside me, urging me to face whatever demons there are to face and get on with my life.

But first I have to talk to Esther and Mary Ann. They may have more to tell me.' She was very apprehensive about the next few months. There would be massive changes in her life in more ways than one. She would have her programme, so Nathan said, but when, what should she put in or leave out? Idly she began to plan in her mind. I am too frightened to write anything down.

She picked up the phone and invited her two friends to lunch on Saturday. There would be plenty of time to think about what to say to them - a few missing links to chase up. Then she remembered something her Tutor at University had said.

"The devil is always in the detail, Maddy, think laterally." 'What devil, what detail?' she thought.

"If Michael and Angela cannot, or will not, help me discover my past I will talk to Nathan about it. Yet, who can help me?" Then it came to her, Bar Lou. "I will go and see her, she is so safe, so understanding, someone other than Nathan who I can trust. There must be a part of her that she keeps hidden. She will understand.

But first, the wedding. Write to him indeed! What can I put on paper? I suppose I should start with those 'five honest working men, how, why, where, what, when.'" At least the answers will ground my dreams.

So she pulled her pad towards her and started to write and dream. She could picture the day with the sun shining, a gentle breeze, her veil fluttering, a simple yet elegant dress and Nathan, in a village church, a happy, happy day. Then a little voice said 'But it will be in January, Maddy, be sensible.' Quite appropriate the date, the three Kings had come to the end of their journey whilst Nathan and she would be beginning another, but having the answer to one question only raised a lot more.

The entrance buzzer sounded. She was startled. 'Oh damn, she thought. I was enjoying the peace and quiet.' At the door stood the florist with a simple bouquet from Nathan. Message said 'I will soon be running out of hors d'oeuvres, can't wait for the main course, love you, only 30 days till we meet again, love Nathan'. She smiled and thought 'neither can I.'

In New York, Nathan was putting the final touches to the first draft of his report. It was nowhere near finished but at least they could all start looking for the flaws. The timetable was tight but it must be right, not quick. He could trust his Cabal, Mark and Gabriella. He hoped against hope that involving them in this project had not put them at risk. 'And Maddy,' he thought, 'she is so a part of me now, I need to make sure she is safe. I could not bear to lose her now. I hope she asks Bar Lou for help with the wedding plans as well as Michael and Angela. Well Angela.' This was, in his view, very much a job for the ladies. He would plan the main course, the setting and just hope he made the right choices.

The more he thought about it, the reunion would be safer held in England, not so many unknowns. Nathan had found in Gabriella, a super personal assistant, just like Dad found in Bar Lou. She would start to reorganise the venue. The girls would stay with Bar Lou and the chaps at Temple Meadows. Somehow he felt happier about that.

So head down, Nathan, this report! Concentrate, get it done, the sooner it is finished, the better. Now that they had Maddy's research the missing links might well declare themselves.

In the Middle East the Sultan and Patra were back at the Palace, but acknowledging to themselves that the best years there were over. To stay would be to court death, but to go would seem like running away. He had to go to the Arab Summit. Patra had been asked by Bar Lou to help her with the re-design of her cottage and Nathan had left a message for her. Her husband could not tear Emir away from the yard, "He will inherit my title but not my country," he thought, "yet he will take what is good into a new life. It is a dreadful thing I must do. This is a journey I must take on my own. There is really only one, or maybe two people I can trust." He decided to contact Perry Bracken, a man whom his father had told him to trust. He would not only look after his finances but would be a good sounding board. It is time to 'scramble', his code for acting in secret. The message to Perry Bracken was simple. 'Marks in the sand of the desert do not last'.

Perry was in his office dictating letters when he received the Sultan's message via the Embassy mail. Well, well, young Nathan was right after all. He made two phone calls. One he simply said, "operation eagle starts now," the other to TM, "it has started."

123

Both men knew that they had only a few days after the Arab Summit to make the whole thing work. It had to be both right and quick. If anything came out, the Middle East would flare up again and the hard won peace would be no more. They needed a plausible cover.

He tapped his pen on the desk. TM's call came in at that moment.

"Thought you might need a new blanket. Mercury is running at Sandwich in 2 weeks, D-day?"

'That's it,' decided Perry, 'it is just inside the window. Patra will already be in England so what could be more natural?' He thought, 'We will go for it'. He made one more call to the President.

Edward and James were sitting in the conservatory at Temple Meadows "James, I have all the papers here for Nathan. I understand that he is coming over for the Bank Holiday."
"That's right," said James. "There will not be much peace that week. Do you think he has any idea of his fortune?"

"No, and I do not think he cares. He has enjoyed playing the stock market. He must have made about 3 million by now and that money is attracting interest in Couttles Bank. If the papers get wind of this, he will be in the centre of some unwanted and unwarranted publicity, especially with this wedding."

"What wedding?" "well, I am almost sure he is about to propose to Maddy, if he has not already done so informally."

"So the 'ice maiden' has thawed?"

"We do not know that, Edward, keep you mind on the job."

"Do you think it would be an idea for him to lunch with TM, Bar Lou and us? It would be less of a problem to deal with in that company. It had better be over there. I will set it up."

Arpinsky and Appleby were standing alone at the Hammerstein Gallery watching the parties move around the miniature displays. "Nothing here anything like what we are seeking," said Appleby.

"I agree, Arpinsky, so let us concentrate on the people. Which are these two men you have been talking about? Are they here?"

"Not yet," said Appleby "but they will be with money to burn, I am told. There they are, just by the door."

"Don't know them," thought Arpinsky, "just another pair with more money than sense."

That was the first big mistake he had made in years. He did not know his enemy. He was so immersed in being he was not focussed.

Dave and Ken had no such problems. They were focussed, "What was it Bar Lou said?" asked Ken.

"Oh, you mean, 'come in to my parlour said the spider to the fly.'"

"Yes, they have taken the first step."

"So have we," said Dave, "is your camera working?" "Overtime," said Ken as they moved around the exhibition, "Brigstock will be pleased."

In their London flat, Angela Allinson said to Michael, "Is it time we gave Maddy her parcel?"

"No", said Michael, "but the time is coming. I have had a letter from Nathan, who wants to come and see us late August. Does that suit you, Angela?"
"Oh, very much," she thought "and I think I know what it is about."

At the yard the Ince Blundells were sitting in stony silence. Natasha, his wife had taken a phone call from Colin. 'Why oh why,' he deliberated, 'does that always means trouble?'

Colin was sitting in a gay bar with Malcolm. "We could start that business, if I could get some capital together, but I am broke. The banks would definitely say 'no'." Pity Malcolm was not rich. Colin would use anyone for his own ends, and he was using Malcolm now.

"I know, I'll phone Dad, or rather mum. They owe me. Tiggy has had the best of everything, now it is my turn. Their finances should have recovered by now. It really was not my fault they lost all that money. Should have been more careful. It is strange though. They never showed the fact that they were almost bankrupt. I wonder if they were telling me the truth. Well, we shall see.

I will go to the Yard for lunch and see how the land lies. Mum at least will be pleased to see me."

The Colonel was decidedly edgy. He had not forgotten the shame he felt at losing their nest egg. It was not going to happen again. TM had saved him from the media last time. Would Colin open old wounds? He would call TM, he has to know.

Tiggy, of course, would be delighted to see him, but would Emir? That young man could see through people. I would not give much for Colin's chances if he crosses him. Tiggy and Emir are as thick as thieves these days, so happy and fun to have around. I wonder if he will go back to Osmantia? Poor Tiggy, but may be not.

The lunch was awkward. Colin was not forthcoming about the real reason he was here, just kept up a light banter. Emir just sat watching, occasionally making a comment.

Then Colin fired the first salvo.

"Well, dad, when did you buy the yard?" asked Colin.

"I didn't," said the Colonel, "it is not mine, I manage it for Emir. Remember I lost out on that investment you suggested, so how could I buy this?"

"Just thought you might have had a bit of luck on the horses," said Colin.

"Colin," said his mother "not at the dinner table. If there is something you want to know, we will deal with it privately afterwards."

Emir frowned. 'So that is what happened. It is obnoxious. Poor Tiggy, she is so trusting. I must tell Nathan. This chap needs watching.'

In Hong Kong, Fing Wah was in his father's study. He knew that he could be in trouble but he did not have an idea what his father really knew. He was about to find out.

"So Fing Wah, what have you got to tell me? Is business going well?"

"Yes, father, quite well. We are opening new markets all the time," said Fing Wah.

"And who exactly funds this business?"

"I joined up with some investors at the start, and they still have an interest."

"And these investors, do I know them?"

"No, I do not think so."

"Don't you? I think you do! I know you do! You were in debt. Do you believe for one minute I would not find out? My people are everywhere. Now you are in so deep you could go under and more importantly disgrace the family. Is that not true?"

"May be", said Fing Wah, "Maybe," said Tsang. "Have you no shame, no sense of family. Have we taught you nothing of our values? Can you get out of this business?"

"No, as you say, I am in too deep."

"That's not the answer I want to hear. Think again. There is an honourable route. You could tell all and shame these people."

Fing Wah looked terrified and said quietly, "I would rather fall on my sword."

"That is not a way open to you. That is for men of honour, you have no honour. How can you be a son of mine? Well, I do know most of what you are up to. You will write down the names of your 'partners' and I will do the rest. You will repay me, every penny it costs, with your freedom, it is lost to you. When I know the details and have them verified, you will join the Monastery at Lantau and there you will stay until I say so. Is that clear?"

"Yes, father."

"Then start writing, your life depends on it. You are my son, so you cannot be all bad. We must chip away to find the good and start again. If you do not keep your part of the bargain, Fing Wah, you will make one more journey from the Monastery, down the hill to the prison. That's a promise."

A few hours later Fing Wah handed to his father a piece of paper. There were 4 names on it.

"Thank you, you will find all you need in your room to join the Monks at Lantau. Go now and get ready. Remember the saying, 'a journey of a thousand miles starts with a single step'. This is your first step to a new life, every mark on this path will show."

Petre Wah and his wife watched as his son. Head shaved, wearing only the garb of a monk, carrying a wooden bowl walked with his companions at the start of his journey.

Petre Wah phoned TM. "You were right, I will hand in the parcel at the Embassy. We are there for a reception tonight."

He put the phone down, nodded to his wife. A small tear ran down his face. He turned and looked to the East, I will only face the West again when this task is completed. He kept his promise.

TM received the envelope the next day. 'Well, well, we really are getting closer, the net is closing.'

Chapter 18

Maddy could not concentrate. She was due in the studios at 4 am the next morning and thereafter for 3 mornings a week whilst Annie was on holiday. At least she did not have to suffer Graham, but did not know who would be her partner.

Before going to bed early she wrote down a few ideas for the wedding. The village church near Temple Meadows would be the venue, the date January 6th, the groom, Nathan Eversley.

The bridesmaids - Tiggy, Esther, Mary Ann and Mai Lee?
The dress – White or Cream?
Bridesmaids – Colour
Flowers – bouquet spring flowers
The bridesmaids - snowdrops and crocus
Church – talk to Nathan
Time – 2 pm
Photographer –
Transport -
Organist –
Choir –
Vicar –
Cake –

'Oh, I must meet with Bar Lou, Angela and maybe even Patra. I cannot do this without help. I'm just not sure that I know what I want, other than I do want to marry Nathan.'

She retired to bed. 4 am came quickly. The news room was busy. Nothing special on the wires, three interviews, 2 sport bulletins.

"Hi Maddy, you will be with Bill Hardy this morning, he is just back from the Middle East." "Thanks." "There is trouble brewing, nothing on the wires." "Talk to him and check the running order. Any changes we will relay via the earphones."

Maddy's ears pricked up at the news about the Middle East. She hoped the Sultan and Patra were safe.

The morning passed quickly. As she was leaving, the director stopped her. "The Boss wants a word about your report on the Liedl paintings. Go now. He is in his office."

"Paul," said Maddy. "I believe you want to see me."

"Yes, how is the programme coming on? When can we schedule it?"

"I'm not sure. There are many loose ends but hopefully before Xmas. That is if we do not run into any problems."

"Fine, keep me up-to-speed. Some drafts as soon as possible."

"Paul, whilst I am here can I sort out a longish break after Christmas. I seem to have worked solidly since my contract started and feel in need of a rest. I was hoping I could take a 3 month sabbatical. I have a few ideas to follow up."
"It is not unusual, Have you problems to deal with Maddy?"

"No, but I thought I may try and trace my family. It has been bugging me for some time. Without the pressure of work, I could do something."

"Ok, I'll try and clear it for you. Will you not be taking leave over the Bank Holiday?"

"Yes, that has been approved."

"I know."

"Until then I am happy to fill in as necessary, as well as completing the schedule for the programme."

"Fine, tomorrow same time? There will be a staff meeting when programmes finish. There are developments we need to talk about, a few changes looming on the horizon, but nothing for you to worry about. I cannot say the same for all the team."

Maddy wished she could be honest with Paul, all this secrecy was bugging her. I just do not know how Nathan does it. Perhaps Bar Lou can help me. I am getting very confused, must be wedding nerves, but that is too easy.

Maddy and nerves were not really a combination that many of her colleagues would have recognised.

She arranged to stay with Bar Lou for the weekend after her meeting with Esther and Mary Ann. 'In fact,' she thought. 'I'll change the date for that get-together. Mary Ann still has the exhibition and Esther will just fit in.'

Having rearranged the date, she would set off to Bar Lou's cottage after the staff meeting. There were so many questions she needed to ask.

Bar Lou was not surprised to hear from Maddy. Nathan had been in contact, he wanted her to help Maddy with the wedding, not that it was official. She doubted that Maddy would mention it this time. TM was coming to Sunday lunch. He may be able to help with the programme she was making for the TV Company.

James and Edward were staying in London so Bar Lou was glad of the company.

Bar Lou was not quite prepared for the line Maddy took. She was desperate to trace her family history. She opened up to Bar Lou.

"I feel that part of me is hidden. I don't know why my step parents changed their surname. I have nothing from my childhood. Nathan is so lucky, you are able to answer his questions. Michael and Angela just clam up when I try to talk to them."

"Have you spoken to Nathan about this?"

"Yes, he says it's the future that matters. He loves me just as I am and tells me not to worry. I don't worry, but it niggles away at me."

"What do you want to do?"

"I don't really know. I suppose you know Nathan's plans. I just wish I had a mother to help me just now. Independence is OK whilst you are carving a career. I know I have done well and want to do better. I did not bank on meeting Nathan or how I would feel about him. It has made me rethink my future plans. I am hoping to take a sabbatical after Christmas, the break will do me good, at least I hope it will."

"Does Nathan know of your decisions?"

"Oh, yes. He said he is hoping to have a break soon. It could work out well for us. So much depends on how the reports we are working on are received. It has been very demanding and quite frightening at times."

"I am sure it has. Now to change the topic, I have been sorting my jewellery. Would you like to help me? By the way I have been admiring your locket."

"Oh yes, Nathan gave it to me before I left New York. Just wearing it makes me feel closer to him. Now let me see your treasure chest."

They had quite a fun afternoon. Trying on jewellery and rings. Bar Lou learnt a lot about Maddy, all of which she liked. She even learnt her ring size. A job Nathan had asked her to do for him.

"Maddy," said Bar Lou, "shall we go up to the house for a swim? It has helped me to use the pool. I do not talk much about what happened in France but I can hardly go swimming with you and not expect you to ask questions.

I never wear fitted clothes because I am not happy with my body. During the War I was captured and tortured. The outcome of which means that there are weals across my back, my face was mutilated. I needed extensive plastic surgery. I do not see me when I look in the mirror. I was in so much shock that I lost weight and was thereafter unable to have children. Nathan's father, Michael, was imprisoned at the same place. He could hear my screams, they made sure of that. He was so kind to me when we were released. If it had not been for him I would not have survived. I am sure that he and Alicia would be so proud of Nathan and, knowing Michael's eye for a pretty woman, would have been more than happy to welcome you into the family."

"Bar Lou, I am terrified, you read about these atrocities but so rarely meet anyone affected. Thank you so much for sharing that with me." She reached out and hugged Bar Lou. "Now, let's go for that swim.

Bar Lou when I look at you I do not see a physically impaired lady. I see smiling eyes, a warm personality, a wicked sense of humour and the sharpest brain I have encountered in years. Be proud of yourself. Although the external marks have faded, it is still in the mind. It is not that the demons find rest.

Perhaps we can fight our demons together and maybe we will surprise everyone at my wedding." "I feel sure you have spoken to Nathan." "Yes, we will marry, all being well, in January next year. Please be happy for us."

"Happy?" said Bar Lou, "I am delirious. You know he used to call me Dippy Dora?"

"I think he has moved on from that," said Maddy. "You will always be our family, you have done so much for him and I can see why he loves you so much. Hopefully I can share just a little of that."

A phone rang "Yes," said Bar Lou. It was Brigstock. Simple message. "Pinky has made his first mistake!" She smiled. 'You little beauties,' she thought. We are getting close, one day my friend, just one day.

"Maddy, I just need to talk to TM to confirm our luncheon date."

"Fine," said Maddy. "I'll get my swimming things together."

"TM" said Bar Lou.

"Yes."

"Perky has made his first mistake. Brigstock has phoned me and, oh, by the way, Maddy is here a few nerves I think. She will be fine. She may have some questions for you on Sunday. I will try to help her frame them. See you at lunch."

"Goodbye, Bar Lou."
"Maddy, are you ready?"

"Coming. You know Bar Lou, I feel so much better. You are so clever. In a few weeks Nathan will be here and our plans will be clearer to everybody. I doubt if they will surprise many.

How will you cope with the extended Cabal?"

"Just as it comes, Maddy. As usual, enjoy the chaos, pretend to be Dippy Dora and enjoy taking the dogs for a walk for some peace. "Rumple, Stilskin go catch a rat" she said, and thought, 'perhaps I will really catch mine.'

Nathan phoned Maddy.

"I just need to hear your voice. How are things going with Bar Lou?"

"Absolutely great. She is a wonderful person but I am sure you know it".

"Yes, I do" said Nathan. "It will not be long before I can say that to you and really mean it. How is your thinking going?"

"Slowly. Things are a bit of a jumble. This weekend has definitely helped. Bar Lou, Patra, Angela and I will meet soon and get down to some details."

"Maddy, you are not to worry about costs. The whole event is just my way of saying 'thank you' to Michael, Angela and you for coming into my life. So please do not worry. Spend whatever, have the wedding of your dreams and mine. See you soon. Love you lots."

"Bye Nathan, see you soon."

She then saw Bar Lou advancing with the hot chocolate. Maddy said "Did you shoot it once or twice? "Oh definitely three times tonight," said Bar Lou. They both laughed.
'What a perfect weekend' thought Maddy.

TM arrived promptly at 12 noon. Bar Lou and Maddy were returning from church. Maddy had met the vicar and fallen in love with the setting and the style of the building. 'Just right,' she thought.

"Well," said TM "how are things with you Maddy? That was a splendid piece of work Nathan showed me. It was quite amazing that these young ladies, working with little or no backup, could sift through so much material and pick out the bones. Well done. It has helped us so much.

I understand that you would like to use your material for the programme. Maybe we will refine it but I assure you that I will release as much as I am able and you can break the story. It would be more than helpful to us."

"That would be great, of course. You will see the tapes before they are broadcast."

"Most definitely. Now that is enough about work, let us enjoy Bar Lou's lunch and a very fine glass of Chateau Neuf du Pape. Quite rounds the meal off well, don't you think?"

Maddy looked up and smiled as only she could. 'Good heavens,' thought TM, 'no wander Nathan played this one long. He had to be sure. What a lucky young man he is. She will be an asset,' he mused. Circle meetings in the future will be quite lively, whatever the future is.

Bar Lou was full of Mercury's progress. "Tiggy phones me every week. We will all go to the races and hope he wins. Maybe there will be more than one reason to celebrate. Did you know that the Cabal will all be here for the Bank Holiday?"

"It will be some reunion. Hannaway is married to that pretty Chinese girl, Mai Lee. I did not think he would be the first to marry. I quite thought it would be Freddie. He is so attractive to the ladies."

"Oh, Bar Lou," said Maddy, "let them take their time. The bond between the friends is so strong. Do you know that between them they speak 28 languages? They swap from one to another with ease."

"Oh, don't I know. When Nathan was 14 he went to stay with the Sultan and Patra in Osmantia. Someone asked Nathan if he could speak Arabic. "Oh yes," he said, "both bazaar and society. It has been difficult keeping up with him sometimes."

Maddy laughed. "Well, who knows" she said, "they might just mature. Anyway, here's hoping. It is good to have friends. Michael told me of a notice he saw somewhere which said

Friends welcome anytime
Family by appointment."

They all laughed. None of them had family to speak of but all were blessed with good friends and oh, how they would need them in the coming months.

Chapter 19

James and Edward had a pleasant weekend at the Club. Edward had finally secured an invitation to the Hammerstein Gallery Miniature Exhibition. I must try and understand the fascination people have with them. Maybe something will click and shed some light on why Michael has written that note 'four miniatures'.

"James, do you want to come to Hammerstein? It is only across the park?"

"No thanks, Edward, I thought it might be an opportunity to look up some colleagues from '1 Corps'. They are in town this weekend. You never know what I might learn. Also, I have some work to do for Nathan."

"For Nathan?"

"Yes, he wants to surprise Maddy."

"Oh," said Edward. "Poor Maddy, her life is going to change so much. She is a bright young woman and those looks! I hope Nathan handles the news about his inheritance well and is able to lead Maddy gently ..."

"Oh, I am sure about the leading," said James laughing "as for the rest, time alone will tell."

Edward enjoyed his walk across the Park to the Gallery. It was a real summers day with just enough light breeze to make for comfortable walking. The Gallery was not crowded. There were enough people milling round for him to see if there were any faces he recognised, may be an old friend or two.

James meanwhile was having a quick drink with two of his particular cronies. Gently word fencing, there were questions he wanted to ask but he had to be sure.

"James, did you know that Arpinsky (now known as Pinkerton) has surfaced? I saw him last week." "Told the boss man," said Nigel 'hoover' Browne. "Is there something going down? The old rumour mill is churning out information. One of my old contacts thinks there is a sting on the way. Thought he might be talking about the Leidl paintings but that was ages ago."

"I get the same feeling, my contacts are jumpy. Appleby was in town as well. Gentleman, this is serious. The past has a habit of surfacing. There are a lot of people who might have something to hide who, after all these years feel safe, but are they?"

"Charles," said James "remember at the end of the war, when we were observing the War Tribunals, we had a feeling that, although they were dealing with the blindingly obvious, the under current suggested there was more. We never did work out what it was. I always thought one of these barristers, Hon. Bart Right Wynne knew too much. I saw his briefs. One or two questions he asked, did not relate to the information he was given - a lucky guess, a quick memo, I did not think so then and I still do not."

"What happened to him?"

"Oh, family fortunes or so it is said, unless you are extremely lucky or avoid death duties somehow. There is no other way to suddenly have millions at your disposal. I know his wife's family had money but there were four children. Perhaps it is worth another look. He has that place in Gloucester, an ancient pile, stuffed full of Victorian art and miniatures. I do not know if he is still alive. He became a recluse, not from choice, so many in his circle shunned him. Suddenly dropped off the invitation lists. It might be worth another look. His son opens up the house and grounds for the National Trust. I've seen him in town, he lent some miniatures to the exhibition at the Hammerstein. That fellow has some sharp friends. Got kicked out of some minor public school, dropped out for a while, went travelling and now has a finger in galleries all over the USA and the Far East."

James' mind did cartwheels. It really had been worth staying in Town. Now they had another piece in the jigsaw.

He said to Nigel and Charles, "Fancy doing a bit of sleuthing, just for old time's sake? If something is about to go down, it's better to be prepared, dib dib and all that."

The two friends looked at one another. "Thought you would never ask. By the way, how is Nathan? Has pseudo fatherhood produced these grey hairs?"

"Not really, it has been so infuriating at times but we have had Brigstock to help."

"Brigstock! Is he still around?"

"Yes. He does the odd bit of work for me now and then. As for Nathan, he has a zest for living that sometimes is in danger of getting out of control. Hopefully he will settle down and marry in the not too distant future." "Charles, he sounds like a chip off the old block." "His father was the same. Do you remember that dining in the night when we arrived at the Mess for the dinner. He had organised a rural pursuits theme and we had a trout stream complete with fish running through the dining hall!! It costs thousands to put right. Good job it was only a short term commission," said Charles.

"Yes, but the hobby horse derby was even funnier. Good job there was no television in those days. Chaps could let off steam without fear of being splashed all over the papers," said Nigel who had coped with more than his fair share of the gossip pages.

"Talking of dining halls," said James, "shall we eat?"
"Thought you would never ask," said Charles.

"Edward did get a surprise at the Gallery. The Honourable Wright Wynne was deep in conversation with two men he did not recognise.

The news that Wright Wynne was given did not please him at all. There had been a 'leak'. Fing Wah had dropped out of sight. "So far, no one knows of his whereabouts. We must find him," said Wright Wynne.

"Believe me, we have been looking," said Davis Brown III.

"Keep trying, now smile and enjoy our booty. Damned clever idea of yours Davis."

Davis Brown III was worried. He, like Fing Wah, loved gambling, knew every Casino from London to Beijing and back and was in deep. 'Pity the paintings had been too hot to handle,' he thought. It was a great sting.
The third person was an Austrian Jew who went by the name of Inky. His partner had recently died in a car crash.

"Maybe it is time to lie low. We can have a break for a while," said Wynne Brown. "Keep in touch, usual channels. I like the one where you use an exhibition catalogue but just leave that for a while. A note in the personal column of The Times will be fine."

"Are you mad?" said Davis.

"No, just like sailing close to the wind."

"Too dammed close," said Davis.

"Sometimes, old chap, just sometimes" said Wright Wynne. "I must go, people to see, places to go."

With that the threesome left. Edward was gadget mad. He was still trying with his new pen camera, so small it was not recognisable. Hopefully it had worked. TM could be very interested. All in all a very profitable weekend.

'Just that job to do for Nathan. Do that on my way back, should be a good game of bridge tonight,' he thought. What more could a man want? Well, there were one or two things but ...

In New York Hannaway was sharing a coffee with Nathan and Freddie.

Hannaway had heard through Mai Lee that Petre Tsang had banished Fing Wah from his home. He said "I heard rumours that people were looking for him but he has just disappeared, no trace. Petre Tsang is almost a hermit, is very rarely seen on the social scene."

"Poor Petre. So he has finally seen through his youngest son." "That is interesting," said Nathan to his friends. But I think the pieces of the jigsaw are coming together. I want to go to Hong Kong anyway, I'll try and see the Tsangs. Maybe I can stay with them."

"Hey Nathan," said Freddie, "Are you dreaming about Maddy or what? Now, about this Bank Holiday romp. What have you got planned apart from spending time with Maddy. Who else will be there?"

"Oh, I have a few surprises in store. Why spoil the fun by telling you? Now, just watch and learn if there is still any room in that brain of yours."

Freddie blushed. "Nathan, is Gabriella coming? I hope so." "Do I have to make it look like a works outing just so you can pursue her?" said Nathan.

"It's serious, Nathe, she is terrific!"

"Good luck, but don't push it. She has got so many relations even you could not escape!!"

"Now, check diaries, Hannaway. I am off to Hong Kong and I will fly from there to Paris and then to London. I need to spend some time there before going to Temple Meadows."

"Nathan, you must have enough Air Miles by now to buy an airline, never mind a seat on the plane."

"Oh, I have given them to Hannaway, we all use them." When he was last in London Nathan had collected his Grandmother's ring from the Vault. He wanted to have it cleaned and reset for Maddy. Gan Gan would be very happy with this arrangement. Now he had her ring size he could get the job done. Petre Tsang would see that only the best jewellers would work on it for him.

He was sad for Petre Tsang and his wife. Maybe if he told them about Maddy it would help lift the very obvious gloom.

Petre was his usual courteous self and was delighted to have Nathan to stay. He readily agreed to have the ring refurbished.

"She is a very special lady, this Maddy then Nathan," said Petre. "Oh yes" said Nathan "very special."

"Good, tell me a little about her."

"Try and stop me," said Nathan. They all laughed. Petre did not mention Fing Wah so he did not ask but he did say to Petre's wife, in Mandarin, "I know of your sorrow. As a friend I share it. Also as a friend, if I can help, please ask."

She smiled.

"Oh, by the way if all goes well next week, Maddy and I will marry in January."

"Congratulations!"
"Thank you. There is so much I want to show her. I'm planning our wedding journey. Could I come here for the Chinese New Year?"

"Nathan, you do not have to ask, of course you are welcome."

"And this is a final request from me. Will you both come to my wedding?"

"That we will think about Nathan. We will reply when the formal invitation arrives."

"So the ring is for Maddy then?" said Petre.

"Yes," said Nathan.

"Your Grandmother would have been very pleased."

The ring was duly delivered to the Tsangs next morning. "It is beautiful," said Nathan, "just right for Maddy."
"Nathan," said Petre's wife. "I have a gift for Maddy which I made myself. It is tradition in my family to embroider good luck wishes on to a special handkerchief for the bride to carry at her wedding. Please give this to Maddy from us both. It has a little pocket in which there are some coins. They signify her independence, I hope she likes it."

"Thank you so much, I see my car has arrived. I am so lucky to have friends like you. I will keep in touch. Now for Paris and Gan Gans apartment. I need to see Clothilde.

Two nights in Paris. Some presents for Bar Lou and Maddy, welcome gifts for Mai Lee and Gabriella and he was off to London. He should be there by midday. He had not told Maddy when he would arrive. He took a taxi to his flat, showered, changed, collected some flowers and went to see Maddy.

He rang her entrance phone and mimicking a cockney said, "flowers for Miss Arlinksy."

"Good heavens, Nathan, I'll need more vases at this rate." She opened her door. It was not the usual messenger. He turned, "flowers for my lady," he said.

"Nathan, oh how super. I was just thinking what to pack."

"Aren't we off to see Michael and Angela?"

"Yes."

"Well, put a move on, I've been planning what to say for weeks."

"You lost for words," said Maddy, "never."

"However, there is one thing I must do first. Come here, I need a hug."

"Only a hug?" said Maddy, as she moved into his arms.
"Patience, Maddy," he said, before he kissed her.

"Now, before this goes too far let's go."

"I have some flowers for Angela and a very special brandy for Michael."

"Bribery! I did not think you could stoop so low," she laughed.

Michael and Angela were waiting. They had never seen Maddy so happy. "It must be good news." said Angela admiring her flowers. "This way," said Michael. "I think it is time Nathan and I had a chat and maybe a brandy." When he saw the label – "on second thoughts, this will keep!"

"Well, Nathan, as if I have to ask why you are here" said Michael.

"Well, that makes it easier for me" said Nathan. "Just one request, may I have Maddy's hand in marriage please. I do love her so, and I will do my best to make her happy."

"I don't think there is any doubt about that. Of course we agree. What took you so long?"

Nathan smiled. "But before we join the ladies Angela and I have resisted telling Maddy about her past. I hear you have been researching her family tree. We have the case she brought with her, complete as the day she arrived. There is a letter from her mother and some pearls and a package from her father. The case has a secret compartment so it arrived safely. She does not know about it. We felt it was important to do it at the right time. I think that right time has arrived."

Nathan was stunned into silence.

"Yes, maybe. Look, why don't you have the use of my apartment in Paris for a weekend. Take the case with you and give it to the Maitres. I hope to take Maddy there for a few days. It will be better if we are on our own and have the time."

"Certainly, now shall we join the ladies?"

Maddy looked apprehensively at Nathan, he smiled and so did she. 'Our new life is beginning,' she thought. Now for the weekend. She wondered what surprises were in store.

It was hectic, mad and very tiring. Meeting up with the gang was fun but she kept thinking, 'when will we get time on our own? There is so much to do.'

Towards the end of the week, Nathan, realising that they had not really had time to talk, said to Maddy "Pack a weekend bag, I am going to take you away for a few days."

"Where?"

"Oh, wait and see, but I am sure you will like it." He explained to James, Edward and Bar Lou his plans. They smiled.

"Life is still like a boys own adventure to that young man," said Edward.

"Let us hope that fortune smiles on them," said James.

"It will," said Bar Lou.

Maddy and Nathan slipped away one evening and took the night flight to Paris.

"Paris?"

"Yes. After all, it is the City for lovers as you will discover. We need time on our own. I have a few surprises in store."

"When we get to Gan Gan's apartment, change for dinner. We are off on a cruise around the City by night. Remember New York, well this is the Paris version. Just two happy tourists enjoying themselves."

'Maddy looks stunning tonight,' he thought. 'I am so lucky.' The meal on a private launch was fun. 'It is the right time now,' he thought.

They arrived at the flat laughing like teenagers. "Come on to the terrace, Maddy, see Paris by night from here." A small table was set, champagne on ice, 2 glasses.

Her heart lurched.

Nathan turned to her, "please sit here. It is a glorious view and I have something to ask you."

"What is it?" said Maddy.

"Madeleine Alinsky, will you marry me please?"

Maddy was stunned. "Yes, please," she said quickly.

He produced the ring and put it on her finger.

There was no need for words. "It is beautiful," said Maddy. "I wanted to ask you here. The ring is a family heirloom, I had it reset for you in Hong Kong."

"Oh Nathan, will I ever really know you."

"Well, we now have a lifetime for you to find out."

"Now some champagne?"

"And the hors d'oeuvres," Nathan

"Well who knows?"

The next morning, or rather later that day, Nathan took Maddy her breakfast. He reached under her bed and pulled out a parcel.

"It's for you Maddy."

"What is it?"

"Open it and see."

"It feels like a picture."

"It is of a sort," said Nathan grabbing his sketch book. 'I can't miss this one.' he thought.

Maddy tore off the wrappings. "It is your family," said Nathan. "Hopefully it answers your questions. Take time to study it, then we have a few things to do today."

"Nathan, this is fantastic. I cannot believe it. O thank you." She kissed him. This time it was different. It said, 'I love you' in a very special way. After a few quiet minutes sitting there looking at her family tree, Nathan broke the silence.

"I must phone Bar Lou and Michael. They ought to be told."

Phone calls made, they left the apartment hand in hand. "We are going to see Clothilde."

"What 'the Clothilde' the fashion icon?"

"Yes. My grandmother helped set her up in business. She might just have a few ideas about your wedding dress and trousseau. We do have to get on with things you know. Remember we have to go back to Temple Meadows and face them all. Bar Lou is arranging a very formal dinner, lots of cutlery and not enough to eat," he smiled. "So find a very special gown that we can take back with us. I am off to the Bank. I think I will need to release some funds," he smiled. Blew her a kiss, then they left to see Clothilde.

She liked Clothilde immediately.

"So what is it you want Madeleine? Do not worry about price. I promised his grandmother that one day I would dress his bride just as a thank you to her. You are so beautiful, a touch of the ice maiden I think." Maddy laughed. 'It is a thaw,' she thought.

Back at the apartment, bags everywhere Nathan showed Maddy Gan Gans room and sitting room. "Now this is to be your arbour, a place to be you. I will only come in by invitation. Talk to Patra, tell her how you would like it and leave the rest to her."

"Now we must pack and get back to Temple Meadows. I am last running out of hors d'oeuvres," he said smiling.

The dinner at Temple Meadows was fantastic. All their friends, partners, relatives came. The setting was magnificent. "I am so lucky," she thought "so very lucky."

Nathan of course made her wait until everyone had found their place. They walked in hand in hand.

"Friends," he said "meet the future Mrs Eversley." It was the first time he had used these words. They felt good. Tonight will be magical, tomorrow, well, we will face that together ...

Chapter 20

It was a very lovely dinner party, full of fun and laughter. After dinner, most guests made their way to the conservatory, chatting informally in small groups. They spent time with Nathan and Maddy, teasing them playfully. It was just too good an evening to spoil.

Nathan suddenly realised that life was changing. He had crossed an invisible line and knew he wanted to take on some of the responsibilities now that he had previously not acknowledged. It was time to look forward, to enjoy the moment. Life was beginning to take shape. He caught Maddy's eye. Together they waited until the guests had either left or gone to their rooms.

Eventually, Edward, James and Bar Lou joined them for a few private moments.

Maddy turned to Bar Lou.

"Thank you so much for tonight, I really cannot remember when I was so happy. I must say, I did wonder what Nathan had up his sleeve when he said 'leave it to me, trust me I am going to be your husband.' The hairs on the back of my neck started to tingle."

She smiled.

"I was not sure what to expect but I feel that wherever we are, or whichever part of the world we visit, this is now where I belong. Thank you."

James cleared his throat. Not given to emotion, or so he would have everyone believe said, "Nathan, tomorrow, well, now actually, you come into your inheritance."

Nathan replied "you mean I get sole control of my trust fund? Edward joined in.

"It is a lot more than that, but now I think tomorrow is time enough. Perhaps over a quiet lunch with Bar Lou. Maddy, take care of this young man, he has far to go, enjoy the journey. Take time to see the view and smell the flowers for it is bound to be eventful."

Bar Lou said "Well I think it's time we retired. Nathan, Maddy, lunch at 1 pm. Perhaps if we get together an hour earlier Edward, James and I can go through the details of your inheritance. Until then I am off. I am off to shoot some hot chocolate and let the dogs out. Goodnight."

The men stood up. "We will walk with you, get some fresh air before we settle."

"Goodnight, you two," they said.

"I've no doubt it will be," said Edward smiling.

Nathan and Maddy sat quietly staring into the distance. He held her hand. It was one of those moments when silence was more effective than words.

"Maddy," said Nathan "shall we do something crazy?"

"Like what?"

"Go skinny dipping?"

"You are mad, but why not? I could not sleep at the moment if I tried."

"Oh, I can think of ways of making you sleep," he laughed.

"Come along or we will miss the best of the moonlight."

If ever Nathan needed to come off cloud nine it was at the meeting in Bar Lou's cottage.

When James had finished outlining the details of his inheritance, Nathan was stunned. He turned to Edward and said, "If you knew all this was coming, why did I need to earn my own capital? Mind you, it has been fun and I would not have missed it for the world."

"Well, it was important that you learned some basic values, how to handle money, to deal with people fairly, to have fun before you decide on your future. I am afraid, Maddy, this soon-to-be husband of yours will lead you a merry dance if you are not careful.

When his parents died, the three of us did our best. None of us had children so it has probably not been the perfect example of child rearing. We have had help from our friends. We could never replace Michael and Alicia but we did our best to create an atmosphere to which he could grow into his own person, knowing himself and caring for others."

Maddy said, "Well, if you could write down your secrets we might learn how to do the same for our children in due course."

"Children," said Nathan, "lets get married first!"

Then he turned to Bar Lou, James and Edward. "I am glad I did not know about all this. It will take me, us, time to digest what it means but whatever the finances and the properties amount to, the best inheritance I could have had is my upbringing. Thank you. Now I am starving, what is for lunch?" They all laughed.

As they drove back to London, Nathan and Maddy were trying to come to terms with all that had happened in a very short time.

"Maddy, you realise, don't you, that we will never have money worries, unlike many of the people we know. What you have or inherit is yours, your own rainy day fund, no questions asked or answers given. So what will you do with your flat?"

"I don't know, probably keep it for the time being. Pay off the mortgage, who knows? Let Michael and Angela use it, for their lifetime. I just do not know. It certainly would help them. I don't know if you are aware that Michael had to start from scratch after the war. A new name, a new life with nothing to fall back on. It has been hard for them. They took me in much the same as yourself, no children, a very frightened little girl and an uncertain future."

"Well, think about it. Talk to Edward. I could always make life easier for them through Cabal Finance. They would never know where the money came from."

"We are almost at the flat. Please stay here for a few days. Are you happy about getting married on Jan 6th next year? The church is available as you know. "Very," she said, "can't wait."

Back in Soho, Pinky and Perky were making plans of a different kind.

"We need to get closer to these two 'suckers' we met at the exhibition. I have an idea they just might be useful to us. We could offload some of the miniatures we have on to them, and see if they are serious collectors! So my friend, the Gallery will know how to contact them, at least, Mary Ann is sure to have a record of them."

"Cute little filly, that one, needs a good man if you know what I mean." They laughed but there was a cruelty in it.

"Yes, that is what we will do. We need the money, you have to speculate to accumulate. My liquid assets are running low. We cannot flood the market with too many paintings or we will attract some unwanted attention so get the details from Mary Ann and we will go on from there ..."

Michael and Angela were also thinking about their future and the forthcoming wedding.

Angela said "I know Nathan is footing the bill, but I would like to do something special for Maddy, but what?"

"We never really looked in that case before I gave it to Nathan for her. Perhaps that is the best thing we could do for her, give her her past. She has always been curious. How much do we tell her? We don't know if her brother survived, where he is, what he might be doing. That is a can of worms I am not keen to open."

In Vienna, 'Inky' was feeling very irritated. Wright Wynne was going cool on their plans and as for that Yank he was a waste of space. 'I wonder why this Chinese guy went missing. Wonder if he holds the secret.' Inky never bothered to find out about his past. "Don't care," he shrugged his shoulders. "Live for the moment is my motto". He had lived in Poland for years with an elderly couple, who he called Hilly and Pop. Hilly was still alive, Pop had died. "Since that researcher came asking me questions it has made me think. Maybe I could be heir to a fortune. I'll go and see Hilly, have a little holiday like, see what's in it for me."

TM was having lunch at the Club with James and Edward. Bar Lou was busy, so she said, probably gone to see that horse again.

"No matter," said TM. "How did Nathan take the news of his inheritance?"

"Well," said James "For once he was silent. When he and Maddy talk it through, it will be fine. No doubt he will spend some time with Edward sorting out the legal papers."

"Do you know how much that young man was worth before his inheritance – 4½ million – he learns very quickly. Now when we tie up all the loose ends, he should be a billionaire. Maddy will ground him, I am sure of that."

"I hope so," said TM, "we will have to keep a watching brief on that situation. Now to business. Our friends Pinky and Perky have been busy I believe". "Yes," said Edward. "Davy and Ken have been contacted by them with a view to their buying some miniatures."

"They have taken the bait then," mused TM. "How interesting." Edward carried on.

"Do you remember Bronsen and Babington, both ex members of the Corps, well they are doing a little discreet digging. If anyone can go through closed doors they can. It is as much as we can do."

"Yes, yes" said TM. "We should see copies of Maddy's final report on the Leidl trail and Nathan has almost completed his – damned interesting his methods. He has built a good team around him. It will have to be handled very carefully from now on. Should any of the media get a hint of what is about to break, we will be in danger of not completing the task."

"TM," said Edward "how well do you know Perry Bracken?" "Quite well, came to prominence after the Cuban crisis. He is a useful contact at present, Uncle Sam seems to trust him. Why."

"Just some information that Charles and Nigel are picking up. Be careful talking to Uncle Sam. May be they should take more of an interest, do a little digging."

"Uh, I hope this is not true," said TM. "If it is, Nathan could be at risk."

"He would not dare harm him," said Edward. "Anyway, Nathan's time with that firm is almost up, the end of September I think. He will need to be here. There is the wedding and his inheritance to sort out. If you get the slightest hint that he might be 'at risk', I need to know. We do not need another Michael and Alicia on our hands."

"Fine by me" said TM.

Esther met Maddy for lunch, chatting about the engagement. "I need all the details," said Esther, "my life is so boring." Maddy was quite happy to tell her about the proposal.

"Esther, what is on your mind?"

"Remember I said I would trawl through the records at Company House?"

"Yes."

"Well, there are some strange bedfellows emerging. The Hammersteins, Wynne Browne, the Foreign Secretary's wife and these other names I don't know, Arpinsky, Appleby and Fing Wah Tsang. It all centres around buying and selling works of art mainly through galleries in America and the Far East. They use several different names. Do you understand it, Maddy?"

"Not really, but I know a man that does, thank you. Have you got the information with you?"

"Yes on disk."

"Are there any copies?" "Only one, mine. Keep it somewhere safe Esther. Clean down your hard drive if possible. This could be dynamite. Say nothing to Mary Ann please. She seems so edgy."

"I agree," said Esther, "got to go I'm afraid. I am at the Bailey for 2pm. Congrats again. Lovely ring. See you," said Esther.

Maddy made a call to TM.

"I need to see you urgently."

"Come right away Maddy. Is Nathan with you?"

"No, he is the States. Back on Friday, for good, I hope."

"I will send a car - 20 minutes."

"Fine," said Maddy.

Chapter 21

Mary Ann had a bad night. She was worried and absolutely sure that the Hammersteins were involved in something which was not above board. She had been checking provenances as per usual. Most pictures came from private collections in this country and some from Europe, a few further-a-field.

Recently three pictures arrived for checking. Although she was given the paperwork, it did not ring true. When she tried to cross reference the information, long time gaps appeared. Not unusual in itself, but the superficial damage suggested they had not been stored or moved for some time, maybe many years.

Normally they would be displayed openly, well lit and known buyers invited to a private viewing. She was never invited to these occasions. Then the paintings would disappear. On these occasions, the Hammersteins did the banking themselves or that is what they wanted her to believe!

Who could she trust? She knew that something was wrong. If she said anything to people in authority, it could be the end of her career. She did not like the limelight, it frightened her, she loved her job. "I will phone Esther, maybe she will know what to do. It is quite obvious something has to happen."

In Poland, Inky was sitting with Hilly in her small but functional flat. He did not remember everything being so grey, so drab, so poor. He remembered the day when Hilly and Pop had told him he was not their child. A friend of theirs who lived in Birkenhau had found this baby wrapped in a ragged blanket on the edge of the woods near the chemical factory. There was a simple note, 'please help my child for I have no hope!' Their friends, like so many in the village, had heard rumours about what happened to people who arrived at the so-called workers Camp. So many arrived but few survived. They knew the numbers did not tally.

Making absolutely sure he was not seen, he put the child inside his coat. It was so thin, too weak to cry, and he made his way home through the lengthening shadows. His wife was so frightened. What have you done, we could be shot. What are we going to do?

"Talk to Hilly, your cousin, you know the one who can't have children. Are they not coming to stay soon?"

"Why?"

"Well, if she looked as if she might be expecting and she stayed longer than usual, it would not seem strange if she went home with a baby, would it?"

Oh, the risks, I suppose she might. Perhaps if I go to see her. I have one visit pass left."

"Do that."

That was how Hilly and Pop became parents. No one seemed to notice or care. They just looked at the baby, helped with discarded clothes, toys and a pram. Pop had spent hours doing up that pram. He was so proud of his son.

"Hilly, why did you want to tell me my real surname?"

"Well, it was not safe in the early years. Even the walls had ears in those days and we did not know. Pop was ordered to report for work at the chemical factory. He was put in charge of a small work force, moving the drums from the factory to the railway sidings. One day, a young man gave him a piece of paper. It said the child's name was Alinksy. If you go to my chest, the one pop and you made for me, I have kept that piece of paper. It is in my beaded purse."

Inky moved quickly. She opened the purse and gave him the piece of paper. When we opened it up, there did not seem to be anything else written on it. I used to keep it in the vase on the fireplace. One day, I needed to sell the vase, we were so hungry. When the paper fell out I opened it again. Some marks appeared. Pop got out his father's magnifying glass. Then we were able to see the words. 'He has a sister, Madeleine.'

By the time this happened, there were very few records. No one really wanted to talk about what happened in that place. We tried through our friends but all the papers had been taken away.

You know now, what happened. We know your mother was shot, she gave a little of her bread to a child. It was not allowed to share. So somewhere you may still have a sister."

He remembered the conversation he had with that guy who said he was trying to find out about his family. May-be somewhere was a fortune, waiting to be claimed. Hilly had fallen asleep. He really loved her. 'I must get her out of here' he thought. One more sting and he would have enough money to get out, make a different life, invent a new family, start again. That was never to happen. He was in deep and he knew it. Some of the people he dealt with were ruthless, especially that Arpinsky. He was not certain in his own mind that the elderly Jew, who ran the gallery, had been killed in a road accident. Inky had never known him to drive at more than 50kph, so how could he have been speeding and come off the road at a hairpin bend - he never left the town. Best not ask questions, he thought.

Never mind, that American Davis Browne II would be calling to collect 3 paintings he had bought. Strange fellow always paid cash. Handy that, thought Inky. I can take my cut now. No one around to stop me. Pity the number of possible transactions were getting fewer, the looted paintings were running out. Could try a good copyist. Yes, I will, bet the old boy never thought of that. If I am careful we could sell some of them twice. Oh what a sting! He smiled for the first time in a long time.

Esther had just come back to the Office from the Bailey when her phone rang. It was Mary Ann. "Esther, I have to see you."

"Why?"

"Not on the phone."

"OK, where?"

"Your flat?"

"See you at 6 pm."

'Now what,' thought Esther. She had been worried about Mary Ann for sometime. Perhaps she will open up soon.

Mary Ann did 'open up'. The story she told Esther that night was to have repercussions beyond belief. Now Esther was involved. Damn Maddy and the Liedl paintings. All this and her job. She did so want to be a good barrister.

Mary Ann stayed the night. She slept. Esther did not. Then an idea came to her. She had to go and see Edward Rayner to discuss a brief he had sent to the Chambers. He was well known in the Art Circles, may be he could help.

Mary Ann was still asleep when she left. She wrote a note, 'Stay put.

Help yourself to whatever. Will bring lunch in. I am due to finish at 2 pm. See you then. Sweet dreams!' and she drew a smiley face.

When she had finished discussing the brief with Edward Rayner and made her notes she said "Edward, could you give me some advice?" and she told him the story Mary Ann had told her.

Edward took a deep breath. "Esther, I will have to think about this. I have one or two contacts who are very discreet. I will get back to you. Where is Mary Ann now?" said Edward.

"At my flat, I hope."

"Go to her, look after her."

Then, changing the subject, he said, "Have you seen Maddy lately?"

"Yes," she smiled. "It is weddings, Nathan, weddings if you get my drift. And as far as this TV programme she is researching, I have never known her be so laid back. No doubt she has told you about the information that came out of Companies House."

"Not yet," said Edward, "but we will meet at the weekend. She is spending it with Bar Lou."

"Are you going to Bar Lou's this weekend?"
"Yes."

"Are you doing anything special apart from wedding talk."

"No, I just want to rest."

"Well, your friend Mary Ann needs a little TLC and a lot of Bar Lou's hot chocolate. Do you think you could invite her."

"Well, fine," said Maddy. "Perhaps I'll ask Esther too." Edward thought, 'Maddy catches on fast, she'll do for Nathan.'

TM's phoned buzzed. No jangling noises in his office.

"It's Edward, are you free for lunch at the Club? I'll book a private room."

"Fine. 12.30 do?"
"Yes, until we meet."

At the club the two men were deep in conversation. Edward told him all he knew. Maddy had some information that her friend Esther researched at Companies House. It really only supplied a few more links.

TM remembered Maddy saying something about Mary Ann. "Ah, that's it, she was worried that the Hammersteins were not completely above board. Well who was completely?" But thinking about it maybe he should dig.

"Edward, can we get Mary Ann out of that place without causing a stir?"

"I think she works on a consultancy basis. I have some work to do for a client, checking the provenance of his collection. Seems that there are two additions of a couple of his Victorian Art Collection. She will be at Temple Meadows with the girls this weekend. She is very good at her job. It will keep her going to the end of the year at least. Then of course there is the wedding."

"Do you know when Nathan is back?"

"Things should be wrapped up as far as he is concerned by next Friday. I will be relieved to have him out of New York."

"Oh, by the way, the Sultan and Patra are going to use the loft. He has agreed to help with that other issue."

"Edward, these could be a momentous few months. I just hope we get everything right."

"Blast Michael and those 4 miniatures. I thought I could work up to retirement, keeping things ticking over. Now this. Well it is why I joined!"

Nathan meanwhile was briefing his team. "I am going back to England. Hannaway is staying here to develop our Cabal work. Mark, Gabriella how would you like to work for us on a more permanent basis? Freddie will still be working for me, but in Europe, so Gabriella, you could, if you would like, take over his project work. It could be the next step for you. You can work together for a while. Think about it. I will ask Edward to write to you more formally when I return to England tomorrow. So how about dinner at the Loft? Is everyone free?

See you at eight. While I think on, the Sultan and Patra will be using the Loft until at least Christmas. Please, no silly phone calls. Now to speak to Maddy. All I will need to say is, 'I'm on my way home, love you lots.'"

Chapter 22

Perry Bracken was sitting at home, feeling most uneasy. Something was not quite right. Ever since he had taken his friend's son, Conrad Parker III, into the business, he knew there would be a reckoning and that day could be coming sooner rather than later.

Parker was one of those people who were always on the edge of any of the working groups – never belonging. He was definitely not a team player. He knew things about people and what he learned was more about their weaknesses than strengths.

His father, Conrad, and Perry had started work on the same day. They became firm friends and in a way their styles complemented one another. Conrad was always dreaming up 'get rich' quick schemes. Perry had the connections, Conrad loved to gamble. Perry was cautious but enjoyed living dangerously. That was to be his Achilles heel. Conrad had got involved with a group of people who frequented casinos, race tracks and clubs. When he looked back now they were 'cash rich' businesses. Conrad and his so called 'friends' were soon involved in money laundering and drugs, a dangerous occupation in anyone's terms. He managed to keep Perry out of it. He even seemed to be short of money.

Perry was the lead accountant for a major audit on one of the biggest leisure company's books. On the surface everything seemed to be in order, but one audit trail did not add up. Perry was a meticulous worker so had started to dig. It was very clever accounting, very creative. He was even more surprised when the Inland Revenue Service became involved. He could tell them little at this stage.

Something niggled away at his brain. He should have gone to the Lead Partner but he had not. Too arrogant, he supposed. Saw it as his big break, more than one step up the promotion ladder. That decision had dogged him through his life.

Conrad and Perry were discussing work. His friend seemed uneasy. "How is the leisure group audit going?" he asked. "Oh, I am close to wrapping it up, should have the draft accounts ready in a week or two," he said.

"Good, then I have an idea. Why don't we have a holiday, friend of mine has a property in the Bahamas. Sun, sea, sand and fun."

"Sounds good. Who is the friend?"

When Conrad remembered the name, something in his brain clicked that was interesting.

"How do you know him?" he asked.

"Oh, we met in Vegas, old college get together."

"What does he do?" asked Perry.

"Works in the family business and will soon take over from his old man."

"Who is he?"

"Frankie Como."

"Not the Frankie Como?"

"Yes, but my friend is OK. He says his father is all reputation. Nobody has been able to produce any real evidence that will bring him down. He employs some very good money men."

On returning to work, Perry looked again at the one audit trail he had been doubtful about. Clever money men. It does not ring true. He spent hours trying to make sense of what was happening in the books. He could not see the formula, but it was there, of that he was sure. Instead of telling his Partner, he told Conrad. Conrad went pale.

He asked, "How close are you to solving the problem?"
"Very," said Perry.
"Friend," said Conrad, "for my sake and your own please do not go there, not now. I am sure the Company will show their gratitude."

"What do you mean, gratitude?"

"A bonus for a good piece of work. Like all young men, Perry either did not see or did not want to acknowledge the implications.

So he wrapped up the accounts. They were reviewed and eventually there was a meeting with the Leisure Company directors. They praised Perry's work and he got his promotion.

He went on holiday with Conrad, at little expense to himself, and came back to New York and back to work. On the flight back, Conrad told him he was going to resign on his return to work. He no longer enjoyed accounting and would be branching out into financial management.

Perry was surprised, "Who with?"

"Oh, that Leisure Group you audited."

"Well, I hope you will be happy."

"Oh, I do too, but it does offer more prospects."

"For what?"

"A chap with ideas. By the way, my future bosses were very pleased with your work. They are going to give the firm more audits. So we could be meeting up from time to time."

Even then, Perry did not see the implications, so Conrad pressed on. "They will ask for you to do the work."

"So?" said Perry.

"Well, you were so clever at not exposing the flaw in the accounting system they want you to succeed. Be very careful not to cross them. They do not ask many questions, they just act."

"What do you mean, not exposing the flaw? I did not knowingly cover anything up. I did miss some papers I thought we had been given, but that was the only part of the audit I really missed."

"I know, I removed them. I am in deep with these guys and now, like it or not, they can make or break you."

Perry sat silent. "What on earth am I into now? Everything I am working towards could go."

"Why did you do it Conrad?"

"Money, fast living. No, I want part of that action."

"But why involve me?"

"You were there, safest pair of hands on the team."

"Too honest for your own good."

"What will happen now?" asked Perry.

"Not a lot, as long as you co-operate," said Conrad.

"What do you mean, co-operate?"

"Well, do as you are told, help them out of a tight corner."

"No!"

"Oh, yes you will. You have to, or let's face facts, you will be disgraced, rumours will fly and the jobs will dry up."

"Conrad, I thought you were a friend."
"Oh, I am", he said, "and always will be but not the kind of friend you would want your sister to marry. I will protect you as a 'friend' and that is as far as it goes."

The rest of the journey was very quiet. Both men knew that today had been a watershed. It was to have repercussions, but much later, and only when Perry moved up the ladder and became a partner, trusted by so many people and 'in the know' at the very highest level.

He had married into a good family, was happy and had two daughters. They lived well and moved across the social scene with ease.

Then Conrad re-surfaced. He needed a favour. Some information. Perry refused until they threatened his daughters, one of whom was really a wild child.. It was a relatively minor piece of information, not really harmful to the state, so he relented.

That was how his 'double' involvement started. He quite liked the excitement until Nathan arrived on the scene. Nathan had got very close to exposing what was happening. Fortunately he had been able to pass it off. After all, Nathan's godfather, Edward, had become his friend, so he could breathe freely for a while.

He had not wanted to employ Conrad's son in the business. If anything he was the most objectionable character who in everyone else's opinion got away with murder.

He had had to bow to pressure.

"You need someone to watch your back, Perry, he will do that for you."

"No, he will do a job, same as anyone else. He will not be in my team."

"Better still," said Conrad.

That was the moment Perry realised he was firmly in their firm's web. He did less of the accounting business but made the contacts in future work and generally tried to establish a good reputation. 'Oh, roll on retirement,' he thought. Take his wife travelling, play with the grandchildren, oh how he wished.

Back in England, TM had requested a meeting with the Prime Minister. The information he was in possession of had international implications. Needless to say it would be a diplomatic nightmare.

It was not an easy meeting.

"Are you telling me" said the PM "that this has been uncovered by two relatively young professionals? Why did we not know?"

"There have been rumblings, but every time we checked our information the responses were not a cause for concern."

"Can these young professionals be trusted? To keep their own counsel?"

"Yes. I am sure of that, Sir," said TM.

"Very well. I will come back with you."

TM left the meeting. Well, at least the wedding arrangements would take up their time. Maddy would get her TV programme. It would be explosive. One last thing, he thought, before she joins Nathan in the Circle.

Nathan and Maddy were at Bar Lou's for lunch. The expert organiser was at work. "Now, where are we with the arrangements? Are the invitations ready?"

"No," said Nathan. "I want to do my own art work." "Well, get a move on," said Bar Lou.

"And you, Maddy, where are we with bridesmaids, dresses, flowers etc?"
"All in hand, I hope. Nathan keeps asking me what I am wearing."

"Oh. I always reply, 'in your eyes, it will be the Emperor's New Clothes,'" they said together.

"I hope it will be a little more," she laughed.

"Bar Lou," said Nathan, "we have to go. The Canon wants to go through a few things with us, order of service and the usual pre wedding chat."

"That should be interesting," said Bar Lou.

"Very," replied Nathan. He smiled at Maddy.

In Austria, 'Inky' kept thinking about trying to find his sister. Then he would do something else. After all, she has not bothered to find me.

Maddy did not know at that moment he existed, but, as usual, 'Inky' thought the worst.

His double scam was working well. He was getting richer. If only he could get rid of that Davis Browne. He knew too much and was getting greedy. He would talk to Arpinsky. He seemed to be up for anything.

After their chat with the Canon, Nathan and Maddy returned to Temple Meadows. They were sitting in the conservatory.

"Maddy, do you feel like a break from all this?"

"Why, do you?"

"Yes, how about I find a jolly little jaunt for a couple of weeks. There is nothing to spoil."

"Nothing too exciting, please" said Maddy.

"When will we go?"

"I don't know, but just a few phone calls and I will be able to tell you more."

"Now these invitations! What would you like? Have a look at these sketches and tell me what you think. If we can agree then I will get the art work for the covers to the printer."

"Then, all we have to do is order the form of service. Josh is keen to provide the music". "What a jazz wedding!"

"No, silly, Labac can play a wide range of music. But it would be fun seeing you coming down the isle to a jazz version of the Rodetsky March."

"Nathan, don't you dare."

"Promise," he said, with his two fingers crossed.

"Now, how about a swim, then dinner, then ..."

"The swim, yes, dinner, yes, but as for anything else I need to be persuaded. Remember the Canon!!!"

"Passion killer," he said, as he kissed her.

The next day Nathan told Edward, James and Bar Lou that he was going to take Maddy away for a few days. "Where?" said James.

"Oh, to Austria. We need to exorcise a few ghosts. Let Maddy become familiar with her past. We will have enough to contend with over the next few months without any unnecessary pressure."

"Well, I think it is a great idea," said Bar Lou. "Then I can move here whilst Patra works her magic on my cottage and we have the last flat race to go with Mercury. It is a good idea for all of us."

Nathan made his phone calls and had the tickets couriered to him that afternoon. He thought, 'I will take Maddy breakfast in bed then surprise her.'
"Nathan, what is in the envelope on my breakfast tray?""Open it and see."

"The Transcontinental Express to Vienna. Wow! But won't we need loads of clothes? I've been getting a wardrobe together for the wedding."

"Maddy, go out and buy some. That's why I gave you the card."

"Oh, I'm to be a kept woman am I?"

"Well, I would not put it like that but yes, I want to spoil you, care for you and even surprise you. It is such fun."

"Yes, it is," said Maddy. "Come here and let me show you what fun can be."

"What, at 9 in the morning?"

"Nathan, just come here."

When Maddy phoned Esther she simply said they were off to Vienna for a few days. She asked how Mary Ann was?

"Better. She is working on a project for James." "Oh, that is kind of him." "Well, she had to get out of Hammersteins. They have linked up with the Foreign Secretary's wife and she made it plain Mary Ann's days were numbered."

"Right," said Maddy. "Well, we will meet up in a few weeks."

"Fine. Have fun."

"We will, of that I am certain," said Maddy.

Nathan meanwhile was sitting in Edward's office going through the legal documents.

"Edward, I had no idea how complicated my trust was or what I was likely to inherit."
"I know," said Edward, "but it was not necessary to burden you with the information. You needed space to grow up and to learn about money and people."

"So that was the great plan," said Nathan. "Well, it worked. Thank you."

"I suppose I need to make a will now that I am to be married. If I write down what I would like to do, as things are now, will you do the necessary?"

"I would be delighted."

"You do realise Maddy will have to do the same. Any will she has in force will be invalidated on marriage."

"Well, I will talk to her about it. This visit to Poland, Vienna and Paris may well answer most of the questions. She still wants to be clear about her past."

"So not just a romantic interlude?"

"Well, that too," said Nathan. "I must go. Maddy will have lunch ready and I want to see what she has bought."

"See you in two weeks." "Thank you, Edward, for everything. Now, all I have to do is have lunch with Maddy, go over our itinerary, arrange some foreign money and just have a quiet evening with her alone. What could be better?"

No phone calls, no faxes, just pack the cases, arrange for his car to take them to Waterloo, then relax and enjoy themselves.

Back at the flat Maddy was singing away to the radio. 'It's ages since I've done this. I am so happy and very very lucky. Life is never going to be dull with Nathan around. Wow, the Continental Express, the people, the places we will see, time alone together. Life is great.'
That might have been the aim, but as she said to herself, life with Nathan would never be dull as she was about to find out.

Whilst they were going through the itinerary, he said, "Maddy, we will be able to visit some of the places your family came from. So you will know a little more. Hopefully you will want to do that."

"Oh, yes please, good, bad or indifferent I need to know."

"Well, you shall," said Nathan, "and so will I. It will never change how I feel about you, Maddy. In a comparatively few weeks we will be married and I am so looking forward to that!"

Chapter 23

TM was still wrestling with the information he had received. He knew he faced a difficult hour with Edward. He had to tell him about Perry Bracken. He hoped Edward was stoical enough and would deal with the consequences quickly and efficiently. 'No wonder he was so good in I Corps,' thought TM.

"Edward, where are Nathan and Maddy?" said TM.

Edward looked at his watch. "Just about to board the Transcontinental Express to Vienna. Why?"

"I just need to make sure they are safe."

"Why?"

He began to tell Edward how the story was unfolding. When he finished, there was silence.

"The stupid fool!" said Edward. "He had everything going for him. Even had the ear of the President!"
"I know," said TM, "and I am very sorry for you."

"Don't be. Sometimes it crossed my mind that he was too good to be true. I must be getting old, TM, to have missed that one. What is going to happen?"

"Well, as you can imagine, it is a diplomatic nightmare. The majority of the decisions are out of my hands. I need you to retain your contact with Perry as though nothing had happened. We have to keep a line of communication open. Maybe, just maybe, he will tell you the whole story."

"I doubt it," said Edward, "but he might tell Bar Lou."

"Why? Well, he had always had a soft spot for her, speaking openly. She is just that kind of person."

"Oh, I know Bar Lou's strengths very well," said TM.

"If I took Bar Lou to New York for a few days, she could see Patra about her cottage and, if necessary, they could fly back together."

"Does the Sultan know about all this?"

"Who knows? He keeps his eyes and ears open, and speaks rarely. He has enough problems of his own to deal with. You know we managed to get him out of Osmantia just in time?"

"No!" said Edward. "What a mess! Is there anything I can do?"

"Not at present. Keep a weather eye out in New York. Perhaps it might be a good idea if either Nigel, or Charles, could join the Transcontinental Express and the other one go to New York. I would feel happier."

"Me, too" said Edward. "Do you know why Nathan is taking Maddy to Vienna?"
"No," he said quizzically.

"Well, Maddy is keen to know about her family background. Nathan had her family tree traced so now they are off to put the flesh on the bones."

"Not another 'jolly jape' that ends in our having to watch our backs?"

"I hope not," said Edward, "I am getting too old for that!"

Hannaway was trying desperately to contact Nathan from New York. Freddy had heard a rumour that Perry Bracken could be in the mire. He had checked it out as far as possible. There were no direct leads, as far as they could tell.

Freddie and Hannaway were sitting together talking about it.

Freddie said, "If I did not think I knew better, I would say someone is trying to frighten him, giving him a taste of what could happen."

"But why?" said Hannaway.

"Grabriella just let drop in conversation that Conrad Parker is getting very close to Perry, now that Nathan has gone back to the UK. Nathan never liked him, you know."

"Where, oh were, is Nathan?" The phone rang.

"Oh, hello Bar Lou. Is Nathan with you?"

"No," said Bar Lou, "he is on the Transcontinental Express with Maddy."

"What, so soon before the wedding?" said Freddie. "Can he be contacted?"

"No, they need this time together. They are following up Maddy's family tree."

"Bar Lou. I, well Freddie and I, would like to take you for lunch. It is important, will you come?"

And so Bar Lou was told what they knew. She did not bat an eyelid.

"Is it not important?"

"Oh yes," said Bar Lou "and those who need to know will be told. You are all coming to the wedding, so I will see you there and thank you very much. How is Mai Lee?"

Inky had returned to Vienna none the wiser really. He knew a lot more about his own early years but no more about Madeleine. He had this idea in his head, that, if she was alive, she could be useful to him but how useful he could not make out.

He was expecting Arpinksy. He did not like him and, from choice, would rather have nothing to do with him but he needed that yank out of the way and fast. The bell on the door to the Gallery tinkled, Inky looked up. He had arrived.

A deal was struck. Inky was glad when Arpinsky left. 'I would not like to cross that man, must keep him sweet.' They had first met when Arpinsky had visited the Gallery looking for miniatures. He thought it strange they had just two. When he first joined the staff, it had been his job to clear the stock room and keep the list of available pictures, sculptures, etc up-to-date. That was when he first saw the miniatures. The old boy had told him some tale about there being two more and if the four were in one pair of hands the riddle of the miniatures would be solved and someone would make a killing.

He had laughed at the time, dusted them down, repacked and ticked his list. They had been one of the first big sales he made. He got more for them than the list said they were worth. He even was paid a bonus. The old man suddenly retired. 'That was surprising,' thought Inky, 'I never thought he would ever leave here.'

The old man was terrified, the miniatures were on the move. Who knew what trouble they would bring in their wake? They had been sold into the wrong hands.

In the Hammerstein Gallery, Miriam Hunter was taking stock. 'Not a bad venture,' she decided. Heatherbourne Castle was just eating money since she had embarked upon her restoration project. This partnership gave her a convenient way of disposing of a number of paintings without attracting too much attention. She knew that her husband, the Foreign Secretary, would not approve, but she needed to do her own thing, however risky. In fact, the greater the risk, the more the adrenaline pumped and she had been short on that lately.

She asked the brothers' Hammerstein, "Why have we got so many miniatures? All these faces staring at one is quite unnerving."

"They are an up and coming market. We have sold about 20 in the last few months, although things have gone a little quiet on that front. The new market appears to be in Victorian water colours."

"Good," she thought, I have a loft half full of them."

Nathan and Maddy were starting the journey through Europe, seeing places she had never been to before and thinking, 'If this is what life with Nathan is going to be like, I'll need the stamina of an Olympic athlete!' She smiled.

"Are you going to share the joke?" said Nathan. "No joke, I was just smiling because I am very happy."

"Good," said Nathan, "are you really sure you want to spend time tracing your family? We could spend time shopping."

"We could do both," said Maddy.

"Don't be greedy," said Nathan, "remember what the Canon said, 'all things in moderation.'"

"So tell me," said Maddy, "where is this place called moderation? In your heart or in your wallet?"

Nathan laughed. "You'll do, Maddy, you really will. I am so looking forward to the future." Deep down he had an uneasy feeling about this need of hers to establish a family of her own, but if that was what she needed to do, then fine by him. The sooner the better. He would rather not have ghosts at the wedding.

"You have remembered that we leave the train at Vienna, have you Maddy?"

"No, but let us enjoy the scenery, the Alps are beautiful." 'Nothing to compare with you,' Nathan thought to himself.

The time to leave the train came quickly, and the car he had ordered was waiting to take them to the Hotel.

The driver said, "Good afternoon, Sir, I have been instructed to give you this packet."

Nathan looked at the envelope. "Good," he said "thank you."

"Nathan, that is not work is it?"

"No, Maddy, I hope it is the tickets for tonight."

"Tonight? Why, where are we going?" asked Maddy. "To a Strauss Concert, what else? If Tiggy and Emir had been here it would have been the Lippanzaner horses."

"I prefer the music," said Maddy.

Back in Surrey, Emir and the Colonel were deep in discussion. The yard had been very successful this year but Emir realised just how much his father, the Sultan, had helped. In the future, they would succeed or fail by their own efforts. Grand titles counted for nothing if you had not got the money to live the life. Whilst he was far from being poor, he knew that he had to be more aware of what was being spent and the return they could expect.

In many respects his life was easier, some of the burdens of the expectation had been lifted. He could pursue his own career. What had started as a friendship with Tiggy was developing into something more, much more. He needed to speak to his father, the Colonel and Nathan about his future.

The discussion with the Colonel went well. The projection for the next year looked healthy enough. The success of Mercury was attracting interest in the yard. They had been talking about forming a link with a yard in Southern Ireland. That was a big step, one he was not ready to embrace just yet.

"Emir, are you still with me?" said the Colonel.

"Oh, sorry Sir, I was day dreaming," said Emir.

"You have been doing a lot of that lately," said the Colonel.

"Oh, yes, well I have had a lot to think about."

"I'm sure. Will you join us for lunch? It will just be Natasha, Tiggy and us."

"Yes please."

He went to find Tiggy. "We are wanted. Lunch is ready," he told her.

"I'm coming," she said.

"Tiggy, before we go in for lunch, you know it is about time we told your parents of our plans to marry."

"Why," said Tiggy. "I thought we were going to elope, run away, marry on a beach in the moonlight."

Emir looked shocked. "Is that what you want to do?"

"No, daft lad, I'm teasing."

"Well," Emir laughed. "Do we tell them?"

"Yes," said Tiggy, "before, during or after lunch?"

"Oh, after I think, I'm too hungry to forego lunch."

"Moron," said Tiggy. They went into lunch.

Natasha suspected that something was going on between Tiggy and Emir. She had watched them getting closer, particularly since it was unlikely that Emir would be returning to Osmantia. It would all come out in the wash, she satisfied herself with that explanation.

After lunch she quite expected Tiggy and Emir to dash to the yard. That is what they normally did. Instead, Emir stayed seated. "Natasha, Colonel, I have something both to tell you and ask you."

"And that would be?" said the Colonel.

"Well, if it is alright with you both, Tiggy and I would like to get married."

There was a stunned silence. Tiggy could stand it no longer. She turned to Emir and said, "I told you we should have eloped. It is easier than this."

"Tiggy, you would not, would you? said her mother.

"Well, if we do not get an answer soon, we might have to. We could go out in the yard, saddle up two of the fleetest horses and ride into the sunset. Well, dad, what is it to be?"

The Colonel looked at Natasha. "When did you put the champagne in the fridge?"

"Before lunch," said Natasha smiling.

"Do you think it will be cold enough to drink? We seem to have something to celebrate."

"Oh, I think so," said Natasha.

Tiggy squealed. "Oh, dad, it's great news, isn't it?" Emir offered his hand to the Colonel, then turned to hug Natasha.

"Isn't this the greatest day?" he said.

"We'll drink to that," said the Colonel.

"So, can I presume our valuable animals are safe from your mad ideas?"

Tiggy laughed. "I'll bet Nathan would have done it. He would have said, 'I say what a jolly jape.'" "That he would," said Emir.

"Where is Nathan?" asked the Colonel.

"Oh, he's taken Maddy over to Europe to try and help her find out more about her family. I think they should leave well alone, just enjoy the mystery. The alternative might not be too palatable," said Tiggy.
"Nathan will cope," said Emir. "Maddy is very lucky. I wonder if I can get a message to him."

"I can," said Tiggy. "He gave me one of those phones. I rarely use it, but now, may be, I could try it out."

191

Nathan checked his messages. "Maddy, you will never guess."

"Never guess what?"

"Emir and Tiggy are going to marry."

"So, what is new about that?" said Maddy. "A blind man on a galloping horse could have told you that."

"No, they are engaged, it is official."

"I am glad," said Maddy, "another excuse to hit the shops."

"Why?" said Nathan. "When have you ever needed an excuse?" She laughed. They went shopping.

The Strauss concert rounded off, well, almost rounded off, a perfect day. She thought, 'I wish Nathan would run out of hors d'oeuvre, well, not quite, it is fun but ...'

Chapter 24

Brigstock was having lunch with Dave and Ken. They brought him up-to-date with activity at the Hammerstein Gallery.

"Since her ladyship has become a partner, there is an air of unease. Of course, she is well known, so quite a few new faces are appearing. We miss Mary Ann and, I think, so do the Hammersteins," said Dave.

Ken chipped in. "To my way of thinking, this is the lull before the storm. We have been back a few times. I even bought a small picture for my old mum. Bought it from her ladyship. She was just glad to make a sale but the Hammersteins did not seem so pleased. It had been part of a consignment due to go to America."

Brigstock said "Have you given that picture to your mother yet?"

"No," he said "it is for her birthday which is a few weeks away."

"Good, perhaps James or Edward could take a look at it. Mary Ann's working for them at present, so she could trace its background."

"Fine, by me," said Ken. "Do you think it might be worth something then?"

"Not in financial terms, but it may just provide another piece of the jigsaw."

"Dave, is there anything else?"

"Yes, the Hammersteins are expecting some American, Davis somebody. They are keen to get her ladyship out of the way. Seems she has to go to some Charity dinner and needs the day to get ready."

"When is this?" said Brigstock.

"Next Wednesday."

Brigstock already knew the name, Davis Browne II. So he was in town. He needed to let TM know.

"Guys, please stay with your observations at the Gallery for a little bit longer, until after the Hammersteins meet this American. Then we might have to spread our wings a little further."

With that, the meeting ended.

Brigstock was going to Garden Cottage for tea with Bar Lou. He really enjoyed her company. She is a good link to TM as well. It will save me a few phone calls. He did not like using the phone to pass on information. Too risky, in his view.

They had a pleasant afternoon. Bar Lou was full of her ideas for the cottage makeover. It was the first time in years she had felt like doing anything to the interior. 'Patra is so clever, it will be done well,' he thought.

As soon as Brigstock returned to his club, Bar Lou contacted TM. "There is some movement. Can we meet with Edward and James, say, for dinner this evening?" "That is fine. Will I tell them?"

"Good."

"Oh, by the way, Emir and Tiggy are engaged." With that she put the phone down.

There was another meeting that night between Conrad Parker and Davis Browne. They originally met at University, two of a kind, devious, cruel, not lacking in money but equally, both would shop one another if there was anything to be gained from it.

Their money laundering project was going well and had been lucrative. This idea of buying paintings in Europe and selling them on in the States was just perfect. However they both had a major concern. Where was Fing Wah? He had disappeared with no trace. Both men knew that if he had 'turned,' it was time to bail out and cut their losses. But not yet. No news was good news, so they felt reasonably safe for the moment.

Back in Vienna, Inky had a surprise vistor. The old man had come to see him. He had been staying with his sister and her family in Poland.

"Strange," said Inky. "I went back there to see Hilly a few weeks ago. It is very drab now or so it seems."

"They were good to you, were Hilly and Pop," said the old man. "How did you know that?" said Inky.

"Oh, I know a lot more than you think and it is about time I told you. I was conscripted by the German Army to supervise the prisoners' work at the chemical factory in Austria. We did not have a choice. It was 'do it or be shot.' I used to see your mother sometimes. It was me, and a few other prisoners, who organised your, shall we say, release from Birkenhau. It was very risky. She told me where a small packet was hidden and said that after the War, I was to find it and give it to you. It was a couple of little paintings in a silver frame. When I came to work here, many years later, I hid them in the stock room. It was better that they were here, too many prying eyes elsewhere. You had to go and find them didn't you? Hilly just made you too tidy. Then you sold them to that Arpinsky. He used to be in the SS. He was one of the cruellest men it was ever my misfortune to meet. He specialised in 'making the birdies sing', his methods were crude. So now he has your gift from your mother. I suppose you know, by now, you have a sister. I think her name is Madeleine. Your father collaborated with the Germans, in order to get a travel pass for her, his younger brother and his new wife. It was the only way he knew of getting them out of this country. Your sister got a seat on the Kinderzug. They were spirited into Switzerland. If you were in the know, that was possible, but expensive. He was very brave, but also stupid. The Germans realised he did not know as much as they thought, though he was very knowledgeable about art. He had studied it at University, but he did not know where the more valuable pieces had been hidden or, if he did, he took that to his grave. He was shot in the village square, one of ten men taken at random as an example to others who did not co-operate. I was forced to watch. I will remember that scene forever. Arpinsky seemed to take a perverse delight in the whole charade."

"Stop, there" said Inky. "I sold the miniatures to him, I think."

"Yes, you did, but you were not to know."

"I tried to tell you of the riddle of the 4 miniatures but you thought I was just a silly old man."

"Well, I did and I didn't. It just sounded like one of those family stories that, when you check them out, have little substance."

"Do you know who has the other two?"

"Yes, your sister, if she is still alive. If not, who knows? But what I do know is that your father incorporated into the frames the names of four people who had worked in the shadows during the war and now were in positions of major influence. He always believed that they would use a cloak of respectability to hide their actions. They are the bullet makers behind many trouble spots around the world."

"I am tired now, and have not really been too well. It is my heart, you know. You can now do one of two things. Be as brave as your father and extricate yourself from the art racket you have established or go the other way and make misery for everyone you meet. It will bring you money but you will not find it easy to sleep at night. It is your choice. Think very carefully, before you act."

"Goodbye, Inky, we will not meet again."

In Vienna, Nathan and Madeleine were looking for a present to give Tiggy and Emir. Both of them knew it had to do with horses, but what? A bronze or a painting? It was then Maddy spotted a gallery.

"Look at that place. We might find something in there." "These smaller galleries often have some interesting works," said Nathan.

"Really," said Maddy "I would never have known." They smiled at one another and walked into the gallery.

Nathan had spotted some Victorian paintings of horses. He thought he recognised the signature, but was not sure.

"Maddy, how about one of these? Oh, look, there are a pair here."

Maddy was not really concentrating. She had a feeling she knew the Gallery owner, yet she could not remember meeting him. There was just some connection.

Inky was watching her. She seemed familiar, classy, he thought. He liked beautiful women. She turned and joined her companion. "Yes, I think they would be just right."

"It's funny, though, I am almost sure I have seen them, or something similar, before. Well, I will let you haggle over the price. Not that you need to, but if it pleases you, remember to ask for the provenance."

"I am not keen on the owner, Maddy, so arrange for the paintings to be delivered to the Hotel. I will arrange for their safe passage back to England."

She settled on a price. 'That is too low,' thought Nathan, but he did not intend to spoil her day.

As they were leaving he said to her, "Maddy, it might be a good idea for Mary Ann to check them out before we hand them over."

"Fine, if that is what you want to do."

He contacted James who arranged collection for him. 'I wonder what can of worms they will open. It could be horrendous' mused Nathan.

When they returned to the hotel, Nathan asked Maddy if she really wanted to carry on with her quest.

"Oh, yes please," she said.

"Well, there is only one more place we need to visit. It could be harrowing and I am not sure whether you are ready."

"Where?" said Maddy.

"Auschwitz," he said.

There was silence. "I feel I should go there," she said. "I need to see for myself what it was like to feel my mother's pain. In a way, I know, or at least, I hope, it will help me fill in the gaps. I can do this if you are there with me."

"Would I be anywhere else?" he said.

"I hope not," was all she replied.

They had a very quiet evening. Nathan just held Maddy in his arms, words were superfluous. 'Tomorrow,' he thought, 'tomorrow will be a really defining moment. Maddy was mentally strong. He hoped she would be able to let go of this family history project once she had experienced this visit. Now I know, after this visit we will go to Paris. There Maddy can open her case. It will be the right moment.'

The next day they drove to Auschwitz Birkenau. Nathan had arranged a visit for that morning. He had particularly asked for a guide who was sympathetic to Maddy's reasons for being there.

Maddy was almost traumatised by her walk though the concentration camp. She felt as though the lump in her throat would choke her but she carried on, sometimes almost stumbling. 'If I feel like this, how did my mother and all the others feel? It must have been awful. They had been cheated, robbed, demoralised, abused and killed. For what? - some mad man's dream.'

She had taken in a candle, in a red glass holder, as many travellers did. She placed it at the foot of the wall against which her mother had been shot. She lit the candle. It flickered and she stood up. Nathan held her close. She knew, then, that she had nothing to fear, her future was assured.

Nathan sensed peace flowing through her body. He was relieved for it had been a risky venture. They finished the tour and thanked their guide, who said, "Excuse me, are you really Madeleine Alinsky?" "Yes," she said.

"I hoped one day I might meet you. That you would come here to this place. I was here as a small boy." He showed her his arm. "That was my number. You look so much like your mother. I was the little boy she gave her bread to. I have been carrying around this packet ever since, hoping we would meet. Now I am sure you are the one." He handed it over to her.

It was a lock of her mother's hair.

"Thank you, thank you so much."

"We are getting married in January, if we have made all the arrangements. Would you come, please?"

"Yes, I owe you that at least and your mother far more".

Nathan and Maddy travelled to Paris. She wanted to see Clothilde, and Nathan knew it was time he gave her the suitcase.

The next day, Maddy left early to see Clothilde. She was to see her dress for the first time. It was the final fitting. She was excited and apprehensive.

"Bonjour, Madame," said Clothilde, "this way please". She was taken to a private room. There she saw her dress. It was stunning. "I hope I can do it justice." "Please Madame, will you try it on? My assistants will help you."

"Thank you, it looks wonderful. So simple, you were right about the material. It did need to be a bit heavier to get the fall right. Oh, I love it, and as for Nathan," her eyes twinkled.

When she came out of the changing room the staff gasped. She looked stunning. Embarrassed, she smiled, "Is it alright?"

"Fine, Madam, you look wonderful. What will you wear around your neck?"

"I am not sure, but you will be there on the day to assist. Are you pleased, Clothilde?"

"Very, it will not be easy for the High St to copy, but they will try."

"How are the bridesmaid's dresses?"

"Oh, we have some simple adjustments, otherwise, OK."

"Thank you all so much". Maddy walked on air back to the apartment. Nathan was making coffee.

"Coffee for you Maddy?" "Oh, yes please."

"A successful morning?"

"Very," she smiled.

"There is a light lunch ready on the tray. Shall we take it into the sitting room by the fire. There is a distinct nip in the air today."

"That would be fine. Do you want me to carry anything?"

"No, just sit down. I will bring it in for you."

"When we have eaten, I have something to show you."

"Oh yes," said Maddy provocatively.

"Oh yes," said Nathan.

They talked about the wedding over lunch.

"As it gets nearer, half of me is excited, the other half panicky. I so want it to be the best day," said Nathan. "Well, we shall just have to wait and see," she said.

"Now, what is the surprise?"

He left the room and came back with the parcel wrapped in sacking.

"What an earth is that?" she said.

"Open it and see" he said.

She gently unwound the sack cloth. "Oh Nathan, it is my case, how did you come by this?"

"Michael and Angela kept it safe for you. They knew that one day you would ask questions and really need the answers. If you look carefully you should find everything you brought with you on the 'Kinderzug'.

"I can hardly bear to open it. Look, my name is painted on the top, and my age." She took the key from Nathan and gently turned it in the lock. The clasps snapped open.

She saw the coat she had worn the day she left, her shoes, her doll, her dresses, socks and a photograph. Was she really that small? As she lifted each piece out, she found a shawl her mother had made for her. She held it to her, the tears ran down her face. She stared at the photograph of her mother and father on their wedding day. She looked again at the dress. 'How strange,' she thought, 'it is almost the same design as the one I have chosen.'

"I think that is all there is". Nathan put his hand in the case and felt around the sides. There was a packet behind the lining, very cleverly hidden. "Maddy, look, you will have to undo the stitching." She cut away the false lining gently and withdrew the package.

She opened it and stared. There were two miniatures of her grandparents in silver frames. "Oh look," she said to Nathan, "as you said, faces to names." There was a small oblong box. As she looked inside there was a letter and a string of pearls. She opened the letter, which read as follows:-

Austria 1943
My dearest Madeleine,
    If you are reading this letter, then I know that you are safe and well and about to marry. I asked Michael and Angela to keep it safe, but, with all that was happening, I could not be sure you would reach freedom or how you would grow up – so I am writing in hope. If the pearls arrive safely and

you like them, please wear them for your wedding as I did for mine and my mother before me. I so wanted to be with you on that special day, to guide you to see the man of your choice and to embrace him in our family.

When you boarded the Kinderzug I cried for many days and nights. A bit of me died that night. Also I was carrying another baby. All the older women say it is a boy. I will not know in time to tell you. I hope one day you meet, if he survives this dreadful war. He will have been given the other two miniatures.

Your father etched into the frames a message. When all four are together you will have information which he said was of national importance.

Please do not feel badly about your father. He was a kind and gentle man in an ungentle world. He did what he did to try and set us free. I hope you will understand that one day. It is better you hear this from me and not anyone else. I fear it is now too late for me to leave this country and what my fate will be I do not wish to even think about it.

If your brother does not survive, try and seek out Haime Finklestein. He will be about Gallerie Madel in Vienna. If your brother does not survive he will tell you how to find the other two miniatures and perhaps, I hope and pray, tell you where your brother might be, probably in Poland.

Be very, very careful how you use the information etched into the frames. It could make you, or destroy your future happiness. I hope you find a man who cares for you as much as your father did for me. A good man will help you do the right thing.

I am going to have to finish now. I will kiss this letter for you. I love you so much, to see that little 3 yr old girl staring at me through the window of the house was a sight I will never ever forget. I wanted to keep you with me but I had to be happy to hold you in my heart and not my arms.

All my love, Madeleine. Be happy, be healthy and above all, be true to yourself.

Mamma
XXXXXXX

She finished reading the letter and handed it to Nathan to read. When he had read it he turned and held Maddy in his arms. "Well, now you know what you came to find. You have a family, a loving caring family, who gave their lives for you. What a gift from them! It is the best

203

possible present we could have received, is it not?"

She nodded.

Nathan also knew he was possibly on the way to understanding the message his father had left on his pad.

Chapter 25

"Maddy, before we leave Paris today, we need to decide where we go after the reception. We have 48 hrs before we start our honeymoon journey. We could come here, or stay in London, or book into a hotel. What would you like to do? Where would you like to go, what places do you want to see? Did you ever make out a travel wish list?"

"No, well, not really. I used to dream about spending some time on an island far away, just swimming and lazing around. We could go skiing or take the train through the Rockies or go on Safari. Why don't you just organise one of your special surprises. I would like that."

"Fine, so you would not mind if we stay at the London apartment for the first two nights, then take off around the world. These are papers you will need to sign, to access bank accounts. We could just pretend that no one else exists and just take our time, making each other happy."

"That is the best idea yet." "Now, we have to pack. Whilst we are away, Patra will do my sitting room so I suggested that she and the Sultan may wish to stay here. They do so like Paris."

"You know, if my mother were here, I could honestly say to her, 'Yes I have found a good man.'"

"Now, we should move, back to London."

"What will I do with the miniatures?" "Take them with us, of course. While we are away they could be cleaned and verified."

"Will you wear the pearls?" he said.

"Wait and see, just wait and see."

Inky was sitting in his office at the Gallery. He had done little else but think about the miniatures. Maybe Arpinsky would sell them back. Maybe he should try and find his sister. If his plan was to work, he needed all four. He felt he could solve the riddle and then, who knows, he could be rich beyond his wildest dreams.

Why had Haime, the old fellow not spoken to him before? Oh, it was all a mess, yet quite exciting. If Davis Browne was off the scene, he could breathe much easier. He needed to see Arpinsky. I wonder what he will want in exchange? He decided to leave a message for him.

Arpinsky was in London. He was due to meet with Appleby, Conrad Parker and visit the Hammerstein Gallery. Hopefully, that overbearing woman would be out for the day. She was a pain, her eyes looked right through you. He could enjoy getting rid of her. After all he had seen off stronger persons than her. He smiled for it was not a pretty sight.

Conrad Parker had jumped into a taxi to reach the Gallery. His brief case was secured to his wrist. If he was lucky, he could off load this cash and crate up a number of pictures to sell in the US at a vastly inflated profit. He was beginning to get careless, though he could never be fingered. He had been just too clever. Little did he know he had been followed, every movement had been logged. He should not have threatened Perry Bracken, it was the wrong move.

Davis Browne had been none too pleased with him. Parker was a little in awe of Browne. He had a few too many connections for him to be genuine. He was also not aware that Arpinsky or Gregory had been tailing them both.

Conrad's taxi pulled up outside the Gallery. Good, that awful woman was not there. Igor and Leon were learning fast. He could do the exchange, have the paintings sent air freight to Vienna and, from there, after they had been copied, to New York. Might as well make a few bob on the deal.

Arpinsky received a telephone call in which he learned about Conrad's little scam. Time he was taught a lesson. He knew too much. They needed Perry Bracken in post, not falling on his sword.

The evening tube train was crowded, hardly any room on the platform either. Parker saw the lights of the approaching train. That was all he remembered. He had somehow fallen on the line. So many people had seen him fall. The Police were now recovering his body. Arpinsky smiled, one down, one to go. Watch out Mr Browne!

Dave and Ken had seen the whole thing from different vantage points. They recognised Arpinsky. Ken moved to follow him whilst Dave moved in to the side of the accident to try and hear what was being said. One policeman said to the other, "he is a gonner." "Any identification?" said the second man.

"Yes, a passport. Conrad Parker, an American citizen, art dealer. The Embassy will have to be informed." Dave left the scene and found a telephone to contact Brigstock.

Brigstock listened. Then he phoned Bar Lou. "One pigeon is dead," is all he said.

Bar Lou said, "It must be a wrong number."

The line went dead.

She contacted Edward. All he could think was, 'I hope Perry was not behind this. But Arpinsky, why here, why now, why Parker?'

Arpinsky smiled for it had been a successful day. One down, one to go. He called in a favour. By the end of the day he knew that Davis Browne was travelling Intercontinental to Vienna. So would he, the only difference being Browne would never arrive. He would then see Inky a little matter of payment.

Greg Appleby was going through his stack of miniatures looking for the two with the silver frames. He was sure they were here. He remembered Arpinksy giving them to him and he had put them in the display at the Gallery. He knew he had sold some, to raise some spending money. Then he went cold. He could not have sold them. Oh no, Arpinsky would go ballistic! That would not be a pretty sight. Who had bought them? He went back to the Gallery to the sales ledger. At least Mrs High and Mighty would not be there. Sandra, Mary Ann's replacement, quite liked him, so he was confident he could get the information he wanted.

He was right. He got the information. It was those Johnny come latelys who had bought them. They paid cash and took them home so there was no contact address. Mary Ann would have known just where to look because she had sent out the invitations. He would wait for the Hammersteins to come back to lock up. He could spin them a story about how he had seen details of a sale of miniatures and as those two had been buying, he thought he would let them know.

He had about 48 hours to find them. Neither Dave nor Ken realised that, in the box of miniatures they had purchased at local sales, were the two that TM was looking for. However, they had done as Brigstock had asked and left them in the bank vault. You can never be to careful he had said.

Appleby finally obtained a contact address. He called. "Hi, I just thought I would let you know that there is a selling exhibition of miniatures in Brighton. Thought you might want to off load one or two of that set you bought at the Hammersteins."

Ken was worried. How did he get this address? A little startled, he said, "well, actually, we have already sold some to a friend, by now they could be anywhere. He has galleries all over the world. He could be interested in some more in the longer term. See how this lot go first."

Immediately Appleby left, Ken and Dave moved. In less than one hour there was no sign that they had been there. However, it was being watched. Somewhere there was a leak, they had never given the address out. Who ever wanted them would be back but it was not their problem.

Maddy and Nathan arrived back at the London flat. Nathan called James. "Are you free? We would like to come and see you and you need Maddy's signatures, I think. We have a lot to tell and show you. You should prepare to be amused."

"Come right away. Would you like to have dinner with me when we finish? I know of a new little place, the food is excellent. How is Maddy?"

"Fine," he said. "We will be with you in 20 minutes.

"Maddy, we are going to see James. If we take the miniatures, that will be one less thing to do later. I will send for a car. Please dress down or I shall have the Guardians spiriting you away to be an old man's darling."

"Rubbish, I am ready. I thought I would show him the letter as well. He might be able to find out more about my brother. Will Mary Ann be there?"

"I do not know. Come on, the car is here." Half an hour later, they were sitting in James' office. "Before we begin, would you like tea?" "Good idea," said Nathan. He ordered the tea and pastries.

"Oh, I should tell you, Edward can join us, I hope that is fine."

"No problem," said Maddy.

"Now whilst we are waiting, tell me about your trip. Clearly you had an interesting time."

"Yes," said Maddy. "I feel so much happier knowing about my background. What has Nathan told you?"

"Not a lot," said James.

She described her week. James was flabbergasted. "You actually had a present from your mother?"

"Yes," she said.

"Two miniatures and a string of pearls. She did try to warn me in her letter."

"A letter," said James. There was a knock at the door. That would be Edward. "Wait a moment, I am sure he will like to hear this."

"Yes, Mamma had secreted the gifts in a false lining in my case. Once I had arrived, Michael and Angela had put everything I had brought with me in the case and stored it in their loft. They told Nathan, so he invited them to have a weekend in Paris and to take the case there for me. They never found the right moment to tell me, so Nathan, knowing how much it meant to me, said he would do it."

"Going to Auschwitz had really shaken me. It took me almost 2 days to get warm. I think you know that my mother was shot, for sharing her bread with a small boy. Well, quite by chance, I think, we met him. She had given him a lock of her hair, hoping one day he might meet me. Isn't that just fantastic? Once that happened, Nathan decided to give me the case. It was then we found all my clothes and the package. Inside the pearl case was this letter. She handed it to them to read.

210

It was very quiet in the office.

Edward said, "Maddy are they the miniatures?"

"Yes," she said.

"May I see them?"
"Of course."

Edward tried to suppress his real interest. They are really very good. Do you know who they are?" "Yes, one is my father and mother on their wedding day and the other picture is of my grandparents."

"Would you like me to get them cleaned for you whilst you are on honeymoon?"

"So," said James, "now you need to trace your brother."

"If he is still alive, yes."

"I will see what we can do," said Edward.

"By the way Nathan, those two pictures you bought for Emir and Tiggy, they are genuine. Mary Ann has checked the provenance. They are ready for you to take with you. Such a delightful and generous present."
"Do we know where they were before going on the market?"

"Yes, Heatherbourne Castle."

"Oh, right." Maddy had certainly got a bargain!

"Time for dinner, I think," said James. "I have booked a table for five."

"Five," said Maddy. "Is Bar Lou coming?"

"Oh, no, but Mary Ann is."

"Brilliant," said Maddy. "Now we will be two roses between three thorns. What fun."

The evening passed quickly. Nathan and Maddy took Mary Ann home, she seemed much happier. They went back to the flat, tired but happy.

James and Edward contacted TM. He was as surprised as they had been.

"Do you think that these miniatures are part of the four Michael referred to?"

"Could be," said Edward.

"Curiouser and curiouser," said TM "and where do you think the other two are?"

"Maybe in Europe with her brother, or who knows? It is a job for Nigel and Charles."

"Yes, I think you could be right," said Edward. "I will get on to it right away."

"All this and a wedding too" said James.

"And do not forget Christmas," said Edward.

"As if I could ... I wonder what will happen next year?"

Chapter 26

Appleby was feeling really ill. He had sold the two miniatures in error. Where they were now was anyones guess. The two men he had been to see, seemed to think that they could be in different parts of the world. Going to where Dave and Ken were staying was mistake no. 2. He just had not given it any thought. He was too pre-occupied, wondering what Arpinsky would do to him.

Arpinsky, by now, was in Vienna making his way to the Gallerie Madel. As he predicted, Davis Browne had started the journey but 'got lost' on the way. He would not be found for some time. He had fallen into a little visited ravine. As far as he knew, no-one had missed him. Arpinsky had removed Browne's luggage from his room. He needed to go through it to remove anything incriminating before leaving it at the left luggage in Vienna.

At Gallerie Madel, Inky was waiting. He was unsure about the payment Arpinsky would demand. He never seemed to be short of money, so that might not be an option. Paintings, very few originals in, plenty of copies though. The door bell tinkled. Inky looked up. Arpinsky said "I believe you are awaiting these paintings. Mr Browne was unable to deliver them personally, so I obliged."

"Very kind of you," said Inky. "I assume that, because you are here, the job is done."

"It is."

"Good," said Inky. "He was getting very greedy."

"Now, as to our arrangement," Arpinsky whispered in his ear. Inky blanched. He could never do that.

"Fine," was all he said.

"Before you go," said Inky, as he handed over a substantial amount of money. "Any chance you may want to sell a few of your miniatures? I'm particularly looking for 2 silver mounted paintings to make up a set."

"I'm not sure what has happened to our miniature collection," said Arpinsky. "I do not have much use for them, as far as I can see."

Inky could not believe his ears. This guy, was he stupid or what? Inky shook his head. Then he said, "If you have the pair, we can trade."

"I will see," said Arpinsky, thinking that if he wanted to trade, there must be something more to the transaction.

Inky was glad to see him go. Arpinsky had asked a heavy price for his work. He had chosen Inky to pay. Where am I likely to get that kind of money? Rob a bank, blast a money van, hold up a building society - he listed more and more options. By which time he had convinced himself he could do it. In reality there was little chance. He had to think his way out of this one.

Once Arpinsky had sent him the original miniatures, he could go in search of his sister and, by hook or crook, persuade her to hand them over. Then he alone would be in the money. He smiled. He loved money, just stacking it up gave him a thrill. He had always wanted to be a banker, but lacked the education.

He looked around the Gallery and thought, 'This is a nice little concern, all the same. Specially since Browne was a no show.' Then he looked at the parcel by the door. He had not seen it delivered or signed for it. 'Strange,' he thought, and opened the crate. They were the paintings Davis Browne had told him about. 'Well, it's an ill wind,' he thought.

Back at Temple Meadows Maddy, Tiggy and Bar Lou were planning Christmas. Nathan having had enough of the wedding plans, went for a walk taking Rumple and Stilskin with him. Come on, go chase a rat.

He was dreading the idea of a stag night, but his friends were pushing him to suggest what night. He was not the first in the group to marry but it was the first wedding they knew about. He would have to talk to them. Then he had a better idea. Why not do something glamorous instead, much more fun. He would make a few phone calls.

He was looking forward to Christmas. The house would be full, as were the holiday cottages. It was the first year he was master of the house and had decided to invite both his close friends, Maddy's friends and her parents, Tiggy's family and Emir's all to stay. 'Then they will be here for the wedding, less pressure,' he thought.

'Christmas Eve will be brilliant. What theme can I dream up?' He had enjoyed the Xmas parties when his parents were alive. 'I know I'll make Maddy's dream come true, oh what a jolly jape. Their faces should be a study and it could be done if they all go to the midnight service. I'd better get on to it now. It will work out well, have a brilliant Christmas Day with all the carols and a meal in the evening. Lounge around on Boxing Day, deal with wedding arrangements once and for all, then spring his surprise.' He laughed.

The oldies can have the place to themselves for a few days and we can have fun.

In New York, Perry was finding it hard to concentrate. Conrad Parker

had not phoned. Relief as it was, it worried him more. What if he had
gone to the Press or tried to kidnap his daughters? Thank goodness
they were going to England, straight after Christmas, for both Nathan's
wedding and some sightseeing. He would love to talk to Edward. He
must come clean, whatever the consequences, though after the wedding
would be better.

At that point his secretary knocked and walked in to the office. "I
hope you have not forgotten the partners' meeting?, and there is some
bad news."

"Oh!

Who? What?" said Perry.

"The Embassy are on line 1 from London." He picked up the handset.
"Perry Bracken here, how can I help you?"
He listened, stunned partly but mightily relieved. Conrad Parker had
fallen on the electric line while waiting to get on the tube. He had died
instantly. No further action would be taken. Most likely outcome at the
coroner's court – death by misadventure. His family, well his mother,
the only family he had, was being informed at that moment.

"Thank God, or whoever. It is not my job to go and see her. We will
have to make sure that she is well provided for, within limits, of course.
Sad for her, as her husband died some months ago. He had gone to that
funeral and there were some strange fellows present.

Well this changes the state of the game, maybe I do not have to speak
to Edward after all. Perhaps it will be a happy Christmas at home with
the family." It would certainly be an expensive one. Good job that extra
money had appeared in his account.

Arpinsky did not celebrate Christmas, on principle. He had decided
to spend it in France. He had booked himself into Le Petit Oiseaux.
He had heard it was under new ownership; however nobody seemed

to know who the new owners were. He knew the place well. It was the scene of some of his greatest achievements. During the War he had been in charge of the SS Interrogation Unit. All foreign prisoners of war, of officer standing, were brought there. Arpinsky had his own particular brand of making them talk – scream, yell, shout, cry or even die. He did not like the ones that gave in easily. Only one person had really got under his skin, That was a woman from the OSS. No matter what he did to her, with his whips, knives, and pliers, she would scream alright but she never talked. Some name like 'Champian', and the fellow she was, with he was stubborn, even when he left her naked and bleeding in front of him. In a funny sort of way he admired their strength. Yes, he would enjoy Le Petit Oiseaux, the food, the wine, the memories. He wondered if anyone would recognise him. 'Doubt it,' he said to himself.

In Poland, Haime sat with his sister, both of them in their 80's now. Not much left to talk about until his sister said, "Did you tell Inky about those tiny pictures?"

"Yes, but the silly boy had sold them. In fairness he did not know their value, nor the way to solve the riddle of the four miniatures.

That poor woman! You know the one who told you about them? Remember when you smuggled out that baby for Hilly and Pop, she wanted her children to have them to remember her by. Now he will not ever see her. Inky will never have a picture in his mind of his mother."

"Did he ever find his sister?"

"No, I do not think so, neither do I know if she is alive or even knows she has a brother. Just two lost souls living in parallel, destined never to meet. Strange world isn't it," he said. They sat in silence.

Then his sister said, "Will you go back to Vienna?""No," said Haime, "there is nothing else to do now. Inky is not the person I thought he would turn out to be. Just think of all the love he had as a child. Why, oh why, has he turned out like he has?"

"Oh, I don't know. Turn on the radio, there is always nice music at Christmas. I like listening to it."

Maddy had gone to the Television Centre to start work on her report. She needed to know the time slot allocated to it. That would affect her presentation. She had the outline ready but the content was still withheld. She had hoped to complete before the wedding, but that was looking unlikely. She would have to talk to Nathan. She was due back to work in April, which could be a good time. "I will have to see if the department agree. It would be a pity to lose it altogether."

She handed in her programme plan and her report, hoping that it would be a short visit. There was so much still to do in London. It did not quite work out that way. News came in about the death of Conrad Parker. She was sure that was the person who had annoyed Nathan. There was something niggling at her, she knew the name from elsewhere. Had it been when she had looked at the researchers' video material? It really annoyed her, when she could not recall information. Maybe Nathan might know.

Mary Ann was really happy working for James and even more delighted when she was asked to research the two miniatures which Maddy's mother had left to her. Mary Ann thought it was very romantic and was pleased for her friend. They looked extremely good, there was no provenance. This was a job where all the stops would be pulled out. However, the two pictures Nathan and Maddy had bought in Vienna for Tiggy and Emir were a surprising find. The last listings she could find showed them as being displayed at Heatherbourne Castle. So how had they turned up in Austria? She would point this out again to James. There had to be a link somewhere, with a gallery in this country but which gallery? Then it came to her. It must be Hammersteins, it must be something to do with Miriam Hunter. Her family owned Heatherbourne Castle.

Chapter 27

Before talking to Edward, she decided to visit the Hammerstein Gallery. Maybe she would see or hear something that would help her. She purchased two bottles of fine brandy for the brothers and some chocolates for the girl who had replaced her. Mary Ann had grown in confidence, working for James and Edward. They seemed to know so many people yet it did not change them at all, they remained affable and friendly, yet so worldly wise. She was so happy.

The Hammersteins brothers, Leon and Igor, were delighted to see her. Miranda Hunter was not there. "I expect she is hung over. She went to some big dinner at the Palace last night." "Oh," said Mary Ann, "very posh."

They all giggled. She asked how business had been. The brothers were non-committal.

"Well," said Igor, "the miniature business slowed, but we are going great guns on Victorian paintings. There was a time we could buy them for a song at auction but now the prices are rising almost daily."

Leon added, "Yes, it must be the new money. Many of our older clients are selling rather than buying."

"That's true," said Igor. "It almost feels like the market is being manipulated in some way. I knew that the Victorians often invited young artists to teach their children to water colour. I could not imagine that there would be two, or even three, copies identical, even if the same view were painted over and over again. I wish you were back here, with our doubts. We need to be so sure of the provenances."

"Well, I cannot come back, it would not be wise, but if there is a particular picture that puzzles you, talk to me. A 'one off' I could do in my spare time."

She gave them the brandy and left the chocolates at reception.

"I have another reason for coming. My friends, Nathan and Maddy, are getting married in January. I would love to give them a nice picture or two but my budget is limited."

Igor looked at Leon. "We might have just the thing. I was at the country house sale a few months ago and bought two pictures. Not very big, they are silhouettes of a bride and groom, beautifully crafted and not too expensive."

"Oh, they sound just right. May I see them?" Mary Ann glanced at the silhouettes. Why did they seem familiar?

"Are they English?"

"No," said Leon. "We both think that they are probably European or, more likely, possibly looted during the last War."

"Really," said Mary Ann. She knew that she had to purchase them.

"I think they will be just right, so now let's talk money."

She walked back to the office smiling, enjoying the winter sunshine. 'Life is good,' she thought. 'It does not get much better than this.' She had so much to tell James and Edward. It felt good to be able to help them for a change.

Back at Heatherbourne Castle, Miranda and her husband were talking over lunch. Neither was very hungry and her husband was not in the best of moods. Over the table in front of him, was a stack of bills.

"Miranda, we just cannot go on spending money like this on restoration. Why are we doing it? There are no children to inherit."

This was a sore point with Miranda. She had developed rheumatic fever as a child and it had left her with a weak heart. The doctors had told her that having children was out of the question. Yet she had been so happy when she became pregnant, only to have to make the agonising decision to have the foetus aborted.

She had never really recovered. Oh, physically, she was much better but mentally, that was a different picture.

She used her abundant energies promoting good causes, which of course boosted her husband's career, and restoring Heatherbourne. She had reasoned that if she could not have children, that would become her baby.

"You know how to hit where it hurts, don't you George? I have been earning money, yes, me, earning money from sales of paintings through the Hammerstein Galleries. I love going to country house sales for them. I knew so many people and there are still friends to be made."

"Miranda, what you earn, as you call it, would not pay the bill for the paint."

"So," she said, "what now?"

"Well," said George, "we scale it down to what can be achieved without facing financial ruin."

Miranda was seething.

"This place means nothing to you. Oh, you enjoy bringing your visitors here, playing at 'Lord of the Manor'. This place has been swept so often by your people, I can almost do away with the cleaners. It is just not fair, this is my home. History has been made here. I just feel the need to make up for all the neglect, something is driving me on. I need to finish this project."

"And if you do finish it, then what?"

"Well, we could have some open days, raise monies for charity."

"Charity has to begin at home, Miranda."

"I know, perhaps I could sell some unused items. If I remember, when Daddy died, there was an inventory. I could look at that and the valuations."

"Fine, but talk to me before you do anything."

Little does he know! She had already started, but all she said was, "Yes dear. Now can we talk about something else?"

"What about Christmas? Will we be here or should we go to Ireland? There is that other ancient pile to look at. There has been some interest in buying it. Some rich young man, I believe, wants to start a stud there. Very appropriate when you think of its history."

She laughed.

"George, what do you think?"

"Ireland is not quite the place for me to go to with all the problems there are. Too much of a security risk. But as a follow-up on the sale, it could be quite profitable."

"Then it is here for Christmas. Fine at least I know."

TM was looking forward to Christmas. He took his family to Temple Meadows. They had one of three cottages and joined in the celebrations there.

His two children, twin boys, absolutely adored Nathan. They were in their final years at Firedown. He had never felt the same about Christmas since his wife died. He had married late in life, she had meant so much to him. It still hurt to this day. Not that he showed it to the outside world. His sister lived with them. She had never married, so she had mothered or, in his view, smothered the boys. He was glad to get them into Firedown.

All he could hear, from the boys, was 'Jolly Japes' and swimming in the new pool with a machine that could be turned on to create waves. TM thought, privately, 'You two did not need a machine to make waves!'

Nathan never ceased to surprise him. He would drop a sentence into a conversation, and whether he did it knowingly, TM was never sure, but it would be a 'gem', a real piece of intelligence.

Now he was Master of the Manor and about to get married. TM liked Maddy, she reminded him of his wife. Those wonderful eyes and that smile! She would have a full time job curbing some of Nathan's more outrageous ideas. The wedding should be quite something as everyone was expecting the unexpected - 'even me,' he thought.

Nathan, meanwhile, was in deep discussions with Brigstock. "Everything has to happen in the one and a half hour time slot when everyone, and I mean everyone, goes to the midnight service. When they come home I want to see the surprised looks on their faces. Can we do it?"

"Of course," said Brigstock. "What is this? Have you taken over the challenges these days?"

"No," said Nathan. "I could never do that, but you do not know how much I loved coming here, so excited, wondering what you had cooked up this time. I do not remember ever saying 'thank you'. Come back and live here again. You could bring your sister." Brigstock grimaced. "You could have the cottage by the gate. I'll have it done up just for you. Then you could see Bar Lou every day."

"I would appreciate that, Nathan. Retirement was not a good idea." "Have you really retired?"

"No, not in my mind, Nathan."

"Good, now down to business. Is everything ordered?"

"Yes."

"And the men know the score and we have agreed the bonus payments?"

"We have."

"Oh good, Maddy will be surprised, I hope."

'More than Maddy,' thought Brigstock.

It would be quite a Christmas, one that those present would never forget. Nathan and his 'Jolly Japes'! He had grown into a very special young man and with Maddy as his wife, he would go far.

Inky decided to spend Christmas with Hilly. She had not been very well. I will bring her here to Vienna. She will love the gaiety, the markets, the shops. Yes, he would spoil her. He was not sure how but he would try.

In all the years she had known 'Inky', he had never once asked them, her and Pop, to Vienna. It was almost too much, too late, but she felt he needed her. So she would go. At worst it would be something to tell her friends about when she got home in the New Year. She did not realise just how much she would have to tell.

Chapter 28

Gabriella and Freddie enjoyed working together on the Cabal projects. She was surprised how much she would miss him when it was time for him to return to England for Christmas although she was due to follow, once Hannaway, Mark and she had agreed the accounts and completed the forecasts for the next year. She thought, 'He is not really my type.'

"If we work late for the next two nights, it should be possible to close the office early for Christmas. There will be little business transacted over the holiday period," said Hannaway. Are we all agreed?"

Gabriella and Mark nodded. They were delighted at the thought of an extra day to see their families, before they left for England to attend the wedding.

Whilst they were having a coffee break, Gabriella asked Hannaway if he had any more news about Conrad Parker.

"Only that it was death by misadventure."

"Oh well, he was full of himself," she said. "I got the feeling that he had some kind of hold over Perry. Just lately, everybody had been saying how stressed Perry looked. Maybe he will feel different after the Christmas break."

"There was some talk that he might retire at Easter," said Mark, "but that seems to have died down. He does not do much work in the audits now. There was a bit of a to-do about some major accounts a few months back. One of the leisure groups, I think. Now he is mainly working with the Corporate Holdings Unit. It cannot be as challenging as the Audit Teams. He was always so on the ball until last year."

Hannaway let them ramble on, some of the information was new to him. He just sat and listened. He must talk to Nathan. He remembered Nathan had been worried about a set of accounts for a Leisure Group.

Freddie met Nathan at his London flat. He had asked for a private word. He had enjoyed working with Hannaway, but was more than happy with Gabriella's work. She was really bright and brilliant with people. He wanted to test the water to see if Nathan would be prepared to consider letting him start an office in Australia, to cover the Far East. He had done some research, which suggested that, within a decade, those markets would open up.

Nathan listened to what he had to say, but wanted to give it more thought.

He said, "When all the Cabal are over here, perhaps we could spend a day working out where we are going and who will do what."

"Fair enough," said Freddie. "Are we travelling down to Temple Meadows tomorrow?"

"Yes," said Nathan. "My work is almost complete. Just a few more phone calls. Then I have to wait for some papers to be couriered here. Suppose I phone Edward and James and we all have dinner together?"

"Do you know when Neville and Jos are due in?" said Nathan.

"I know Jos is due in London tomorrow. He said something about seeing the parents, then motoring down to Temple Meadows on Christmas Eve."

"Neville is talking about joining a major expedition to the Arctic, as a doctor. I do not think he will ever settle back in Wales. I know he has been making a name for himself in sports medicine. It is a new field and he is well respected. He also has a steady girlfriend and his coveted Welsh jersey."

"Oh, I did not know that," said Nathan. "Can you phone him? He should ask her here, over Christmas, and definitely for the wedding."

"Sure," said Freddie. "Did you know that Jos has decided to go full time with Labac? That is where his heart is."

"I did hear," said Nathan. "They are playing at the wedding."

"How did that come about?"

"He offered so I talked to Maddy, who was not altogether sure, so we compromised. They will play some suitable music whilst Maddy and I sign the register. Apparently he has written a special piece for when we leave the church. My heart is a bit in my mouth, but Maddy and I will be married by then, so I suppose she will expect the unexpected."

"Nathan?" "Yes!""About your stag night."

"Yes," said Nathan.

"Well, I thought to wait until we are altogether and sort something out then. It ought to be special."

"Oh, it will be," said Nathan. There was a knock at the door. It was the courier. Nathan signed for the parcel, he looked very pleased.

He leaned to Freddie. "Are we ready to meet Edward and James? Good I am hungry."

Freddie shook his head. He thought, 'Nathan really does not change. I thought his inheritance might get to him. This Maddy must be someone extra special ...'

Maddy, Tiggy, Esther and Mary Ann were at Maddy's old flat, just happy to be together over drinks and food. The dresses had arrived for the bridesmaids -they were stunning.

"I'm going to enjoy this," said Esther. "I will never be able to afford a Clothilde dress for many a long year". "It would not be my first priority," said Tiggy. "Mine neither," said Mary Ann, "but I am so excited about your wedding. I never thought that Nathan would be your husband, he's always seemed a little wild."

"A little," said Maddy. "You do not know the half but he is so considerate and very romantic with me. I feel so good when he is here. We will have a lot of adjusting to do, but I am confident."

"Have you thought about your 'hen night?" asked Esther.

"No, and I am uncertain about it. We are very much in the public eye so our old haunts are out. Why don't we wait until we are together at Temple Meadows? I think Brigstock is picking us up tomorrow, so we will take the dresses to Bar Lou's cottage and meet up with the men."

"Sounds good to me," said Tiggy. "At least I will get a chance to see how it is done."

"Yes," said Mary Ann. "When are you two getting married?"

"We are hoping in September. There are still problems in Osmantia affecting Emir's family, so we will have to wait and see."

"Good luck with it! Just imagine, if Patra has anything to do with the organising, it will be a stunning wedding," said Maddy.

"Oh, by the way, Nathan and I bought you a present when we were in Vienna. I think he has taken it to Temple Meadows. Perhaps when Emir arrives, we can give it to you then."

Patra and Bar Lou were just about to see how her cottage looked – Bar Lou was so excited. Once they arrived at the cottage, Patra said, "Will you go in first?" which she did.

"Oh, Patra, it is wonderful. I did not expect it to look so homely and the alterations look splendid. Thank you so much. I must settle your fees."

"No, that has been done."

"Oh," said Bar Lou and they both said together "Nathan."

"Well," said Bar Lou, "let's have a drink to celebrate then we need to make our way back to the house. Christmas is going to be wonderful this year. I hope I can find the energy to enjoy it."

Patra asked, "Is Clothilde coming early for the wedding? I would so like to meet her. I have some ideas for a fashion range. Do you think she would help me?"

"You can only ask but why not ask Nathan? He is really our contact with her."

"Isn't it interesting, how Nathan has suddenly become the one everyone turns to, for help, advice and fun?"

"It's not so sudden Patra, he has been building up to it for years. He was always the one for a laugh but when he was made Head Boy at Firedown, things began to change. Oh, he still laughed and organised his jolly japes but it was as if he grew up over night. He has a way with people which is quite extraordinary. In Maddy, he has found someone who can manage him. She is very clever. He absolutely adores her yet he does not even try to control her. It is as if it is not necessary. They used to call her the 'ice maiden' at University. Now she is softer somehow, more rounded and a very good listener. Must be the journalist in her. That smile is devastating. Just imagine what kind of children they will have."

"It does not bear thinking about," said Patra. "Emir and Tiggy hope to marry next September. I hope she will let me help."

"Why not talk to her parents whilst you are here? It must be a welcome change, planning a wedding rather than worrying about Osmantia."

"Yes, it is. No more of this. We need to go back to the house for supper. Come along, best foot forward."

The Hannaways were enjoying their flight to England. Mai Lee said, "I've never travelled first class before. Isn't it wonderful? What is the matter, you have been so very quiet? Is anything wrong at the office?"

"No, it is not that. I had a call from my old Headmaster at Firedown, he is retiring. He has asked me to consider applying for the post."

"Really," said Mai Lee, "and how do you feel about that?" "Well, I was stunned. I have enjoyed working with Nathan and I have learned a lot from him, but I do not want to do that work long term. I loved my time at Firedown. It would be my dream to go back there as the Headmaster. Do you think I am too young?"

"No, if you are good enough, you are old enough. Have you told Nathan?"

"No, you are the only other person that knows. If we can separate Nathan from his jolly japes for an hour or two, I shall talk to him. Nathan is so happy now with Maddy. I remember when his father and mother died, it was dreadful. It was the first time I met Bar Lou. She glided down the drive in a flowing dress. I did not know she was so old, or at least she seemed so to us. Like a Grandma. She sort of enveloped Nathan. I could just see the top of his head. They looked a sad couple as they walked to the car. I did not think he would come back to Firedown. But he did, after Christmas. Now he is getting married after Christmas. Strange, isn't it?"

"No," said Mai Lee. "How did you become such good friends?" "Well, we were in the same year but not the same house. Nathan was appointed Head Boy and he asked me to join his team along with Jos, Walshy, Jacko and Emir. We became the 'Famous five'. He had gone home at Summer break but did not ask Emir to go with him. Said he had a lot to do, if he was to be Head Boy as things needed changing. If the Head had heard him, I think he would have withdrawn the offer straightaway. Because his parents were dead, he had guardians, all manner of people. He went round them all asking questions. Then he came back here with a plan. The Head was very good. He knew that there was merit in 'some', but not all of his ideas, and let him start with one or two which led to more and more.

That is how the 'Cabal' was formed. We met in the Head Boy's rooms on Sunday evening. They drank loads of dark coffee, well mainly," he smiled, "and set about bringing Firedown in to line. It was the best year of my life at school."

"Mai Lee, I really want that job, but would you be happy as the Headmaster's wife?"

"Do you have to ask, but wouldn't we have rather a large family?"

"That's true," said Hannaway

"Darling?"

"Yes."

"I have some news of my own."

"What is it?"

"Well, you know I went to the doctor's before we left?"

"Yes. Mai Lee what is wrong?"

"Nothing. It is just the best news, we are having a baby."

"A what? When?"

"August, may be."

"Oh," said Hannaway, "oh I am so happy. You are wonderful. Wait till I tell the Cabal."

Mai Lee smiled.

Dave and Ken were sharing a Christmas drink with Brigstock. It was his last night off, as it were, before the Christmas guests arrived. Then the place would be a mad house. How so many different personalities would get on, he had no idea, and Nathan was up to his tricks again.

Ken said, "Briggie, Dave and I will be at my mum's over Christmas but if we can help, just ask. Mum would rather have her old cronies about. We thought we would take them to the pub and then disappear."

"That's fine, if I need you, and I suspect I will." He thought for a moment. "How do you fancy being chauffeurs? With everyone staying and more arriving for the wedding, we shall have to hire in cars to cope."

"Great, do we get a uniform?"

"Oh yes, smart suits, white shirts, a cap and a tie."

"Oh well," said Dave, "we finally have to conform."

They all laughed.
"Now," said Brigstock, "please bring me up-to-date."

"Well, it has been quiet. The strange thing is, we have not seen that Davis Browne, you know, the Yank, around. He has not been at the Gallery. Now he is a missing link. It might be worth following up."

"We never did find out who rolled over our flat. It was a very professional job. Fortunately there was nothing to be found but we did move out very quickly."

"What shall we do with the Arpinsky stuff we bought?"

"At the moment, it is in the Bank."

"Leave it there. There is time to decide about that once this affair is settled. I have an idea it just might be coming to the boil."

"Now chauffeuring duties, you know that also means some bodyguard duties. I think Bronsen and Babington will also be around. I understand that TM will get us altogether."

"By the way, do you know a coach driver? Nathan wants Maddy to arrive at Church in a coach. Can you imagine it?" "What about Ince Blundell? He was Horseguards and he has that stable in Surrey," said Ken.

"What a good idea! I am sure he would be delighted to organise it or even do it himself."

"It's going to be a big do, is it, this wedding?"

"Yes, it is. People are coming from all over the world. It will need a sight more time sorting everything out."

"Wait till I tell my old mum," said Ken.

"Not until afterwards, please."

"Fine," said Ken.

"Dave, you have been quiet." "Yes, I know. Who'd have thought that we three would be asked to help. We don't have the best of backgrounds."

"Forget it, the past is the past, enjoy today. I'll see you on 27th. We have lots of ground to cover. I am living in the Gatehouse now, back on the Estate. Couldn't stand it with my sister, not her fault. I've just got set in my ways. So you can bunk with me. It will be more than useful."

Ince Blundell was very surprised to get a phone call from James, after all they would be meeting in the next few days.

"Just want to run a few things past you before we meet," said James. "This wedding. Nathan would like Maddy to arrive at the Church in a coach, driven by four white horses and then they will make the return journey to the house in it afterwards. He is opening up the old coach path from the church to the house."

"Well, I never," said Blundell. "As a matter of fact I have just bought an old coach at auction. It needs quite a lot of work. I bought if for a gimmick boost for our PR, don't you know? If we put a move on, it could just be ready in time, and, no, Nathan is not footing the bill. It will be Natasha's and my wedding present. I will be the coachman and I am sure some of the lads would not mind earning a few extra pennies. Consider it sorted."

"Great," said James. "You know Nathan has planned everything down to the last detail. We've all been given jobs to do. He get more like his father every day."

Appleby, meanwhile, had dropped out of sight. At least he thought he had. There was no trace of the miniatures. He was really in problems. He had really scoured that flat, nothing. Little did he know Arpinsky had worked it out that the miniatures were missing. He was not best pleased.

Chapter 29

"Nathan," said Maddy. "I have thought about my flat in London. We will have so many places to stay." "But Temple Meadows will always be our home, you know, that don't you?" said Nathan.

"Yes I do, but, about the flat. I have decided to pay off the remaining mortgage and ask James to arrange for my parents to live there rent free for the rest of their lifetime. It is a good compromise."

"Maddy, that is great. Now I have a confession, I have already asked James to organise clearing the mortgage."

"Nathan, I wanted to do that."

"I know, but bear with me. I want you to have your nest egg to invest or to keep for a rainy day. Something that you will own and can do what you like with."
"For your own expenditure, you will have a new account. Money is not going to be a problem but we will be judged on how we handle it."

"I know and I trust you completely, Nathan, but that does not mean I will just say 'yes' all the time. It is not in my nature."

"Oh, I know that. Hadn't we better get ready for dinner?"

"It's a buffet," said Maddy. "Very informal. It is easier with so many people here."

"Clever you! Come here. See this piece of mistletoe? I put it here, just for you and me to be very traditional." "Nathan!" "Maddy." He kissed her. "Not long now to the main course." "No," she smiled, "I feel the same way. The presents are all wrapped and ready under the tree." 'It is a pity it will not be a white Christmas, so much more romantic,' wished Maddy.

"Well, we can't have everything. Come on, let's get ready to greet our friends."

It was a super evening with people laughing. TM's two boys did the honours with the angel on the tree and the Christ child into the crib. The oldest boy Samuel, sang solo in 'Once in Royal David's City'.

"Its magical," said Mai Lee, experiencing her first Christmas outside China.

"It's time we left for church," said Nathan. "I think there are enough cars to take everyone there but I suggest we walk back along the old coach path. It is only a few minutes away. The little village church was packed out. It was a good service, the Reverend was on good form and people were happy.

After the service, Nathan had arranged for the choir to lead his party back to the house. Lanterns were carried by the men, who gallantly escorted the ladies. As they turned into the coach path there was a gasp, the ground was covered in (artificial) snow. Fairy lights decked the trees, all the way to the house, while snow was sprinkled liberally as far as the eye could see, even on the roof of Garden Cottage.

"Nathan, how did this happen?" said Maddy.

"Oh, just a little Christmas magic," he replied, "for my bride to be."
"What are we going to do about the pre-wedding celebrations?" "Oh,
let's get Christmas over first, we'll worry about that later."

TM strolled over. "Nathan, thank you. My boys are having such fun.
Just look around you and see the smiles and hear the laughter. You are a
very special person. Happy Christmas."

"Thank you. It is a special time for me as well, and it will get better.
This is only the beginning. I just hope my parents, wherever they are
tonight, or rather this morning, can feel our happiness."
Nathan and Maddy were the last to leave the conservatory. They
walked hand in hand up the stairs. It was a beautiful starlit sky. They
smiled at each other, there was no need for words.

Next morning Nathan and Maddy delivered their presents to the
families on the Estate. His father had started the tradition and he was
determined to continue. Maddy had arranged hampers for the adults
and presents for the children.

Breakfast was in full swing when they returned to the house. The big
tree, this year, was in the conservatory, with presents piled high around
it.

TM's two boys were really excited. They had already discovered
their pile, Nathan, Maddy, James, Edward and Bar Lou, as hosts, handed
out the presents. The floors were awash with paper. There was more
laughter and a few tears. Nathan turned to Maddy. "Well, lady wife-to-
be, this is from me to you."

It was a relatively small package. Maddy looked at him, "I have
already had so much, why give me more?"

"Well, if you come with me, we can slip out for a few minutes for
some quiet time. Everyone will drift around, dinner is at 4.30 pm, so I
am sure we can find 'something' to do." He smiled.

239

Once in their own sitting room, Maddy opened her parcel. There were 2 boxes, one contained a pair of pearl earrings which were a suitable style and colour match to her mother's pearls and the other a diamond necklace, bracelet and earring set. Maddy started to cry. Nathan held her close.

"I know," he said, "I know."

"Please wear the diamonds tonight. They were my mother's. I had them reset for you. I would just like a bit of her to be with us tonight. Are you going to wear the red dress?" "Wait and see," said Maddy, "just wait and see."

After dinner, Nathan stood up and made his first speech as Master of the Manor.

"I am so happy to be here with you all and I hope today has lived up to expectations. It is also Maddy's first time here, as it is for so many new friends. I hope it will become a tradition. So please raise your glasses. Happy Christmas and a great New Year. I know I am looking forward to it." Raucous laughter followed his remark. Maddy blushed. She looked stunning in her red dress and her diamonds. They almost matched the sparkle in her eyes.

"Before I sit down, as is traditional, there will be a cooked breakfast for you tomorrow. Then the staff go home to their families. Lunch will be a buffet and in the afternoon we are all off to the Pantomine where you can hiss and boo to your hearts content. We have tickets for the matinee, then do as you will. Thank you."

On the day after Boxing Day, Gabriella and Mark arrived – they were a little overawed. All the younger members of the party gathered in the conservatory.

Jos said, "Well Nathan, this stag night, where will it be?" Esther joined in with, "Come on Maddy. What are we doing?"

"Well, it is a departure from tradition. As you know, it would be difficult for us to have the usual party so I have organised something just as special. Maddy has some envelopes to hand around. Open them altogether." "The New Year's Ball in Vienna. Wow" said Gabriella. "Yes," said Jos. Mai Lee asked her husband to explain. Tiggy looked at Emir. "What will I wear?" "What a wonderful, wonderful idea -four days in Vienna."

"Think of the shopping," said Gabriella and Mai Lee in unison. "Yes, just think," said the men, hands on their wallets. "Tiggy, there is a special display of the Lippazaner Horses on New Year's Eve at 2 pm. We have tickets for everybody. It also means that the oldies can have some space. We leave on the 29th and are back here on the 2nd January. No need to remind you what we will be doing after that."

Nathan said a silent prayer, hoping that nothing would happen to spoil the fun. He was aware that there were loose ends to follow up. He needed to spend some time with James, Edward, TM and Bar Lou. Now he had been invited to join the Circle. He was immensely proud of this decision and needed to be brought up-to-date.

He had planned one more surprise for Maddy. He had set things in motion to try and find her brother, if he was still alive.

This started a chain of events the like of which, no-one could have foretold the outcome.

Inky was enjoying showing Hilly around Venice. She was very popular with his friends and loved spending time in the gallery. He was so comfortable at that time and was completely off guard. He had made significant money on the sale of the Victorian paintings. Those he did not choose to sell, he had sent to the States. With Parker dead and Fing Wah missing, there were not the same controls. Cracks were beginning to develop. There had been no news of the fate of Davis Browne II, no body had been found as far as he knew. Yet he was wary of Arpinsky. Inky was desperate to purchase the two miniatures so he would go along with Arpinsky for the time being. He had the first payment ready for him when he showed up. He had taken most of it from the last lot of money from Davis Browne, which he had been waiting to launder.

Arpinsky had had enough of the chateau. It was not as interesting since it had been converted to a hotel. There did not seem to be anyone around who ever gave him a second look, much to his chagrin. He was looking to build up his cash reserves. The deal with Inky for the miniatures seemed a good investment.

He decided to go to London and catch up with Appleby. Then it would be a simple matter to pick up the miniatures, return to Vienna and complete the deal with Inky. He, too, was surprised that no one had found Davis Love's body. Perhaps he would go walking in the area where he had disposed of it. At least it would satisfy his curiosity.

Appleby was unaware of Arpinsky's decision to return to London to collect his miniatures. Little did he know they had been sold. Appleby had not made any further enquiries as to their whereabouts. Certainly those two fellows who attended the Gallery did not appear to know about them. When he had searched the flat he had found nothing, it was almost too clean for two fellows on their own.

Perhaps he ought to try again. If the miniatures were in England he should be able to find them before Arpinsky returned. It was a very faint hope.

Then he had a thought. If Arpinsky was out of the way ...

Chapter 30

Dave and Ken were sharing a cup of tea with Brigstock. They had enjoyed the Christmas festivities more than they thought they would.

Dave said, "He is some bloke, that Nathan. Is he very rich? His wife-to-be is quite a looker, phew."

"Briggie, do you think we could have a day off? It is quiet, we have swept the grounds, there is nothing out of the ordinary. I would like to see a few mates and my mum. We could be back tomorrow."

Ken said, "Yes, I asked a pal to keep an eye on the flat, just in case someone came back. You never know."

"Fine," said Briggie. He was feeling very tired but he was determined to see all the arrangements through. Anyway, he had promised to set a special challenge for TM's boys and a few friends from the village. Today would be ideal.

Edward was having a similar conversation with Bronsen and Babington. "It is a good time to have a break. We are all safe enough here. Have some fun, see what you can find out. See you tomorrow evening."

Edward was sitting quietly in the small lounge at the Dower House. He had been thinking a lot about retirement lately. Now that Nathan was about to be married and seemed to be settling down, it could be the right time. There were people at the office who could take more of the work on board. He would still keep his hand in ... just a few special cases. He was enjoying the respite. They would all be back tonight, then the fun would begin again.

The next morning, as he sat reading his paper, there was a knock at the door. "Come in," he said. "Oh, Mary Ann what can I do for you?" "Is it a good moment, there is something troubling me. You remember you asked me to check the provenance of the two pictures Nathan and Maddy bought for Tiggy and Emir?"

"Yes". "Well, when we were in Vienna ..."
"Oh, did you have a good time."
"Brilliant. Maddy is so lucky, but the best thing is there is no side to either of them, they make everyone feel so comfortable."

"Now, back to what I was saying. In Vienna we went to Gallery Madel and there I saw two, what I am almost sure, were copies of the same pictures. Maddy and Nathan had gone off on their own so they are not aware of this. But what is even stranger, I saw two original Victorian paintings which were on the Antiques Squad list and there are copies at the Hammerstein Gallery."

"I am puzzled. You knew I worked at the Gallery for a while. Nothing like that happened whilst I was there. I would have known. Yes, people did come in wanting to sell pictures, Igor and Leon always showed them to the office. I did not see anything of note."

"It was only when Miranda Hunter became a partner and I was almost pushed out, that there seemed to be secrets. That chap, Davis Love, used to be there on a regular basis, bringing in pictures and taking some away, but the export documents looked funny to me. Why send paintings to Vienna, then on to the States? Now I know why. The Antiques Squad have discovered quite recently that there are a group of technically good painters at work, copying originals. It is said that they were sending some work to the States which was original, but there would be some dubious provenances with the copies. A young Chinese man was a key figure, also a young American, I think his name was Parker. They were the contacts in New York. I do not know if it makes sense to you."

"Yes, it does. Thank you. I will see that those who need to know are told. But may I ask you one more thing, will you keep this information to yourself? If we are to go further, time is of the essence."

"Of course, having told you I am now off to join the others. I am so glad the information is useful," said Mary Ann.

Edward found TM and James. There is a major development and he told them what Mary Ann had said.

"It all ties up," said TM.

"So far the Austrian Police, who found the body of Davis Love, have kept the information out of the public domain. He had papers on him linking him to the Hammerstein Gallery. I heard today that there is a stranger in the village where the body was found. Says he is on a walking holiday."

"Walking, in winter" said Edward.
"That is what I am told. He is being watched. We have decided to see what happens."

"Dear me," said James. "I hope we get through the wedding before it breaks."

"We can control things," said TM. "We are quite a distance from breaking this story. Anyway, we need Maddy back here, for you remember she will front the television programme. We are months, rather than years, away from finding the truth."

"James, do you know where Nathan is planning to take Maddy?" "What," said James, "Nathan tell me that! I doubt if Maddy knows. They will be in the London flat for a night or two. Maddy has a few papers to sign before they fly out, if that is what they are doing."

"I will have to see Nathan, even if he gives me the itinerary in a sealed envelope. It may never be opened but I think I will err on the side of caution."

Esther, Maddy, Tiggy, Mary Ann, Mai Lee and Gabriella were regaling Patra and Bar Lou with the exploits in Vienna. "It was such fun," said Gabriella, "and the shops, wow!" The whole city laughs," said Mai Lee, "so different from my home."

"Well, I realised that you shopped, all the bags are testament to that." "Oh, I am keeping these," said Gabriella. "I have a great collection at home."

"Why?" said Esther.

"Something different, I suppose. I love shopping and I can look at them and remember my mistakes, and there have been plenty, and the things I still enjoy. I've been collecting since I was a teenager."

"Mad," said Tiggy. They all laughed.
Patra said, "I think I have a few that you might like. They are all from big names in fashion around the world. I will send them to you."

"Oh, thank you, Patra. I think my favourite will be the Clothilde one. Maddy, I do not know how you managed to get her to design our dresses."

"Well, I felt I could only cope with three bridesmaids, but I wanted you each to have a special dress."

"But what is the connection with Clothilde? She is so particular about the clients she accepts."

"Need you ask?" said Maddy. "Its Nathan. Everywhere we go he meets an old school chum or someone his father or grandmother have helped. It is absolutely annoying and another thing, he speaks so many foreign languages and he can swap so quickly from one to another. I feel like saying sometimes, 'Will the real Nathan Eversley please stand up!'"

Bar Lou smiled then said "He always liked languages. His father was the same but I like his sketches. I have his book here from when he was quite small. I can show you one or two." "Which ones?" said Maddy, beginning to blush.

"Oh, I think the ones when we stayed with Patra."

"Do you remember, Patra?"

"Oh I do. He gave the Sultan, Emir and I some he did himself. If there are any more of Osmantia, do you think he would let me have some?"

"No doubt," said Maddy, "he is so very generous. Leave it to me. I think I have ways of persuading him." They all laughed.

"I'm sure," said Esther, "and we can guess what they might me."

"Now, to the wedding. Bar Lou, can we see your outfit." "No, not until the day. Now, hairdressers." "Oh, Bar Lou, have a glass of wine, we can do that later."

In the small village of Dansee, Arpinsky, in the guise of an elderly vicar, was walking in the mountains. He had heard the Intercontinental express go by so he knew he was near the spot. What he was not aware of was that he was being watched. He was so arrogant, he had let his guard slip – another mistake.

In the guest house last night, he had asked if there was any likelihood of avalanches and managed skilfully to bring the conversation around to accidents. The information he wanted was not forthcoming. He did have one anxious moment. 'Could he be alive, that dammed Yank?' No, he was dead. He dismissed the idea from his mind. He scanned the ravine with his powerful binoculars but there was no visible sign. He thought he saw a glint of light but when he looked again, decided it must be the sun on the snow, so he could move on.

Nathan had not been happy to tell TM about his plans. "I want Maddy to be the first to know. What about a compromise? I am sure I will not want to drive to London after the wedding. We do need to be there and two days later we will be leaving for our ultimate destination. You arrange a driver for me and I will hand him the information you want in a package at the airport."

"Fine," said TM, "consider it done." Somehow he felt relieved. He had wanted to provide a driver, remembering what had happened to Nathan's parents, albeit quite a while ago now, but he did not want it to happen again.

Unbeknown to them all, the Vienna papers were full of photographs of the Ball. One in particular caught Inky's attention. 'English visitors enjoy their evening.' One name stood out, 'Madeleine Alinsky.' That just could be her. He wondered! He went to the office to get a copy. Once Hilly went home, he would follow this up.

The wedding morning finally arrived. The sun was shining and real snow was falling gently to the ground. Maddy looked out of the window. 'So this is it,' she thought. She could feel the butterflies in her stomach already. 'Funny,' she thought, 'I do not remember anyone telling me how I am getting to the Church. Perhaps Dad has arranged it. Well, I hope someone has.'

Bar Lou knocked and came into her room. "Well, how are you my dear?"

"Nervous," said Maddy, "but excited. It is so like a dream come true. I feel I will wake up and find myself staring at the screens in the news room."

"It's real, alright," said Bar Lou. "Angela will be here soon. It is her privilege to help you dress."

"Oh, right," said Maddy. "I thought Clothilde was doing that." "She is, but there are things a mother should say to her daughter on a day like this. What are you reading?"

"Oh, the letter my mother wrote to me. Remember we found it with the pearls. Would you like to read it?"

"Oh yes," said Bar Lou. After she had finished reading, the tears were flowing. "I vowed I would not cry," said Bar Lou. "Now, a hot chocolate." "Yes but do not shoot it." "Would I do a thing like that?" said Bar Lou smiling.

In another part of the cottage the bridesmaids were getting ready. Clothilde was fussing around. Her poor assistants were running hither and thither. 'It needs a stitch here. Do it, please.'

'Oh, I do love dressing beautiful women,' she thought. When the photographs come out, I must have some for the salon walls. These are by far my best creations to date.

She still had to dress Maddy. They had agreed that no one would see her dress before she left for the church. Her father would, of course, and her mother. "Clothilde has said 'a little bit of mystery at a time like this adds to the day.' Hope she is right."

Maddy looked at her dress, simple, classical and stunning. She hoped she would do it justice.

Finally, she was ready. Clothilde, Patra and Bar Lou had left for the church.

"No doubts?" her mother said.

"None whatsoever," said Maddy.

Just at that moment her father arrived.

"Michael, what do you think?" said Angela.

"She looks so much like her mother standing there. Maddy, you look absolutely beautiful. Nathan is in for a big surprise."

"Come along, Angela, your car is waiting."

"Is that my car?" said Maddy.

"No," said her father. "Just look out of the window. Maddy saw the coach & horses. She could hardly swallow.

"Oh, Dad!"

Michael helped his daughter out of the house into the coach. She looked at the coachman it was Colonel Ince Blundell in his full dress uniform.

"Thank you," she mouthed.

"It is a big moment for you," Michael said to her.

"How do you feel?"

"Strangely calm. I almost feel a reassuring hand on my arm, and so very, very happy." They took the old coach route to the Church.

There were gasps from the villagers as she stepped from the coach.

Michael took her arm. The bridesmaids saw her for the first time in her dress.

They smiled at on another. "You look absolutely ravishing," said Esther. "Now, let's get this show on the road."

250

The wedding march started, and they moved off in to the church.

Nathan and Emir turned around. "You lucky man!" said Emir.

"Not luck, old friend, judgement," said Nathan.

Maddy arrived at his side. They smiled at each other reassuringly and with love. The rest, they say, was history. After the photographs, the coach drew up and they drove slowly to the house.

"Hello, Mrs Eversley. I love you," said Nathan.

Maddy just smiled.

"Oh, what did you think of the Labac music? Jos wrote that piece just for us. We have the original score from him to keep. It's called 'Maddy's Dream.'"

"Really," said Maddy. "I realised it was not quite his usual style, but he wrote it just for us?"

"Yes."

"How wonderful."

The reception went well. With all that had happened, Maddy had not really noticed Bar Lou's dress. It was not the usual creation. When she stood up to say a few words, Nathan, Emir and Maddy were riveted.

"What a fantastic dress! She looks wonderful. It isn't flowing everywhere," said Emir.

"This day is full of surprises," said Maddy.

"There are a few more to come," said Nathan.

"Oh," said Maddy "I wonder what they are."

The dancing was in full swing, Maddy and Nathan had changed but she was still wearing her mother's pearls. They moved around their guests, chatting, laughing, shaking hands. Then it was time to leave. Bar Lou was waiting at the entrance. They hugged. She whispered in Maddy's ear, "Thank you for helping me to find myself. This has been a big day for me as well."

Her father and mother were also there. Nathan handed her mother a small packet beautifully wrapped. "This is from both of us to say thank you."

Then they left for London.

"Where are we going after London?" asked Maddy.

"Wait and see. We have a few things to do before then." He winked. "Oh, we are finally getting to the main course?" They laughed.

Meanwhile, Tiggy's brother has been watching, taking note of the house contents. 'If Dad won't give me the money, maybe his friends will contribute indirectly,' he thought. He would just have to be careful. He knew he needed money desperately and by now did not care how he got it. Just one painting would be enough or a few jewels?

Ken had been watching him for some time. 'Silly blighter,' he thought. He nudged Dave and indicated Colin. "Sure," said David. "I'll talk to Brigstock. This could be interesting."

Brigstock spoke to TM. They agreed to watch him, if he took anything to follow. 'I hope he is not involved in the art scandal,' thought TM. 'It would just be to bad.'

'He is clever,' thought Brigstock. 'He is after the small painting in the hall. It would go under his jacket and with a coat over his arm, few would notice. Very similar to the Leidl painting snatch.'

Colin thought he had got away with it. 'Out of the mouths of babes.' It was easy. He made straight for a meet with Appleby.

"This pays off my debt, then," said Colin.

"Just about," said Appleby. "Any more where this came from?"

"Could be," said Colin, "could be. The money will have to be right. Or other needs met," said Appleby, giving him a knowing look. "But this is private, just between you and me. Now I have another commission for you ..."

Chapter 31

Arpinsky left Dansee and made his way to the airport. He needed to find Appleby and the miniatures. The rest would be easy. He was still unaware that he was being tailed. On the plane he slept. 'Too much mountain air,' he thought. 'It has been a useful diversion, very pleasant in fact.' Soon they would be landing at London Airport. He had pre-booked a hotel and was looking forward to a bath, a good meal, fine wines and a sound sleep.

At the Penthouse flat, Maddy and Nathan were giggling. Bar Lou had somehow managed to leave a parcel in each of their cases. Intrigued, they had been opened. Two bright red night shirts and a cap bearing the inscription, 'in case of fire'.

"Why unpack?" said Nathan. "We will only have to repack." "I just want to make sure that nothing else has found its way into the luggage."

"Maddy come here, sit with me by the fire. It is very comfortable. It is time we dispensed with the hors d'oeuvres and went straight to the main course."

"Oh, I don't know so much. I quite like the starters. It gets me in the mood," she smiled.

Slowly Nathan removed her dress, "You look fantastic but I think we can dispense with the diamonds."

"Why are you still dressed?" said Maddy. "It is so warm by the fire, I know I will join you in a minute."

"Don't be so untidy," said Maddy, "fold your clothes." "Maddy." As she looked up he kissed her and that was the start of their married life.

Next morning Nathan wore his red night shirt for a laugh as he prepared breakfast. He had not wanted the night to end. After breakfast, Nathan found his briefcase. "Nathan, do we have to?" "Well, we could wait for an hour or two."

Bar Lou, James and Edward had been busy saying goodbye to the guests. It had been quite an exercise. Hannaway, Mai Lee and Mary Ann were staying on a little longer. The Sultan and Patra were on their way to the States. The Ince Blundells had returned to the stables with Emir, but Colin, he seemed to have disappeared.

Maddy's parents were deep in conversation with Edward. "Does this mean we can move in?" asked Michael.

"Yes," said Edward. "I understand the lease is up on your house." "That's right" said Angela. "The new rents are a little too high for us." "That is what Maddy said to me," replied Edward. "Move as soon as you like. I hope you will be happy there."

"I am absolutely sure we will," said Angela. "I have always liked that flat, so central yet quiet. She is so thoughtful." "They both are," said Edward. "I agree," said Michael and with that they left.

James, Edward, Mary Ann and Bar Lou had a quiet meal. They looked around the conservatory. "Strange," said Edward, "yesterday, full of noise, bustle, people and laughter now we are back to normal."

"Not quite" said Bar Lou. "Where is the picture, the small one? It used to hang here. I think it was a still life."

"Colin stole it," said James. "Do not worry, we will get it back. He is being watched. He is a nasty piece of work, that young man. This time, he will not be able to blame anyone else. You know he tried to insist on his partner coming to the wedding."
"No," said Bar Lou. "What did Maddy say?"

"I did not hear," said James "but I understand it was short and to the point."

"Oh," said Bar Lou "I can imagine. Oh, by the way, Hannaway and Mai Lee are staying at Garden Cottage. I thought they would enjoy the privacy. I am staying here tonight."

"Did you know that Hannaway has applied for the Headship at Firedown?" said Edward.

"Does he stand a chance of getting it?" asked Bar Lou.

"Oh, I think so. Nathan has been lobbying on his behalf, but I doubt he knows that. At least he knows the schools traditions. Mai Lee is very clever. She will be an excellent Headmaster's wife if the appointment is confirmed."

Inky had taken Hilly back to her flat. She was so grateful she had chosen her present, a picture for her flat. A copy, of course. Inky hung it for her. It looked good. At least it added something to the room.

He made his way back to Vienna. 'Tomorrow I begin to find out about my sister Madeleine.' He had not banked on a visit from Arpinsky a few days later. He had not brought the miniatures.

"Just one more job for you to do," said Arpinsky "then the miniatures are yours."

"What job?"

"There is another picture on the way. I need it copied quickly as we have only borrowed this one. The original needs to be returned as we have no provenance, if you get my meaning. It will be a personal delivery. An obnoxious young man will hand it to you. Can you arrange the work quickly?"

"I think so," said Inky. "I will make some calls now". "Do that, my friend," said Arpinsky. "Don't fail me, or the consequences could be unpleasant, to say the least."

"Now, where is the money you owe me?"

Inky handed it over. He had an idea. If he told the Customs it was dirty money, Arpinsky would be stopped and maybe out of his hair for good.

Arpinsky was not that slow. He had outlets where he could swap the money Inky gave him and bank the new money instead. He knew a traitor when he saw one.

Once Arpinsky had gone, Inky turned his thoughts to finding Madeleine. At that moment, the Gallery bell tinkled. It was Babington. He thought that he had located Maddy's brother and was about to check him out. He needed some form of proof. What that would be he had not yet decided.

Inky was elusive, showing him picture after picture. Babington feigned interest, asking questions as he went.

"What is that small picture over there?"

"It is a Victorian still-life."

"Is it for sale?"

"Not yet. There is some slight damage so it will need to go to the repairer. It has only just arrived at the Gallery. A young man sold it on behalf of his sister, who needed the money. It happens a lot."

"Oh," said Babington, "that is interesting. May I look at it?"

"Yes, of course."

Babington moved to the light. "I am right," he said to himself. He had seen the mark on the frame. This is the picture stolen from Temple Meadows.

"Do you think the young man will have any more to sell? I particularly like Victorian art."

"I could ask," said Inky, "but I do not know!"

"Thank you. I will call back next week and maybe we can talk money."

"Thank you. Good morning," said Inky.

Now to find my sister.

Babington contacted Edward. When they had finished talking Edward said, "Do you think it was young Ince Blundell who sold the picture?"

"From what I can glean, I am almost certain Sir. There is something not quite right here. At the moment I am having some difficulty working it out. Shall I stay around for a few days?"

"Yes," said Edward, "do that, but keep in touch."

Babington settled himself in the coffee house. He could watch the Gallery from there with ease.

It was two days before the next significant event happened. He had almost given up hope. A young man, not known to him, arrived at the Gallery with some paintings, all the same size. He seemed to haggle with Inky. Some money changed hands and he left.

Babington watched keenly. Inky made a phone call. He was able to see. It was the painting from Temple Meadows he had looked at. But there appeared to be three of them! He contacted Edward, who told him to stay put. "I will get some help from the local people. We may be on to something useful."

Edward had a very clear idea of what was happening. Mary Ann had almost put her finger on it. From the information Babington had given him, it was becoming clearer. He made contact with TM who advised the Commissioner. The Arts and Antiques Squad were alerted.

Edward was convinced that it would be just like the Leidl paintings. The original would be returned to Temple Meadows. He thought, 'if we can really uncover this deception. it will have international ramifications.'

TM phoned Bar Lou.

"Will you go to Vienna? I need you to help Babington. We are reasonably close to uncovering a real scandal in the art world. Ask Freddie Jackson if he will go with you. He has a specialist knowledge of Victorian art. The Austrian police will have wired the place for sound. Now we need to know what pictures are there. We do not want to close the place down yet. There is more to come from this one."

"Good," said Bar Lou. "I love a good mystery. Time for Dippy Dora to emerge. Freddie will enjoy a break. He seems to want to move on, but I will know more on my return."

Meanwhile, Nathan and Maddy were in blissful ignorance. They were staying on an island in the Indian Ocean. Very private. The owners had furnished a bungalow tastefully. The fridge and cupboard were well stocked. The feature Maddy liked most, was the glass panel in the floor of the lounge. The bungalow was built on stilts out over the sea and they could see fish and other sea creatures swimming by.

It was paradise, or as close as one could get. Nathan was amazing, he had friends all over the world. She was just beginning to realise what marriage to Nathan could mean. She knew, at some point, she wanted a firm base somewhere, where they could be free of work, live simply, entertain friends and just be happy. It may be a pipe dream just now. But sometimes dreams do come true.

Nathan broke into her reverie.

"Maddy, how long do you want to stay here?"

"Forever," she smiled.

"I agree. However, there is a big wide world to be explored, people to meet, things to do."

"What do you suggest?"

"Well, we could stay until the weekend, then fly to India. I know you always wanted to see the Taj Mahal and there are other places just as beautiful."

"We have been invited to Hong Kong for the Chinese New Year celebrations. We will be staying with the Tsangs. They are a super couple."

"Oh, is that where my special handkerchief came from?"

"Yes."

"Then I will be able to thank her personally."

"Yes."

"Fine, let's do that."

Back in England the Hammerstein gallery had reopened. The brothers were getting very fed up with Miriam Hunter, who was trying to take over.

"She will have to be stopped," said Igor.

"I agree," said Leon, "but how?"
"We could talk to Wright Wynne, he seems to know her. It is not going to be easy".

"What is?" said Igor.

"Now about the Spring Exhibition, Victorian paintings I think. We can keep her busy arranging loans from her friends."

Miriam was delighted when the brothers told her of the plan. "Oh, it's just like opening my own gold mine. Nothing could be simpler. If we get some really good paintings, they could be copied and no-one would be any the wiser. The restoration will be completed and I can leave this place and get on with my life. Oh, and I thought it was going to be boring!"

Mary Ann had coffee with the brothers. They told her about the planned exhibition. They seemed very excited. Mary Ann told Edward, who relayed the message to TM.
'Well, its all starting to move now,' TM said to himself. Michael must have been working on this. Funny though, we know where two of the miniatures are but what about the others? If we can find them, we may just be able to find the solution to a lot of unanswered questions and lay some ghosts.

Then,' he thought, 'I can retire, see more of the boys and settle down. That would be great.' He had heard the gossip in the department. 'There might even be a book on who is likely to succeed me. Little do they know!'

Inky went to see Haime Finklestein. He had been around for a long time. He might know more if he would only tell. He needed just one snippet of information to start him on his way. Haime   was not very helpful, saying he had told him all he knew.

"Why do you not go to Prague? I hear that they are establishing a library of information, dedicated to the Jewish struggle. Maybe there, you will find your answer. I do not know."

Inky thought for a minute and said, "Old man, you might be right." "I am just playing for time" said Haime. He had worked for a while with Michael Eversley. He did not know of his death, so he wrote to him in England. Somebody needed to know, as he did not like what was happening.

Chapter 32

"Leon," said Igor, "I cannot contact Wright Wynne. I phoned a few times with no result. I was going that way to look at some potential paintings for the exhibition so I decided to call. It was a bit risky as he does not like callers. Did I get a surprise? He has gone, moved out and left everything just as it is. He is now living in Brazil."

"Brazil?" said Leon. "Something is not right, to go to Brazil. He is either very frightened or he is into something shady and it is about to come to light. It is a case of 'watch this space'. Wait until I tell Mary Ann."

"Why Mary Ann, Leon." "Oh, she once mentioned them to me when she was checking provenances."

"No other reason," said Igor.

Leon shrugged his shoulders.

Edward and Bar Lou were having coffee in the conservatory when Brigstock came in with the post. There were a few letters for Bar Lou, general household correspondence, a letter for Edward, and one addressed to Michael Eversley.

"What?" said Edward, "Let me see it."

"Ring TM," said Bar Lou.

"Really it should wait for Nathan to return."

"No, let us at least ask TM's opinion."

They moved to the office, another Nathan improvement. He had also found Maggie Lamb, to help them with secretarial work at home and to coordinate estate matters. Bar Lou liked her and so she thought, did Edward.

"Good morning, Maggie. We just have a few calls to make. The post has arrived and I think it is time for coffee. Brigstock is in the conservatory. We will join you in a few minutes." Maggie did not understand the need for secrecy. As far as she could see, it was a fairly straight forward job and she liked it so much. Nathan was a great boss and as far as Maddy, what a super young woman she was. All in all, she was happy, except, of course, for her daughter Emilie. She did choose such unsuitable boyfriends. Maggie really did not like her current companion. Oh, he was well mannered but there was something not quite right about him. She was sure he was using Emilie but for what purpose? She tried to recall his name - Colin ... 'That's it, Colin Ince Blundell. Even though he is the son of one of Nathan's closest friends, I cannot take to him.'

Bar Lou spoke to TM about the letter addressed to Michael Eversley.

It was decided that Edward and Bar Lou would take the letter to London and meet at the Club. TM had agreed that in strict legal terms, it should go to Nathan. However, he was away and not due home for some weeks and the rate at which things were moving elsewhere, this letter might be important. He felt sure that if Nathan knew everything that had happened, he would not raise any objections.

His instincts were right. He handled the letter very carefully whilst they were waiting for the meal. The writing was quite difficult to read and the sense of it difficult to make out, but he read on. It was from Haime Finklestein.

As he finished the letter, all he could say was, 'Good heavens.'

Edward looked up, surprised.

TM explained. "It is from a chap in Poland. He did some work for Michael. I think he was the one Maddy and Nathan met at Auschwitz. Remember, she said he had given her a lock of her mother's hair. He was the little boy Maddy's mother had given some of her bread to. She was shot for doing that kind deed."

Bar Lou nodded "Yes, they wanted him to come to the wedding but he felt unable to travel."

"Well, he writes about Inky. Apparently he has been asking about Maddy, question after question. Haime says he told Inky nothing, but wait until I read this out to you."

"I fear for Madeleine, Inky is her brother. I was asked by her mother to keep an eye on her son if I survived. He had been smuggled out of Auschwitz and was brought up by a relative of mine. He now runs the Gallerie Madel in Vienna. I thought he would grow up to be a fine young man. Hilly and Pop were so caring. They did their very best for him. Somewhere along the line, he turned. Now he is a sly, greedy, power hungry grabber who thinks only of himself. He has original paintings copied, provides dubious papers and sends them all around the world. I have seen crates of them go to America and Hong Kong. The Leidl paintings were in his gallery for a while.

He has a lot of visits from a man called Arpinsky, a nasty bit of goods. It is said, by friends of mine, that he was in the SS during the war, and was known as the Torturer. There is some good in Inky, I am sure, but I doubt if he could go straight if he tried. Protect Maddy from him for he could be very dangerous.

Oh and one last thing. His mother had hidden a package for him in her mother's grave. She asked me to find him and give it to him at the appropriate time. I moved the package to a strong room at the Madel

Gallerie. When Inky first started at the Gallerie, it was his job to write up the stock book. He found the miniatures but did not realise their value to him. Then, one day, he sold them to an American whom I have seen with Arpinsky. If this is right, then that man has half of the miniatures you were trying to find, Michael. It may be that Maddy has the other two. You know the key to the riddle because I have told you. Try and recover the miniatures. If Arpinsky gets even an inkling of an idea that Maddy may have them, I fear for her. He will stop at nothing.

Do this for me, Michael. Maddy's mother kept me alive in that place, so please look after her daughter and please an old man. Signed Haime Finklestein.

"Phew," said Edward. "Does anyone know where Nathan and Maddy are?" Bar Lou shook her head. "They could be anywhere. I know he was hoping to meet the Tsangs for the Chinese New Year which is anytime now."

TM explained that he had asked Nathan for an itinerary and how reluctant he had been to give it. In the end, we compromised and he gave me a sealed envelope which I agreed only to open in an emergency.

"Open it," said Bar Lou, "they could be in danger." TM took the envelope out of his pocket. "I do not know why I brought this with me," he said, "it was just instinct."

"Well, open it man," said Edward.

Bar Lou watched eagerly. TM looked at her and nodded. "You are right," he said, "They are with the Tsangs."

"Then speak to him TM. He must know what we know. You could say that you would like Maddy back for a few weeks to do her programmes. Then they can resume their travels." "Oh is that what you call it," said Edward smiling. It broke the tension.

TM excused himself. "I have to talk with some senior people. Perhaps we are almost ready to release information."

Bar Lou and Edward sat in silence, then Bar Lou said, "But where are the other two miniatures? Arpinsky may have bought them but he would not necessarily have realised their importance, of that I am sure. I remember Mary Ann talking about a miniature exhibition at the Hammerstein Gallery. I will invite her to tea. May be she will tell me more."

Meanwhile Maddy and Nathan were staying with the Tsangs. Maddy and Su Ming were getting on famously. They had a wonderful Chinese New Year celebration, with fireworks and super food. Maddy was talking with Su Ming.

"I wanted to say a big thank you for that beautiful embroidered handkerchief with the coins. Nathan explained its significance to me. I did carry it on my wedding day. I know it pleased Nathan.

He has told me of the wonderful times he has had here, with you and your family and how much your husband helped him. He also talks of your sons. Are they doing well? I know he hoped to meet them."

"Oh, they were incorrigible when they were together. They even invented their own version of Chinese. They could talk away and neither Petre nor I could understand a word they said."

"Perhaps it was just as well!!"

"Su Ming," said Maddy, "I thought the fortune cookies were great fun, quite similar to our Christmas crackers."

"Has Nathan taken you to Lantau yet?"

"No, we are going tomorrow."

"Tell Nathan I asked the farsighted one to write the message this year. He will know what I mean."

"Oh, I will," said Maddy "now about this dressmaker you know ..."

Petre Tsang and Nathan were in his study talking.
Nathan asked quietly, "Petre, can you tell me what happened to Fing Wah?"

"He is not of my family at this time. He disgraced us and now he is paying the price."

"Where is he?"

"Why do you want to know?"

"Well, I hear that some dangerous men are looking for him." "That would not surprise me but he is safe. He has accepted my punishment, he had no honour. I would not allow him to fall upon his sword for there are other ways."

"Well, I am sure you are right," said Nathan.

The phone rang on Petre Tsang's private line.

"Tsang," he said, "who is this?"

"Oh, my old friend, what can I do? There was a panic. Certainly he is here with me right now." He handed the phone to Nathan.

"Eversley," said Nathan. "TM why are you contacting me? It is not Bar Lou, is it?"

"No, Nathan, when will you be leaving Hong Kong?"

"In three days time. Why?"

"Can you come home? I think it is time for Maddy's programme to go live. At least, it will be in a month or so. It is very important Circle Business."

That was the clincher. Nathan knew he had to go. He told Maddy about the programme news. She was excited, but a little sad. "I am enjoying our honeymoon so much. I really do not want it to end."

"We do not have to travel to faraway places for it to be a honeymoon, Maddy. What we have is so special. I am sure it will last a lifetime. Indeed, I intend to make sure it does. Now, come here Mrs Eversley and I will show you what I mean."

"Nathan, don't you ever think of anything else?" she said laughing, as she moved into his arms.

They did go to Lantau. It was their last day in Hong Kong. Maddy was fascinated, sailing the China seas to so many little islands. She loved the peace of the Monastery and remembered what Nathan had told her about his visit. He spoke to one of the elderly men who shook out the fortune sticks for them. Nathan spoke to him in Chinese.

"What did he say?" "Oh, he was too overcome with your beauty to say much. He said we would make a long journey together through life. That is good enough for me." He had not told her all that the farsighted one had said. Thinking about it, he realised another piece of the jigsaw was in place.

They had a wonderful banquet that evening. Three of Petre and Su Ming's sons were there with their families. They were so pleased to see Nathan and were captivated by Maddy.

Before they left, Nathan went down to the town. He had a parcel to collect from the jewellers and he wanted some sketches framed for Petre and Su Ming. He had kept up with his sketches. Some were very personal. He had completed a series of family pen portraits for Petre and Su Ming. In one picture, Fing Wah was just in the shadows. He showed them to Maddy on his return. She thought they were wonderful. Su Ming had demonstrated the 'Tea Ceremony'. She had dressed Maddy in the correct wear and they were going to surprise their men.

It was really fun. Maddy was not sure she remembered all the correct protocol. Nathan was so proud of her. Together, they gave the framed prints to the Tsangs.

"You did these for me Nathan?"

"Yes. I always have a sketch book with me. Bar Lou will tell you that this has been my hobby since I was at Firedown. She keeps them for me. One day, I hope my children will be able to look at them and see their history, not just feel it."

"I hope that Fing Wah will emerge from the shadows, Petre, and be the son to you that he can be."

"And you, Nathan, there is no doubt you will be happy for it is already written. Life often challenges our beliefs. Be strong for Maddy. She has not finished her journey yet. It will be for the best that she walks this path. She needs to find that last little bit of herself. Give her the space to do that. I know you are capable of giving her time and the intellectual freedom she will need but be patient."

"What are you two saying?" said Su Ming.
"We were just thinking and talking mens' talk".

They all laughed.

"Now my geisha wife, what other ceremonies has Su Ming taught you? I think we should find out," said Nathan.

Chapter 33

Leon phoned Mary Ann and asked her to visit the Gallery. He sat waiting for her to arrive. He had been very upset when she left the Gallery. He liked Mary Ann for she was so gentle.

Mary Ann arrived, somewhat flustered.

"What is it you want to know, Leon, and why is it important?"

"Well, we were going through our records of the sales of miniatures. The stock check and the book numbers do not seem to tally."

"That is strange," said Mary Ann. "Show me the sales, Leon. Maybe I can find it for you. We were rather busy, as I recall. If you remember, it was an 'invitation only' first day."

"Oh, I remember that," said Leon.

"I do remember seeing two men, I thought at the time that I did not know them. You know, they had come into a lot of money and wanted to 'buy some art'. They were quite loud. I think they bought two pictures. One of them, the quieter of the two, bought two miniatures, the ones in the silver frames. I did not get a chance to check the provenance but they did need cleaning."

"Ah, here it is, in the ledger." She pointed to the entry.
2 Victorian flower paintings – artist unknown.
2 mins to buy price £1000

"That's probably why you did not find it. It looks like, whoever was entering the sale did not finish writing it up. It is not my writing."

"Well, that's one mystery solved and another raises its head. Hopefully, I can find out who they are. I do not remember them coming again."

TM had a lengthy conversation with the Prime Minister and his Advisors. He outlined the current position and offered a few suggestions for the way forward.

"Clearly, we have a situation, if handled incorrectly, which could blow up in our faces. In diplomatic terms, it is a nightmare. The effects will resonate around the world. There are some big names in the frame."

You remember that my protégé, Nathan Eversley, married the TV presenter Madeleine Alinsky. Well, she stumbled on the same information, which intrigued her at the time of the theft of the Liedl paintings. She was about to make a TV programme and tell the world of her findings. It would have been a real scoop for her."

However, I had to stop it, the paintings were only the tip of the iceberg. She was disappointed. After some discussions with you, Sir, we agreed that she could make the programme at the end of the investigation."

"We are not at the end, by a long way. However, if she made the programme under our guidance, we could smoke out the rest of the information we need. I think Nathan would agree, as long as we guaranteed her safety. Maddy need not know everything, but she is very sharp, so what do you think?"

"Isn't Eversley on honeymoon?"

"Yes, but I have asked him to return to the UK for a few weeks."

"Has he agreed?"

"Yes, they will be home by the weekend."

The men looked at one another – they nodded.

"Then proceed with care."
"I will," said TM, "and of course I can liaise closely with your nominee."
The meeting ended.

Brigstock called Ken and Dave to meet him at Firedown. "Come in a hire car, use your chauffeurs' uniforms then it will be less obvious to any prying eyes.

Nathan and Maddy are due home at the weekend so it would be normal for me to be making arrangements."

"Fine," they said, "what kind of car?"

"Oh, I will arrange that and let you know."

Meanwhile, Charles Babington was still in Vienna. The young man he had seen in the gallery with Inky ran a local art school. It was extremely popular with visitors, who could buy direct. "That is it. The paintings go there, are copied, returned to Gallerie Madel, then the originals are returned and the copies sold. Nice work if you can get it."
Charles looked over towards the Gallerie Madel. He saw Colin in a heated discussion with Inky. As he watched, they shook hands and Colin left with a small package. It looked the right size to be the paintings from Temple Meadows. "Well, my friend, little do you know what is about to happen."

Charles contacted Edward, to say that Colin would be picked up in England. The whole process would be kept very quiet.

He thought, 'I can go home.' But that was not to be, Bar Lou and Freddie would be arriving soon.

Nathan and Maddy were due to land that evening. The steward approached them.

"Excuse me, Sir, Madam, we have been told that a car will meet you at the airport. Once we have landed, I am to escort you through customs to the vehicle. I hope you have enjoyed your holiday." They smiled at one another, "Oh yes," said Nathan.
"Nathan are we going to the flat or Temple Meadows?"

"I think the flat first, collect the post, then make our way to Temple Meadows later. Is that fine with you?"

"Of course," said Maddy. "It will give me a chance to see Esther and Mary Ann."

"More girlee talk! Remember you are a married woman now!"

"How could I forget?" she said.

Just as Charles was about to leave the coffee house, he saw Arpinsky enter the Gallery. 'Curiouser and curiouser,' he thought, 'now what can he want?'

Inky did not appear to be happy, he was shouting. Arpinsky was very annoyed. He left in a hurry, empty-handed. Charles followed him. He went straight to the station and boarded the Intercontinental Express. Charles nodded to the two members of the Austrian Force who were helping him. "Follow him. Whatever you do, try not to let him out of your sight. Keep your HQ informed of movements. He is a very slippery customer so be careful."

Meanwhile, Appleby was panicking. He had returned to the flat that Dave and Ken had used. It was still empty. He went in, just the same, but nothing had changed – well, not quite 'nothing' - a camera had been installed and it was taking pictures of his every move.

As he left, he thought, 'There is nothing for it. I either tell Arpinsky, or give him two miniatures in silver frames which are not the ones he wants. But how would he possibly know?' He decided on the latter cause of action.

'When I have done that,' he told himself, 'I will leave England for good. Somewhere quiet, as I do not fancy meeting Arpinsky on a dark night!'

On their return to the flat, Nathan had insisted on carrying Maddy across the threshold.

"Fool," she said.

"Oh, that is what you think. Well, fools are supposed to be entertaining and I know where this show will start."

"Nathan, put me down please."

"Ok, but in the bedroom, I think."

"Nathan, please."

"Oh, you do not have to beg Maddy. I am more than willing."

They were lying contented in each others arms when the phone rang. Nathan picked up the handset.

"Eversley," he said, then he listened.

"Yes TM," was all Maddy heard.

He put the phone down.

"Maddy, you will never guess, TM has said you can go ahead with your TV programme."

"Really?" said Maddy. "Oh, I must contact Esther and Mary Ann."

"Well, get dressed first, please."

She smiled at him.

"Go and have a shower, you are driving me to distraction."

Nathan had not told her of the risks involved. Why worry her at this stage? She would be well protected. Anyway, he reasoned she needed a clear head. He realised that there could be repercussions, some of them aimed at Maddy herself.

She seemed happy enough. She was singing in the shower. No doubt the flat would soon be full of chattering women, so he decided to go and see Edward and James. 'Perhaps,' he thought, 'I will phone Bar Lou, she might like to join us. It will be easier for me to tell them, altogether, what I know and of course they can bring me up-to-date.'

He told Maddy of his plans and, as he had anticipated, she was expecting Esther and Mary Ann.

"Good," he said, "but before we start, I need those papers signed. Then I can give them to Edward to process. Shall we have a meal with all three tonight? It would be good to see them."

"Great idea," said Maddy.

She signed the papers, gave them back to Nathan, then said, "Move. My friends will be here soon."

He kissed her, then left. She was smiling.

Maddy put a call through to Paul Tinyman, to advise him she was back in town and had sufficient information now to make the programme. She needed studio time.

She thought to herself, 'This could be the last programme I make for some time, so it has to be good.' She did not know just how good it would be.

She picked up a paper for she had seen so little news. It was time to catch up before the girls came. There was a small column on page 6 which caught her attention. 'Baronet leaves England to live in Brazil.' The article was full of innuendo. 'They are fishing,' she thought. She had heard of Wright Wynne but in what context? Somehow, it seemed important. Then the bell rang.

The girls were in session. They wanted to know where she had been, who she had met, in fact everything.

"Come on," said Esther, "spill the beans."

"Well," said Maddy, "it was absolutely the best time. We ..."

Colin Ince Blundell had contacted his friend, to meet him at the airport. He did not want to have the painting in his possession for a moment longer than necessary. He needed to get it back to Temple Meadows as soon as possible. But how, that was the question. It could be tricky.

He was totally unaware that he was being followed. In fact, he was so arrogant it did not even cross his mind. This latest operation seemed to be rushed. It was not usual for him to do so much. Colin thought he usually contacted Davis Browne, then had no more to do with it. But he had disappeared from the scene, strange that! Even Inky did not know where he was to be found. As far as Colin was concerned, they needed to stop for a while.

279

Miriam Hunter, meanwhile, was gearing up for one last push. She had not enjoyed the strictures her husband had tried to impose. Too stultifying! 'My money would not even pay for the paint,' she realised. 'Well, I will show him. After this exhibition, I will be quids in and the restoration of Heatherbourne Castle shall be completed. She had no idea how foolish she was being, or if she did, she chose to ignore it.

Appleby was most upset that he could not find the two men who had bought the miniatures. However, he was happy about his own little plan. He was on the way to the Gallery to collect 2 miniatures. He would buy 2 silver frames and just hoped against hope, that Arpinsky did not notice.

Then he needed to get as far away as possible, but where? Arpinsky had a very long reach.

Perry Bracken was sitting in his office. There was still no news of Davis Love. In one way he was delighted, less to worry about. He had not been in touch with Edward since the wedding. Nathan was still away on honeymoon. 'Lucky devil,' he thought. He did think he would have heard from Fing Wah, but assumed wrongly that he might still be working in the Far East.

He had been impressed with Nathan's piece of work. Perhaps, he thought, Forensic Accounting was the way forward. He had been very interested to discover that Nathan was one of the brains behind Cabal Finance. Perry had been annoyed when Nathan recruited Gabriella and Mark Heaney to work for them. Since Christmas there had been little movement of funds from Cabal but it was quite a dormant time nationally, so he did not give it any credence.

At the Cabal Finance Office, Mark and Gabriella were wondering what the future might hold for them. Freddie was working in Europe whilst Hannaway and Mai Lee were still in England. Gabriella, not one to let the grass grow under her feet, suggested that they review all the prospects undertaken so far and start to plan how and where they might attract others. Mark was in agreement.

"We really should phone Nathan," said Mark. "He might have other ideas."

Nathan had been giving some thought to the New York Office. He felt sure Hannaway would get the Headship and he knew Freddie wanted to move back to Australia. 'It is fair enough,' he thought. 'I need a new figure head.' He had a glimmer of an idea in his head. It would need some work on his part but he thought he could pull it off. He would talk to TM first. He was looking forward to having supper with Edward, James, Bar Lou and Maddy. It would be like old times. At the same time, he felt there was an edginess in the atmosphere. Almost the lull before the storm. Everything was too busy. He would ask Maddy what she thought.

Bar Lou was really pleased to see them both. They looked so happy. Edward and James had arrived with Nathan, and Maddy came on her own from the flat, having shared a taxi with Esther and Mary Ann. She, too, had registered an atmosphere, but she could not put her finger on any one reason. It did not worry her unduly. She was so excited by the prospect of getting her television project off the ground. She had little time for anything else. Tomorrow, there would be discussions with TM.

The supper party went well. They talked mainly about the places visited and the people they met. Edward was surprised that they did not meet Fing Wah.

"He was away," said Nathan. "His father had sent him on a journey with tasks to perform. It is unlike Petre Tsang, but he must have thought it a good idea."

"When are you returning to Temple Meadows?" asked Bar Lou.

Maddy looked at Nathan. "When?" she asked.

"We will definitely be there for the weekend, but Maddy will need to be in London next week if she is to work on her programme. So I guess we will be there in the week. I would like to go to Paris the following weekend, as there is some business I need to complete. I have a property to check out. You remember, Edward, it was in the papers of my father. I will have to decide what to do with it. Possibly Maddy will have some ideas. I have not discussed it with her as yet, and do remember we are still on honeymoon."

They all laughed. "I think," said James, "it's going to be one long honeymoon for you two."

"I hope so," said Maddy. "If it is, we shall be very lucky."

Chapter 34

"Bar Lou, when are you off to Austria? Freddie is quite excited at the thought of escorting you to Vienna."

"Is he? I shall have to be careful, people might get the wrong idea! A young handsome man and an older woman."

Nathan got the message. Whatever she was going to do in Austria was not up for discussion.

"There is something I would like you to do for me when you are there. Perhaps we can talk about it at the weekend."

"Fine," said Bar Lou.

"Well, Maddy, how have you managed to keep up with this globe trotting boy of mine?"

"Bar Lou, that's a leading question. It has been absolutely wonderful. Some of the poverty we saw in India contrasted with the opulence, so it was very thought provoking."

"Oh dear," said Bar Lou, "I feel another TV programme coming on."

"Nathan, be quiet," said Maddy.

Despite the almost careless banter, there was something in the air. Nathan's brain worked overtime. 'Maybe it will come to me. I hope so.'

As they made their way home, Maddy took up the question of making some programmes for television with Nathan.

"Would you mind?"

"Only if it doesn't take over. Otherwise, I will help you. There are some old stables at Temple Meadows, may be they can be converted for you."

Maddy was stunned, "Just like that?"

"Yes, well, not quite just like that, for we will need planning permission. Why don't you work on the idea? It is a fast developing medium."

"Now, no more work today, I have a few other ideas as to how we might pass some time."

Colin was visiting his parents. He wanted time to think, a place to stay and somewhere to stash the paintings for now. They were so busy with the horses and the wedding, no one really noticed he was there. That suited him.

Then Tiggy gave him the perfect opportunity.

She said, "Do you know that Maddy and Nathan are back? We have all been invited to lunch on Sunday."

"All of us?" said Colin.

"I suppose so," said Tiggy, "but if you come, no problems please. Sometimes you can be perfectly awful."

He pulled a face at her. 'Perfect,' he thought, 'it could not be better. With a bit of luck I should be able to get the pictures back safely.'

Bar Lou was talking to Freddie.

"It will be best to fly to Vienna, I think, then we will be less obvious, just looking like a couple of tourists. I need your specialist knowledge. When we have settled in Vienna, no big hotel this time, just a small guest house, Charles will meet us. He has photographs for me to see. If I am right, there will be faces I know. That alone will help us understand what is happening."

"There is something else you should know. Charles thinks that the young man who runs the Gallerie Madel could be Maddy's long lost brother."

"Good heavens, does Nathan know?"

"Not really, he is cross checking our leads."

"Who is doing it for him?"

"Nigel."

"Good, he will miss nothing. We used to call him Hoover."

"What, he is not violent is he?"

"No, whatever gave you that idea?"

"Oh, there used to be an advert, the words of which were 'All the dust, all the grit, hoover gets it every bit because it beats as it sweeps as it cleans.'" They all laughed.

The meeting with Charles left Bar Lou perplexed. Arpinsky again! Would she never get that man out of her life? But Colin, how did he get involved and if Inky was Maddy's brother, there could be storms ahead. Especially as she was likely to be very high profile after the TV programme. I hope TM knows what he is doing."

Freddie had gone to the coffee shop with Charles. They had arranged to breakfast there. Bar Lou made her own way. Her arthritis was playing up but she was determined not to let it get in the way. 'With two young men to do the running around, I should be fine.' Famous last words!"

Dave and Ken were sitting talking with Brigstock. He told them that Appleby had been back to the flat. It is just a matter of time before we see some action on that point.

"Now, Ken, I have a special assignment for you. Maddy is going to need a car and chauffeur. Watch her back. The project she is working on could ruffle a few feathers, if there are leaks. Keep your eyes and ears open as unobtrusively as possible. I need to know if anyone in particular is hanging around. Use the lapel camera. It is barely noticeable. She is moving in Nathan's world now, which is not really as secure as the one she has left. There are risks, as you know."

"Understood," said Ken, "you can rely on me. Which car shall we use? It may need a few refinements if you get my meaning." "I think Nathan has ordered a new car. I will ask him this weekend."

"Fine."

"Now, Dave, Perky, you know what you have to do. We need his every move logged. He will slip up. You know what is very strange? That Yank, Davis something or other, has disappeared. Even worse, young Colin Ince Blundell seems to be the new courier."

"Briggie," said Ken, "I would worry more about that toffee nosed Miriam Hunter. She is using the owners and I wonder if they realise what her game is. I'm not sure either, but it is something to do with pictures. She was very thick for a time with the Honourable Wright Wynne, the one that scampered to Brazil." "Doesn't she live at Heatherbourne Castle?"

"Yes. Her husband is the Foreign Secretary."

"Wow," and he whistled.

"I have spoken to TM. It might be an idea if you revisited the Gallery. One never knows what little gem of information will result."

"Ok. Fine by me."

Maddy had gone back to her old flat to see her parents. She had some presents for them and she wanted to say a personal thank-you. Nathan would collect her from there to go to Temple Meadows.

She was so excited about her TV programme. Pity she could not tell them. All in good time, all in good time.

She enjoyed her meal. It felt strange at first, being back in that place and not being in charge. Little did she know that Michael and Angela felt the same. They need not have worried. There was so much to talk about the time passed quickly. It was only when Nathan rang the bell that they each looked at their watches.

"Nathan, come in," said Angela. "By jove, you look well. Thank you for making Maddy so happy." Nathan gave her the flowers he had brought. She was delighted.

He walked over to shake hands with Michael. "Oh, I found this in a small off licence on my way here. I understand it is a newly imported brandy. Let me know what you think."

He sat by Maddy, and they held hands.

"I am sorry to break this up but it is time Maddy and I made our way to the house. The weekend will go quickly enough. Nice to see you both here. I hope that you are settled." With that Nathan and Maddy left. She took a look around. "Angela, you have made this room look so cosy. Now I know where to come for some extra tlc."

Nathan laughed. "She thrives on it, you know, quite the tiger," and he winked.
"Nathan, enough information, thank you."

On their way to Temple Meadows, Nathan told her about the car. It comes complete with a chauffeur chosen especially by Briggie. It will save on time and energy and at least I will feel happier that you are using your own car and not hopping in and out of taxis. You will be busy enough."

When they had settled in at the House as Nathan called it, he had one more job to get out of the way. This one was a little more sensitive. He had arranged a bank account for Maddy at the largest private bank in London. She had even signed the papers, really without reading them, a point to make to her as well. He did not think that the account itself would be the issue, it would be the balance. Well, no time like the present.

"Maddy, have you got just a few minutes to come here and sit with me? You can arrange all those another time. Maybe we could take some to London and the rest to Paris."

"Fine," said Maddy, "now what?"

"Remember these papers you signed in London?"

"Yes."

"Did you read them?"

"No, why should I? I trust you absolutely."

"Thank you for that darling. They were the papers to open your account at the bank I use. You have met the Manager. He was a friend of my father's."

"Oh, yes, at the wedding."

"Well, here is your cheque book, cards and first statement."

He gave her the envelope.

"Thank you. She put it on the table."

"Maddy, what have I just said about reading papers?"

"Oh, if I must, I was thinking of other things I would prefer to do."

"You are incorrigible, open the packet."

There was silence. "Nathan, what is this all about? I can hardly take it in."

"Well, you see, I always wanted to marry a millionaire. That was a fantasy of mine but you mean so much to me, and I love living out some fantasies, so I thought, 'why not?' We have money more than enough, so learn to handle it. I will not ask any questions. There are instructions at the bank for you to draw down from the main account. I hate the idea of you asking for money. It is yours as long as you do not run away with the first handsome man that comes along. Use it as you will."

He looked at her. Tears were falling down her face. He took out his handkerchief and gently wiped them away. They sat in silence for a while. Then Maddy said, "Lets go to bed, or I might go looking for that handsome young man ..."

"Then I shall come looking for you and throw you over my shoulders, just like this," as he picked her up, "drag you to my cave and well, order you to make some tempting food, suitable for the Gods."

"Now, where were we? Oh yes, bed." He turned off the lights and made for the bedroom.

"Good slaves get their reward you know."

"Oh yes, and some were especially trained to please their masters. I never did explain to you what Mai Lee taught me. I'm looking forward to learning. Now come here," said Nathan.

Arpinsky went looking for Appleby. He needed the miniatures, if only to tempt Inky, so the sooner he collected them the better. He could return to Vienna. After that, there was little else to do unless, of course, the miniatures were worth more than he thought. Maybe they had sentimental value. He knew the price of everything and the value of nothing.

Appleby was very elusive, not in his favourite haunts. He phoned again, no reply. 'This is stupid. I am wasting time. No matter, I really do not have much more use for him. He is expandable.'

He made his way to Soho and started cruising the bars. Just by chance, he saw Appleby going into a Casino. What did he want there? He waited. As soon as Appleby appeared he walked up to him and said, "I believe we have a little business to finish, so where have you been? Ducking and diving?" "I think we should slow things down."

"Why?" said Arpinsky.

"I just have a feeling that we might be attracting some attention. One of the chaps I followed came into the Gallery today, just looked around and left, no purchases, just a quick look and he left."

"Do we know who he is?"

"No, but there is something familiar."

"Where are the miniatures?"

"Back at the flat."

"Shall we go and collect them?"

"Yes."

Appleby lived in the top flat of three. It was quiet now, but around midnight it could be very noisy.

He handed the package to Arpinsky who did not check the contents. He merely slid it into his jacket pocket.

Appleby offered him a drink. "Just a quick one," he said. He walked up behind Appleby. His next move was quick and decisive. Appleby was no more.

He had been careful not to touch anything around the flat. He put off the lights and left. There had been nothing of importance lying around. It would be a few days at least before he was missed. It would be easy to find other couriers, more reliable.

The Ince Blundells arrived for lunch. It was a happy afternoon. Even Colin seemed to be on his best behaviour. It was the first time Emir had had a chance to speak to Nathan since the wedding.
"I need to have a private word when you have time."

"After lunch do?"

"Fine," said Emir.

After lunch they had coffee in the conservatory. Colin excused himself. He collected the painting from where he had hidden it on arrival. To make sure he was on his own, he looked around, but he did not see Brigstock in the shadows.

"Got you at last," he said.

"The photographs will be useful. Silly, silly boy."

"He phoned TM."

"Shall we deliver him?"

"No, just follow. He is small fry, but nasty."

"We need the principals."

"That could be difficult."

"Fine."

Nathan and Emir crossed the hall to the study. Nathan saw Brigstock.

"When was the picture returned?"

"Recently, Sir."

"How recently?"

"Today."

Emir looked shocked, Nathan angry.

"Why was I not told?"

"We have only just found out."

"Emir, this way," said Nathan, "we can talk freely in Arabic. What is worrying you?"

"My father, the Sultan, is talking of going back to Osmantia. Evidently someone has been in touch. It cannot be right."

Nathan said, "It is a difficult one. We have no grounds for detention. Maybe it will be less problematical than you think."

"I don't trust them," said Emir.

"I will alert TM. He may have some ideas. Is Patra going with him?"

"No, that is strange too. I believe she is hoping to stay with Bar Lou."

"If not, she can either stay here or London, whichever she prefers."

"Maddy and I will be in Paris next weekend. I have some business to conclude. Are you still going to Ireland to look at the Stud?"

"Yes, do you know who owns it?"

"No," said Nathan.

"Miriam Hunter."

Nathan was quiet. "They should not be short of money then, for her husband is the Foreign Secretary."

"As far as I understand it, they are refurbishing Heatherbourne Castle. It is eating money. She works at the Hammerstein Gallery. The brothers Leon & Igor are getting annoyed with her overbearing manner. She is very driven. There is a big throughput of Victorian paintings she is borrowing from Galleries and friends for the exhibition."

293

Nathan was surprised.

"We ought to go back to the ladies," said Nathan.

"Let me know when, or if, you go to Ireland. It is very pleasant at this time of year."

"Oh, by the way, has anyone heard from Hannaway?"

Edward said, "As far as I know, he is at Firedown. He has the interview on Monday."

Maddy and Tiggy were just about to go for a walk. "Are you two going to join us?" said Tiggy.

"We might as well," said Nathan. It was a nice afternoon. He whistled up Bar Lou's dogs. He thought that they needed a good walk. What a pleasant way to spend a few hours, they were lucky.

"Maddy, go towards the old stables," said Nathan. "We can have a look around, I will phone the architects on Monday."

"Are you going to alter them?" asked Tiggy.

"I don't know yet," said Nathan. "It is part of the ongoing refurbishment."

Maddy smiled. "He is clever."

Tiggy took one look. "Good heavens, Nathan, it will cost a small fortune to restore these."

"Oh, the building itself is sound. As to the rest, who knows?"

"What do you think Maddy?"

"Oh, I like them. There is a good atmosphere."

"Shall we go back?" said Emir. "Tiggy, we need to go back to our own stables. There is work to do before we settle for the evening."

They returned to the House, Colin was sitting watching the television, the others were chatting.

"Dad," said Tiggy, "we need to go back to the stables. Are we ready to go?"

"Yes, of course. Thank you, Nathan. Lovely to see you Maddy. It will be good to have you here at Temple Meadows."

"Thank you. The coats are in the hall." As they waited for the guests to don coats, Maddy spotted that the picture had been returned. She was about to say something when Nathan put his arms around her shoulders. She smiled at him.

"Goodbye," they said, "see you soon."

"When did that picture come back?" "Today," said Nathan. "Do not worry."

Chapter 35

The phoned buzzed in TM's office. He was expecting Maddy. He wanted her to work on the TV programme and needed it to get underway. He had decided just how much to tell her.

He answered the phone. His secretary said, "Will you please contact the Commissioner? The PM will call in two minutes."

"Fine. I am expecting Maddy Eversley. Will you make her a coffee please?"

He picked up the scramble phone and dialled three numbers. "Yes, Commissioner." He listened. "Another body. Who is it?" "Your 'friend' Appleby. We are not releasing details, but I do need to let the Ambassador know."

"Can you put that off, please, for say 48 hrs? The Ambassador's home keeps cropping up in our information. Can I phone you back? The Prime Minister's call is coming through."

"TM, good morning."

"There have been a few developments Sir."

"Is there anything I can tell the President? I shall see him tomorrow."

"I know it is difficult, Sir, but we need a little more time. Things are on the move."

"When the TV programme is ready to go, I will make sure you have your copy and one for the President. Is he not in Paris in three weeks? That is the sort of time scale, give or take a week or two, we are probably looking at."

"Fine." The phone went dead.

TM walked to open the door.
"Maddy, hello! Do come in. Sorry to keep you waiting. How are you?"

"Now, about this TV programme. The information you will be given is highly sensitive. We will not be filming at the TV Studios."

"Oh," said Maddy, "but I am more familiar with the equipment."

"That is as maybe. We have studios available. The equipment is the same so you will be alright, I assure you."

Maddy left his office shell-shocked. Nathan was waiting. "Come on, let's go to the flat. Your car is waiting."

She managed a weak smile. "Oh yes, it is very comfortable Nathan. This job is scary."

"I know, but you will be brilliant."
"Oh, I hope so," said Maddy.

TM made one further call to the Commissioner.

"It is all systems go. What has been started today will be a diplomatic nightmare. I am due to see Edward, James, Ince Blundell and Nathan this afternoon. Do you wish to join us?"

"No, Bar Lou," said the Commissioner.

"No, we have an unwanted complication in Austria. She is there with Freddie and Babington. The PM is getting nervous."

"Only getting, that is an understatement!"

"Do you think Maddy will cope?"

"Oh yes, she is very bright and she has Nathan and that Cabal of his, to call on for help."

Bar Lou was feeling extremely tired. It did not help that Arpinsky was back in Vienna. It was like living her worst nightmare all over again. 'I will have to talk to TM. It is time to begin to hand over to a younger group. We are all getting too old and carrying too much baggage. I know I need to retire and enjoy my cottage. I must move myself. Charles and Freddie will be waiting.'

In another part of Vienna, Arpinsky and Inky were deep in discussion. "Well, I have the miniatures for you. I hope they are worth it. Many lives have been sacrificed for these."

"What do you mean?" said Inky.

"There is no more to say. I have checked my bank, the money has arrived. Here is your parcel."

Inky looked at it quickly.

"Then it is goodbye."

"Oh no, my friend, you will do exactly as I say in future."

"But it would be ridiculous to keep reproducing original paintings. The Gallerie is attracting visitors from all over the world. One day someone will work out what is happening. Technically, the paintings are brilliant, the paints are aged, but an expert would easily spot the differences."

"You will do as I say! You wanted money, you are getting it. Now, you have one choice. Do as I say or there will be consequences. Now, go. I will be in touch."

Inky was shattered. For the first time in his life he was really frightened. He sat down in his apartment and started to unwrap the parcel. Maybe there was a short cut. By now, he was certain that Maddy was his sister and if Haime was to be believed, she could have the other two. Maybe, just maybe, that was a more lucrative way to go.

Then he looked at the miniatures, put on the special light he used for looking at paintings, then held the miniatures around it. He turned them this way and that, there was no additional engraving.

Arpinsky had made another mistake, this time I will be calling the shots said Inky to himself.

He was not wise enough to realise that only one person had got the better of Arpinsky and lived to tell the tale.

The meeting in TM's secure room was tense.

"Gentleman, the court dance has started" said TM. "There will be strikes in Europe, here, America and the Far East. They are all time co-ordinated, once the code word is received the operation will start in 12 hours."

"Maddy is working on her script for the programme," said Nathan.

"She is a bit shocked but very determined. She appreciates being trusted."

"Good," said TM.

"Are we being fair to her" said James.

"That's what worries me," said Edward.

"Maddy will be fine," said Nathan. "There are issues close to home, like finding her brother, that are intriguing her more."

"And on that point, Nathan, we know who he is. But she cannot be told now for he is a part of the link in this issue. By the way, my information is that he knows who Maddy is. He has some powerful acquaintances, well, ruthless would be a better word. Are you still off to Paris this weekend?"

"Yes, I hope so."
"Good," said TM.

"Now, gentleman, this is what we shall be doing ..."

In the racing yard, Emir was not really concentrating. He had not heard from his father for a few days, neither had Patra. 'I do wish he had not gone back to Osmantia. I have this awful feeling in the part of my stomach. He was so meticulous in his preparations. Normally, he is so confident, just goes, but this time ...'

"Emir, the horses need feeding now, not next week."

Emir looked up, "Oh yes, sorry."

"Is it your father you are worried about, Emir" said Tiggy.

"Yes, it is and I know my mother is as well."

"Where is she?"

"I think she is using Nathan's flat. Would you mind terribly if I went to her? I've got an awful feeling about this one." "Why don't we both go? Dad will cope. We are not entered for any races for 2 weeks. Perhaps we could plan our wedding and maybe Mum could come for the day. Then Dad could slip off and meet his old cronies. Has he talked to you about retirement?"

"Yes, and I think he is right, it is something we have to consider."

"But what would he do without horses?"

"Maybe there is a way," he said.

"Now, suppose we finish here and go to Patra."

"Can't wait," said Tiggy.

Maddy and Nathan had arrived in Paris. Neither of them had seen the work Patra had done. Maddy in particular was hoping everything they had planned worked.

Nathan seemed preoccupied.

"Nathan." He looked up at her. "What is worrying you?"

"Oh, not a lot just thinking what we might do with the rest of our honeymoon."

"What would you like to do, Maddy."

"Nothing too exciting. Why not find a chateau, rent it and move in there, just the two of us. So much has happened very quickly, I think we need to stop and take stock. We cannot possibly carry on at this rate."

"I think I know just the place. We could look at it tomorrow. When

I was told of the details of my inheritance, there was one property my mother had just bought. She realised, just as you do, that sometimes we need time, peace and quiet. Just to be."

"Oh, Nathan the philosopher. Is there no end to your talents?" "My talents! What about yours? Mai Lee must be a very good teacher and you an apt pupil, but I have a few ideas of my own."

"Oh, really! Well, not now if we are going to look at this property. There are a few arrangements to make." "Do you know much about it."

"Not really, it is an estate property. It is being run as a hotel at present. We could just book in and stay overnight."

"Remember," said Maddy, "I need to be in London by Monday lunch time. You make the phone calls whilst I pack. What transport will we use?"

"Do you fancy going by helicopter? There is a firm I an thinking of using. It is a clear day so you would be able to see more as we fly down."

"I've never been in a helicopter before, always fancied it though. Well, get on with it."

Maddy started to pack. Then she saw the two red nightshirts. She packed them. 'Just in case of fire,' she smiled.

It was a wonderful weekend. She liked Marin and Julie Chanson, who ran the place. There was an instant rapport. Nathan, on the other hand, did not understand why his mother had bought it, in the middle of nowhere, overlooking a sleepy village. It must have some other significance.

Maddy was still asleep when he left the room. He wanted to talk to the Chansons. It was cosy in the kitchen. He spoke French like a native, so conversation was easy.

He explained to them that his mother had bought this property before she was killed in a road accident. He had not been told about it until recently.

"I thought you reminded me of someone," said Julie.

"Michael," said Marin.

"Yes, that is it."

"So what do you intend to do with the Chateau?"

"Well, I have not spoken to Maddy yet, but I would like to restore it and turn it back into a family home. Not that we have a family as yet," he laughed, "we have only been married for a few months."

"If we did that, would you stay on? We have lots of friends who might like to stay."

"That would suit us," said Marin. I have a small farm to run and Julie needs to take things easier. I am relieved, at last, to know. It has been a long time waiting."

"I am sorry about that," said Nathan.

"Now I had better take my wife some breakfast. I think I will have to push her out of that four poster bed. On the other hand maybe I will join her. Are any other guests here?"

"No, we had instructions from James to keep this weekend clear." "Oh, have you? Well he is quite right. I promise I will keep you fully advised of my plans. Would you like to look at one of the cottages which you could live in? We can modernise them. Then my friends can stay. It might be better for you."

They smiled. "Will you change the name, Nathan?" "I do not know,

I think I will leave that one to Maddy, which is where I am going now."

"Don't worry, I will take the tray with me. We can breakfast on the terrace."

Maddy woke slowly and looked around. No Nathan, she noticed, as she turned over and lay on his pillow. Just another five minutes.

Meanwhile, Nathan had set breakfast on the terrace. He woke Maddy with a kiss. "Breakfast is ready sleepyhead. The sun is shining so get up. Here, wear yours, I found it in the case." "Oh, very flattering," said Maddy. "I am not sure red is my colour." They both laughed.

Nathan put his ideas to Maddy over breakfast.

"What do you think?"

"Well, we will definitely keep that four poster bed."

"I wonder why?" said Nathan.

"Well, its comfortable, cosy and private, I like it."

"So I've noticed," he said.

"But seriously do you think that you and Patra could give this place a makeover. I have a feeling that she will need something to get her teeth into very soon."

"I have spoken to the Chansons. If we keep it as a family home, they will be happy to look after it for us." "So, I could be persuaded," she said, smiling. "Now, why don't you try?"

Chapter 36

Emir and Tiggy arrived at Nathan's flat, Patra seemed relieved to see them.

"I am so pleased to see you both, I do not seem to be able to settle. Your father did not want me to go with him. He even shunned the idea of my going to the airport with him."

"He has been very edgy since we left Osmantia. It is a good job Nathan has been so kind. He seems to be so aware of our situation."

"Patra," said Tiggy, "that is what friends are for. Mind you, I do agree about Nathan. We grew up together. underneath that jolly jape approach to life he is clever, very sharp and the best of friends."

"When his parents died in the car crash, he was devastated. We used to talk and talk. His mother was pregnant and he was so looking forward to having a brother or sister. Then he read about an Indian Tribe somewhere who 'swore brotherhood'. It was a ritual where they cut a finger or wrist, not deeply, and mixed the blood."

Patra shuddered. "Really Tiggy."

"Well, we were only children but somehow he has always been there for me and I for him."

Emir said, "He seems to have that effect on people. I was unhappy when father said that I must go to Firedown. I wanted to stay home with you. But he was right of course, and I met Nathan, Freddie, Jos and Hannaway".

"Oh, the Cabal," said Patra.

"Yes mother, you have met them all. Firedown was strange at first but by the time I left I knew I had friends for life. No matter what happens, one or all will be at my side. Nathan is also my brother. Do you remember when he came to stay and we used to slip away and go to the bazaars?"

"Do I" said Patra, "I was so worried."

"It didn't matter for we both spoke the language. We were just two young boys out on a jolly jape."

"Oh, don't mention those 'japes'. They were fun. I thought he would grow out of it but ... not Nathan. Poor Maddy!"

"Oh, I think Maddy understands him, she is clever enough not to try and change him. Didn't she have a beautiful wedding? Everyone laughed, chattered, it was like a family party, only better," said Patra.

"Now, you two, shall we spend a little time talking about your wedding? Where shall we begin?"

TM was also worried about the Sultan's return to Osmantia. In fact he was downright annoyed. What on earth did he think he was doing? Well, he is truly on his own, we are so stretched. Another rescue mission is out of the question.

In discussion, the Sultan realised he had made a mistake and a big one. He had believed it was his duty to return, to help his people, with little or no thought to the consequences. He was not even sure who were enemies or friends. The Palace had been taken over. His horses, well he did not know what had happened. It was a good job they had been able to get the best of them to England. I have to face up to the fact I may never leave here alive. My son will not follow me here as ruler. It has been a long tradition but now it is ended and Patra. I am so sorry ...

He did not return to England. His mutilated body was left at the gates of the American Embassy. When the news broke, it made headlines around the world. Fortunately Nathan was still in England and able to go with TM to see Patra and Emir.

Patra knew as soon as she saw them standing at the door. TM was most uncomfortable, but Nathan, well he took over and spoke to her in Arabic. Emir could say nothing, only hold on to his mother.

Nathan said gently, "Patra, would you like me to make some arrangements to bring his body here? He might like to be buried at Temple Meadows."

"Thank you, but sometime in the future, I will take his ashes back to Osmantia. We had a favourite place and it is there I will scatter them."

"Whatever you both want will be done. I promise you."

"Now, why don't I take you both to Bar Lou, away from the press. I am sure Edward would prepare a statement for them, but I warn you, if Bar Lou offers hot chocolate and says 'one shot or two,' say just 'one'. They are lethal but guaranteed to give you a good night's sleep."
They all smiled.

Nathan said to Emir, "I will bring the car around at five pm but Maddy will be over before that. She can help Patra pack. Have you told Tiggy?"

"Yes, she will make her way to Bar Lou."

The two young men held each other for a few seconds. Words were not important.

Bar Lou had returned to England. She was tired, apprehensive and concerned for Maddy. She knew now was not the right time to tell her about her brother, even Nathan agreed reluctantly. It was more important that she got this TV programme right.

Her phone rang, it was TM. She heard what he had to say.

"Oh no, and they are coming here?"

"Yes," said TM.

"Who is with her?"

"Emir, Nathan and Maddy."

"Could not be better, and Tiggy?"

"On her way to you, as we speak."

"Fine. TM before you go, I have completed my debriefing. Have you had the tape?"

"Yes."

"Sometime, we must talk. It is important to me". "I understand only too well, Bar Lou, soon, I promise. There are so many changes coming."

Hannaway had just received the news. He was to be the new Headmaster of Firedown, well, if Mai Lee agreed. He was so excited.
At that moment Mai Lee walked through the door. One look at his face told her all she wanted to know. She ran to him. "I am so pleased, when do you start?"

"I am not sure, I think I will work with George Green for a while, then take over in September. Just think, a new baby, the best job in the world and you to share it with me."

"Good. Now phone Nathan, whilst I organise a special celebration for just the two of us," she laughed. He kissed her. She knew how strong the bonds were with the Cabal.

"Nathan," said Hannaway, "I've got the best news. I am going back to Firedown as Headmaster."

"Brilliant," said Nathan, "we must celebrate, but not just yet. Emir's father has been killed in Osmantia."

"What on earth was he doing, going back there?"

"I do not really know," said Nathan.

"Whilst you are on the phone, I have some news about Fing Wah," said Hannaway.

"Come here to Temple Meadows for the weekend. Celebrations will be a little subdued but Emir would be glad to see you. Walshy will be here on Sunday. Freddie and Jos cannot make it yet."

"Fine," said Hannaway, "Mai Lee will be keen to talk to Maddy. Do you think you two would make good godparents?"

"Bye."

For once Nathan was speechless. We are not even parents – godparents! Wait till I tell Maddy.

Charles and Freddie were on their way back to England. They had enjoyed working together. They felt that they had done all they could in Vienna. Now it was just a waiting game.

Then they saw Arpinsky on the plane. No sign of the police, who had been watching him. Freddie nudged Charles and pointed.

"Gracious," said Charles, "what can we do?"

"Not a lot," said Freddie, "just wait and see."

"Perhaps I will ask to see the flight deck," said Charles, "then we can get a message to London."

"Good idea. As Nathan would say, another 'jolly jape,'" 'but perhaps not so jolly,' thought Freddie.

Freddie was glad Bar Lou had gone home earlier. He was concerned about her and knew he had to speak to Nathan. Vienna had been one project too many as long as Arpinsky was alive.

This latest piece of information was relayed to TM in a form only he would understand.

He phoned through to the studio where Maddy was working. He was mightily impressed with her work. She is so professional, the early clips he had seen were excellent.

"Maddy?" "Yes." "It's TM."

"Oh, I am sorry, I did not recognise your voice. Nathan is not here, if you wish to speak to him."

"No, it is not Nathan I need, it is you. How is the programme coming on?"

"Well, we are about to start editing. Your man is very thorough, the best I have worked with."

"Good, but how long now?"

"Two, three days at the outside."

"Fine."

He phoned the Commissioner. "We have set a date. It needs to co-ordinate with the TV programme. Maddy says her work will take two or three days. I think we should me with the PM. He leaves for America in 48 hrs. I will call you back, or someone will."

He dialled the direct line, pushing the scrambler button.

"Sir, TM here. We are ready to set a date. Have you a time slot in your diary?"

"You have? That will be fine. The Commissioner will be with me."

"Well TM, Commissioner, tell me the worst. How many people are involved?"

TM handed him the list.

The PM blanched, "Oh heavens, a reshuffle just now. The Press will have a field day."

"I'm sorry, Sir, I do not think he is personally involved but his wife certainly is."

"Can you be sure that you will be able to move simultaneously in 5 countries?"

"Yes, it is all carefully planned."

"And you are observing all the protocols?"

"Yes Sir."

"Keep me informed. I will arrange a line for you. Do not use our normal channels. What will be will be, I suppose."

"We have no choice, Sir."

"I understand. And the TV programme?"

"The tape will be with you in time to take to America."

"And the presenter is?"

"Maddy Eversley."

"Have we made arrangements for her safety for she will be hounded for a while, I hope that there are no skeletons."

"Not as far we know." He reckoned without Inky.

Inky had worked out that his father had collaborated with the Nazis and, as a result, many valuable works of art had gone missing. He intended to use this to blackmail Maddy. He had his story ready to sell to the highest bidder. If only he had the real pair of miniatures. Could he bluff that? His annoyance was to be his downfall, but not before he had leaked the information to the media. He thought that he was untouchable. Even if anyone found out about the paintings, he had a bargaining counter so he was safe.

Safer still, if he could find the other two miniatures. He also had a score to settle with Arpinsky. It was sheer stupidity to think he could outwit him, but Inky did not read it that way.

He knew from his talks with Arpinsky that the miniatures had been in the possession of the Hammerstein Gallery. He would check the place out, in fact he had time to look up the list of exhibitions. If he were lucky, the Hammerstein might feature. He thought he remembered someone saying that it would be a good cover for their own project. Inky had not been happy with the throughput. Too many pictures, too many people involved. Well, there were three less, the Chinaman and two Americans. He did not trust Colin. In his view, he was not the best conman but he did have a connection with his sister Madeleine, at least, he claimed that he did.

'We will see, we will see,' he mused. 'Suddenly everything is going my way.'

Colin, meanwhile, had teamed up with Miriam Hunter. He was trying to persuade her to consider setting up their own outlets and ignoring the existing connection. After all, Inky was not keen to carry on much longer.

Miriam could see that she could make more money that way and her dream of completing the work at Heatherbourne Castle would be that much nearer. However, she had her doubts. It had been fun and lucrative but she was more interested in selling the estate in Southern Ireland. She needed the cover of that money to provide for her slightly more risky ventures. There was a potential buyer, some ex Horseguards Colonel, perfectly respectable. The offer was reasonable, not quite as much as she thought she would get but enough. She thought it would be relatively easy to make up the difference. She would show that husband of hers.

Colonel Ince Blundell, Tiggy and Emir were talking to Nathan. They were in a dilemma. The Sultan had intended to buy the estate in Southern Ireland. Without his money, or until Emir knew what the position was, following his father's death, it looked as though they might have to withdraw the offer.

Nathan and Maddy already knew this and she agreed with the idea he had put forward. She felt sorry for Tiggy and Emir, so close to their wedding. Emir's father had been killed. He had to do something, for he owed Tiggy's family so much. That brother of hers had a lot to answer for, as he already knew.

"Look," said Nathan "I had intended talking to you both anyway. Edward, Maddy and I have a suggestion. Colonel, Tiggy I owe your family so much. I needed help when my parents were killed and you were there for me, no questions asked. Now I want to return that compliment. I did not know how I could do that without embarrassing you, until recently. I know about the estate in Southern Ireland. Edward has had a look at it. What I am suggesting is, we can afford to make a better offer then you have. It is a legitimate business you are proposing to run so if you agreed, Edward will arrange the purchase quickly, then make the property over to you as a wedding present."

"Oh, Nathan," said Tiggy, "my wonderful blood brother."

"Colonel, Emir, this would give Maddy and me so much pleasure. We will be your first visitors. Use what monies you have available to refurbish the stables. How about if we ask Patra to redesign and refurbish the house? It would help her and you."

"Have you decided how you will run it?"

"Yes," said Emir. "Tiggy's parents will live there and we will have a stud manager."

"Well then, Sir, perhaps Natasha, Patra and Tiggy could get on with some ideas. I'm sure Natasha will have plenty. Now how about a toast?"

"To the future, may you never find a mouse in your cupboard with tears in its eyes."

"Nathan, really," said Tiggy, as they clinked glasses. "Just one thing," said Nathan "do not charge Bar Lou for her horse, give me the bill." The conversation between Nathan and Edward was brief. "Show the purchasers as Cabal Finance. I have cleared it with the others. It must be done quickly before it becomes entangled with other things. I am sure you understand."

"I thought this might happen. I have everything necessary to complete the sale. Will you transfer the money today?" said Edward.

"Yes," said Nathan, "it is on the way to you as we speak."

"See you soon Edward, thank you."

On the way home, the three of them were silent.

Tiggy said, "Emir, just a quiet wedding please, you know I do not like fuss. If we get the date right we could honeymoon in Ireland. What do you think?"

Emir and her father looked at one another. "We agree," was all they said.

Chapter 37

Freddie sat down with Nathan. He was hesitant at first, then he looked at his friend and began to talk. Nathan had known for sometime that his friend was uneasy in his work. He did it well enough, in fact he was one of the best.

"So you see, Nathan, I went to America to fill in a gap when I left the Army. The whole experience has set me thinking and I have some ideas to run past you. At first, I was keen to settle back in Australia and develop the Far East connections, but on reflection, there is time to do that later, because I will go home.

Working on this art project has opened my eyes. America is a voracious market. This leaves the door open for the syndicates to move in and clean up. All they want is money or a way of laundering it. No-one cares who gets hurt. Working with Charles Babington has been an experience and to some extent shaped my thinking.

If we were to change the focus of the work in America, and put the emphasis on funding for the arts, it could have some amazing results. That country is just ready for such a move. I think Charles would relish such a challenge. He would be so good to have on board. With Gabriella, Mark and myself we may have the nucleus of a fantastic team. There is much more to come from Gabriella. If we are to open up the ethnic markets, she would be ideal. What do you think?"

"Well," said Nathan, "that is quite an idea. Maybe after Emir's father's funeral, the Cabal will meet. I am sure that there will be no problem. We could look at a start in the New Year. Be careful, though, the next few months will shake the Art World but we will have to wait and see. I was expecting a slightly different kind of news."

"Oh" said Freddie, "and what other bit of inside information are you expecting?"

"Well I rather hoped that you might tell me when you are going to marry Gabriella."

"How did you know, we have not told anyone."

"When you are happy yourself, Freddie, and I am deliriously so, you sometimes see that same spark in others."

"Oh, another Nathan insight, I see. Well you are right. When the current investigation is completed, we will set the ball rolling. Will you be coming to New York at all?"

"I hope so. Maddy will be glad of a break very soon. She takes her work very seriously. The programme she has been working on will be broadcast and we have a honeymoon to resume."

"Has it ever stopped?" Freddie asked.

"Not really," said Nathan, "we have a plan for a month or so, then I will be back in harness. Before then, I will fly to New York and see all of you, provided the situation here does not blow up in our faces."

"Thank you, Nathan, now I can plan for the future as well. Oh, what do you think of Hannaway's appointment?"

"I am delighted for him and Mai Lee." "Did you know they have asked Maddy and I to be godparents?"

"No, so it is true Mai Lee is expecting. Gabriella thought she might be. Oh no, I feel a major shopping expedition coming on."

"Freddie, just a thought, why don't I ask everyone here? Maddy and I may need you all, it might be easier to cope with."

"Look, sort out some dates with Maggie Lamb and she will organise everything."

"Now, Freddie, I must move, I am meeting Maddy and Patra for lunch, the funeral you know, but it has to be done."

Nigel was talking to James and Edward. "I have finished the investigations you asked me to do. I can confirm that this chap Inky or Stephan Allinsky is Maddy's brother. They did not know of each other's existence and they are as different as chalk and cheese.

He has an outsize chip on his shoulder, he thinks money automatically buys power and that is what he thinks he has, by the bucketful. You would think that when two very ordinary people saved his life and in doing so ran a terrible risk, he might have turned out differently. As you know, he has a pivotal role in the art scandal. I did go and speak to Haime Finklestein. He is an amazing man, he knew Maddy's mother. Did you know that she was killed for sharing a small piece of bread with him? He said, many times, that he felt so guilty and that he had some responsibility to try and watch over Inky."

"He thinks, in fact I know, that Inky has information relating to his father and in order to be able to use it, he needs to bring together four miniature paintings. Haime had stored two of them in the stockroom at Gallerie Madel. Inky found the packet, cleaned them and promptly sold them to Arpinsky." There was a sharp intake of breathe from James and Edward. "Well, it does not end there. Greg Appleby, thinking that

Arpinsky had bought them as a blind and wanting to ingratiate himself with the Hammersteins, lent them to the gallery for the spring exhibition, where they were sold in error to two chaps who had suddenly come into money. Told some tale about winning the pools." They smiled.

"Do we know where the miniatures are now?"

"Well, it gets curiouser and curiouser. Greg Appleby is dead, he completed the sale, the records were never completed and the person who bought them used a false name."

"Well," said James, "Maddy has two of them. If we could put all four together, we would have the missing links."

"That's important," said Charles, "I have had some thoughts. Has anyone thought to ask Brigstock?"

"Brigstock?" said James.

"Yes, he had two of his contacts working on this as well. Well, that is what Charles and I think. If it is the two we know, they are a bit rough and ready but excellent in a crisis. They can blend into any background. Charles thinks that Maddy's new 'chauffeur' is one of them. Perhaps a meeting with Brigstock could clear that up."

Inky is over here at present. I suspect he is not happy. Apparently Arpinsky gave him two miniatures which Inky thought were original but they were not and he is after revenge. That could be why Appleby died, if he had double crossed Arpinsky in the first place ..."

"We are getting into the realms of conjecture," said Edward. "Arrange for a thorough, but silent, search of Inky's room or flat and we need him watched around the clock. As to Maddy, if Brigstock has set something up, then it will be at Nathan's request. I will confirm that and I will have to bring Nathan up to speed. I would not like to be the person who even tried to harm Maddy. There would be nowhere they could hide ..."

Maddy had gone into the studio to see the final edition of the programme. It would not be a live presentation, which she would have preferred. Having run the film through a few times she was satisfied. Four copies were made, each was stored in a special container, the seal of which would only be broken immediately before use and in the presence of witnesses. She would take the other three copies with her. Two would go to TM on her way home and one put in the bank vault. She could not even show it to Nathan.

She was still very apprehensive about the content. She knew that the after programme interviews, which she would attend, could be gruelling. She was not to know just how hurtful they were to be, nor the way other events would cast a long shadow. It was a good job really. She began to get an idea of the importance of the film when there were two people accompanying her.

Ken said, "Brigstock thought it would be an idea if I showed Dave, here, the ropes. We can then share the driving. Do you mind?"

"No," said Maddy. "Now can we move off? I need to deliver this parcel quickly and then get home to Nathan at the London flat."

"Fine," said Ken.

So the film was delivered. TM looked relieved. As soon as Maddy left, he arranged a viewing and invited the Commissioner. The two men were very impressed. "It is very professionally done. The camera likes Maddy Eversley, she is very good indeed. When is D-day?" asked the Commissioner.

"Well, the PM sees the President tomorrow and no doubt he will contact the Presidents of the countries involved. Expect fireworks once this film is networked."

"Who owns the rights, TM."

"We do, and we will handle the release."

"And Maddy Eversley, she will need protection."

"That is arranged, unobtrusively of course."

"The film is only the beginning of a chain of events, some of which will be intensely personal but Nathan will cope."

"But will Maddy?"

"Yes I am sure she will."

"Do you know what she will do after this?"

"Well, Nathan is taking her away for a month or so. Then she has some ideas about future programmes. Nathan is having a studio built for her at Temple Meadows."

"She will be a loss to the TV company."

"But our gain, I think."
"Quite."

Maddy was showing Nathan the programme. He was stunned. "Darling, you are wonderful, the camera loves you, it is really very very good." In truth his heart sank. Not long now and we will be in for some flack.

"Come here, Maddy, how about an early night?"

"Nathan!"

"Well, the programme cannot go to the bank until tomorrow."

Chapter 38

Miriam Hunter took a final look around the Victorian Art Exhibition. The Gallery lighting had been restricted to enable her to show off each picture at its best. It had been relatively easy for her to persuade friends and other galleries to lend pictures. The pieces for sale were good examples of the era and the painters of the time. Some people, including her, might rue the day they sold these works.

Miriam was happy on another count, the house and stables in Southern Ireland were sold. Some finance house had bought it for an investment. Now she had nearly all the money she needed to complete the restoration of Heatherbourne Castle. However, she could not resist the temptation to send just a few more pictures for copying, not because she really needed the cash, just for the thrill. That was to prove to be her downfall.

Igor and Leon came through from the office. They, too, were pleased with the display. There were quite a few pictures for sale and, thank goodness, all had good provenances. Mary Ann had checked them thoroughly so they could rest easy.

The morning of the Exhibition dawned. Invited guests would

arrive at midday and the public viewing started at 3 pm. It was the only exhibition of its kind this spring, so the brothers were hoping it would be a success.

Miriam knew it would be popular. There was a distinct and growing interest in the period. She knew that, with a busy day, she could move at least six paintings for copying and have the originals back before the exhibition was due to close. There would be so much movement it was the ideal cover. She was waiting to hear from Vienna about the arrangements for collection. It was strange that two of the most experienced couriers had dropped out of sight. She was not too keen on using Colin, especially since he had proposed an alternative to the existing system. Why mend what is not broken?

She was surprised to see that man, Pinkerton at the exhibition. There was something about him she did not like. He was taking a good hard look at their pictures. Strangely, they were the same ones she had earmarked. The switch was relatively easy as there were three other works, not dissimilar, by the same artist.

She saw Pinkerton blanche, he had seen Inky come in. As she turned to look at the visitor, Pinkerton seemed to have vanished into mid air. Now where was he? The last thing he had wanted was for Inky to blow his cover. Inky walked around the exhibition. He was impressed, it was extremely well done. There were a few pictures that, once copied, would sell well in America. If only the chain had not weakened. Well, he could always store the copies, they would keep.

He was not really clever enough to realise that he was out of his depth, greed had overtaken common sense. What he wanted, he wanted now. He recognised Miriam from a photograph he had been given. He made sure that he attracted her attention. He introduced himself as Allinksy from Gallerie Madel, Vienna. Miriam blanched. What did he want, he should never have come here, it was too dangerous. He passed her a piece of paper as they shook hands. The numbers corresponded to the ones she had thought suitable.

"Is there anyone I can talk to about selling some of these pictures in my Gallerie?" he asked.

She pointed out Igor and Leon.

"Thank you," is all he said.

'Well, that must be the easiest way I know of getting some of the paintings to Vienna. I hope that Igor and Leon agreed.' Then she would no longer have to come to this gallery again. She could resume her social life with a vengeance.

Little did she know that there was more interest in the Exhibition than that from the art lovers and other dealers. Cameras had been installed in strategic places. She had not realised, when the two men, posing as insurance employees arrived to check security, were anything other than what they said they were. If she had been concentrating, she might have asked a few more questions.

Inky had half expected to see Arpinsky (Pinkerton) at the Gallery. He was disappointed. 'You will keep,' he thought, 'time is on my side for once.'

Arpinsky had other ideas. He was tired of Inky's demands and wanted rid of him but at the moment he could bide his time. Too risky to do anything in this country. Too many prying eyes. Just how many there were, he had no idea.

As the various agents reported in to TM's office, he realised that nearly all the people directly involved in the Art heist were here in London. He phoned the Commissioner and the Prime Minister.

It was two hours before he received the time for operation pickup to commence. He looked at his watch - 2 hours to go. He was edgy. He had told Nathan to stay close to Maddy, her programme was timed to go out in 48 hours.

Nathan realised the importance of that statement. He tried not to show it. Maddy was simply excited. If this programme was well received she might be able to work on other subjects, especially if Nathan completed the refurbishment of the stables. Work was underway. She would need good staff. She liked the Director she had worked with on the current programme and maybe Annie Wilkins could be tempted. Nathan encouraged her to plan forward.

He made a phone call to Bar Lou. He wanted her up at the house. She could encourage Maddy to come up with ideas for new programmes. He also knew that he needed her. He had so hated keeping things from Maddy. He had tried to get TM to see his point of view, but he was intransigent. It was an attitude Nathan found disturbing, he was a very open person. He was glad that Maddy and he were having a month away. It would give him time to mend a few fences.

He was not the only one who was edgy. Policital leaders from five countries were preparing speeches, hoping to save their futures. Senior security personnel had started the countdown, interview rooms were being prepared. The considerable amount of evidence was ready. Timing and accuracy were the key words. Only the best operators in the world were involved. The adrenalin was pumping.

TM looked at the clock, he counted down the last 10 seconds. The words 'go-go-go' were echoing around the world. In less than an hour he would know the success or otherwise of the operation.

It was 2 hours before he knew just how successful. News wires were clattering. He knew that the Press onslaught would begin. They used the intervening time to prepare, he had tried to look for some errors. He remembered his old boss had warned him, when he was starting out, always looking for the joker in the pack. Take it out first. Try as he could, there was no clear joker, no unknown source. He would just have to wait and see.

He was waiting to hear that Arpinsky or Pinkerton was in custody.

He had waited a long time for this day. He always took the loss of his staff personally. This man, Arpinksy had to answer for the death of Michael and Alicia.

When would the news hit the wires? He reasoned it would be about midday, Greenwich Mean Time. He checked out the timing around the world. Yes, midday here would be about right. So Maddy's programme could go out in prime time on Thursday, today being Tuesday. He made two phone calls, one to the Chairman of the TV Company, the second to Maddy and Nathan.

His phoned buzzed, it was the Commissioner. All he said was, "All present and correct. There may well be more to come. Who knows what we will be told?" "Thank you," said TM, now he could wait for the joker.

The next phone call was from Brigstock. 'Surprising,' thought TM, 'what can he possibly want?'

"Sir, I have been to the Bank. In among the paintings that my chaps purchased when we started out, are two miniatures. They look old and in need of a clean. The lady in one of the pictures reminds me so much of Maddy. What do you want me to do?"

"Bring them here, yourself, now."

Could this be the joker? If Brigstock was right, he may well be able to solve the riddle, if there was one.

The red light flashed on his phone.

"Yes," he said.

"Oh, Prime Minister, when did you get back?"

"Oh right so far as good. I think that there could be a resignation on your desk soon."

"As far as I am aware, all the listed persons are in custody somewhere. The news could well break about midday, in 45 mins."

"Thank you, Sir."

He put the phone down. There was a knock at the door. It was Edward and James. They could tell by his face, operation pickup had been successful.

"No jokers?" said Edward.

"None so far," said TM.

"I have had one surprising piece of news. Brigstock thinks that the two missing miniatures are in his possession. Apparently, two of his lads bought them as a blind. He put all the purchases in the Bank. It is only now that our part of the operation is nearing completion, he thought he should see what there was and arrange their disposal.

If they are the two missing miniatures, there could be more revelations to come."

The Foreign Secretary left his office for the last time. He had his resignation in his inside pocket. He was on his way to 10 Downing St to deliver it personally. "Damn Miriam and Heatherbourne Castle. Well, they could jolly well leave. There was that place in Ireland". Little did he know, there was no hiding place.

In America, Perry Bracken's family were distraught. Their world was collapsing around them. Their dad a cheat? How could he have led such a double life? There were no answers, only questions.

One of the hardest-hit families were the Ince Blundells. They could not believe that Colin had been so stupid. What a disgrace! How could they face their friends? Now he realised why he had not been to so many circle meetings. TM must have known Colin was involved. He had only been kind. The Colonel felt he had no option but to resign, which he did forthwith.

Tiggy was sitting on a straw bale talking to Emir.

"What do you think will happen?"
"I do not know"

"I want to talk to Nathan. How many people do you think know?"

"It is impossible to tell. Would you like me to phone Nathan? I think he is at Temple Meadows."

"Nathan," said Emir, "can Tiggy and I come over?"

"Fine, see you in an hour or two."

He spoke to Tiggy's parents and asked if they wanted to go with them.

"No, we will stay here. There are things to be done. I will have to talk to the Lord Chancellor's office," said Natasha.

"That bad?" said Emir.

"That bad," said Natasha. "It could not get much worse. I hope it will not affect the yard."

"We can recover," said Emir, "we have good friends who will stand by us."

With that Tiggy and Emir left for Temple Meadows. Bar Lou and Maddy were in the conservatory. Nathan was in the office. Tiggy joined the ladies, Emir went to find Nathan.

Nathan was sitting with his head in his hands. "Oh hello, Emir, I did not realise that you had arrived."

"How bad is it Nathan?"

"Enough and it will get worse. We still have Maddy's programme to go out. Who knows what to expect? I worry for Maddy."

"Why?" said Emir.

"Well, she is so vulnerable. If only we could find those other two miniatures. I am absolutely sure my father would not have been interested in them for nothing."

"Well, they could well turn up," said Emir.

"The fallout from this art sting may just open a door."

"Hope you are right," said Nathan.

The phone rang, it was Petre Tsang. He spoke in Mandarin. "Fing Wah will be investigated. I have been with him. He has changed, he will not leave the monastery for he liked the life and is happy. Oh, the far sighted one said to tell Maddy her journey will bring happiness."

Chapter 39

Inky had returned to his hotel to plan his next moves. The conversation had gone well with the Hammersteins. He had agreed with them to take the unsold paintings to Vienna. He smiled, it would be a nice little earner, yet there was still something niggling at him. He had been delving into his family history. He knew, now, that his father and mother had been killed by order of the Germans. I suppose they could be almost war heroes. That had been his first thought, then he had discovered that his father had been a collaborator.

If that got out, it would destroy his work, take away his power base but hopefully it would not happen. As far as he knew, no-one else was interested. Maybe apart from Madeleine. She was too well off to care! He had forgotten that the courier, Colin, had been in his office alone, for 20 minutes, whilst he dealt with a customer.

He did not like this courier, too nosey, to keen to please, always asking questions - in other words, a nuisance. Little did he realise that Colin had read the report on his desk and now had in his possession all the information he needed to blackmail both himself and Madeleine.

Colin high-tailed it back to England. He had a few connections with freelance journalists and he wanted to pursue them. All he could think about was 'pay day'. He could leave this country and assume another life, live check by jowl with the rich and famous and move with the high rollers.

He had hinted to his journalist friend about a big scandal about to break. An arrangement was made whereby, if Colin was in trouble, his friend would collect a package from a safety deposit box and go with the story revealed. If he failed, then others could be caught in the net. Little did he realise that his information was common knowledge to the people in the know and almost peripheral. In the hands of a 'stop at nothing' investigative journalist, it would be headline news. Colin did not care anymore, he felt safe. Knowledge was power.

Inky was packing in readiness to return to Austria. Arpinsky had gone to ground yet again. That man was an enigma. Inky needed him out of the way but that could wait, his time would come.

There was a knock on his door. He opened it. Two men pushed their way in.

"Mr Alinsky?"

"Yes," said Inky

"Stephan Alinsky?"

"Yes."

"Come with us, please, you are under arrest for your involvement in a series of art thefts. He started to say, "anything you say will be given in evidence."

Inky did not hear the rest. His mind was all over the place. He was being led down the corridor to a side door and bundled into a waiting car.

The words 'go-go-go' had rung around the world. All the known participants were arrested, their premises searched and documentation removed. It was done quickly, quietly and efficiently. They had about 24 hrs before the news broke, to question their suspects. They needed a head start before legal advisers galvanised into action.

As to the legal advisers, most of them had participated in a sweep. Match the solicitor/lawyer with the perpetrator. Someone could win a tidy sum of money. They had not used the usual centres so the worry about leaks was diminished.

Everything was done by the book. Questioning did not start until the order was given. It was timed in such a way to be a simultaneous action with every suspect. This operation was carried out with clinical efficiency.

Arpinsky was at the airport, it was safer to get back to Europe. What was the hold up? They had been waiting in the Customs queue for 20 minutes. Once through the doors to the waiting area, he would feel safer.

He tried to see what was happening. Two men were arguing about their passports. They kept pointing to a child, oh, someone must have forgotten to put the child on the passport. He watched, highly amused.

He did not feel the arm on his sleeve at first.

"Mr Arpinsky?"

He turned to find three men blocking his movement.

"No, you have the wrong person. My name is Pinkerton."

"Oh yes sir, we know about your various aliases."

"Now, sir, please come with us."

They took him to a nearby office. "Mr Arpinsky, also known as Pinkerton, you are under arrest on suspicion of the murders of Conrad Parker and Davis Browne." He continued with the caution ...

Aprinsky took no notice. All he kept saying was "There has been a mistake. You have the wrong person."

"Come with us, sir." He was taken to be questioned, there was no escape.

He thought, 'I know more than they do about making people talk. They will not break me. Soon I will be free and I will have my revenge.'

In all there were ten arrests, with possibly more to follow. It was a very busy 24 hours whilst information was processed. It was a very complex operation. There were teams of people checking and cross checking information around the world. Fortunately there were few obstructions.

In England, the Commissioner had his statement prepared and was ready to join the hastily called news conference. Coordinating the information release needed fine timing. As he was speaking, the people arrested were getting legal advice. They had each made their one phone call. Colin did not seek a solicitor, he phoned his journalist contact.

The Commissioner walked in to the news conference, looked at the clock on the back wall, then started to speak. "Ladies and gentleman, we have today five people in custody in relation to a number of matters including murder, theft, attempted blackmail and numerous other offences. This is part of an international operation. You will be given a copy of my announcement before you leave. You will appreciate that the matter is sub judice. I cannot discuss it further. Thank you for your time today." With that he left the room.

Similar meetings were held in Germany, New York and Hong Kong. The names of the principals involved would not be released until the next day, after they had appeared before the Magistrates or their equivalent.

The news wires were burning. This was a big story and every journalist worth his salt was looking for an angle. Editors were pressing, contacts made, usual sources tapped. No-one was able to break the wall of silence.

However, there was one person sitting reading a letter from Colin Ince Blundell. He did not see the significance of the information at first. Thought it was just a disappointed boyfriend wanting revenge. He put it to one side. 'One never knows,' he thought. He would wait until the names were released before trying to make the connection. He would go out and hang around with some of his crowd, try and see who knew what, if there were any leads.

Absolutely no-one was prepared for the list of names that emerged the next morning. The Prime Minister was due to make a statement at midday. As usual, the television companies were preparing their programmes. He liked the presenters on Inter News, so he decided to tune into their station.

Nathan, Maddy and their friends sat watching her programme go out to the public. Maddy had concentrated on the art scandal and was beginning to expose the sequence of events. It was an impressive piece of television journalism seen in Countries all over the world.

As the programme finished the phone began to ring. Nathan had anticipated this might happen and had arranged for Maggie Lamb to intercept all incoming calls. He was worried for Maddy. He wanted her to stay at Temple Meadows but realised that she would have to go to some carefully selected interviews the next day. TM had given him a list of approved times and interviewers.

One person, and one alone, was more concerned with the presenter than the content. He had an idea that her surname used to be Allinsky. He needed to do some digging. Maybe Colin had given him some useful information after all. He could hear the cash tills ringing.

TM's office was a hive of activity but he still found time to contact Maddy.

"Well done! A really professional piece of work. I am to offer the Prime Minister's congratulations as well. He will write to you."

Maddy was dumbfounded.

"Thank you," was all she could mutter.

"Are you prepared for the interviews tomorrow?"

"I think so," said Maddy.

"You do realise that Ince Blundell's son is involved?"

"Yes, but I can handle that, at least I hope I can. I know most of the interviewers, so it should be fine.

I will be glad when it is over and we can go to France."

"I am sure you are. Give Nathan my regards."

She put the phone down. "It was TM, he seemed pleased."

"So he should be," said Bar Lou.

"We are all very proud of you."

"Hot chocolate, anyone?"

They all laughed. "One shot or two?" she persisted.

It had been a dreadful day for the Ince Blundells. Natasha had sought advice regarding her appointment as a Magistrate. She thought she might have to resign. She knew her husband was devastated. This was the last, in a long line of problems, Colin had laid at their door. But this time he could stand on his own two feet. Had she known what was to follow she might have dealt with the problem differently. The one thing that sustained them both was the support they had from Nathan, Bar Lou, Edward and James.

Edward had said, "Eventually there will be other news. Really Colin's involvement is small but because of the nature of the whole case it is given more prominence than it warrants."

"I understand that," said Nathan.

"But why did he do it?" said his father.

"We have backed him, to our cost, all the time and supported him, yet he seems to feel we owe him more. He resents Tiggy's friendship with Nathan. I suppose, now that Tiggy is to marry Emir, he feels more left out than ever. But to steal from Nathan I just do not understand him at all."

"Natasha, I have come here to seek your assistance. Do you remember Angela Allison, Maddy's mother?" said Edward.
"Yes."

"Well she, like you and Bar Lou, had a specialist skill that we need, to try and break a code based on numbers. We do not want to give it to the boffins at the moment because we do not understand its significance. Would you be prepared to help?"

"Of course," said Natasha, "when would you like us to start?"

"Is tomorrow soon enough?"

"Fine," said Natasha.

"Well, Bar Lou will contact you. TM is providing some space for you to work in. I am sure you will get on well with each other. After all, you are not strangers."

"No," she laughed, "just keep Bar Lou away from the hot chocolate!"

Maddy walked into the news room. It was to be the first interview of the day. She was a little nervous. Annie was the first to greet her.

"Wow, Maddy, you look fantastic, married life must suit you. What a programme! We are all a little jealous or rather envious. Now that you are famous, will you still have time for lunch?"

"Of course. Now which studio are we using?"

By 10 pm that night Maddy was exhausted. Talking about the programme had been marginally harder than making it. She had to be very careful about her replies. All in all, she felt quite happy with how things had gone. She was glad to be back at the flat with Nathan, just sitting quietly, after a relaxing bath. She liked those private moments with her husband.

"Nathan?"

"Yes."

"When are we going to France?"

"Maybe at the weekend. Certainly no later than next week."

"Good," said Maddy, "I am so looking forward to it."

"I have spoken to Patra, she might stay for a few days. Is that okay with you?"

"Yes, as long as it is a 'few days'. We could do with some time to ourselves before we return to the treadmill."

"Now, come here, Mrs Eversley, I have a few suggestions as to how we might enjoy ourselves ..."

The events of the last few days were to change a number of lives in different ways. Some families had to face up to changes which would radically alter their lives, others would grow into roles they had never envisaged for themselves.

But before that could happen, two pieces of information would come to light. It would upset the status quo for a while.

Chapter 40

The morning papers went to town on the events of the last 24 hours. Almost everything there was to know about those persons arrested was read and re-read. Reporters were camped outside their homes and offices.

The Prime Minister's statement had given them one piece of information that was unexpected. The Foreign Secretary had resigned. The speculation started. Was he involved, what did he know, why had his wife been arrested? Order went out from the editors, 'we need information and we need it fast.'

The Colonel's friends from the Jockey Club had been in touch, very sad for this very genuine man. They pretty well knew what Colin was like. Many thought, 'serve him right.' Natasha had been in touch with the Clerk to the Magistrates to get her position clarified. She stood down from the Bench until the case was over. Then she thought, who knows ...?

Their son, Colin, was hoping against hope that his journalist friend had retrieved his letter and had made the connections. If Maddy was discredited, it might help his position. In his mind, he invented various scenarios. After all there was little else to do. The Duty Solicitor had advised him that, for the present, he should be careful what he said. "Until we know what the evidence is, do not make any statements, particularly written ones. It is very unlikely you will get bail, so prepare yourself for that. If there is enough information, when you return to Court, an application will be made then."

That advice shook Colin. 'Go to prison. What for, carrying a few pictures back and forward?' He could not believe what he had heard, now he was really scared. His mind was working overtime. What if he tried to make a deal? They might be interested in Maddy's father. He knew where the paintings were copied. But he was not that brave. The people he had been working with had too many connections. That journalist might just do the job for me. He heard the key turn in the lock of his cell door.

"Come along, Ince Blundell, there are a few people who need to talk you," said the policeman.

"Is my solicitor here?" said Colin.

"Possibly, now move yourself."

Miriam Hunter fared no better. She was a strong woman, but the indignity of the whole proceedings was getting to her. All she had wanted to do was to restore Heatherbourne Castle. Nobody had been physically hurt. She was naive enough to think that with her and her husband's connections, she would soon be released but that was not to be the case.

She too heard the key turn in the lock. She looked up and saw a policeman and a sergeant.

"Mrs Hunter, we need to take you to an interview room for further questioning. Come this way."

Miriam suddenly realised it was not going to be as easy as she thought. On the way to the interview room, she caught sight of a headline in a tabloid paper, 'Foreign Secretary resigns'. She stumbled, 'What have I done?' she said to herself.

Maddy and Nathan were having breakfast at the flat whilst watching the news on the television. It was beginning to dawn on Maddy that, what had started out as a straightforward case of art fraud, had major ramifications.

She turned to Nathan and said, "This is frightening, I just had no idea."

"We very rarely do," said Nathan.

With that the phone rang, Nathan answered it.

"Eversley," he said, then listened.

"Maddy, it is Annie for you."

Maddy looked at him, shrugged her shoulders and took the phone from him.

"Annie, what can I do for you?"

Then Annie explained in detail how some information had come into the newsroom regarding Maddy's father. They say he was a collaborator in the War."

Maddy said nothing ... her mind was in a whirl.

"That is not all," said Annie, "Bill Hardy is following it up. He is not your friend, Maddy. If there is anything to be found, he will find it and you can guess the slant he will put on it. Be very careful. I must go. I could get into awful trouble if anyone knew what I was doing!"

"Bye Annie," was all Maddy said. She sat back on the sofa stunned.

"Maddy, what is it?" said Nathan. "Tell me, let me help you."

Maddy shook her head. Nathan knelt in front of her and held her hands, he hated to see her like this.

"Tell me, Maddy, or do you want me to phone Annie back?"

"No, don't do that, but get hold of TM. It is important and we may need Edward's advice." Then she told him what Annie had said.

Nathan phoned Edward. All he said was, "The joker may have been played. Ask TM to contact me urgently and will you come to the flat please? We need your advice."

"I will do both," said Edward, "just sit tight. I doubt if TM will come, but I will ask him."

Maddy looked at Nathan.

"I am so sorry," she said, "you don't need this."

"Maddy, I love you, please remember that. You are my first priority. No matter what has happened or will happen, we will face it together. We will not be alone either, our friends are strong and they will be there for us if we need them. So cheer up, Edward will be here soon and I'd rather he saw you dressed."

"Oh, golly, yes! I'll have a shower and be with you in a few minutes."

Nathan tried to work out who could have had the information besides himself. Even he did not know the truth. Nigel Bronsen was still following up some additional leads, then it clicked. It could be her brother, but she did not know about him yet, but what did he hope to gain? He picked up yesterday's paper. There it was in black and white, Stephan Alinsky had been part of the art fraud.

When Edward comes I shall have to tell her. She is going to be devastated. The sooner we get away the better.

The entrance buzzer went. Nathan picked up the receiver.

"Yes? Oh Edward, come up."

He opened the door, Edward and TM came in.

"Good morning, I did not expect you TM but I am pleased to see you. We need to bring Maddy up to speed with the information we have about her father."

The two men nodded.
"Maybe it will help if I do it," said TM, "then you can pick up the pieces Nathan."

"Fine," was all he said.

Maddy came into the room. "Oh, hello, would you like coffee." She went towards the kitchen. She had that awful sinking feeling something bad was about to happen.

Nathan followed her.

"You go back into the room, I'll make the coffee, you sit down for a minute."

TM asked Maddy what she knew. She explained about the phone call, she knew she had a brother but as far as she was aware had not met him. She remembered her mother's letter. I have talked to Michael and Angela about it but really it all happened so long ago, they knew less than me."

"Well, let me tell you a bit more," said TM.

"As you know, your father did work with the Germans and before they shot him he engraved a message on the silver frames of four miniatures, two of which were packed in your suitcase, the other two we now know were hidden. They have recently come to light. Now we have all four miniatures."

Nathan interrupted, "so that was what Dad was working on."

"Yes," said TM, "to continue, we are now working on trying to break the code."

Something clicked with Maddy. "Michael and Angela got out of Austria into Switzerland so it is just possible that they may have taken something to a Bank."

"You could be right," said TM. "Now, as to what we do next. James, work on a statement with Maddy, give us as much time as possible."

"Is anyone else involved Maddy?"

"I do not know, but Annie said that Bill Hardy was digging about. He is no friend of mine."

"Who is this Hardy?"

"He is the foreign affairs specialist at Inter News."

"Edward," said TM, "find out what we know about him, if necessary set some false trails. Anything to keep him busy for 24 hours."

TM turned to Nathan and Maddy.

"Will you both stay in London for the time being? It will delay your departure to France for a while but we need you on hand. Maddy, you may have to go on TV about this but we will give you enough information for you to pull the rug from under this man Hardy."

With that the two men left.

"Nathan, did you know all this?"

"Not all of it. I do know who your brother is. When we were in Vienna, do you remember we bought two pictures for Emir and Tiggy."

"Yes."

"Well, the man who sold them to us was your brother."

"Why did you not say anything at the time?"

"It was only confirmed to me later and the moment had passed. Now it appears he is part of the art scam that you uncovered."

"Oh my goodness" said Maddy "is there any more to come?"

"No, well not yet. You heard TM if the code is broken there may be more to come, we shall just have to wait and see."

Maddy started to cry. He wiped her tears away gently. "This is just a hiccup, which hurts I agree, but we have the rest of our lives to get over it. We did not fashion what happened way back then. It is not your fault; it is just so-so that you are involved. Now, I don't remember seeing you smile today."

She hit him with a cushion. "You fool" and she smiled.

Once back at his office TM joined the code breakers. He relayed the information Maddy had given him.

"Yes, that is right," said Angela, "we did go to a bank but I thought it was just for some money."

"Why don't you ask Michael? He is at home today."

"I will send Edward round," said TM.

"Do you want me to phone him?" said Angela.

"That might be helpful," said TM.

"TM," said Bar Lou, "what if Maddy saw these miniatures. If she sees all four she might remember something".

"Good idea. I'll phone Nathan and ask him to bring her over."

"How was she?" said Bar Lou.
"It was hard to say. We did not know what this art fraud was going to lead to so how could she? It has hit her hard but she will recover."

"I hope so," said Bar Lou.

Maddy and Nathan arrived after lunch. Maddy was delighted to see all four miniatures. They are beautiful but they are not in the right order. I used to play a game with my father, he would jumble them up and I had to put them in the right order. It was his favourite game and we did it over and over."

"Maddy, can you do that now?" said TM quietly.

"Oh easily," she moved them round.

"There you are. He made up a number game so I would remember."

"What was it? Oh yes."
"One and one makes three, two and two make four, three and four made me so I was five."

"Maddy, you are great. It is a bank safe box code. I am sure your father is not all bad, whatever happens, remember that."

350

Bar Lou wrote down the numbers 1132245 or any combination.

"No," said Maddy, "he used to often say when we played numbers, add up every other one, then come back along the numbers taking away the remaining numbers. So it should read 13254214."

"Maddy, you are fantastic," said TM "if your husband can remember which bank Natasha, we may solve this riddle yet."

Michael remembered the bank, the name of the manager and the date he made the deposit.

Chapter 41

Arpinsky maintained his silence. It was a frustrating time for the interviewees as they could make little progress. They returned him to his cell. He continued to refuse legal advice. He did not believe that he could be brought before an English court, after all he was German. His logic was flawed. He had not given himself time to think about the consequences of returning to Germany for trial.

There were more consultations with the Commissioner whose advice was to circulate what information you have to Interpol and contact the Jewish group trying to trace War criminals, the name escapes me. One way or another this man will face justice.

Colin asked to see his solicitor again. He had made up his mind to come clean, irrespective of what might happen to him in the future. He wanted his solicitor to pass this information on. He thought naively that it would prove to be the only way he could save his own skin. He did not know that much, but maybe it would be enough to deflect from his own situation.

Meanwhile, his journalist contact had heard that Bill Hardy was digging information about Maddy's background. He was enjoying this assignment. If she was permanently out of the frame, his prospects were great. He was ambitious and really did not care who he trampled on to get what he wanted. When he received a message to meet a freelance who may just have the information he was seeking, his face lit up. 'Got you at last, Golden Girl.' If he had not been so blinded by jealousy, he might have considered just what evidence he needed. What were the questions to be answered?

He went to the meeting. The information he was given just fuelled the flames. He agreed with the journalist to tip him off when the story was about to break on TV. Concurrent press headlines could be very useful indeed, gave him a bit of a smokescreen. On his return to the studio there was another message for him. Another source had come forward. Good, he thought, the more information he could get the better. He rang the number on the pad, no reply. He'd try again later. He started to write his copy, well, the first draft. He thought, 'I can always modify it if other information comes in.' He phoned the second contact three times. Ken and Dave were enjoying stringing him along. The fourth time he phoned, Ken answered.

"Hello," said Ken.

"Oh, this is Bill Hardy, Inter News, you left me a message."

"Oh, yes, heard you were looking for information about that TV presenter".

"Well, not her, I am looking for background information, thought it would make a good story."

"Oh," said Ken "I might have something and I might not. How much are you paying?"

This stumped Bill for a few moments.

"Depends what you have, I may already know it."

"Doubt if you know this," said Ken.

"Shall we meet, say 12 noon at La Bistro. Is that okay with you?"

"Fine," said Ken "bring your wallet."

Ken and Dave smiled at one another. They phoned Brigstock who spoke to James. He seemed pleased.

"Brigger," said James, "we need to keep this chap on the move and away from a studio for 48 hours. I will see that you get some information which will arouse his curiosity. Tell your chaps to 'string it out.'"
"Understood," said Brigstock. "If this chap Hardy hurts Maddy, then he hurts Nathan and that was not going to happen." Then he had an idea, he would run it past Nathan.

He could be given just enough rope to hang himself, then Maddy would move in with the truth.

Nathan listened to what Brigstock said to him. He liked the idea but suggested it needed careful handling. He did not want Maddy hurt. He told Brigstock to hold off until he had spoken to TM and then Maddy. If she said, 'no' that was it, no further action.

TM thought it would just work. He was waiting to hear from the agents in Switzerland. If the information in the deposit box helped, then it may be safe to proceed with Brigstock's idea.

He decided to meet with James, Edward, Bar Lou, the Commissioner, Nathan and Maddy later that day. It was important that every step they took was analysed carefully and everyone understood the reasoning. He needed total agreement on this one.

The somewhat expanded meeting was tense. Maddy was very apprehensive, she had not realised such a group existed or that her husband could be part of it. She sat back and listened whilst TM

355

explained the course of action he proposed. Nathan held Maddy's hand. When TM had finished, Bar Lou said, "Maddy, there is no pressure on you to do this. We may be able to get a result, not as good of course, another way."

Maddy said nothing. What was she getting herself into?

The Commissioner said, "Maddy, I really understand your initial reluctance, this is all tied up with the fall out of the Art fraud. There are matters of international importance coming to light. We need to smoke out one or two people. Using this chap Hardy, would give us a lever, but it is up to you."
Maddy took a deep breath. She looked at Nathan.

"I have one question. Is there any information to suggest that my father was or was not a collaborator? If he was, this ploy fails. If you know differently and I can be privy to that information, then I will do what you ask. If Bill Hardy wants his day, then fine. There are better journalists around than him and if he is undermined, it might give others a chance. I hope that you realise that this is very personal for me on two levels. There is the Bill Hardy issue, but more importantly it is about my family, my 'brother'. Well, I think he could be my brother in custody, and now this collaborator business. It hits where it hurts at mine and Nathans' happiness and the effect it could have on our future. Nathan, how do you feel?"

"Maddy, you have my full support for whatever course of action you take. I agree with your idea. Let us find out what is in this deposit box, reserve your right not to proceed."

"I think that is the correct move," said Edward. The others all nodded.

"When will the papers arrive?" said James.

"They are on their way with Nigel Bronsen, he had done a remarkable job on this case."

"Shall we adjourn now?" said Bar Lou. "I think Maddy and Nathan could do with a break. So could I."

The meeting was adjourned.

The Commissioner went straight back to his office. A decision was about to be made in conjunction with the Home Office as to when all the principals would be taken before the Court. It had to be in the next 24 hrs. It was a simple enough procedure. The Stipendiary would hear an outline of the case, then defence solicitors/barristers had a chance to respond. As the initial remand would only be for 7 days, he did not anticipate there would be any bail applications. It would however put all the names in the frame and that could be a two edged sword. He thought to himself, 'I will just have to live with it.'

Nathan and Maddy had returned to the flat. They were both very quiet. Maddy needed a few questions answered. She felt that she really did not know this man she had married and that disturbed her a little. Would he be able to tell her? Why had he kept his work so secret? She thought he worked in international finance.

Nathan broke into her silence.

"Maddy, come here and sit with me, there is a lot I need to explain to you. I have wanted to tell you this for a long time. I knew when I first saw you at the Rugby Club Ball that you were the only woman I wanted to spend the rest of my life with. There was just something in our chemistry. Can you imagine how I felt having to wait before I could tell you? You know, now, about my collection of videos of your work. It sounds daft now but I was in America, you were here, not easy. I also knew that I wanted to follow in my father's footsteps. He worked as a very senior intelligence officer in International Finance. There was more to his work than that. Both he and my mother were killed in a road accident, but it was no accident. Like you, I wanted to know what happened to my parents, but at the same time, if I followed the path I have outlined and I could persuade you to marry me, was it fair to put you at risk? I am developing some experience in more precise form of accounting so I decided to spend some time learning all I could and assessing how it would help in the world wide money markets. Thanks to my education and the kind of opportunities I have had, my contacts stretch around the globe, mainly among the younger high flyers, some of whom you have met. What it boils down to, Maddy, is that you have only had about half of the information about who I am and what I do. Now you have much more. You are intelligent enough to fill in the gaps. What is really important to me is you, you are my life, I love you so much that I would happily change direction to keep you. I really do not need to work to earn money. I think you realise that. We could spend more time on the Cabal projects. It would be satisfying and you could make lots of TV programmes. So think about it. I will make us something to eat whilst you take in what I have said."

"Nathan, don't go for a minute. I had no idea about the depth of your work commitment. I am glad you have told me. Now I understand some of the phone calls. I do not know if I would have felt differently about you had I been party to this information. It is a bit scary, not more jolly japes, - it is the real thing. Whatever the future holds, I dare not think about, but I know this. I am happier with you than I have ever been in my life. I wake up each day thinking how lucky I am and wanting to enjoy my life as your wife. The more I know about you the more I love you. There are moments when I am perplexed but they pass, you make what we do seem so natural, so caring. Your parents must have been super people. I cannot say that I am looking forward to what Bill Hardy will think he knows but I will face him if necessary." She smiled at Nathan. "I do love you. I think you know that, so are all the secrets out in the open now?"

"Yes," said Nathan. "Come with me, we can miss tea. I think we will enjoy our own main course don't you?" He kissed her as they walked towards the bedroom.

"Nathan, do you realise it is early afternoon, there is work to do."
"Who cares?" said Nathan, "work can wait for both of us. There are other more important things in life than work."

"Oh yes," said Maddy, "and what may they be?"

"Well, come with me and I will show you ..."

Chapter 42

Arpinsky sat in his cell, most unperturbed he really thought he had the upper hand. He was convinced that the English Police could not prove he had anything to do with the art fraud. As to the possible charge of murder, they were just fishing. He was quite sure that he would be free to go home that morning.

Bar Lou had gone back to the cottage to think. She was absolutely sure that Arpinsky had been the person who had tortured her in captivity and been responsible for physical damage to her person. The evidence relating to the art fraud was a bit thin and she thought that the chances of the murder charges sticking were remote.

The Commissioner had said they would get this man one way or another. She could provide the other way. If he was tried for war crimes, she could give direct evidence. She was strong enough to do that and may be others would come forward. She decided to phone TM.

He was not surprised to receive her phone call, he knew how she had been mutilated in captivity. It had been Michael Eversley who had given her the will to carry on. He was in awe of her courage. They would all support her. Surprisingly, it was Maddy who was most likely to be able to understand Bar Lou. He had noticed their growing friendship.

He had intended to phone Maddy and to show her the letter that was found in the deposit box. After all it was Maddy who had broken the code. Her father had listed every item which had been looted and by whom, and as far as he knew where it had been either stored or displayed. There were several names listed of persons now holding Public Offices in Europe. The arrests that were about to follow would make headlines for days. Maddy's father had been a brave man who dealt with the situation honestly and with stoicism. Maddy could be proud of him. As for Inky, he would learn a hard lesson, whether it would change him who knows? 'Silly fool,' thought TM.

The next morning, TM was really surprised to see the tabloid press headlines.

'TVs golden girl's father was a Nazi Collaborator'. He could guess what followed. The news stations headlined the story as well. What on earth were the editors playing at? There had been no attempt to check out the story. He phoned Nathan.

"Eversley, hello""Oh TM, what can I do for you?"

"Have you seen any papers or heard the news?"

"No, what is happening?"

"Brigstock's plan is working. Bill Hardy is in it up to his neck."

"Can Maddy correct him with any supporting evidence."

"She surely can, her father was a very clever double agent. There are people being arrested at this minute who must have thought they were home and dry."

"No doubt your phone will be ringing nonstop, expect the media pack to camp outside your flat. From their point of view, it is a good story. I am trying to arrange for Maddy to be interviewed by one of the global networks. We are taking advice on that at present. Maybe tomorrow will be soon enough. You can tell Maddy she will see all the material we have this afternoon."

Oh, one other piece of news, Bar Lou has decided to testify as to Arpinsky's war crimes. Our case in the art fraud is not strong. The Jewish group are delighted, they have sufficient statements to ensure he will not be free for a long time."

"What will happen to Inky? After all he is Maddy's brother."

"He will be sent back to Germany to stand trial there. The extradition papers are on the way as we speak. He will go down for some 10 yrs. The Austrian Police have been most efficient, all the workshops have been raided and artists arrested. We are not yet in a position to know exactly how many copies have been made, no doubt someone will tell us."

"As to young Colin, Tiggy's brother, he is likely to get a shorter sentence, but it may be all he needs."

"And Perry Bracken?"

"The Americans are handling that. He has come clean about the paintings and the money laundering. You might be needed to give evidence on that Leisure Group set of accounts."

"Now about Maddy's interview? I have just heard we have the right person lined up so she has nothing to fear. In fact she will come out of it very well indeed, so will her father and mother".

"Will she get the miniatures back at the end of the trial?"

"Certainly, did she tell you how the riddle was solved?"

"No, did Maddy do it?"

"Oh yes, it was quite cunning."

"She never ceases to surprise me," said Nathan.

"So when can we plan to leave for France?"

"Shortly after the interview. I think it would be a good idea to let the dust settle."

"Thank you". Nathan put down the phone.

"Maddy," he called, "you are headline news again."

"What," said Maddy "why?"

"Mr Hardy has just put his big size tens in it."

"Nathan, stop talking in riddles, what is happening?"

"Well, Brigstock's plan worked."

"TM has arranged a global TV interview for you to rebut the information. Your father worked as only he knew how, kept meticulous records and now many people who thought they had nothing, thanks to the war, can lay genuine claims to their inheritance. It will make a good feature programme in time, when you start working on your own label."

"Sending me out to work, are you, and what will you do?"

"Take you to France, then develop my interest in forensic accounting. I'll be able to start with scrutinizing the household accounts."

A cleverly armed cushion caught him off guard. He laughed, "I'm glad that we will be free of tension once and for all when this is over although it will be months before all the participants come to justice."

"Did anyone say what will happen to Fing Wah?"

"Oh, did I not tell you?" said Nathan, "he absolutely loves the life of a monk. He will stay in the order. The Government there have too much on their hands to want to be bothered. Petre and Su Ming are relieved. They hope to come and stay with us soon. We will have to arrange for Mai Lee to meet them."

"Did I tell you that Mary Ann phoned" said Maddy.

"No," said Nathan "what did she want?"

"Only to tell me that once the trials are over, she and Leon will be married."

"Leon?"

"Yes, Hammerstein, you know the Gallery owners? They have decided to move the Gallery into Chelsea and start again. Mary Ann will be a full partner in the business."

"Well, it has been quite a day for news, so much it is difficult to take in. I will be glad when we will be free to go to France. Have you had any ideas about refurbishing Le Petit Oiseaux."

"Oh, yes, Patra and I have quite a few ideas to talk over with you, it is a very exciting project and likely to be expensive."

Nathan just smiled. Maddy was happy, so was he. It was to be some time before he would realise why his mother bought the Chateau and what had happened there to his father and Bar Lou.

"Has Emir been in touch with you?"

"Not yet," said Nathan, "all this business with Colin has rather overshadowed their plans. Tiggy's father and mother are off to live in Southern Ireland. It is quite possible that Emir and Tiggy will marry there. I think Patra has finished supervising the refurbishment and restoration. It will give them a fresh start. Tiggy and Emir will run the racing stables. No doubt Bar Lou will be taking a keen interest."

"Speaking about Bar Lou, TM has told me that she will give evidence against Arpinsky, He is to be extradited to Germany to stand trial for his war crimes."

"Nathan, is everyone absolutely sure that Bar Lou is ready for the stresses and strains it will bring in its wake?" asked Maddy.

"Well, we are hoping that you will be able to give her that support, friendship and wise counsel. She trusts you absolutely and she has told you what happened to her at his hands. Even I do not know as much as you."

"Of course I will, then she can come to Le Petit Oiseaux and we can spoil her."

"That is fine by me," said Nathan.

"In fact, there is a cottage in the grounds she could have for her own. I am sure that the Chansons would look after her."

"What a great idea," said Maddy.

"I have an even better picture in mind."
"What?"

"Well, when you become chatelaine, will you walk around with one of those fancy belts with all the keys dangling and the purse? You could wear sexy fishnets and high heels."

"Nathan, stop right there, these fantasies are getting out of hand."
"Not to my mind," he said "they are only just beginning to make me realise how much fun we can have. Maddy, I hope we can fill the Chateau with laughter and have our friends around us. It will be our retreat, something we start together."

The phone rang.

"Yes?" said Maddy, "oh, good morning TM."

"Are you in a fit state to face this interview. Mr Hardy has had his five minutes of fame. It is time to give him a lesson in good journalism."
"I have been thinking where would be the best place? Perhaps we should use the studios where you made the programme."

"Why not at Temple Meadows? The conservatory would be ideal from a sound point of view. I would feel more comfortable, less exposed, and Nathan will be there waiting for me."

"That is a brilliant idea Maddy. I will arrange it for tomorrow. Whilst you are at Temple Meadows, find a little time for Bar Lou. No doubt Nathan has told you what she is planning."

"Yes, but you did not doubt her bravery did you?"

"No, of course not, in a funny sort of way it might just help her come to terms with herself. If she had gone on stage, she surely would be a theatrical dame of the British Empire by now."

"The mind boggles," said Maddy "now back to this interview. We will probably travel down to the house tonight. It will be an opportunity to spend some time with James, Edward and Bar Lou."

"Thank you very much Maddy, you have been such a help to us all. Nathan is a lucky young man."

"So am I," said Maddy, "I am looking forward to living a reasonably normal life."

"Some chance, with Nathan around Maddy, but I think you already know that."

There was a click as the observation window in his cell door opened. All Arpinsky could see was an eye looking at him. Then he heard the key in the lock.

"Well, Sir, you are getting your wish, you are going back to Germany to stand trial there. The papers are being signed at this moment."

"Good," said Arpinsky. He thought, "I have so many people in my pocket, this move signals absolute freedom. Then I will be able to seek my revenge." He smiled as he imagined the 'fun' he would have.

"It may not be as 'good' for you as you think, when you read the papers the Duty Inspector shows you. It may not be the soft option you seem to think it is."

Arpinsky frowned. Little do they know. I am far too clever for them.

It was a different story as he stood in the Custody Suite whilst the Inspector read out the deportation order. He thought he had heard wrongly.

"Can you repeat that?"

"With pleasure Sir, you are to stand trial for War Crimes."

"Now sign here."

"Gentleman," he nodded to the two German plain clothes men, "he is all yours" and good riddance he thought as he closed the file.

He looked at his list, then thought, 'it will be a long day but give me an 'honest to goodness local criminal', rather than his sort,' With that he turned and left the area.

Nathan was on the telephone to some friends. He hoped to arrange a surprise for Maddy ...

Chapter 43

Freddie had invited Charles Babington to New York to see what projects Cabal Finance were sponsoring. He had learned a lot from Charles when they worked together in Austria. There was a great deal of mutual respect.

Charles felt very much at home in the New York office. He thought they were a tremendous team, he liked the way they worked. He also realised that Freddie and Gabriella were very close. Mark had been very suspicious of Charles at first but that was soon dispelled. They talked at length about the arrest of Perry Bracken, although they knew it was coming. The scale of the deceit had shocked them.

Charles knew that it was time for him to start thinking about the future. He knew that changes were coming back in England. He felt he needed a new start, a new challenge. He would welcome the opportunity to work for something like the projects he had seen on his visit. 'This is how money should be used,' he thought. His three weeks in New York flew by, he did not know when he had enjoyed himself so much. He had spent most of the final day with Mark, talking about the future of the project. He found that they had similar ideas. So engrossed were they when Freddie returned to the office with Gabriella, they hardly looked up other than to say "Hi."

"Is that all you can manage?" said Freddie. "Hey guys we have some great news. Gabriella and I are engaged to be married." "What took you so long Freddie?" "Congratulations, Gabby, be happy."

Freddie opened the filing cabinet and liberated the last bottle of champagne and four glasses.

"Before this drink goes to our heads, how about a celebratory meal?"

"Great idea, but where would we get in."

"Oh, I think I can sort that out" said Freddie reaching for a phone.

"That's done. We are off to the trendiest place in town. Now I have one more phone call to make."

"Nathan, it's Freddie, the visit has been brilliant, as you thought. Charles is really impressed with our work. It would take little persuasion to encourage him to join us and just one more piece of news, Gabriella and I are engaged."

"Freddie, that is marvellous news, are you celebrating?"

"What do you think?"

"Where?" When Freddie told him, he whistled. "Must be paying you too much. Will Gabby's parents and brother be there?"

"Of course."
"Well have a great evening. I am sure Maddy will phone you herself and congratulations to both of you."

Freddie went back to the inner office and joined his friends.

Nathan, meanwhile, was making a series of transatlantic phone calls.

If he could not be at the celebrations, he could still be part of them. When he put the phone down he smiled. Now to go and tell Maddy.

Maddy was coming to the end of her interview. She looked pleased. He heard her say, "There is just one quote from my mother's letter to me which I received just before my wedding to Nathan." She read on 'please do not feel badly about your father. He was a kind and gentle man in an ungentle world. He did what he did to try and set us free. I hope you will understand that one day.'

She smiled at her interviewer. "I think that says it all, don't you?"

When the interview ended, Maddy turned to see Nathan smiling at her.

"Are you fine?"

"Yes, really I am, now who is for tea?"

When Nathan saw the unedited film, he was really impressed. She told the story simply and very well and looked terrific. He looked across to where Maddy was talking to the crew. He thought she really loved that world and was very good. The sooner he gots her project underway, the better.

As the crew started to leave he went to stand by Maddy's side.

"Well done darling."
"Thank you."
"I've got some news to tell you."

"What?" she said as she waived goodbye to the crew.

"Well, it can wait if you are too busy."

"Nathan!"

"I've just had a phone call from Freddie, he is in New York."

"Yes, I know that."

"Oh, if you know." She just looked at him.

"Carry on."

"Well, he and Gabriella are engaged."

"Oh brilliant, what took him so long?"

"Who knows?" Nathan had that faraway look in his eye.

"What have you done Nathan?"

"Well, I just arranged a few surprises, all good I assure you."

"Are we all having dinner together tonight?"

"No, James and Edward are in town and Bar Lou is spending the weekend with Patra. She wants all the news from Ireland," said Maddy.

"Well, we could go skinny dipping in the pool, have a lazy meal and an early night."

"Great," said Maddy "last one to the pool makes dinner."

Hannaway and Mai Lee were in their sitting room. It would not be long before their child was born and they were starting a new life themselves.

Mai Lee broke the silence.

"You know I cannot get used to hearing you called 'Headmaster.' Does it sound strange to you."

"No, it did at first, but this place, with all its traditions, is home to me. I was a scholarship boy which put me apart from the rest. Nathan was very kind to me. He only had guardians at the time his parents were killed in a road accident. That is how our friendship started."

"We have our first Governors' meeting tomorrow so Nathan will be here with Maddy. You two can have a good gossip."

"Oh yes, I will find out all the news, pity we cannot go shopping, but that will keep. I feel too heavy and ungainly to be walking far."

"You do not look like that to me, you look beautiful and I am really looking forward to holding our baby."

There was a knock at the door.

"Come," said Hannaway.

"Headmaster?" said the young boy.

They both smiled.

"Yes Fenner."

Jocelyn and Walsh were having a meal together. They were due to play at the Jazz For All night and Walsh was in town for a meeting to talk about how the growing drug menace was having its effect on sport.

They both had discussed this topic on many occasions. It was going to be a difficult exercise particularly at international level.

"Oh, let's forget about work," said Jos "Have you heard that Freddie is engaged to Gabriella?"

"You mean that super girl from New York? So another wedding, another get together and Mai Lee's baby is due any time."

373

"Well," said Jos, "we are going to have to get our skates on."

"Why," said Walshy, "we have plenty of time but in saying that I have met someone rather special and I think she feels the same way."

"You old dog, when do I meet her?"

"Not before she has my ring on her finger."

They both laughed.

"We have all come a long way, have we not Walshy. You have your coveted Welsh jersey. I have my England caps. We have all travelled the world yet we remain the best of friends. That last year at Firedown made all the difference to us," said Jos.

"Talking about Firedown, I have been asked to join the Governors."

"So have I," said Jos.

"Strange, isn't it?" then they both said "it's Nathan again."

Colin was sitting in the interview room with his solicitor. He knew that the next half hour could change his life. He had found it hard trying to live up to his parents expectations. He was not keen on horses and certainly did not want to join the Army. That had caused ructions. Left to his own devices he had made a few, well more than a few wrong choices. He needed to be liked by people. All he could think was, 'I am just a failure. I've hurt my parents, my jealousy of Tiggy is all out of proportion and now I am sitting in a police station with a solicitor probably facing a spell in prison so I just have to pull myself together and start again. This is the first step on a long, long road. He looked at his solicitor and grimaced. He heard the interview room door open and two men walked in. They were from the Serious Crime Squad.

"So Mr Ince Blundell, what is this information you have for us?" The tape was set, the initial statements made. His solicitor spoke.

"I have to tell you that my client is doing this interview at his own suggestion."

"Colin, it is time to start."

He cleared his throat and began. He was clear and concise and therefore soon into his stride. There was not a lot of new information for the record, but it did tie up various relationships and to that extent it was most useful.

There were many questions to which Colin answered openly.

At the end of the session, Colin was exhausted and relieved. He had a brief word to his solicitor and was returned to his cell. He thought to himself, 'I can face the future now, whatever happens, I will cope.' Then he slept.

Maddy and Nathan were enjoying a lazy Sunday morning at Temple Meadows. It was a relief, in a way, just to relax. When Maddy looked back at the time since her wedding she realised how much had changed in her life. She now knew about her parents, she had a brother, she had missed the buzz of working in a TV newsroom, but now she was married. She was more settled, very happy and looking forward to the future.

"A penny for them," said Nathan.

"A penny for what?" said Maddy.

"Well, you were miles away, we ought to make a move. A few friends are coming for lunch."

"What?" said Maddy, "now he tells me."

"Calm down, it is all in hand. Don't worry, we have at least an hour before they start arriving."

That hour passed quickly, as she bathed, dressed and tidied the room. Somehow today, she did not mind she felt different, happier if that was possible.

The lunch was a great success. It was so pleasing to see Mary Ann so happy. Leon would be good for her and Esther had news to impart. She had been offered a partnership in her law firm. Annie Wilkins joined the group for the first time. She had decided to join Maddy's TV programme-making project. At first she was overawed but she soon relaxed. So many interesting people, some had only been names to date. One person in particular was taking a keen interest. Jos. He thought she was super. Pity he was going abroad but he did have a few days, perhaps he would invite her to dinner or maybe wait until he returned. He felt like a schoolboy again.

James said, "Nathan, when are you off to France?"

"Probably midweek. Maddy has an appointment in town on Tuesday, so any time after that."

"I think Patra will join us for a few days to go over some plans for the Chateau."

"Chateau, what Chateau?" said Bar Lou.

"The one mother bought before she died."

"Oh," said Bar Lou, "I did not know that."

"Well, I look forward to visiting you there."

"Good," said Nathan, "we will expect a lot of guests, you are all invited."

"Nathan," said Maddy "we need to get the place habitable first."

"Oh, it's not that bad, we will be doing a nice line in four poster beds!"

"Nathan, too much information," and she smiled.

She had enjoyed that four poster bed.

Chapter 44

Miriam Hunter sat in her cell, feeling cold, upset and wondering what the future would hold for her. She had not told her husband about the sale of the Irish property. She was having her doubts about living in Heatherbourne Castle. There was another property in Scotland but she had not been there for years.

Her solicitor had not been hopeful about her sentence. She had discussed this with him before deciding to plead guilty. Her only hope was that she would be given credit for her early plea and that her Barrister would make a good case in mitigation.

She had not seen her husband since he had resigned his post as Foreign Secretary. She wondered if he would be in Court. She knew that he had arranged her solicitor and Barrister but other than that there had been no contact.

What could she say to him? 'Sorry' was inadequate, if not insulting. She knew that she would be remanded to prison the next morning. It was very difficult for him to go anywhere at present without being followed by the press pack. She decided she would write to him as soon as possible. Maybe in time, they could rebuild their shattered relationship but who knows?

Her husband was staying at his club. He could not bear to go back to the Castle. It had been a busy few days since resigning. The Prime Minister had been kind to him but the facts were, he was to return to the back benches. He had thought hard and long about his resignation speech, the words would just now flow. Most of his colleagues had been sympathetic but no doubt the opposition would have a field day at his expense. So he left for the House, dreading walking the corridors, packing up his office, saying his goodbyes and thank yous. Then into the House he went. When the time came for his speech, he was suddenly nervous. Strangely, the mood of the House was generally supportive. He read from his prepared text, added a few personal comments and sat down. 'So this is it,' he thought, 'twenty years of hard work, late nights, committees, constituency business, bazaars, fetes, presentations etc, now it had ended in ignominy. Oh Miriam, why?' He thought.

There were some complimentary and supportive comments from others in the House, but he was glad to leave. All his personal boxes were packed, he had signed all the necessary forms. It was time to face his constituency, another resignation, another speech. When would it all end? Perhaps he would go to Ireland for a few weeks, it was reasonably safe to do so. He would go to Court the next day to surprise Miriam. The idea that she would be remanded in custody filled him with horror.

Miriam had passed the letter to her solicitor to give to her husband. It did not make pleasant reading. She had written about the sale of the Irish property. That would be a blow to him.

As for Heatherbourne Castle, she would not go back there. It could be offered to the National Trust. She would eventually go and live in Scotland. 'What a mess,' she thought, 'and it is all of my doing.

Just think, all of this came to light because of one or two silly mistakes and those four miniatures. The ripples have affected four continents.' Suddenly she realised that it had not been worth it. She had effectively lost her home, her integrity and maybe her husband, life would never be the same again.

It was the morning of the Court appearance. Inky was apprehensive. His solicitor had told him that he would be going down on remand for seven days in the first instance. He had no idea what was to face him, the indignity, the confinement, the fear ... He started to tremble, then it hit him. 'Who cares, who really cares?' and he had to answer, 'No-one. I do not have any true friends. Now I have lost everything.'

The Gallery will have to be sold. There is no future. He hated the drive from the prison to the Court. He had no contact with anyone else.

As he walked up the steps from the Bridewell to the Court Room, he was full of foreboding. In the dock was Miriam Hunter, Colin and himself. Arpinsky was not there. 'Where was he? Oh,' he thought, 'I am not taking the rap for him.'

The Clerk asked him to identify himself which he did, Miriam and Colin did the same.

"Sit down for a moment, Mr Allinsky."

"Miriam Hunter and Colin Blundell listen to the Clerk whilst he reads the charges to you."

When the Clerk finished, their Barristers stood up in turn and advised the Court that no plea would be entered or bail application made at this stage.

"Very well," said the Judge. "Then Miriam Hunter and Colin Ince Blundell, you will be remanded in custody for seven days. Go down with the Officers."

"Stand up, Mr Allinsky. Is there an application for this man?"

The prosecuting Barrister stood. "Your Worship, I have an application from the Austrian Police for a deportation order to be made, to return this man for trial in his own Country. I think, my Lord, you have all the papers in front of you."

"Thank you, yes."

Inky's solicitor stood up. "Sir, my client is aware that this could be the outcome. Therefore, I have no further comment."

"Mr Alinsky, you will be deported to Austria where you will stand trial with others for your part in this fraud."

"Go down with the Officers," said the Clerk.

Miriam Hunter was taken to an interview room.

"You have a visitor, Mrs Hunter." With that, her husband walked in. She hung her head.

Then she said, "What have I done to you? Did you get my letter?"

"Yes," he said, "that is why I am here. Was life so bad with me that we could not be honest with each other? I thought you enjoyed our lifestyle, meeting people from all over the world. I just do not understand, was restoring Heatherbourne worth all this?"

"No," she said quickly. "It became like a drug, I just could not stop and when you made fun of my little job at the Gallery it spurred me on, now I never want to see the place again."

"What happened to the place in Ireland?"

"It was sold to a Finance House. It was a drain on my resources. We never went there, so it seemed logical to sell and of course the monies raised completed the refurbishment of Heatherbourne. Will you please start the negotiations with the National Trust? Oh, and as to where we, or you, can live, there is the lodge in Scotland. The existing lease has run out so it might provide a place of shelter for a while."

"Miriam, you are a foolish, foolish woman. As to what I feel at the moment, it is not possible to put into words. I will stand by you through the trial, then we shall have to see what happens after that."

"There will be no trial," said Miriam.

He looked up at her.

"I will plead guilty. I have already made a full statement to my Barrister. He will be in discussion with the police this week. Colin has done the same. As to the rest, I do not know."

"Miriam, there are families on four continents facing problems just like ours, because people are greedy. I hope you understand that."

She shook her head.

The policeman returned. "It is time to go, Mrs Hunter."

She just looked at her husband. "I'm sorry, so very sorry."

He left as he had come, through a side door, and into a waiting car.

Maddy had just been told that her brother was being deported. She felt sad, she ought to make contact with him somehow. It was a matter for her to discuss with TM. But not today. She was meeting Mary Ann and Esther for lunch, then she had one more appointment before meeting up with Nathan. They were off to Paris in the morning. She was excited about seeing the renovations Patra had carried out.

The lunch was just what she needed, a good old gossip with friends, the plans for Mary Ann's wedding. "By the way Maddy, that TV interview was terrific," said Esther. "What happened to Hardy?"

"I have not heard," said Maddy, "neither in a way do I care. He should have checked and cross checked his facts."

"No love lost there," said Esther.

They chatted on, three friends happy and safe in each others company. Three lives which would continuously intertwine for many years to come.

TM was having lunch with Bar Lou, Edward, James and the Commissioner. They had much to discuss. This latest affair had made them all realise just how wearing the Circle work was becoming.

It had been an excellent but tedious case to work on. Their resources had been stretched and the original objective of solving the conundrum of the four miniatures completed. TM had given them back to Nathan that morning.

"Well," said James, "Nathan is more than ready to join the Circle and we can help him as we have done for many years now. He is so like Michael, sometimes I think it is him standing there. He will eventually build his own team, then watch our world."

"I think I agree," said TM.

"Bar Lou, have you anything to add?"

"Yes. I am beginning to feel very tired. As you all know, I shall be in Germany in the late Spring for the War Crimes Trial. An event I am not looking forward to very much, but that man has caused such misery, I have to go on with it. I will need my diaries and reports that I made at the time, please, TM."

"Maddy has said that she will be with me, as will Nathan. It will be as though Michael and Alicia are there. Whether I shall ever know if he was involved in their death, I do not care, so many people have come forward to testify, he cannot escape this time. After that I shall retire. I have a good friend in Patra. She would be an ideal candidate for the Circle, by the way, as, in my opinion, would Maddy."

James said, "Does anyone know what Nathan is doing today?"

"No, oh well I suppose it will come out in the wash. He was very excited about something."

"Maybe it is the thought of having Maddy to himself for a few weeks," said Edward.

TM smiled. "Who wouldn't? No, back to business. Arpinsky we know about. Alinsky, Maddy's brother is to stand trial in Austria next month. Perry Bracken, well that case will run and run for a while. So much has been uncovered, there are numerous gangs running for cover. It will be a tremendous piece of work. When it comes to the fraud jury, Nathan will be giving evidence. No doubt a book and film will follow in due course."

Miriam Hunter and Colin are on prison remand. Both have pleaded guilty to the lesser charges which has been accepted. Sentence will be passed next week.

Alinsky will stand trial in Austria and work has begun on the process involved in tracing the owners or descendants of much of the art work that has been recovered, or will be recovered, in the fullness of time."

"Yes, I hear that Mary Ann has been commissioned to trace and check the provenances," said Edward. "It is a big job but she will do it well."

"Doesn't she get married soon?" said Bar Lou.

"Yes," said James, "it will be a quiet ceremony, even with Nathan involved. I hear that Nigel Bronson will be helping Mary Ann."

"That's right," said Edward, "she will need someone with his skills, it will be a mammoth task."

"Well," said TM, "that brings us up-to-date. I now have to brief the PM."

Chapter 45

Natasha and her husband were busy packing their belongings. Neither of them was very talkative. Both had been to Court. Natasha saw the look on her son's face, as he was remanded to prison for seven days. For a moment, he was like her little boy who needed her comfort but she could not respond. She would have to go and see him in prison. She needed to talk with him. There were questions that needed answering. He needed to understand that, despite everything, he was still her son whom she loved.

"Natasha," said Colonel, "will you mind giving up your life here and moving to Ireland, it will be a big change."

"Yes, I know, but maybe that is what we all need. Emir and Tiggy will run this place efficiently and I think, with success. I always dreamt of the day she would marry, the local church, lots of friends and family, gorgeously dressed and a reception at home, full of laughter and happiness. Now she is insisting on a quiet wedding with no fuss."

"It is difficult, I know," said her husband, "current events have cast a long shadow. If she wants a quiet affair, why do we not suggest that she gets married in Ireland? I am sure her friends would be happy to travel. Shall I talk to her about it?"

"If you think it will work."

"There is no harm in trying. Why don't you prepare lunch. I will finish here, then we can both talk to them."

"Before we do that, what about Colin?"

"What about him?"

"Well, I do not feel that I can just abandon him."

"Natasha, he has been nothing but trouble. We have tried."

"Yes, I know he has made some silly decisions. Moved with the wrong crowd, tried to impress, but all that happened was, he was never part of a supportive group of friends, not like Tiggy or Emir. Do you think he might come to us in Ireland?"

"Natasha, I do not think it would work, unless, of course, we could try something. I hear there is a residential centre on the outskirts of Dublin which specialises in rehabilitation. If he were willing, then perhaps I could arrange it. That might be a way forward."

"I would like to go and see him in prison, see if he is in the mood to take on board such a suggestion. He needs to know we care. There is a lot of good in that young man, we just have to find a way to release it."

Lunch was a simple meal served at the kitchen table. Natasha raised the question of the forthcoming marriage.

Tiggy looked at Emir who said, "I have spoken to Patra and Nathan."

"A lethal combination," said the Colonel.

"No, please hear me out, we both realise that to marry here would be somewhat difficult in the light of the current situation, so we thought..."

"We would like to get married in Ireland" said Tiggy.

"Are you sure?" said Natasha.

"Oh yes, it could be very romantic. Nathan has this friend who owns a castle and specialises in weddings. All sorts of famous people have been married there. We can stay in the Castle, be married in the Chapel and celebrate with a typical Irish party."

"Nathan strikes again," said her father.

They all laughed.

"Is that what you want Emir?" said Natasha.

"Yes, it would be different but I would like to build into the ceremony some of my traditions. Like it or not, I am a Sultan and if I ever return to Osmantia I want the people to know that we have observed any traditions."

"How would it differ Emir?" said Natasha.

"Well, I think it is better if we talk with Patra who, by the way, wants to pay for the wedding, that is one tradition which is different in my country. Please let her do this."

Tiggy said "Mum, this is going to be a wedding with a difference, East meets West, isn't it the best idea?"

One look at her daughter's face told her that it was. It would be a super wedding after all.

"Mum, what will happen to Colin?"

"He will probably serve a prison sentence, then afterwards, who knows? It is unlikely that he will be at the wedding." "That is a pity," said Tiggy. "What a fool he has been. Are you going to see him in prison?"

389

"Yes, I hope so."

"Can I come?" said Tiggy.

"Of course."

"Now about these wedding plans," said her father. "I suppose I could wear No 1 dress uniform, must put on a show you know."

"Emir, what will you wear?"

"I don't know, possibly my official outfit, but I want to talk to Patra first. Although I have inherited the title, I have not been sworn in. So it is one I shall have to think about. Maybe it would be better to wear just ordinary clothes, like at Nathan and Maddy's wedding."

"Is Nathan to be your best man?" asked Natasha.

"Oh yes," said Emir, "I wonder what he will do this time?"

"Nothing too awful, I hope," said Natasha. "Now we had better get back to work. Have you decided what furniture you want? It is pointless taking too much with us. I would like to buy over in Ireland, it would be fun."

"No, we will do that today," said Tiggy, "but we want to make a few changes as well."

"That is fine by your father and I."

'Perhaps, just perhaps, things are going to work out in the long run,' she thought, or rather hoped.

Brigstock and Bar Lou were sitting in her garden having afternoon tea talking about old lives and the current situation.

390

"Are you happy about the War Crimes Trials, Bar Lou?"

"Not happy exactly. Of course, I am glad that Arpinsky is finally having to answer for his cruelty to others so to that extent, I am relieved. He will be out of my shadow at last. I never quite got rid of that feeling that he could still hurt me and he did of course. I am sure it was he who was behind Michael and Alicia's death. Did you know that there will be 10 people giving direct evidence of his involvement. Isn't that wonderful? Nathan, Maddy and Patra will be there with me."

"Yes, well that could be a mixed blessing. Nathan can be a handful."

"Not with Maddy around. This is too serious for one of his surprises."

"Did you know that they own Le Petit Oiseaux?"

"No, do they know what happened there?"

"I doubt it. Patra has been telling me of the refurbishment plans. It should be different. Nathan and Maddy want to take me back there, after the trial. I am not sure I can face it. I did not even know Alicia had bought the place and what's more, I do not think Michael knew either. She did not have time to tell him. Nathan has much of her personality, off the cuff decisions, full of surprises. Fortunately he has inherited a little of his father's determination and caution. I suppose we must be thankful for small mercies."

"I agree," said Brigstock, "Nathan has been like a son to us all. It could have been a disaster when you think about it, but he has survived and with Maddy by his side, the future looks reasonably assured."

"I hope so," said Bar Lou, "I really do. I hear he is to employ your two lads on the estate, doubling up as chauffeurs when necessary. That is good news for I like them both."

"Yes, it is good news. They are useful lads, quite resourceful and more than capable of handling themselves in a crisis."

"Did you know that Charles Babington is going to be his Estate Manager? He will be responsible for looking after the maintenance and development of all the properties."

"Nathan has chosen well, the people he is appointing now are tried and trusted and will look after his interests and those of Maddy. Did you notice that Charles was taking more than an interest in Maggie Lamb?"

"No," said Bar Lou, "I do enjoy a gossip. Do tell me more."

Maddy was putting the final touches to their packing. Where on earth was Nathan? He said he would be an hour, not half a day.

The phone rang.

"Hello, Maddy Eversley."

"Maddy, it is Hannaway. Mai Lee and I have a daughter, both are doing well. Is Nathan there?"

"No," said Maddy "but he should not be long. We are supposed to be leaving for France this evening, but you know Nathan, easily distracted."

"Maddy, we are so happy, the job is fantastic and the pupils love Mai Lee. Ask Nathan to phone me please."

"I will and congratulations to you both." 'Our first godchild,' she thought, 'we will have to think of a present and an outfit for the Christening.'

Nathan arrived about an hour later full of apologies. "There were things I had to sort out and it took longer than expected, but I am here now, so give me a kiss."

"Nathan, we have had a call from Hannaway, Mai Lee has had a little girl."

"Oh wow!" said Nathan, "I bet he is like a dog with two tails. We will have to think about a present. As godparents-to-be, we have a special responsibility, so it has to be something good."

"Nathan, have you forgotten we are supposed to be on honeymoon? When are we going to France? We will never make the check in time at this rate."

"Oh we will, it is sorted."

"What does that mean?"

"It is a surprise."

"Nathan!"

"Just wait and see."

An hour later they arrived at the Airport.

"We do not normally fly from here, Nathan, what are you up to?"

"Just updating our transport pool, I have bought a company plane. It has been so hard keeping it a secret from you, but now we will not be tied to using commercial flights. We can take off when we like. I hope you like the inside. It is a lot more comfortable than the standard first class, at least I think so, and its tax efficient as well."

"Nathan you are amazing. I can see that life is never going to be dull with you around and I hope that will be for a really long time."

"Now are we going to Paris or the Chateau?"

"Oh, definitely the Chateau, we have about four weeks to relax and get things we want. The Chansons are delighted with how it looks, they will have dinner ready for us. Now, let's board this plane and fly away."

Maddy sat in the lounge area of the plane absolutely delighted. There was an office and a sleeping area. She thought she recognised the pilot. Was he another of Nathan's cronies, well who cared!

It was late evening as they drove to the Chateau. It looked wonderful in the twilight. Just magical. She was yet to learn its history. It would be fun to trace back the various owners, she thought.

The Chansons were waiting to greet them.

There was a super log fire in the entrance hall and in the lounge. It was the first time Maddy had seen the refurbishment. She was entranced. Just the right blend of comfort and formality, a real family room.

Patra had kept the same sympathetic blend of old and new in the dining room. Maddy loved the colour schemes. She was really happy with the changes. Nathan could not wait to show her the conservatory and the swimming pool. He had surprised himself this time. It had been designed to blend in with the existing building so well that it looked as though it had always been there.

He had built out from one of the smaller rooms, which now provided an easy entertaining area.

"Wait until you see the bedrooms, Patra has done a wonderful job."

"I think I can wait just a while for that pleasure. Why don't we have a meal and talk to the Chansons about the coming months and how we propose to use the Chateau. I have this idea that it might be fun to research its history, they may be able to give us a few leads."

"But not tonight, Maddy, let's have our meal then finish exploring the changes. I have other ideas as to how we might pass the rest of the time."

She smiled at him, "and I have a surprise for you too but it can wait a while longer."

Chapter 46

Edward, James and Bar Lou were spending an evening together at the house. They knew in their hearts that changes were on the way which would affect their lives. They all knew that Temple Meadows would be their home for as long as they wanted it to be. Eventually Maddy and Nathan would fulfil their roles and start running the place to their own liking.

Bar Lou broke the companionable silence with a question. "Did you know that Nathan and Maddy now own Le Petit Oiseaux?"

"I did," said Edward, "Alicia bought it just before she died. She had some ideas for its use but never lived to tell me. In fact, she was on the way to see me when the accident happened".

"After the War, the then owner ran it as a Hotel. When Alicia bought it she continued with that tradition. Kept most of the same staff. It is a couple by the name of Chanson who run it, or did so until Nathan and Maddy went to see it."

"That is where they are now," said Bar Lou, "and they want to take me back there after the War Crimes Trials."

"Oh," said Edward, "we need to tell them both of its history". James intervened. "Maddy is already thinking of researching its history and maybe making a TV documentary from it, she has this idea for a whole series."

"So what do we do?" said Bar Lou.

"Didn't Patra do the refurbishment?" said Edward.

"Yes, she did. I only know because she collected some keys from me and read the deeds. She is very thorough."

"And very clever," said Bar Lou. "Maybe it will be different now and after the Trials maybe my more negative thoughts will fade away, once that man cannot hurt me again."

"Has Nathan ever asked for details of what his father did during the War?"

"Not recently, Edward. When he was made Head Boy at Firedown he did ask then. He wanted to know more about his father. The way he read it then, it was one big boys own adventure. The only person I have told outside the Circle is Maddy. She is a super young woman. I was really annoyed with that TV reporter when he did that 'so call' exposé on her father. Don't people check their facts any more?"

"Apparently not," said James. "I had some strong words, as did TM, with the Chief Executive of Inter News. I think TM went to the Chairman of the Board."

"Maddy's interview on the Global Network was brilliant. She just dealt with the facts without rancour I believe their viewers figures were fantastic. I hope she will do more work for television. Have you seen the studio conversion in the old buildings?"

"I've looked in" said Bar Lou, "but it was just an empty shell, no doubt Maddy will tell me more."

"Did you know Nathan has now acquired a Company plane?" said Edward.

"No, when did this happen?" asked Bar Lou.

"Oh, quite recently, it is a good investment from a time point of view. Financially, I just do not know. He seems to know what he is doing."

"Perhaps he will fly you to the Trials, Bar Lou."

"The last time I went flying at Nathan's request was in that balloon for my birthday. On reflection, it was marvellous, at the time I was petrified." She laughed, then said, "He is quite an astonishing young man, older than his years and very clever. Now with Maddy at his side who knows?"

"Yes, it is wonderful to see them together," said James.

"Did you hear that Natasha and Tiggy went to see Colin in prison? He is on remand and due to be sentenced tomorrow. He did not say a lot. Tiggy was really shaken and Natasha keeps blaming herself," said Bar Lou.

"Well, he did not play a major role in the fraud, apart from taking the paintings from here and I do not believe it was his idea. He made a full statement to the Police so that will count to his credit. He has been on remand for one month as well. It will be interesting to see what sentence is handed down."

"What do you think will happen to Miriam Hunter?" asked Bar Lou.

"That is a much more interesting situation. Most of the paintings which were copied, were from her own collection at Heatherbourne and she has also given a full statement to the Police. She totally exonerated the Hammersteins. Interestingly enough, the information she gave suggests Arpinsky murdered Appleby. They are both small fry in this fraud. In reality, their sentences should reflect that but there is always the determent factor to build in. Well, we will not have long to wait to know the answers."

"I feel sorry for her husband. He was making a good name as Foreign Secretary. The Government will miss him. He is a member of my Club and often stays during the week. There is talk of them going to live in Scotland, if the marriage survives. I believe the National Trust are very impressed with him, he has been organising the handover of Heatherbourne Castle. It could be that he will accept a role with them."

"These next two months will be very interesting," said Bar Lou.

"I like this young man Bronsen, who is looking after the Estates. He is very thorough, and is already called 'eagle eyes'!"

"A title that suits him well," said Edward. "He is an excellent choice, quite a linguist as well. With Nathan's capacity for buying property around the world he will need it."

They all laughed, three friends who respected one another and enjoyed being together.

Bar Lou said, "I have been thinking I might write a book."

"A biography?" said James.

"No, a thriller," said Bar Lou, "after all I have enough material."

Esther sat at her partners desk. It was her first week in her new office. Already the briefs were beginning to flow, too many at times but she was not complaining. She would take what she could get at first. In her heart, she knew that she wanted to specialise in Company Law. She had enjoyed the cut and thrust of the Criminal Court and the complexity of relationships in Family Division but she preferred Company Law. Listening to Nathan talking about applying the processes of forensics to accounting had whetted her appetite. As a pupil she had spent some time on a major fraud case and had enjoyed every moment of it, the research and seeing just how the forensics had been manipulated through various companies appealed to her.

The other partners had assumed that she might specialise in Family Law. As a woman, they supposed she would be more suited to these cases. She had been given some time to think out her options. Now she had made a decision. How to tell the other partners, it was a very traditional firm so they might not take kindly to a woman wanting to work in Company Law.

The meeting was scheduled for 4 pm. Until then she had court appearances to make and she was having lunch with Mary Ann. Maybe it would help to talk it over with her. At least she could listen, she might have an idea of the best way to present her decision. Fortunately, her two briefs were remand cases which could not proceed for lack of reports, so her clients had waived their right to attend.

The courts were very busy, lots of media folk around. Twice she had been asked if she was acting in the Hunter case. Then she remembered it was today that Miriam Hunter and Colin Ince Blundell were to be sentenced. She spotted Mary Ann in the corridor, so made her way forward to where she was standing.

"Hi Esther, we are waiting to hear what happens to Miriam Hunter, and by the way, this is Leon Hammerstein, my soon-to-be husband."

"Pleased to meet you, Leon, will you join us for lunch?"

"No thank you, Esther, I have no doubt that you will have plenty to talk about. Do you know if Maddy will be here?"

"I don't think so. She has gone with Nathan to France. They broke into their honeymoon because of the art fraud scandal and her TV programme, now they are continuing where they left off, as one might say."

They all smiled.

Esther said, "I will go and disrobe and join you in the Gallery. See you in five minutes."

Mary Ann and Leon made their way into Court. It was filling up rapidly, with plenty of interest from the media, with few political observers in Court. On the whole, they felt sorry for her husband.

The usher came in. "Please stand."

The Judge arrived, bowed to the Court and sat down.

The Clerk said, "My Lord, this is case no 1 before you this morning. Crown versus Hunter and Ince Blundell." The two prisoners were asked to identify themselves. Miriam was nervous and suddenly looked older. She had lost a lot of her vibrancy. Colin looked down at his feet.

The Judge first addressed himself to the case of Miriam Hunter. The prosecuting Barrister outlined the case for the Crown. Then her Barrister stood up and made his speech in mitigation of her offence. He was able to say that she had pleaded guilty on the first possible occasion, that her time on remand had been salutary and she deeply regretted her foolhardy actions, though well meaning, in order to restore Heatherbourne Castle to leave to the nation. She had let her enthusiasm cloud her judgment. He finished by outlining her circumstances now, and the effect it had on her and her husband.

"Thank you," said the Judge. "Miriam Hunter please stand up. This is a sad case, your actions were, to say the least, foolhardy. You have had a privileged lifestyle and with privilege comes responsibility, not only for your own actions but to understand the effect they have on others, particularly your family."

I have given you credit for your early plea and good character up until this series of actions. I note, from the evidence, you have been open and honest in your own statements. Therefore you will be sentenced to two years imprisonment." Miriam blanched and gripped the brass rails on the dock to steady herself, she felt faint.

The Judge continued, "But this will be suspended for two years. If you commit any further offence in that time and are found, or proved, guilty, you will go straight to prison for this offence. Do you understand?"

"Yes. Thank you."

"Go down with the Officers. You will be released in due course."

"Colin Ince Blundell, stand up please," said the Clerk.

His Barrister rose to give his speech in mitigation, but there was not a lot he could say. "Mr Ince Blundell, you are here today because you have participated in a fraud, you set out to deceive innocent people. To you it was easy money, you even stole from your friends to gain an advantage.

I have given you credit for entering a guilty plea at the first opportunity and for your remorse. I note from your records you have a previous conviction for a drug related offence but that the time on remand is the first taste of prison life. You will go to prison for 18 months. Take him down."

Natasha and Tiggy gasped. The awful reality of what he had done, came home to them.

"This sentence will make or break him," said Tiggy, "but no doubt we will stand by him this time. For me he is in the last chance saloon."

Natasha nodded. "I cannot support what he has done or condone what he did to your father, but he is our son and I will go to see him in prison, if only to let him know that and to try and persuade him to make the best of his time there, get some qualifications and do something useful."

"Well, perhaps we ought to go. Did you see Esther and Mary Ann in the gallery?"

"Yes, I knew Mary Ann was coming because she phoned me."

"By the way, Emir is taking us to lunch with Patra."

The news of the sentences was passed to TM, who in turn informed the Prime Minister's office.

He was lunching with Edward and the Commissioner. They thought it was a fair result.

Edward felt sorry for the Ince Blundells. Colin had always been a bit of a misfit, never concentrating on anything for long, always truculent. Maybe prison would sort him out, at least he hoped so.

The three men had met for another purpose, to discuss the future of the Circle. The PM was keen for it to continue as it was, a source of useful advice and information. It was the best way to proceed that was exercising their minds.

The Commissioner spoke first. "I am very impressed by Nathan Eversley and am delighted that he has agreed to join the Circle, as have Jocelyn and Hannaway. They are a good combination. I am not sure that it is the right time to involve Maddy, although she is someone for the future."

Bar Lou said, "I agree but there is someone in whom I have confidence and who has a good grasp of international politics, that is Patra. She is so diplomatic and moves across continents with ease. She is also a competent linguist. Her design business is taking off and would be a good cover. I could sound her out. However, I think you all understand that after the War Trials, I want to stand down from the daily responsibility. I feel I have done enough."

"I quite understand," said TM, "and I am sure that we will respect your wishes. The Trial will take a lot out of you I am sure. What will you do afterwards?"

"Nathan wants me to go to Le Petit Oiseaux with him and Maddy, as I have told you already."

"Are you going?" asked TM.

"Yes, I think so. Although I am apprehensive about the memories it will evoke, maybe I can lay these ghosts to rest as well. Who knows?"

"Will you be sure to tell Nathan and Maddy what happened there?"

"When it is appropriate," said Bar Lou. "I just do not want to spoil their enjoyment for the Chateau and its surroundings. What happened to me was a long time ago."

"Edward," said TM, "what about a transition period. If we meet in tandem with our new members for a while, then we can retire as they begin to understand how important the role is. We do not all need to leave at the same time."

"I agree," said Edward, "this is the only workable solution."

The Commissioner nodded. "I agree too."
Bar Lou smiled "Michael and Alicia would have been very proud today, Nathan following in his father's footsteps. It should be interesting to watch ..."

Chapter 47

Esther sat in the partners' meeting. It was the first time she had attended in her own right. She was surprised by how much time they spent on what might loosely be called, domestic arrangements, like coffee making facilities, parking, uneven distribution of briefs, and allocation of office space. She did not really know what she had expected. Finally the senior partner, George Parkinson, directed a question to her.

"Well, Esther, your first meeting, we do get around to questions of law sometimes. Have you decided which area of our work you would regard as your specialism, remembering always in your early years to take as wide a range of briefs as you can manage."

"I have been doing just that," said Esther, "but I would really like to specialise in Company Law. It has always fascinated me from my university days. There is a great deal of new legislation either on the statute book or about to be introduced. I know it is not a major area of work in chambers at present, but I feel it will be in the future."

There was a stony silence.

One partner said, "Do you think that Company Chief Executives or even Board Rooms would be prepared to take advice from a young woman, how ever proficient?"

Esther responded "I am not saying it will be easy or that I would be first choice to advise a Company, but I would not be responding to actual business decisions, only on the legal implications. Advice can be taken or rejected in any area of the law. In my own view, if the advice is good enough and explained properly, then it should not matter what the age or sex of the Barrister. The quality and accuracy of the opinion is what matters."

George Parkinson intervened. "As a principle, I agree with you, but in practice, I have two reservations. Firstly, we do not have a senior specialist-in the Company at present and secondly we have not talked about whether Company Law fits with how we are perceived by those whose briefs we receive at present. In fact, I cannot remember when we were last asked for an 'opinion' on a company law matter. Have you thought about any other specialism?"

Esther looked around the room, then said, "I rather get the impression that my ideas are not exactly what you all expected of me. I can only be true to myself, therefore I have been straight with you. I could go on accepting criminal and family briefs and do them very well, but I feel we have an opportunity here to develop a new specialism, one which will reflect the changes in legislation as they affect companies large and small. There are many business forums operating now. Many, if not most, have their headquarters in London. I feel sure that they would at least listen to me and the kind of service I feel can be offered. After all, good legal advice early on will be cost effective in the longer term and the country needs businesses to be successful."

"Esther you are sounding more like a politician than a Barrister," said George Parkinson. "Will you please think again? Perhaps we can discuss this further in my office next week."

Esther went home feeling very depressed. Why should it matter that the advice is given by a woman? Had the partners but realised it, their attitudes displayed by so many men in the City, made her more, not less, determined. She felt absolutely sure that there was a future in Company Law, but where to turn for advice?

Maddy and Nathan were still in France but they were due to return to be with Bar Lou at the War Crimes Trial soon. That just might be too late. "I wonder if Edward might be able to help me."

Esther did feel a little bit on the outside of the group, mainly because they were all marrying and up to their eyes in arrangements. Even Mary Ann, who could always be relied upon to listen, was preoccupied. The art fraud trial had taken up a lot of her time of late, it had been very worrying for the Hammerstein gallery. She understood perfectly and knew in her heart, if they knew of her dilemma they would rally around.

The next morning she phoned Edward Rayner. She had always felt that there was more to Edward than appeared on the surface. At the very least, he would listen to her.

Edward agreed to meet her and suggested they talk over dinner at a quiet fashionable restaurant. She accepted his invitation gladly. It was a fairly long time since she had sat in civilised surroundings and enjoyed a quiet meal with one other person. They agreed to meet two days later, the day before she was to see George Parkinson.

She found that, more than once, her thoughts wandered into the realms of what she should wear.

The dinner was a great success and Edward listened patiently. He could see where the partners were coming from but there was something about this young woman which suggested she could just succeed. He had, of course, done his homework, her university dons expected that she would do well. In fact, one predicted she might even return to academic life in the future.

That was good enough for Edward. There was a similar expectation throughout the profession. So, he mused, we have a tiger by the tail.

Sticking to her guns could leave her isolated with chambers expecting her to fail. He could always look to putting some work her way, but that might not be the answer.

He laid out the options for her and suggested what might be the consequences. Then he had an idea. Every year, some of the bigger companies funded a sabbatical year for bright young lawyers to spend time working alongside law companies in other countries. If Esther were accepted on such a scheme, it might just open up opportunities to test her theory against some of the sharpest minds in business.

He explained about the scholarship, how it was funded and pointed out that she might be on the young side on her first application but, nothing ventured, nothing gained. He said he would send the papers for her to consider. Her brain was working overtime, it would be a wonderful transition.

They finished their meal, happily talking about Bar Lou and the forthcoming War Trial, Nathan and Maddy and the fallout from the art fraud. In fact, they had a most enjoyable evening.

The next morning she went to chambers knowing that the meeting with George Parkinson would either confirm her belief that chambers were not ready to agree to her proposal, or they may suggest she looked elsewhere in due course. She had not quite realised how valuable an asset she was to chambers, and what a loss she just might be to them.

Unusually Esther asked George Parkinson if she could map out for him her ideas. As usual, she was concise and very clear about why she thought her future lay in company law, despite all the obstacles that may be put in her path.

She also explained about the scholarship.

"Are you not a little young to be applying for a "place?" said George. "No, I do not think so, it is aimed at new barristers and solicitors to give them a wealth of experience to bring back to the profession in this Country. After all, we are the seed corn of the future. Just think, Sir, the prestige that would accrue to this chamber, if I were accepted."

George smiled. "Yes, Esther, I can see that, well I will contact my senior partners today. I feel sure we can support your application."

Esther said, "Thank you. I appreciate your time."

As she left the office George thought to himself. 'There goes a future Law Lord, if some young buck does not succeed in domesticating her. Whoever it was would be a fool to try.'

Bar Lou was sitting with James, Patra and Edward in the conservatory at Temple Meadows. They were expecting Maddy and Nathan to return the next day. The forthcoming trial was uppermost in their minds.

Bar Lou felt strangely confident. She had such good friends around her, she knew that the next few days would be a watershed in her emotional life. She had been carrying the baggage for too long. Oh, no doubt about it, she had enjoyed her life with Nathan, James and Edward. It had been a lot more demanding than she had thought it would be. It was a good job that she had been able to balance that with her work for the Circle and her other abiding passion, horse racing. She now owned four horses, all stabled with Emir and Tiggy. So far, she was on the right side financially, although she suspected that Nathan was bearing some of the costs. How he did it, she did not know, but she never saw many veterinary bills.

There had been so many changes in the last decade, just where had the time gone? She, like Nathan, had fallen under Maddy's spell. She was so right for Nathan, she would keep him grounded without him really knowing. He adored her and, although he might just go overboard from time to time, at least he would make her life interesting and fulfilling. He understood very well that she needed time and space to develop her own interests, and television might well be the major communication medium of the future.

411

Patra said, "where are you Bar Lou? You seemed to be deep in thought."

"Yes, I am sorry. Where were we?"

"Well, we were talking about the coming week, the arrangements for travel and where we will stay."

"Oh, did I not tell you, Nathan is taking us all in his new toy, the aeroplane. Maddy says it is so comfortable and we are to stay in a Schloss, belonging to some friend of his that he met at the International College, so no need to worry. It will be quite exciting in a funny sort of way."

Patra frowned.

"Please understand me, I know that the next week will be a roller coaster for me and once it starts, there is no going back, but I have to find the same reserves of strength that I did when he had me in his power. Now it is my turn, not for revenge but justice and that is what will happen. He has only one defence that he could possibly proffer, that he was only obeying orders. But his life since then has hardly been one of remorse. He seems to have gone on killing people. It has to stop. If I am the first to apply the brakes, then so be it."

"Well," said James, "I am really proud of you Bar Lou. I always felt that you would find a way to rationalise what happened to you, but to be able to be so objective at this time is amazing."

"I agree," said Patra.

"James, do you know that, after the trial, we are flying to France to stay at Le Petit Oiseaux."

"Oh, good heavens," said James "haven't you told Nathan yet?"

"Told Nathan what?" said Patra. "I thought his mother owned the Chateau."

"She did," said Bar Lou, "but during the War, Arpinsky reigned supreme, there questioning, as he called us, 'spies'. But he did not confine himself to the spirit of the Geneva Convention, he applied physical torture, just to remind us."

"Us?" said Patra, "Does that mean you were tortured in that Chateau?"

"Yes," said Bar Lou, "and Michael, Nathan's father."

"Will it not come out in the Trial?" asked Patra.

"Probably," said Bar Lou.

"What about telling Nathan and Maddy?"

"You are right, they will be here tomorrow. Tell me Patra, you have done the refurbishment at the Chateau, is it very different?"

"Structurally no, but internally, very different. It has been updated in a sympathetic manner. Even Nathan seemed to realise that it needed restoration, not rebuilding, though he did take some persuasion."

"I am sure," said Bar Lou, "then I have little to fear from going there. I will emphasise with what has happened to the people as I did at Auschwitz. But it is the future that matters and I have this feeling that it will echo more with laughter than tears."

Chapter 48

Miriam Hunter and her husband were sitting in the lounge of the hunting lodge. The scenery was stunning, acres and acres of heather clad moorland. It had not been an easy three weeks since her release. They had been busy packing the items bound for Scotland, yet leaving behind the furniture and fittings which made Heatherbourne Castle what it was. When she went around for the last time with the curator from the National Trust, she remembered more laughter than tears. Maybe Heatherbourne was telling her to look to the future, she could not change the past; what did the future hold?

She looked across at her husband. These last six months had taken their toll, he had aged, he missed the work he had been doing, the cut and thrust of international politics. Never a man to make a hasty decision, he had taken to his post a steadying influence, considered opinions blended with optimism. She, and she alone, had taken that from him.

Now they sat opposite to each other, isolated from everything and everyone who, to some extent, made them what they were. She did not know if her marriage was strong enough to withstand the stresses and strains. They had both been so busy with their own interests she could not remember when they had sat together in one room for any length of time. The silence was awkward.

Her husband looked up and said, "Well, are we just going to sit here saying nothing? I think it is time we discussed what has happened, how we feel and turn our thoughts to the future."

"I agree," said Miriam.

"Do you want to start?" said her husband.

She looked at him, remembering the young politician, full of ambition, championing his constituents cases, desperate to be called to speak in debates, rising through the party ranks and finally into government itself. She looked down at her hands, especially at her wedding ring.

"I am having difficulty knowing where to start. You know all the fine detail only too well. What you perhaps are asking me to do is answer the question Why? I really am not sure, what made Heatherbourne take over my reason for living, driving me on and on to complete the restoration. It was almost as if it took me over. It became the child I never had, to be nurtured and moulded to face the future. The social life I had, paled into insignificance. Oh, I enjoyed meeting people and always tried to be a credit to you. I must admit, I loved the state occasions and in the early stages of our life together, to sit in the strangers gallery and listen to the debates. I hope I gave to the role as well, Heatherbourne was always an attraction when you wanted to talk to visiting dignitaries in private. It was then I began to see its potential, its future, if you like. I was devastated when I was told that I could not conceive children, as I am sure you were. I suppose, in a way, I was happy to be able to fill the void in my life. The social occasions have been so much part of my lifestyle they are now second nature. I was treading a well worn path, one which had become my destiny. It was just something I did well. I am not sure I ever gave a thought to its likely place in history, there was a job to do and I did it.

Now, and in the future, I hope I can rebuild your trust in me. I know it will take time. I feel so empty inside, almost as if my emotions are frozen. I suppose, now, the thaw is starting. When I was locked in that prison cell, I did a lot of thinking. I am not sure I found many answers, there was so much anger within me. The young girl who shared my cell once said to me, 'Why don't you just be you and not someone that you think people want you to be? I am not educated, never did like school, had three kids before I was twenty-one, married a wastrel, lived in squalor and he forced me to go on the game. So I got into drugs just so I could face the punters and perform, if you know what I mean. The rest I am sure you know. But you are different, you listen, you know what to say and how to say it. I will not forget sharing this cell with you, we come from different worlds don't we?'

"So who am I really, wife but not a mother, a socialite but I find some of the idle chit chat boring. Oh, I do my bit for charity, but am I charitable? I am working through my baggage, I don't know if I can do it on my own. I need you, want your wisdom, your understanding, your caring. If that is forthcoming, maybe we have some hope of building a new life."

He looked at her, seeing probably for the first time how vulnerable she was. Once the socialite veneer was stripped away, he saw glimpses of the person she could be. He was still hurting, he hated seeing the pity in men's eyes as they patted him on the back or nodded as they passed by or, worse still, went out of their way to ignore him. Even young politicians, whom he had spent hours helping, found it difficult to look him in the face. He had not realised how, not having children affected their relationship, but in truth he loved his wife in his own way.

"Miriam, we have to decide what is important to us, where we have firm ground on which to rebuild. Our lives have changed through circumstances and maturity. It will not be an easy exercise and it will only work if we are almost brutally honest. I believe we can do this and I for one want to try".

Miriam looked at him and said, "Oh so do I, so do I."

Gabriella and Freddie were planning a trip to Europe to meet his family and friends. She knew Nathan and Maddy and had met most of the people in what he called the Cabal. She thought it was comforting to know that he was so loyal to his friends. He had made a really good impression in America, now she wanted to do the same in England. She had never really thought about her colour before, her parents had not made a fuss about it, neither had her school friends. There had been odd comments at university but she rose above them, determined to get the best degree she could achieve. She knew that, in one way, she was blazing a trail. Since she had met Freddie she had found an inner strength, a contentment she had never experienced before. Now she was to spend time with his family. What would they think, would her colour get in the way, was she the kind of woman they wanted for a daughter-in-law, most of all could they be friends? "Well," she said, looking at the mirror, "you will soon have some answers."

Freddie called to her. "Gabs, are you ready? The taxi is here. It's time to go."

She came racing down the stairs. He smiled at her. "You look fantastic," he said. That was just what she needed to hear, good old Freddie. 'I do love him,' she said to herself and that is what matters.

The visit to his parents was awkward at first. They were all trying too hard. One morning, she walked into the kitchen and helped his mother prepare the meal. They talked and laughed, peeled vegetables, washed up, made endless cups of tea. The ice was broken, she felt comfortable and, what is more, she liked her in-laws. Freddie was mightily relieved. The next day they were going to Firedown to see Hannaway, Mai Lee and the new baby. Gabriella, as usual, had hit the shops and bought nine presents for them. It would be good for Freddie to show her his school, help her understand how much it had helped him and how the friendships he made there had sustained him. He felt she would be surprised, it was not exactly first class living. He smiled to himself. In fact it had been hard to settle in, when he first arrived. Mai Lee and Gabriella had a mutual interest in shopping, no doubt a day out would suit them both.

The next port of call would be to join Nathan and Maddy at the Chateau. He had already offered them the chance to stay there for their honeymoon so that they could explore Europe. Maddy thought they would prefer the Paris flat but she would sort that out later.

Little did she know Nathan was planning a whole scale reunion, their very first house party. He would tell her after the War Trials. He was sure she would enjoy it. But then, he did not know the surprise she had in store for him.

In the meantime Maddy, Patra, Bar Lou, Nathan and Maddy were all gathered at Temple Meadows prior to leaving for the War Trials. Bar Lou had spent time re-reading her old diaries and reports. How they brought back memories. It had been a tremendous challenge at the time and exciting as well as highly dangerous.

She still had to tell Nathan and Maddy about his father's and her own time at the Le Petit Oiseaux. She hoped he would not be upset. Whilst she knew that this had to be done, she wanted to talk to them in her own cottage, perhaps over crumpets and tea by a roaring fire. They might even toast marshmallows. Nathan and Maddy were on good form. They seemed to have settled into an easy relationship and, although they enjoyed their quiet moments, they just loved having their friends around. In some ways, for both of them, they took the place of their family.

Maddy knew that, very soon, they would have to decide where their permanent base was to be. She loved the Chateau but realised it might not always be practical. Inevitably, that meant Temple Meadows was the only choice. She was happy with that. She had that nesting instinct, it was almost time to tell Nathan. Fortunately, she had not been too troubled with morning sickness but she did notice that she had started peering in prams and looking at baby clothes. Then there was a nursery to prepare.

She also wanted to see Esther and Mary Ann before they left for Germany. There was so much to discuss with them, especially Mary

Ann's wedding. She also wanted to catch up with Esther's news. She suspected that being a partner in Chambers had not been a bed of roses. Edward had hinted to her that Esther needed to talk to a friend. Maddy had invited them to the flat for the day before she left for Germany. She needed some new clothes, to accommodate her slightly expanding waistline. Even Nathan had noticed that but for a bright man he had not put two and two together, for which she was grateful.

She also intended to spend some time with Annie on the plans for the studio. She would need a good crew. She already had a few ideas for programmes, especially the one that explored the history of places like the Chateau and there must be many others. Nathan had so many friends all over the world that it could be a great series. Preparation would be the key. Annie was dying to get her teeth into a good project. Watching the studio develop and arranging its equipment had been very time consuming but she not only learned a lot, she enjoyed herself. She hoped Jos would come this weekend. She had seen him once or twice. They had a meal together at the Jazz Club. She loved jazz so found much to talk about with him. Jos liked Annie, they sort of fitted, as he explained to Walshy. He knew that he had to think about his future. Travelling around the world, either playing cricket or composing with Labac, was beginning to pale. He wanted to do something else, preferably in the entertainment business. He would talk to Nathan about his ideas. When he had the answers and could see a way forward he would ask Annie to marry him.

The conversation between Jos and Nathan had proved fruitful. Nathan had told him about the way sports management was developing in America. He advised Jos to go and have a look at it. "You could stay in the loft. Talk to Charles and the staff at Cabal offices. Charles, in particular, has his finger on the pulse. Freddie and Gabriella would make you very welcome. I am sure they could set up some meetings for you, after all you are not unknown over there." Jos smiled. Nathan had matured so much. If that was what marriage did, well, roll on the happy day.

Nathan looked at his watch, it was time to find Maddy, they were due at Garden Cottage for tea. Just like old times thought Nathan, crumpets dripping with butter and honey and his two most favourite ladies altogether. What could be better?

What indeed?

Bar Lou was as delighted as ever to see them both. There were some subtle changes in Maddy but she did not dwell on that thought. She was apprehensive, it was not going to be easy telling them what had happened at Le Petit Oiseaux but it had to be done, after crumpets and tea.

Nathan looked at Bar Lou, she seemed a little on edge. "Bar Lou, are you worried about something?" asked Nathan. "Is it to do with the Trial?"

"No, but I need to talk seriously to both of you and before you ask, Maddy there is nothing physically wrong with me, so let me carry on please."

"Fine," they said in unison.

"You know a little, Nathan, about the work your father and I did during the War. Special Operations was a necessary part of the War effort. It was exciting and dangerous. Michael and I worked as part of the same cell. There was always the risk that we would be caught, the Germans were everywhere and so were the collaborators. One night, the farm where we were held up was raided. We could never be sure whether it was by chance or as a result of a tip off. We were both captured and it did not take a vivid imagination to realise what might be in store for us. At first, we were taken to Paris, then the SS moved us to their 'place of correction', a euphemism for the most degrading experience of our lives. At times, I felt that death might be preferable. It was there that I came face to face with Arpinsky." She saw the startled look on their faces. "Yes, it is the same vile creature now facing the War Trial. His boast was 'he could make any little bird sing'. I shouted and yelled in agony, as nails were pulled off, slash marks criss crossed my back, I was raped, sometimes

421

subjected to blasts of cold water, always I was naked. He even brought your father in to watch. He heard me scream, saw the pain and I have no doubt felt it, but neither of us told him what he wanted to know. Stupid, you might think, but we knew that was to be our last mission. The allies were advancing rapidly on a number of fronts. The Germans would have to surrender. Your father Michael was beaten, threatened, whipped etc. He possessed a wonderful ability to cope with the pain, tried not be scream, he must have been in agony. He used to call to me from his cell. It was his strength which got me through. All of this will come out in the Trial. I can see how distressed you are, but let me finish, there is not much more you both need to know. I was so disfigured, I needed hours of plastic surgery, my back bears the scars to this day. Maddy has seen some of them because we swam together. The disfigurement and the subsequent operations gave me a face I did not recognise. It was nearly the face of that young woman who went to France but not quite. It was like a mask had covered the real me. In the very early stages I could not look in a mirror. I would always see Arpinsky in the background, grinning at me, working out his next move. Your father, Nathan, was wonderful as was TM, he was my spy master. It was five years before the reconstruction was completed, the final blow was when I was told I would never have children. Michael was also impotent for some time. Where did this all take place you might ask? At Le Petit Oiseaux. I did not know that Alicia had bought the place or even that Maddy and you were planning to restore it to a family home."

"It did have a weird feeling at first, as though it wanted to give up a secret but now there is a wonderful atmosphere, very welcoming, we have really enjoyed our time there."

Nathan interjected, "Do you want to see it Bar Lou, we can change the arrangements."

"No, don't do that, once the Trial is over I need to go back and face up to what happened. It might just square the circle for me."

"Well, you do not have to stay in the house, we have prepared a super cottage by the river for you, so you can go anytime and have your friends to stay," said Nathan.

"Bar Lou, I owe you so much, the last thing Maddy or I would want to do is to add to any problems you might feel you have. If it is too much then say so, we can always stay in Paris or even go to New York. It is up to you. Do not decide now, tell us when you are ready". He moved across to where she was sitting and held her in his arms. She appreciated the gesture.

There was a knock at the door, Patra had come back from taking the now ageing dogs for a walk.

"Can I come in?"

"Yes do," said Maddy.

"How has it gone, Bar Lou?"

"Very well indeed, I feel so much better." She turned to Maddy and Nathan. "I confided in Patra and she has helped me to see that period for what it was, history, I have so much to be grateful for now."

"So any more crumpets or tea, we still have work to do."

They all laughed. Maddy kissed Bar Lou, then Nathan, and they walked back to the house hand in hand, not talking as there was no need. Temple Meadows was bathed in a rosy glow from the setting sun. They looked at each other, smiled and walked on into the future.

Chapter 49

When the time came for Patra, Maddy, Bar Lou, Nathan and Edward to leave England for Germany there was a quite palpable tension in the air. It was going to be emotionally exhausting particularly for Bar Lou. Maddy and Nathan had been horrified after they heard what had happened to her when she was captured. They had talked about it long into the night and had even debated whether they should keep Le Petit Oiseaux. Nathan wished he had known what his mother intended to do with it, but he felt he wanted to use it for a family residence, a place to invite friends and spend holidays, enjoying all that the local area had to offer.

In a way, he could understand how Bar Lou might have reservations. On the other hand they would wait and see, it just might be fine. The new aeroplane was much admired, particularly for its comfort. The flight to Germany was smooth and without incident. A car was waiting to take them to Schlos Verdl, which was owned by a friend of Nathan's. It was very convenient for the Halle where the trial would take place. It looked like a fairytale castle with red turrets and slit windows, yet inside it was very comfortable. There was great excitement about the circular rooms. Patra, in particular, took note of the design features. Their evening meal was held in the old banqueting hall by candlelight.

"It is a great shame that tomorrow we have to go to the trial," said Bar Lou, "it is so relaxing here. That view down the river is quite something."

"Never mind, Bar Lou, I am sure Hans and Barbel will invite you back sometime. Their hot chocolate is almost as lethal as yours." This latter statement made everyone laugh. "Before you go to bed," said Hans, "put on your jackets and walk down the path to the gate. As you walk back again, it is a wonderful sight."

Full of curiosity they did as he suggested. There was much laughter, once they started the return journey for their way was lit by glow worms, their little tails flickering in the moonlight.

"What a surprise," said Patra "what makes them do that?" "I have no idea," said Edward, "we must ask Hans."

Morning came too soon. It was a very quiet breakfast table, nobody really wanted to eat but they did try. Maddy had been feeling very sick. Oh heavens, she thought, what a time to develop morning sickness. Nobody really noticed for which she was thankful.

Hans had arranged transport for them. The German prosecutors were waiting to tell them what would happen. There was a big crowd outside the Halle. Bar Lou was glad to get inside.

It was not long before Arpinsky was brought into court handcuffed. The officers accompanying him were armed which, at first sight, was very intimidating. Proceedings were soon underway. The galleries were packed out. Those persons giving direct evidence were heard first. Bar Lou was called after lunch. Patra had sat with her. Edward had joined TM. Maddy and Nathan sat in the gallery. It was an impressive occasion, almost theatrical. The proceedings were held in German with simultaneous translation into English and French.

Bar Lou was called at 2 pm. She walked with much dignity to the witness stand. She took the oath with a clear voice, which belied her 70 years. There was absolute silence in the court when she described what had happened to her. She was so glad that she had told Nathan and Maddy before they left England. It was better that she was not distracted by what they might be feeling. Some of the women in the gallery sobbed openly. Arpinsky sat motionless. He had not recognised Bar Lou at first. You have seen a very good surgeon, he thought, as he remembered how he had made cut after cut about her body. She was too brave for her own good and the only woman he could not make sing. He tried, day after day, stubbornly believing that his mind and actions would dominate. If he had listened to his officers, Bar Lou and Michael would have faced a firing squad but he left it too late to organise and managed to leave the Chateau just ahead of advancing forces. He regretted not having finished the job.

Bar Lou was cross questioned by Arpinsky's lawyer. She stood up to it well, when under severe pressure she turned to his lawyer and said, "If what happened to me had happened to you, do you think you would forget a single thing? I think not." With that she sat down. Arpinsky frowned at her. So he had dominated her after all. He smiled. 'I will always win,' he thought.

He had refused to give evidence. This surprised the court. His lawyer would open proceedings in his defence on the fourth day. The Trial summaries and accepted paper evidence would also be exchanged, over 2000 items were submitted in all.

The English party left the Halle together. Nathan had arranged that Bar Lou would be interviewed by Maddy for Inter News, who would syndicate the programme. A room had been set aside at the local TV studio. It was to take place at the end of the Trial when the outcome would have been announced. Bar Lou was happy with that and felt that she did not want to return to the Halle for a few days. Barbel, Maddy, Bar Lou and Patra went shopping. Nathan and Edward returned to the court.

He had also received information that Maddy's brother, Inky, was due to stand trial the week after this trial had finished. He had talked to her about going to see her brother. She had not really been keen at the time. Nathan felt it would help her in the long run but it had to be her choice. Hans could arrange for her to see her brother in prison. She did not have to attend the trial. Haime Finkleslen had been called as a witness, as had Charles Babington and Freddie Jackson. Bar Lou had been excused.

Inky had little idea of the weight of evidence against him. He was quite surprised when his lawyer spelt it out for him. It had been suggested to him that he plead guilty, the reason being, it could shorten his sentence. He was thinking about it. He had another few days before he had to make a final decision, so he spent the time watching the Arpinsky trial. He thought he saw Maddy leaving the Court but could not be sure.

Therefore, it was with some surprise that he was told, by the prison guard, that he had a visitor. The last person he expected to see was Maddy. He suddenly felt very, very ashamed. She tried very hard to understand why he had got involved but could not make rhyme nor reason of his replies. So she turned her attention to the Gallerie Madel. "If you go to prison, what will happen to the Gallerie?" she asked. "It will be sold to meet legal costs and damages, which could be punitive. It may not raise a good enough price to meet all those costs.

"Was that originally father's Gallerie?"

"Yes, but I have made many changes, and Vienna has changed, it is a good property."

"Yes, I know," said Maddy. "If I was to get a proper valuation, would you agree to my purchasing it from you"?

"Well, I suppose it is half yours anyway."

"I am not bothered by that," said Maddy, "do you agree to my proposal?"

428

"Yes, why not."

"What will happen to the money?"

"My husband will arrange for a local firm to pay off your debts, then hold the rest on deposit until your release."

Inky thought for a moment. "I would like to settle some money on Hilly, she has little to live on and she did so much for me as a child."

"That can be done," said Maddy.

"Will you leave all the transactions to me then?"

"Yes, if papers are drawn up, I will sign them for you, giving you power of attorney over my affairs."

Maddy tried to tell him that she would do her best to help him when he returned to civilian life and that she would visit him when she could.

He smiled and looked at her. "You look a lot like mother in the miniatures. I never did find out what happened to them or if the four ever came together so that the riddle was solved."

"Yes, they did," said Maddy, "it appears that father, far from being a collaborator, was an honourable man."

"What a turn up for the books," said Inky.

He looked at her, then said, "Thank you for coming. I really do not deserve it, maybe one day we can be friends."

Maddy left the prison. She felt grubby and not a little defiled. 'What a terrible place,' she thought to herself. Nathan was waiting for her in the car, she looked across at him and smiled. He knew all was well.

429

Maddy told him all about the Gallerie deal. He was somewhat stunned. "What will you do with it?"

"Oh, I will talk to Mary Ann and Leon but I think if I let them have it on a peppercorn rent, as a wedding present, then maybe Igor would run it for them. I knew he would like to return to Austria. Haime Finklestein had said he would be willing to help get things going again. It could be a good result all round."

"Quite the little business woman, are you not? I shall have to keep an eye on you in the future." They both laughed.

"Now, all I want to do is get back to the Castle, have a bath and a relaxing evening. I do like Barbel, she is very interesting. I told her about my idea of researching various homes around Europe and making a series of television documentaries. She thinks they would be quite keen."

"Maddy, will you please stop working for a few hours?" said Nathan.

"Fine, I give up. How long do you think it will be before the Arpinsky trial concludes?"

"TM thinks it will be another 3 or 5 days."

"We are all having dinner together tonight so we can ask him then, if you like. Are you going to wear one of your new dresses."

"Why?"

"Well, I just want the others to realise what a lucky man I am."

"Oh, I think they know that already."

"Well, if you were to wear that blue dress, you know the floaty one, this might just be the ideal jewellery to wear with it." He handed Maddy a jewellery case, which she opened.

"Oh, Nathan, this is stunning, what beautiful stones, where did you get it from?"

"Oh, I went for a short stroll around the town and spotted it in a jewellers window, but if you are not wearing your blue dress, then my effort will be in vain."

"Of course I will, stupid." She leant over and kissed him. "You are very special, Nathan, and I do love you so much."

"Careful Maddy, I think we should wait until we are back at the Castle before taking this little episode any further."

Arpinsky was on 24 hr watch whilst in the cells. It was important that his trial continued with no slip ups. This man was a disgrace to his country, so there was no way he would be taking an easy exit.

He was still convinced he would get off. His defence was simply that he was acting under orders. He forgot one small thing, he had no written evidence to support his assertion. All documents had been thoroughly researched and nothing could be found.

He was to hear this in Court the next morning when the prosecutor rose to make his closing speech.

Arpinsky was not listening as intently as he might have done. He was away in fantasy land, planning how he would deal with Bar Lou and the rest of them who had given evidence. When he did realise what had been said, it was too late. In opting not to give evidence himself, he had played into the prosecutor's hands.

He was defeated. Well, he would just have to arrange another exit for himself. It should be easy once he returned to the prison. He could arrange anything from his cell. When all the speeches were finished, the senior judge present said that they would announce verdicts one week hence. The prisoner would remain in custody.

At dinner that night TM suggested that maybe Maddy should do the interview the next day, instead of waiting for the verdict, then leave for France. It would be better to be away from this area, to avoid any unnecessary attention.

Maddy was happy to fall in with the suggestion, she had already been to the studios and explained how she would like to set up for the interview. She had also given Bar Lou a list of the questions she had prepared. Annie could rehearse them with her when she arrived tonight. Then it should be plain sailing. Annie or TM would take the tapes back to England.

Afterwards Patra, Bar Lou, Nathan and herself would fly on to the Le Petit Oiseaux and help Bar Lou recuperate, if that was really necessary.

It all felt like an anti-climax. The build up had been so intense, now they were just waiting for a result. Maddy thought Nathan looked a bit edgy. He obviously had something planned, she would ask him later.

The next morning Maddy dressed with great care, checking every angle of her dress to make sure it fitted perfectly. She was satisfied with her hair and would repair any makeup at the studio. It was time to find Annie and Bar Lou. Patra and Barbel were going shopping, for a change.

It was a short drive to the studio. Bar Lou was a little apprehensive. She had not done a televised interview before, Annie had done her best to answer her questions. Maddy turned to her. "Just think about it as a fireside chat, without the hot chocolate." "Shame," said Bar Lou.

The studio manager was waiting to greet them. They were to have use of one of the dressing rooms whilst they waited. The manager was keen to talk to Maddy. He had seen some of her earlier work and was impressed. She went with him to the studio. After discussion about the camera placement, the lighting plan and sound checks, she was happy to start. Annie brought Bar Lou through and the interview began. Maddy soon had her confidence and Bar Lou told her story with little prompting from Maddy. After a while, Bar Lou did not notice the cameras, she spoke to Maddy and retold her tale for what she hoped would be the last time. Maddy skilfully brought the interview to a close and went to the gallery to see the re-run.

"Looks OK to me," said the editor.

"Fine," said Maddy "I need all these copies sealed into their carriers. They are going to London tonight. Thank you for all your help."

"What a stunner," said the studio manager, "the cameras love her. I hope she does some more work here one day."

"I hear she is going to run an independent company from England. It will be worth watching out for her output."

The return journey to the Castle was quick. They had all packed, ready to leave late afternoon for the airport. With luck, they would be at the Le Petit Oiseaux by supper time.

On the flight back, Maddy turned to Nathan and said "Well, what are you planning?"

"Moi," said Nathan smiling.

"Well, I thought it would be a good idea to have a house party, not so intense, as all the usual suspects arrive tomorrow."

"Do the Chansons know?"

"Oh yes, they are looking forward to it and Bar Lou's cottage is ready.

She might prefer to sleep there with Patra."

"Right, and when were you planning to tell me?"

"I just have," he said. She shook her head. "Nathan, Nathan."

Chapter 50

As their party arrived at Le Petit Oiseaux, Nathan put his arms around Bar Lou.

"This time, you will be enjoying yourself, entertaining my friends and yours. There is nothing to fear, we are all here for you. Do you want to come to the Chateau first or would you prefer to go direct to your own cottage?"

Bar Lou shook her head.

"I just do not know what I feel at present. Just numb, I suppose. I never saw the surrounding countryside the first time. We just bumped along in an old van. The guards kept looking at us and laughing. They did not realise we could understand what they were saying. As a result, I suppose I thought it was the last journey I would ever take.

Now, it looks like any other Chateau, standing proud in the evening light, mellow and serene, yet I did not dream what happened to me here!"

"No, you certainly did not," said Nathan.

"Just think, Nathan, the last time I drove up this road it was with your father. We were being returned to England. He, like you are today, had his arms around me, letting me draw on his strength just as I am doing today from you."

I realise, probably for the first time in many years, I have nothing to fear. I am so lucky to be here at all, so as the poet said 'Begone dull care'. I want to enjoy this week, my memories will never leave me but hopefully they will fade now that Arpinsky cannot hurt me anymore. He is no longer in my head. I think it was during that interview with Maddy, I realised I was talking history and that is where it should remain, in the past. Thank you so much, to both of you, for helping me to see that."

"I think I would like to go to the cottage first, with Patra. Maybe we could have our meal there. Tomorrow is another day, the first day of the rest of our lives. I will definitely make a new start with old friends. Nathan, you are the son I was never able to have. It has meant so much to me to be part of your life, to see you succeed, to marry Maddy, yet you have never forgotten me."

"How could I? I always felt so secure when I was with you even if you did wear some crazy outfits. All my friends loved you as well. You see, I was able to choose who would be my family. I doubt if I could have done better. My mother and father guided me well... you have helped me make the journey towards whatever is my destiny. Now I think you should relax. There is a super new swimming pool at the Chateau. Now Maddy and I will come with you to the cottage, then we will walk back to the chateau."

As Nathan and Maddy turned to wave goodnight to Bar Lou and Patra, he thought he saw his reflection in the cottage window, but that was impossible, it must have been a flick of the light, but it looked real. He wondered.

Maddy held her husband. "I think it will be alright, you know. Bar Lou suddenly seems at peace. Now, as for tomorrow, who is coming and when and what are we going to do?"

436

"Oh, the Cabal, their partners, yes, they all have close friends. And there are one or two surprises. Michael and Angela, Per Osmason and his balloon, Mark, Mary Ann and Esther, TM and the boys, Edward, James and his other special guests. It will be great, the chateau will ring with laughter, the best housewarming I could imagine. The Chansons are delighted and on Saturday evening I have arranged a special event for everyone from the village. It is best to let us satisfy their curiosity, then we can all settle down."

"Maddy, you are very quiet."
"I know, will I ever be consulted about your jolly japes?"

"Oh, they might not be as jolly or a jape if I told you beforehand. Our life together is just beginning. Where the journey will end I do not know, neither my beautiful wife do you, isn't that exiting?" She smiled as only Maddy could.

Back in Vienna, Inky was just leaving the prison for his court appearance. He had decided to plead guilty, having heard his lawyer's view of the evidence. There was no choice. He would just have to take what was coming to him. What a mess his life was. There was one good thing. Maddy had been to see him. He thought, 'She is really beautiful and kind, if only I had met her earlier.'

The prison transport drew to a halt. All those attending court were ushered through a side door to waiting cells. He wondered how many others would be here today. His case was not called until 2 pm. It had been a long morning. He had advised his lawyer to tell the Court he would plead guilty. "I might as well face facts, the sooner I know what is to happen to me the sooner I can get on with it and as Maddy said, 'Grow up, Inky this is the real world. Whatever happens take your punishment like a man.'" She had promised to come and see him when she could. He had lots of bridges to build ...

In America, Perry Bracken made his fourth appearance in Court. Today, his lawyers were to ask that his case be dealt with as a separate matter. He was not sure that this plea would succeed. The District Attorney was taking advice which might lead to some plea bargaining that he could accept. The sooner it was finalised the better, it would be for him and his family. In his view, they had suffered enough. Then there was the blackmail issue. It had all become very complicated, especially with the death of Conrad Parker. He hoped it was accepted that he knew nothing of his death. Perry knew he was facing a prison sentence. He had been stupid, now he had to wait.

Arpinsky realised he would be imprisoned for life. He was determined not to serve any more time than he had to, he had contacts and he would use them. He was arrogant enough to believe no-one could, or would, defeat him. He was in for a rude awakening.

Inky was more relaxed than he had been for some time. He was due to be sentenced the next day. The guilty plea had been accepted and a few minor charges were dropped. He knew Hilly and Haime were very disappointed in him and that hurt. Meeting Maddy had made a difference, he trusted her. Hopefully, when all this was over, they would meet and spend some time together. He had heard about the sentences for Miriam Hunter and Colin Ince Blundell. He had no reason to believe he would be as lucky.

Nathan and Maddy were planning the house party with the Chansons, guests were arriving. It was just a little chaotic but nobody seemed to mind. TM's boys were running around, happily playing with the Chansons' grandchildren, telling them lurid tales of Uncle Nathan's jokes and japes.

Edward walked in with two very special guests. Maddy looked up. "Nathan, look who it is."

"Who?" said Nathan.

Then he looked up from testing rows of bulbs. "Oh, Petre and Su Ming, how wonderful. I am so glad you are here, so everything is settled in China?"

"Well almost," said Petre. "I did promise Su Ming this journey, once Fing Wah had paid his due. He is staying with the monks."

"I had heard," said Nathan, "he is very brave."

"Now I think I can agree with that sentiment."

Maddy joined Nathan. "Would you like to see your rooms, then we will do the grand tour. I, too, am so delighted that you are here."

"Thank you," said Petre, "shall we follow you."

"Yes, your suitcases will be in the room when you get there. Su Ming, have you ever slept in a four poster bed?"

"No, I have not, what a strange custom."

"It is an old custom, the Castles and Chateaus were so draughty, it was one way of keeping warm!"

Dinner that evening was noisy, happy and very interesting. Nathan and Maddy looked at each other down the length of the table. To have all their friends and family here was just fantastic. Bar Lou had been hesitant but she was chattering away with hardly a care in the world.

Before they rose to move to the lounges, Nathan rose to say a few words.

"Friends, family and guests, well everybody, welcome to Le Petit Oiseaux Chateau. I hope that this will be the first of many visits we will share in the years to come. These last few months have been difficult for all of us, especially Bar Lou. We have all been affected by what has happened. I think I can say we have achieved what we set out to do, right a few wrongs and bring justice to those who have cheated, stolen and murdered. A few of us have married and we have at least four more to come during this year. Hannaway, as is usual these days, or should I say

Headmaster and father, has managed, with the help of Mai Lee, to start off the next generation. Congratulations!

With weddings, christenings and other special occasions, gentleman, I can assure you that retail therapy will head the expenditure list for some time to come.

TM has just handed to me a note, we now have all the trial results. Perry Bracken was sentenced to five years and Inky, he looked at Maddy, 8 years, up to 3 years of which can be suspended at the President's discretion. Arpinsky to be imprisoned for life, initially in solitary confinement." He looked at Bar Lou, she was very quiet.

"Now as for tomorrow, we will be entertaining the village, ending with a hog roast and fireworks. Please help us make this a great day. They have much to remember, as we have.

Otherwise the order is, enjoy yourselves. If the weather is right, Per Osmason has his balloon here and will be organising flights. Maddy and I will take the last flight, I would love to see this place in the evening sun from the air.

Oh, we will need a cricket team. Josh will organise that, if he can tear himself away from Annie for a while and the villagers have challenged us to petanque. I think that is a job for you to organise TM.

Finally a toast, to friendship."

"To friendship," echoed around the room.

Nathan and Maddy moved around their guests. It felt so good to have all their friends with them this night. It was quite a gathering from the Americas, Australia, China, the Middle East, Wales, Ireland, England, Norway and Scotland, just like a mini united nations.

"We are so lucky, Maddy. Whatever the future holds, I do not know, as long as we are together. That will be fine by me."

"Look," said Maddy "most people have retired, so shall we say goodnight to the Chansons and thank them, then we can do the same."

"Good idea. He was thinking about the surprise he had in store for her."

Maddy looked at him. She wondered how he would take the news.

Eventually, they made their way to the master bedroom. Nathan went to close the curtains.

"Please don't do that, I love looking at the stars, they are so bright tonight."

"Fine by me," said Nathan.

"Before we climb into this wonderful bed, I have a surprise for you."

On a small table were not four, but six miniatures. He had a special one of their wedding and that of Michael and Alicia.

"Nathan, they look wonderful but ..."

"But what, Maddy?"

"Well, we may need some more. How do you fancy being called Papa?"

"What did you say?"

"Well, I asked how you would fancy being called Papa?"

"Maddy, you're not, are you?"

"Well, yes, we are having twins."
Nathan sat down. "I cannot believe it, we are going to be parents.

Oh Maddy, you are so very clever."

"Well, you did play your part, you know."

He smiled and pulled her to him. "What a surprise, what a wonderful surprise! The best yet, but who knows ...?"

THE END

About the Author

Kate Nelson was born and educated in Cheshire, England. Her love of words started when as a small child she read a series of books called 'Tales the Letters Tell'. From there onwards words fascinated her as did travel. Attendance at creative writing workshops and writing groups, as well as meeting with established authors developed the interest even further. This, her first novel in her own words "...is a story written for fun to be enjoyed by those who share her love of words".